A WHISPER AWAY FROM EVIL

by

Gabriel Blake

A Whisper Away From Evil

First published in 2023 by DRF Publishing.
Copyright © 2023 by Gabriel Blake

Print ISBN: 978-1-9996636-5-0
eBook ISBN: 978-1-9996636-4-3

Cover by DRF Publishing
Edited by DRF Publishing
Written by Gabriel Blake

www.gabrielblake.com

'Oh, what a tangled web we weave,
when first we practice to deceive.'
— Sir Walter Scott, *Marmion* (1808)

1

December 18

9.10 p.m.

Propelled by fierce winds, rain pelted down on the Kent motorway. Numerous emergency vehicles with flashing blue lights lined both sides of the incident, illuminating the gloom. Twinkling like stars, thousands of tiny glass fragments littered the road. In the midst of it all lay the wreckage of an old white Ford Transit van and a dark blue Mazda MX-5. The southbound section of the M2 between junctions four and five had been closed, much to the annoyance of tired motorists eager to get home and out of the dismal December weather. Strewn across the saturated road were unrecognisable parts of both vehicles. On its side, the van took up both lanes, while what was left of the overturned Mazda was a good four metres or so further ahead on the grass verge. A black four-door saloon pulled up beside a police car. A man dressed in a dark suit and tie stepped out.

A uniformed officer wearing a high-visibility jacket approached him and said with a broad Welsh accent, 'I'm Owen Carrick, Roads Policing Lead Investigator. And you are?'

'Detective Inspector Harry Baxendale. I've been assigned to assist in the investigation. Please tell me why I'm out here in the pissing rain?'

'Possible homicide. Just over an hour ago, a van rammed into the back of a car that was parked on the hard shoulder.'

'It happens far too frequently, but surely it's an accident. No one in their right mind would plough into a stationary vehicle on purpose,' said Harry, who considered it a waste of his time being called to a road collision.

'A witness says the Ford Transit accelerated along the hard shoulder towards the Mazda instead of braking to lessen the impact. A passenger in the same vehicle concurs.'

'Maybe the van driver was distracted or dozed off.'

'I start every road death investigation with the mindset of unlawful killing, and usually, I'd agree. However, I've been doing this for a long time – something is definitely off with this one.'

'Fair enough. I'll bow to your experience,' said DI Baxendale as he approached the van. He pulled a pair of latex gloves from his side pocket and slipped them on.

'In the van, we have a twenty-nine-year-old deceased male. The Forensic Collision Investigation Unit is on the scene and has discovered the gentleman's wallet.' Owen checked his notes. 'Vincent Perry from Chatham. The deceased has significant injuries, so I hope you have a strong stomach, Detective.'

Harry cast his eyes over the severe damage to the front of the vehicle and peered through what little remained of the shattered windscreen. A short burst of camera flashes gave him a brief glimpse of the driver's broken body. The camera flashed a couple more times before the FCI emerged from the back of the van holding sealed evidence bags containing the wallet, an iPhone, and various scraps of paper. Harry turned his attention from the bags and asked her if it was okay to take a closer look.

'Be my guest,' she answered, and turned to Owen Carrick. 'You can have the coroner remove the body now.'

'Thank you, Sally.'

Rain rattled against the side of the van above as Harry crouched down and poked his head inside the cab. He spied the word 'DAD' tattooed across the middle fingers of the dead man's left hand. Owen Carrick wasn't kidding about the man being messed up. Harry observed the severe damage to the side of his face and skull and the cloying, metallic odour of blood in the air. He noted Perry hadn't been wearing his seat belt. If you were going to intentionally crash into someone, wouldn't you want to protect yourself as much as possible?

As though listening in on his musings, Owen said, 'You've noticed the seat belt, haven't you?'

'Yeah.'

'Doesn't make sense, does it?'

Getting to his feet, Harry answered, 'No, it doesn't. Unless he didn't intend to survive.' He looked towards the second vehicle and approached. 'Who do we have over here?'

'Now, this is where it gets strange,' said Owen.

'I'm all ears.'

'Despite the vast amount of blood on the steering wheel and dashboard, there's no victim. We're still checking the vicinity, but so far, we've failed to locate a body.'

Harry's puzzled expression fell away as he closed in on the overturned car, taking in the extensive damage. Although a two-seater, the back of the car had been crushed forward, almost into the front seats.

'Jesus,' he said, crouching down to examine the interior. He stood, glanced along the hard shoulder, and pointed to Sally, who was taking measurements with a member of her team. 'Is that where the van struck the car?'

'Yes. There is still a lot of work to do, but Sally is confident the driver made no attempt to brake. The position of the van suggests he may have changed his mind at the last second and tried to swerve around the Mazda.'

'So the van collided with enough force to push a stationary vehicle nearly fifteen feet?'

'Yes. Sally estimates the van was travelling at more than seventy miles per hour, and the handbrake not being applied in the car didn't help. That's usually the first thing you would do if you'd pulled up on the hard shoulder.'

'Unless you're preoccupied. Though it does seem strange,' said Harry. 'I can't imagine anyone would have got out of this car alive, let alone walked away from it.'

'You'd be amazed at what I've seen people walk away from.'

'I'm sure,' said Harry. 'Could there be another explanation for the blood?'

'Well, this is where it gets even more bizarre. We have several witnesses who claim to have seen a young woman in the driver's seat a second or two before the crash. They pulled their vehicles over further along and trekked down the hard shoulder, half-expecting to see the poor woman's remains. But she'd vanished.'

Harry raised an eyebrow. 'Vanished? That's absurd.'

'Hey, I can only relay what the witnesses have stated, Detective Inspector.'

The rain continued to fall as Harry scanned the carnage, trying to assess the situation. He wiped the rain from his forehead and said, 'Okay. It's a strange one, I'll give you that. But it's not murder until we find a body. I'm assuming you've already expanded the search of the surrounding area?'

'Of course. I've called for more officers, and I'm hoping a police helicopter will be here shortly. Meanwhile, I have officers checking recent admissions at local hospitals. With any luck, we'll find the driver within the next couple of hours.'

Harry said, 'The witnesses would have been driving past at *some* speed, so we can't rule out the possibility they are mistaken.'

'I'm not ruling anything out, but the witnesses were pretty adamant.'

'And yet none of them saw her crawl out of the wreckage and leave,' Harry argued. 'Are there any traffic cameras along here?'

'Yes. Across the motorway, up ahead, and further back down this side. I've already got the ball rolling on getting them examined.'

'Great,' said Harry. 'I'll follow up on the witness statements tomorrow. Let me know when you've confirmed the identity of the deceased driver, and I'll find out all I can about him.' Walking away, Harry stopped in the tracks of his wet footprints and turned. 'Oh, and if you find the woman, give me a call.'

Harry hastened to his car to escape the heavy rain. Before heading home, he called Detective Chief Superintendent Malcolm Falconer and left a message updating him about the new case. Through the water cascading down the windscreen, he observed the scene once again. Despite his initial reservations about the collision, he sensed something dark.

2

December 18

Harry arrived home soaking wet and tired. Upon entering the house, he removed his suit jacket and hung it on the overcrowded shelving rack between his wife's duffle coat and his daughter's anorak. On the shelf above were two family photos: one of Harry and his wife, Jenna, and their teenage daughter, Leah, standing outside the front door of their new house. In the other, they were about to board the train at the end of Southend Pier. Harry stared at the photo and smiled, always reminded of the day Leah got her stick of rock tangled in her mum's hair. Jenna laughs about it now, but she certainly wasn't happy at the time.

'Harry!' a woman's voice shouted from a room along the hallway. 'If your jacket is wet, don't you dare hang it up next to the others.'

He glanced to the heavens and answered, 'Of course not, love.' But he left it on the hook anyway. Harry kicked off his black leather shoes and squeezed them onto the crowded three-tier wooden shoe rack beneath the coats.

Along the hall, he popped his head around the door of the living room. Jenna was on the sofa watching television with a glass of white wine in one hand and her phone in the other. He glanced at Leah in the armchair with her feet tucked under her. With a tablet on her lap, she swiped the screen with one hand while texting on her phone with the other, probably conversing with friends about whatever she was looking at. Beside her chair was the immaculately decorated Christmas tree with its static white lights and perfectly spaced purple and white baubles.

Jenna turned her head away from the lame reality show she was watching. 'How was your day, hon?'

'Shit!'

'Language.' She nodded towards their daughter.

Leah looked up and asserted, 'Mum, I'm seventeen. Hi, Dad.'

'Hello, sweetheart.' He smiled back, but her focus had already returned to her devices. 'Right,' he said. 'I'm going up to take a shower.'

'Okay, babe. Do you want me to put your dinner out, ready for when you come down?'

'What is it?'

'Spaghetti bolognese,' she said, concentrating on the television.

'I'll sort it when I'm ready, thanks.' Before heading upstairs, he lingered in the doorway, staring at his wife and daughter, seemingly oblivious to his presence. Was this the daily routine in most households – a lack of attentiveness to loved ones and taking the unity of family for granted?

Slightly wet from his shower and with a large towel wrapped around his moderately flabby waist, he perched on the edge of the bed to examine his phone. He hoped for a message from Owen Carrick, telling him they'd found the woman alive and well. He remained doubtful someone could have climbed out of the crumpled car, but if they had, he suspected they wouldn't be alive now. It seemed unlikely there would be any news until morning.

He finished drying himself and put on his comfy shorts and a blue T-shirt, which had become a little tight around his midriff. The dreaded middle-aged spread – creeping up on him. He needed to get back to running before work and lifting weights in the garage.

Harry entered the kitchen, and despite telling her not to, Jenna stirred the bolognese while the spaghetti boiled violently on the hob. They had only lived in the house for a few months, having moved from Ilford to Kent. Jenna, a solicitor with over twenty years' experience at a small but notable company, had been headhunted by a highly reputable law firm in Maidstone with strong ties to London. Having been demoted after the fallout from his last case, Harry didn't need much convincing. Not that he'd done anything wrong as far as he was concerned. A serial killer had been stopped, and the infamous murderer, Harper Darmody, was presumably no more. Two for the price of one.

The impact of both cases coursed along the chain of command, and a few were made scapegoats, him included. When he'd reached out to Kent Police, he was offered a position soon after and was happy to make the switch, unlike Leah, who'd found it a little more upsetting to leave her friends behind. But, being motivated and ambitious, she hoped to join up with them again at Cambridge University, where she was determined to go a step further than her mother and become a barrister.

Harry moved up behind his wife and put his arms around her, snuggling into her back while she stirred the spaghetti. He planted a kiss on her neck. 'Want me to take over?'

'No. It's almost done.'

'I said I'd sort it.'

'Well, you know I like to look after my man.'

'Yes, you do.' He kissed her neck again. 'So, how was your day?'

'Good. I love my job, you know that. Was the road accident a waste of your time?'

Harry removed his hands from her waist and stepped back. 'No. They were right to send me. One fatality and a missing woman. I'll know more tomorrow.'

'I'm sure you'll get to the bottom of it. Go and make yourself comfortable. I'll dish up and bring it in.' Harry fetched a nice cold beer from the fridge on his way to the living room.

Later, when Jenna and Leah had gone to bed and left him watching television alone, he received a text message from Owen, letting him know they hadn't located a body and that the search would continue in the morning. Comfortable in the armchair, he reflected on the crash and sipped from his third bottle. Though unwilling to accept the collision could have been intentional, his earlier sense of unease remained. Deliberately targeting a vehicle on the road in such a way wasn't unheard of; however, it *was* rare. Once he had more details and questioned the witnesses, he hoped to get a better idea. He finished the last dregs of his beer, switched off the television and the lamp, and drifted upstairs to bed.

Walking along the landing, a muffled voice, followed by a stifled laugh, slowed him down. Most probably Leah, talking to a friend. Nearing the main bedroom door, he recognised Jenna's voice, which quickly fell silent. Darkness spilled from the room as he opened the door. He glimpsed Jenna rolling over in bed, apparently asleep. The glow of her mobile phone on the bedside table faded into the background. Harry marched into the en suite, switched on the light, and closed the door. He turned on the cold water tap and stared at himself in the mirror, his face red with anger. Gripping the sink with both hands, he squeezed hard on the porcelain. Jenna's affair was supposed to be over; not the main reason, but certainly one of the few that had encouraged their relocation from East London to Kent.

Benjamin Knightley was a solicitor who worked at the same firm as Jenna. The pair had been having an affair for eight months before Harry found out. He'd seen little signs but brushed them off, blaming his insecurities and paranoia. Then his world came crashing down.

After interviewing a suspect one morning, it occurred to him that he wasn't far from his wife's office, so he dropped by to surprise her with sushi (her favourite) for lunch. The young receptionist knew him well and waved him through to Jenna's office. He opened the door, and to his horror, Jenna was bent over her desk, being taken from behind by Knightley. All hell broke loose, and he almost strangled the life out of him. Coming to his senses before it was too late, he removed his hands from around the bastard's neck and fled the building. After several costly weeks in a flea-bitten hotel and numerous late-night, emotionally charged phone calls, they talked things through and chose to work on their marriage. He'd often considered whether her affair was payback for a foolish one-night stand he'd had nine years earlier.

Should he confront her now or wait until the morning? Surely she wouldn't do it again, not after everything they'd talked about and the promises made. Perhaps his concerns were unwarranted. Harry brushed his teeth and washed his face. When he'd calmed down, he turned off the bathroom light, took off his T-shirt, and slipped quietly into bed. For now, he would wait and see how the situation progressed.

3

December 19

The dark sky made for a dreary morning. At least it was dry. Instead of going to the station, Harry drove straight to the scene of the previous night's crash and parked among a multitude of police vehicles. Barely 7.45, and already he wanted the day to be over. He'd hardly slept, tormented by thoughts of Jenna and Benjamin. A long, depressing shift lay ahead, and if the witnesses were correct, the discovery of a body was imminent. Assisted by a family liaison officer, he'd have to inform her family – a part of the job he hated. Every copper did.

The mangled vehicles had been cleared overnight, and the outside lane of the motorway had reopened several hours earlier. Traffic cones lined a large section of the inside lane and hard shoulder where the Mazda had come to rest on the grass verge. A police helicopter hovered above the field over the ridge, unhampered by the low clouds – something that could soon change. Harry scrambled up the wet grass of the small slope.

Impressed by the number of available officers taking part in the search, he spotted Owen Carrick passing out instructions. Harry walked towards him and said, 'I take it there's still no sign of her?'

Owen looked over his shoulder. 'Morning, Detective Inspector. Not yet. But there was a call to the station about an hour ago. A seventeen-year-old girl has been reported missing.'

'I see. The girl's name?'

'Rebecca Heaton.'

'Young girls are reported missing all the time. It might just be a coincidence,' said Harry, having recently journeyed out in the early hours to collect *his* daughter after she'd been caught in a lie about where she was spending the night.

'Not in this case. Rebecca Heaton was not at the boyfriend's address supplied by her mother. And it turns out the Mazda is registered to the girl's boyfriend, Ryan Levinson, at the same address.'

Harry didn't show it, but this new information concerned him. It added a new layer to the investigation, and in his experience, it decreased the chances of finding her alive. Time to start interviewing the witnesses, beginning with the Ainsworths.

Philip and Vanessa Ainsworth lived in Ashford, another part of Kent that had undergone quite the transformation over the years. The married couple, both in their mid to late fifties, confirmed their statements about the van speeding past them on the hard shoulder.

Philip, who had been driving, said, 'The van was directly behind me for about four or five miles. The driver showed no eagerness to overtake until he indicated left to enter the hard shoulder. From there, he put his foot down and sped past us. He must have been going at least seventy miles per hour, aiming directly for the parked car.'

Vanessa said, 'I glanced up at the man as he zoomed past, and although it was dark, he was staring straight ahead, fixated, eyes wide.'

The couple added they did not see if there was anyone in the other car and were lucky not to be involved in a motorway pile-up.

On his way to see the next witness in Sittingbourne, Harry contemplated whether he'd been a fool to think this was anything more than an insurance job and doubted his previous sense of unease.

*

Mrs Hillingdon welcomed him inside, showed him to the living room, and hastened to fetch her daughter. In her early twenties, Melanie Hillingdon had been a passenger in her boyfriend James Harding's car. She was a sweet young lady with short black hair and freckles who remained visibly shaken by the collision.

Melanie's words fired rapidly from her lips. 'We were on our way back from the cinema. There were flashing hazard lights up ahead, and as we drove past, I saw a woman in the driver's seat.'

Other than the woman having blonde hair, she couldn't offer a better description.

She continued, 'There was a loud bang, and James saw part of the incident in his rear-view mirror. He immediately pulled onto the hard shoulder to see if we could help. A property maintenance van that had been in front of us also pulled over, and the three of us hurried towards the scene. Other cars stopped, with people getting out to help. I remember the traffic edging around the van in the outside lane, people staring and taking a good look at the crash before speeding up.'

She didn't recall much else, just that the van driver who'd walked beside them feared for the girl he'd seen in the car. The trio were baffled when there was no sign of her.

In his car outside the Hillingdons, Harry called Craig Bishop, the driver of the maintenance van. Mr Bishop had told Owen Carrick the night before that it would be best to call his mobile as he would be at work. Over the phone, Mr Bishop claimed to have seen the hazard lights on the hard shoulder and thanked his lucky stars he wasn't the one who had broken down on such a miserable night. The woman stood out because of her long, curly blonde hair and her head resting against the driver's side window.

'Perhaps she was asleep,' he said. 'I remember thinking to myself, she shouldn't even be in the car. She should be standing away from the vehicle on the verge. I know it was chucking it down, but it's just not worth the risk.'

Mr Bishop had over-elaborated on his last statement, sometimes a tell-tale sign of deception. He certainly wasn't buying Bishop's responsible citizen act. But he did corroborate Miss Hillingdon's account of a woman being in the car. Harry told Mr Bishop he'd be in touch if he had any more questions and to call if he remembered anything else relating to the incident.

Harry's mind raced. His doubts and uncertainties were no longer tenable. Owen had told him he'd be amazed at some of the collisions people had walked away from, but she had been seen *seconds* before the car was struck. It didn't seem conceivable she could have survived and walked away unharmed. Harry glanced at his Tag Heuer watch, a present from Jenna last Christmas. Eleven thirty. He made another call.

'Hey, Owen, it's Harry. I have one more witness to interview, but two have reaffirmed there was a blonde woman in the car, so she must be out there somewhere.'

'I think we've found her. I've just received word that the reverend of a church in Hartlip discovered a young girl in the grounds a short while ago. It's about a mile or so from the crash site. The helicopter is on its way, and I'm about to head over there now.'

Harry asked the only question that mattered at this point, 'Is she alive?'

'I'm afraid I have no further information at the moment.'

'Okay.' Assuming the worst, Harry's shoulders slumped. 'Text me the location. I'll meet you there.'

4

December 19

Harry didn't have to travel far from Sittingbourne to the small village of Hartlip. Up ahead, two police cars and an ambulance were parked on the kerb outside St Michael and All Angels. The road being fairly narrow, he followed suit. Climbing from his car, he looked around. How on earth had she managed to walk so far from the motorway? It wasn't confirmed if she *was* the young girl they were looking for, but . . .

He showed his warrant card to the police constable guarding the lychgate and walked along the path under the shadow of a large tree. Either side of him were ancient gravestones scattered among the rich green grass in front of the old church. As he neared the rear of the stone building, he saw the police helicopter in the field belonging to the school next door. Owen Carrick looked his way and approached. Going by his excited smile and the urgency of a paramedic rushing into the church, Harry got the impression good news was on the way.

Before he had the chance to ask, Owen hollered, 'She's alive.'

An intense rush of relief washed over Harry. He hadn't expected her to survive, but so far, there wasn't much about this case that had gone the way he'd imagined. 'Considering where we are, it seems appropriate to say thank the Lord. Is she badly injured?'

'After seeing the wreckage, you'd certainly think so, right?' The bemused expression on Harry's face prompted Owen to continue.

'Other than a few scratches and a small abrasion on her head, she has no life-threatening injuries.'

'What? That can't be! You saw the car and the blood.'

'I'm as shocked as you. They'll carry out a thorough examination at the hospital, but other than being confused and distressed, she appears to be in good physical health. She hasn't said a word so far, mind. The paramedics have checked her over and will shortly be transporting her to Medway Hospital.'

'Is it definitely the young lady we are looking for?'

'She doesn't seem to be carrying any identification, so we can't be one hundred per cent certain. But she fits the description. It has to be her, doesn't it?' Owen sounded hopeful.

The paramedics appeared at the church entrance and ushered them out of the way as they wheeled the patient along the path towards the waiting ambulance. Harry glanced at the young woman as they passed by. As expected, she looked pale and frightened. A dressing had been applied to her head wound, and her long, blonde hair fanned out around her. The Reverend Rupert Strathearn, a tall, thin, balding man with glasses, emerged from the church. Harry walked over to introduce himself.

'Good morning, Reverend. I'm Detective Inspector Baxendale. Is it okay to call you Reverend? I'm unfamiliar with the social etiquette of the church.'

'I'd be happy for you to address me by my first name if my parents hadn't lumbered me with Rupert, so let's stick with Rev, Reverend, or Mr Strathearn.'

Harry appreciated the humour. 'Could you tell me how you came to find the girl?'

'Now, let's see. I arrived at the church around eight o'clock. At half past ten, I took my usual stroll around the grounds because that's when I have my first and only cigarette of the morning. You can imagine my surprise when I discovered her lying face up on a grave at the back of the church. On closer inspection, she had a few bumps and grazes, and I assumed she'd fallen. As I touched her gently on the shoulder, her eyes sprang open. She immediately became agitated but, strangely, remained silent. I did my best to calm her, and she eventually let me guide her into the vestry, where she gulped down a glass of water. I tried to get her to talk, but she seemed traumatised. That's when I called the police.'

Harry looked in the direction of the graveyard at the back of the church. 'Would you be so kind as to show me exactly where you found her?'

'Of course,' said Reverend Strathearn, and he led both Harry and Owen along the path. 'She was lying right here,' he said, pointing to a grass-covered grave with an old, weathered, and slightly oblique headstone.

Harry asked, 'On the grave itself?'

'Yes. It struck me as odd because she was lying in alignment with the coffin below, head up by the stone, feet at the bottom. I must admit, I was quite apprehensive as I approached. I thought, well, I'm sure you can guess. As I neared, I could tell she was breathing. When I woke her, not only was she terrified, but she didn't appear to have a clue where she was.'

Harry stared at the timeworn engraving on the tombstone.

HERE LIETH
THE BODY OF MARY
ELIZABETH MARTIN,
WHO DEPARTED THIS LIFE
THE 18TH DAY OF DECEMBER
1776, AGED 17 YEARS

'Will that be all, Detective?'

'Yes. Thank you for your help, Reverend.'

Harry turned to Owen. 'When you finish your report on the collision, can you send everything you have over to me?'

'Will do.'

'And when you've confirmed the identity of the victim—'

'Already confirmed. Vincent Perry *is* the deceased driver.'

'Okay,' said Harry. 'I'm struggling for time – is there any chance you could have one of your officers look into Mr Perry and Rebecca Heaton's boyfriend, Ryan Levinson?'

'I'll do it myself when I get back to the incident room. What are you going to do now?'

'I'm going to the hospital. As soon as she is able, I need to ask the young girl some questions. I'll also let Mrs Heaton know we've found her daughter.'

As he wandered along the path towards his car, Owen shouted, 'Harry! Would you let me know if you get anything out of the girl? I am as baffled by this as you are.'

Harry smiled. 'Of course.'

5

December 19

Harry had been in the waiting area of the hospital ward with Police Constable Lucy Fenton for over two hours. Lucy had accompanied him to question the girl. The waiting room was compact, with six chairs, a portable television on the wall, and a small, unloved play area for children. Other than a brief discussion about the case with the PC, not many words were exchanged. He had hoped Lucy might add some insight, but she couldn't come up with anything he hadn't already considered.

Lucy excused herself and headed off to the bathroom. Harry stood to stretch his legs and looked at the small outdoor square below, surrounded by windows and a solitary door. In the centre stood an unusual sculpture he could not make head nor tail of. To the side was a faded wooden bench, offering the promise of a brief respite from the hustle and bustle of the busy hospital. There was no disputing that Rebecca was in the car; two unrelated witness accounts couldn't be wrong. She had been given the all-clear by the doctor, and other than a couple of minor abrasions and bruises, she had no further injuries – a miraculous escape. He had delayed calling her mother, wanting to speak to the girl on her own first. He sipped from his second cup of tasteless vending machine coffee, grimacing slightly as he did so. The brief vibration of his phone alerted him to a text from Jenna.

Hi babes. Hope your day is going well and you've found the missing woman. xx

Returning to his seat, he contemplated the previous night, less confident it was Jenna's voice he'd heard on the landing. Though Leah and her mother sounded alike, the light going out on Jenna's phone as he entered the room left him uneasy. She could have been checking the time. There had been many occasions when she'd messaged him from upstairs to see if he was still awake. If he didn't reply, she'd wander down to fetch him or cover him with a blanket. It wasn't easy to forget what he'd seen that day in her office. What followed was an extremely challenging time in their marriage. He'd found it within himself to move past it, forgive her of sorts, just as she had him for his dalliance. Was he being irrational or ignoring the cold, hard truth?

Harry was about to reply to Jenna's text when Dr Prasad entered the room. Soaring from his chair, Harry asked, 'Can I see the girl now?'

'You can, Detective Inspector. She appears to be in a state of shock and still hasn't said a word.'

'Yes, the reverend who found her said she wasn't quite with it.'

Dr Prasad continued, 'A scan revealed no permanent damage, but it's evident she's suffered some form of head trauma. We've taken a blood sample to run further tests. It would be helpful if you could get her to communicate in some way, though I suggest at this stage you only have a few minutes with her. She shouldn't be pressed too hard.'

'Okay, great. I just need to make a quick phone call.'

Harry moved away from the doctor and called Mrs Heaton to let her know they'd potentially found her daughter. Overjoyed, she was out of her front door before the call had ended and on her way to the hospital. Harry turned and saw PC Fenton had returned from the bathroom.

As the doctor led them along the corridor, Lucy said, 'I hope I'm not crossing a line, guv, but was calling Mrs Heaton a bit premature? Shouldn't we have made certain it's her daughter beforehand?'

'No. It has to be her. But if she doesn't open up, at least Mrs Heaton will be able to confirm it for us. Then hopefully, we can find out exactly what happened and wrap this case up as soon as possible.'

The girl was in the last bed on the left, next to the window. The paper-thin blue privacy curtains around the bed were closed. The doctor pulled them aside and beckoned the officers forward.

In a calm, reassuring tone, Dr Prasad said, 'This is Detective Inspector Baxendale and Police Constable Fenton. They are here to ask you a few questions.' Already sitting upright in the bed, the girl stared blankly ahead. It was difficult to know if she understood. The doctor turned to Harry. 'I'll give you some time alone with her.'

She appeared as frightened now as she did when he caught a glimpse of her at the church. Her face was ashen, and her bright blue eyes were wide with fear.

'Hi, Rebecca,' said Harry, hoping she'd acknowledge her name. She gave nothing away. 'I promise this won't take long. I have some questions about the collision you were involved in last night.' She fixed her gaze on him, but she was hard to read. If he had to guess, he'd say she had no idea what he was talking about.

Harry said, 'Do you remember being involved in an incident last night?'

Her silence continued, and her expression remained unchanged. Harry stared at Lucy, suggesting she give it a try. The constable moved around to the side of the bed but kept her distance so as not to spook the poor girl.

She smiled softly. 'Hello, Rebecca. I'm Lucy. We're here to make sure you are all right and to find out what happened to you. Can you tell me how you are feeling?' She didn't reply and held the same blank stare.

The two officers exchanged glances before Harry faced the window and listened as Lucy tried again. 'I know you are distressed after last night, but we can't help if you won't talk to us.'

Accepting they were not going to get a response, Harry turned and said, 'I've called to let your mother know where you are. She will be here shortly.'

At the mention of her mother, the intense glare in the girl's eyes eased, and her shoulders relaxed into the pillow. The silent treatment continued. All he could do now was wait until Mrs Heaton arrived. Her presence would hopefully prompt a response from Rebecca and provide him with some answers.

'We'll leave you to rest and come back a little later,' he said. Both officers returned to the waiting room. Another bland coffee was on the cards.

While Harry waited for Lucy to return with the drinks, he replied to Jenna's earlier message.

Found the girl. Talk to you about it later. Can't wait to get home. X

Cutting a frustrated figure, he put his phone away and buried his head in his hands. Lucy appeared, passed him his coffee, and sat in a seat opposite.

'What do you think?' asked Harry.

'She's obviously scared, guv.' She pulled the lid from her coffee and took a tentative sip.

'Is that all it is, or is there more to it?'

'Hard to say. I wasn't involved from the start. By your question, I assume you think there is.'

Harry sipped his coffee and sighed. 'Maybe. From what the witnesses say, the deceased van driver had every intention of hitting the car Rebecca Heaton was in. I'm hoping she can fill in the blanks and tell us why he wanted to kill her.'

'There are times when we have to take witness statements with a pinch of salt,' said Lucy. 'We all interpret things differently.'

'I agree, but they were both adamant she was in the driver's seat at the time of impact. That's pretty convincing.'

'What if she got out of the car after they drove past, just before the collision?'

'No. We're talking about zero to two seconds between the witnesses passing the car and it being hit,' said Harry. 'I have no doubt the truth will come to light. It usually does.'

Lucy looked at her phone while Harry put his head against the wall and closed his eyes. His exterior looked calm, but on the inside, he was agitated, desperate to get to the bottom of things. A backlog of other ongoing investigations didn't help. Hearing a commotion at the end of the corridor, he moved to investigate. An excited woman, smartly dressed with short brown hair, came rushing towards him.

'Mrs Heaton?'

'Yes, where is she?' she insisted, anxious to see her daughter.

'I'm Detective Inspector Baxendale. I'll take you to—'

'Mrs Heaton?' Dr Prasad interrupted, appearing from nowhere.

'If you'd like to follow me.' The doctor gestured towards the unit. 'Detective, would you mind remaining here? We don't want to startle the girl any more than we already have.'

'Of course,' said Harry, reluctantly. He'd barely placed his backside on the seat of the chair when Mrs Heaton appeared at the door to the waiting room in an agitated state. Surprised, he jumped to his feet, noticing a distinct look of anger and pain on her face.

'Detective Blacksdale,' she uttered.

'Baxendale.'

'Whatever! I don't know what you're playing at, but that is *not* my little girl.'

6

December 19

It took a while to calm Mrs Heaton. Finding out the young girl in the hospital bed was not her daughter did not go down well. When she'd regained her composure, she levelled her anger towards the detective. There wasn't much Harry could do to appease her. He'd rolled out all the usual police clichés, promising he wouldn't rest until he'd found her daughter. He was as exasperated as she was and now had two teenage girls to deal with – one still missing and another who had seemingly gone mute.

PC Fenton proved invaluable in settling Mrs Heaton, so Harry suggested she take her for a cup of tea in the canteen and try to gain some insight into Rebecca and her boyfriend. In the waiting room, he stared at the image of Rebecca he'd asked Mrs Heaton to send to his phone. The girls bore a striking resemblance to one another. Not doppelgangers, but remarkably similar in build, natural blonde hair, large blue eyes, and the same button nose.

If the mysterious girl along the corridor wouldn't open her mouth, it was time to question Rebecca's boyfriend – Ryan Levinson. Being the registered owner of the Mazda, perhaps he could shed some light on why a seventeen-year-old with only a provisional licence was driving his car.

Harry answered a call from Owen and said, 'It's *not* Rebecca Heaton.'

'Because that would have made life simple for us, wouldn't it?' he replied. 'We'll resume the search. Anyway, an officer has gone through the CCTV on the motorway and found nothing. The cameras were too far away, and the images were blurred due to the severe weather conditions. When I get a chance, I'll check them myself.'

Seething, Harry removed the phone from his ear and mouthed the word, 'Fuck!'

Owen added, 'As of yet, I haven't had the opportunity to look into the backgrounds of Perry or Levinson.'

'No problem. Thanks for letting me know.'

Harry tossed the phone onto the seat beside him. He'd had better days, and at this point, he couldn't see a way to alleviate his mounting stress. His phone pinged with a message from Jenna, letting him know she'd be home late and he was to cook dinner for Leah and himself. Pizza it was, then. He replied and checked the time: 3.22 p.m. He'd find out if Lucy wanted to accompany him to interview Ryan or be dropped off at the station. Harry opened the door to exit the ward and hesitated, toying with the idea of questioning the girl once more. He let the door close and walked back along the corridor.

Sitting upright in bed with her head on the pillow, she gazed at the dark grey sky outside the window. The clouds were heavy and ready to burst. Unlike before, she appeared more at ease. On the overbed table sat a plate of untouched food: dried fish, chips, and mushy peas. Harry pulled a chair closer to the bed. The girl didn't flinch and continued to stare skyward. Unsure what to say, and with the day slowly grinding him down, he vented a prolonged sigh and relaxed into the chair.

Eventually, he said, 'Over a period of two and a half years, my daughter spent months in a hospital bed just like this one, next to the window. It was over ten years ago, but it's still fresh in my memory. My wife and I feared the worst and expected to lose her to acute lymphoblastic leukaemia. She was three years old at the time of her diagnosis. So tiny, and yet so bloody brave. She's around your age now.'

He paused to let the silence linger and said, 'I can help if you'll let me. If you tell me your name and address, I can get your parents here. They could take you home.' Harry sighed in defeat and pushed himself up, using the arms of the chair. 'I'll come back tomorrow and see how you're doing.' He parted the cubicle curtains.

'Annalise,' she said, soft and low.

He turned to face the girl, whose eyes remained fixed on the window.

'My name is Annalise Fournier.'

Harry smiled at the breakthrough and immediately detected a North American accent. 'Pleased to meet you, Annalise.'

'You can call me Anna. Most people do.'

'Okay. Anna it is.' He moved closer, leaned against the window, and patiently waited for her to speak.

'Why did that lady get upset when she looked at me?'

'She's the mother of a missing young girl.'

'And you thought I was her?'

'You're about the same age, and finding you the way we did, yes. How old are you, Anna?'

'Seventeen. Is the lady going to be okay?'

'If her daughter is found safe and well, she'll be fine.'

'I hope you find her.'

'Me too. Are you from the USA?'

She frowned. 'Canada. I'm from Toronto.'

'Are you here with your parents? Or visiting friends, maybe?'

'I was on my way home from work.'

'How did you come to be in the church cemetery? Did you get lost?'

'I'm not sure of anything.'

'You've had a nasty blow to the head, so it's not surprising.'

'No, you don't understand. There was this guy. Like, really creepy looking. He tried to force me into his car and injected something into my arm. I managed to pull away from him and ran into a nearby churchyard to hide. I remember feeling tired and falling, and when I came to, there was this old priest guy staring at me.'

Harry took out his notebook and pen. 'It sounds as though you've been through a terrifying ordeal. I'll let the doctor know, and he can find out what you were injected with. It was most likely a sedative. Could you describe this man?'

'He was a white guy, late thirties, six feet, maybe taller. He had long, jet-black hair and thick stubble.'

'How long was his hair exactly?'

'Just below his shoulders. And his left eye wasn't normal. It was like, slanted, or at least lower than the other. It's hard to explain. His hair seemed intentionally longer on the left side to conceal it. He also had an accent, like yours.'

'English?'

'Yes.'

'Anything else about him?'

'He had a stud above his right eyebrow and wore a long leather jacket.'

'Would it be okay if I got a composite artist to drop by? A picture would be a great help.'

'Sure.'

'Excellent! Now, you mentioned his car?'

'It was a dark red SUV, but that's all I can tell you. I didn't hang around to check the licence plate. I was scared and just wanted to get away.'

'I can imagine. Where exactly did this man try to abduct you?'

'The corner of St Clair and Kenwood Avenue.' He scribbled down the address with a puzzled expression, trying to recall the whereabouts of those roads. He couldn't.

Anna continued, 'It's the Christmas holidays, you see, so I'm working part-time at Landucci Pizzeria. I'd seen him in the restaurant the day before. I remember because I caught him staring at me a few times but thought nothing of it. Anyway, I finished my shift at three in the afternoon, and when I got outside, he approached me. He offered me a ride home, and at first, I politely declined, but he kept on pushing. In the end, I told him to get lost and carried on walking. The next minute, he pulled up beside me and attempted to bundle me into his SUV.' She sipped her water.

'I already mentioned the syringe. God knows what would have happened if I hadn't kicked him hard in the shin and gotten away. I tried to get the attention of passing cars as I crossed the road, but they ignored me. So I ran into the churchyard and hid in some bushes. That's when I became light-headed. The next thing I remember is waking up in the graveyard with an unbelievable headache.' She reached up to the bump on her head.

'You did brilliantly. To fight him off and get away took a lot of courage. Your parents must be extremely worried about you. Do you have a phone number for them?'

'Their numbers are on my cell, which is in my bag, but I don't know where my bag is.'

'I'll give the "old priest guy" at the church a call and see if he has it there. What about an address for where you live?'

'I live with my parents at 70 Helena Avenue,' she said.

'What's the postcode?'

She tilted her head to the side, puzzled, and must have guessed he meant area code. 'M6G 2H2.'

The code seemed odd to Harry. 'Is this close to where you were found?'

'Should be.'

'Okay,' he said. 'I'll check this out, find any numbers registered to the address, and get in touch with your parents. I'm sure they'll be relieved to learn you're okay.'

'Detective Baxendale, there's something else. I'm pretty sure the church I woke up in was different from the one I ran into. Does that sound stupid?'

'Not at all. You've been through a lot, and the bump on your head wouldn't have helped. Plus, it was dark. Places often look different in the light of day.'

'I suppose. Could I ask one more thing?'

'Of course.'

'How come everyone has a British accent around here?'

Harry pulled the chair closer and sat down. 'Anna, where exactly do you think you are?'

She scrunched up her face and answered, 'In Toronto, silly.'

7

December 19

Many things didn't come naturally to Lenny Grey, and love was right up there. Though in his mid-fifties, love had eluded him until recently. Not that he'd ever gone looking for it. An investigative journalist for most of his career, he'd thrown himself into his work as he hunted and hounded criminals around the world. He'd also worked as a correspondent during the Bosnian War. He'd taken women out, of course, but rarely did he make it to a second date, be that his choice or theirs. Mostly theirs.

Of all the crimes he'd seen and the horrific atrocities he'd experienced, it was the events of the summer before last that had caused him the most personal grief. While attending a crime scene, he'd met forensic pathologist Olivia Reid. Not the most romantic way to meet, but when you're not looking for love, it can find you in the most unexpected places. Their romance was short-lived, but in Olivia, he imagined he'd found "*the one.*" Things were progressing nicely, and he'd just helped find the notorious serial killer, Joseph Webster, bringing closure to the death of a young boy that had haunted him for years. On his return home later that evening, he discovered Olivia's body in his blood-soaked bed. Knowing Lenny was getting too close, Webster had tracked him down and found Olivia alone and vulnerable in the apartment. He'd settled for her instead.

She wasn't the only person taken from him that summer. Before he lost Olivia, Lenny had teamed up with DCI Colin Hargreaves in the hunt for Webster. They had worked together before and had become friends in the process. Unfortunately for Colin, he'd stumbled across Webster's hideaway, and when Webster returned, he'd murdered the DCI. The experience of losing Colin was traumatic enough, but finding Olivia dead culminated in a bungled suicide attempt, with Lenny shooting off his big toe. But that's another story.

In a café not far from the home of the BBC, Lenny sipped his tea. Less than an hour ago, he'd given an interview to promote his new book about the events leading up to and the deaths of not one but two killers: Joseph Webster and Harper Darmody. However, despite numerous searches, Harper's body had yet to be recovered. Lenny had toyed with the idea of writing the book for a while; it was a difficult decision to make, especially as it meant reliving the horror of what happened first to Colin and then ultimately to Olivia. Continuing his struggle with unrelenting torment, he knuckled down and poured his grief onto the pages.

When his food arrived, he thanked the man, folded the newspaper with '*cafe*' written in biro at the top, and tossed it next to his phone on the table. Biting into his egg and bacon sandwich, the yolk flowed down his chin and dripped onto his clean white shirt. Good job he'd chosen to eat after the interview. He wiped the mess with a napkin, made it worse, and gave up. Sipping his tea, he watched people through the window, wrapped up in layers of clothing to fend off the painfully cold wind.

Taking another bite of his sandwich, his phone rang. Harry Baxendale. What did he bloody want? If the police wanted to talk to you, it was rarely good news, so he let it ring. He recalled Harry proposing the idea of a future collaboration at Olivia's funeral. He hadn't entertained the idea then and wasn't going to now. In truth, he had no idea what he was going to do next. He'd written a couple of books but didn't regard himself as a novelist. There had been some calls from news editors, but he didn't fancy going back into journalism. For a long time, he'd been snubbed by the media, and Lenny was a stubborn old sod.

Taking the Tube from Oxford Circus, he returned to his apartment in Stratford. Within seconds of closing the door, a fluffy black-and-white cat brushed past his leg, welcoming him home with a meow. He'd fallen in love with cats after unintentionally visiting a cat café in Nottingham the previous year. Having accepted the reality of being alone for the foreseeable future, the company of an indoor cat seemed the way to go. The cat was given to him by his friend Elaine, who happened to be the mother of Webster's first victim. Born out of hostility, a peculiar friendship had evolved between the pair over the years. She owned his apartment and let him live there for a modest rent. He didn't see her often as she lived in North Yorkshire; the last time he had seen her was when she'd dropped the cat off back in September.

'Hello, Phoebe Waller-Bridge,' he said, staring down at her as he removed his coat and hung it up. 'I'd love to believe you're excited to see me, but I'm betting you just want to be fed.' He bent down and lovingly ruffled the fur around her neck. 'I'm only joking – I know you don't like me going out.'

Along the hall, he paused at the door to the bedroom where Olivia had been murdered. He hadn't slept in there since – well, not intentionally. Now and then, when he'd had one too many whiskies, he would lie on the bed for hours and cry himself to sleep. Devastated by her death, he wished with every fibre of his being it had been him and not her. The cat's meow spurred him onward to the kitchen, where he filled her bowl with a pouch of salmon. It looked like no salmon he'd ever put between two slices of bread. He observed Phoebe's reluctance; perhaps she wasn't keen either.

Leaving the cat to eat, he walked into what was once the spare bedroom. He caught sight of himself in the full-length mirror and stopped to stare. 'Still a fat bastard,' he said bitterly. Overweight, yes, but nowhere near as big as he used to be. Considering the grief and stress he'd been under over the past year or so, his weight was bound to fluctuate. Giving up smoking and a seemingly never-ending diet, albeit erratic, had certainly improved his health.

Lenny changed his shirt, put on some joggers, and made himself a cup of tea. He planted his backside in the armchair in front of the television, and as soon as he was comfortable, Phoebe settled on his lap, purring like a goodun. His phone rang on the small glass table next to his armchair.

He glared at the name. 'For Christ's sake, Harry, leave me alone.' About to return it to the table unanswered, he changed his mind. 'What do you want?' He muted the TV.

'I could do with your help.'

Lenny replied with a blunt, 'No!'

'You haven't heard me out yet.'

'Don't want to. I'm not interested.'

'Okay, Lenny, fair enough. You go back to watching daytime television, and I'll leave you alone.'

'Good,' said Lenny, and hung up. He turned up the sound on the TV. 'Cheeky bastard, assuming all I do all day is sit and watch the bloody telly.'

A few seconds later, he switched it off and called Harry back. 'I'm listening.' There was a slight pause on the line. He imagined Harry with a self-satisfied smile, knowing he'd call back.

Harry said, 'I've got a car crash with one fatality, a missing driver, and a young girl in the hospital with no idea how she got attacked in Canada and woke up in a graveyard in Kent. I could do with a hand, Len.'

Was this a road he wanted to venture down? It wasn't as if he had anything to lose this time. He caught Phoebe staring at him accusingly, covered the phone, and moved it to one side. 'Apart from you,' he said, stroking her head. 'All right, Harry, what do you want me to do?'

'I don't think these cases are linked, so for now, I'd like your help with the car crash. Just follow your instincts, wherever they might lead.' Harry explained the situation and his suspicion of malicious intent.

'I'll text you my email,' said Lenny. 'Send everything you have so far and everything you receive going forward. If you want my help, I'll need to be kept up to date.'

'Not a problem, but keep this between us.'

'No worries. I'll be in touch if I find anything of importance.'

Lenny hung up, turned on the television, and smiled. His heart raced with excitement. He'd never admit it to Harry, but being involved in a new investigation had reignited his passion.

8

December 19

Outside the Levinsons' house in Hempstead, heavy rain battered Harry's car. Glad to have Lenny on board, he put his phone away and viewed the large detached property and the gravel drive big enough for a whole fleet of cars. Unfortunately, cars were noticeably absent, and his earlier knock had gone unanswered. Questioning Ryan first thing would have been his preference, but after a challenging morning, it couldn't be helped. He'd elected not to bring Lucy and set her to work on verifying Anna's address. Her story couldn't possibly be true. She was either severely concussed, delusional, or lying. On their way to the station, Lucy informed him that Mrs Heaton had called Rebecca's boyfriend a number of times without success and had also failed to find anyone home when she'd visited his address earlier that morning.

A glance at his watch revealed it was nearly half past five. He'd go straight home from here, order in some dinner, and call Owen. With the investigation becoming increasingly complex, it was time to put their heads together and try to make sense of it all. Despite the search teams venturing back out into the fields, there was still no sign of Rebecca. Staring at the house, a curtain twitched from an upstairs window. Somebody *was* home. He left the car and dashed through the driving rain to take shelter under the porch. Harry pressed the bell hard and continuously.

Not wanting a wasted journey, he stooped down to the letterbox, pushed it open, and shouted, 'I saw you at the window, so I know you're in there. I'm Detective Inspector Baxendale from Kent Police. I'd like to speak to Ryan Levinson.' He rapped his knuckles against the door.

At long last, there was movement from inside. The door opened, and in front of him stood a dishevelled young man with short blonde hair, wearing a crumpled T-shirt and shorts.

'Ryan Levinson?'

'Yes. Who wants to know?'

Harry produced his warrant card. 'Detective Inspector Baxendale. I'm here to ask some questions about—' A gust of wind blew hard rain into his back. 'Look, do you mind if I come inside for a few minutes?' Harry noted Ryan's hesitation and the way he peered over his shoulder towards the driveway, as though he were expecting someone.

The young man pulled the door wide open. 'Where are my manners?' he said.

Harry wiped his feet on the not-so-welcome mat and glanced around the ostentatious hallway. Conscious of the immaculate chessboard-tiled floor, he asked if he should remove his shoes.

'No, you're all right.'

He followed Ryan along the hall into a bright and spacious, white-carpeted living room. Black and white appeared to be the favoured colour scheme. The house was pristine, with no expense spared on furnishings. Lingering in the doorway, Harry said, 'Are you sure you don't want me to take off my shoes?'

'Honestly, it's fine,' said Ryan, smiling to play down his obvious nerves. He sat on the black leather sofa and invited the detective to take a seat in the matching armchair opposite.

Ryan asked, 'What is it I can help you with?'

Harry picked up on how articulate Ryan was. No doubt he was well schooled. 'How come you didn't answer the door when I knocked the first time?'

'I didn't know you'd knocked previously. I was asleep. I haven't been feeling too well.' Ryan's handsome face reddened, and more than a few beads of sweat adorned his forehead. His calm and collected act wasn't working.

Harry reached inside his jacket pocket for his notebook and pen. 'Let's get started, shall we? Do you own a car, Mr Levinson?'

'I'm sure you already know the answer,' he said. 'I own a blue Mazda MX-5.'

'Do you have any idea where your car is right now?'

'Of course. My girlfriend borrowed it last night, so I assume it's parked outside her parents' house.'

The young man's confidence grew by the second, ready to answer any questions thrown his way. The cynic in Harry speculated whether he'd prepared his answers beforehand. 'And your girlfriend would be?'

'Rebecca Heaton. Hold on, has something happened?' His newfound concern seemed genuine.

'How long have you been dating Miss Heaton?'

'I'm not certain. About seven months, maybe.'

'Well, Mr Levinson, I'm sorry to have to tell you this, but last night your car was involved in a fatal collision.'

'Oh my God,' he said, raising a hand to cover his mouth. 'I should never have let her use it.'

'No, you shouldn't. You must have known it was illegal for her to drive alone with only a provisional driving licence, so why did you?'

'I know it was wrong of me, but it was pouring down outside.' Ryan got to his feet and walked over to the window, peering through the brilliant white net curtains. He was definitely expecting someone. He turned and said, 'I should have called her a taxi. It just didn't occur to me at the time. Like I said, I haven't been well. She asked, and I – I stupidly agreed. I can't believe this has happened.' He returned to the sofa.

'What time did she leave here with the car?'

'Seven. Maybe a quarter past.'

'Well, that's a little odd,' said Harry. 'The incident occurred just after eight p.m. I'd hazard a guess and say it takes less than fifteen minutes to get from here to the site of the crash. Why do you think it took her so long?'

'I couldn't say. Perhaps she left a little later than I said or stopped at a shop.'

Harry pointed his pen at Ryan and said, 'You know what? I'm sure you're right. What about earlier in the day?'

'We spent most of the day together. I picked her up in the early afternoon, and we visited my friend Sarah, where we stayed until about four. Then we came back here because I wasn't feeling great.'

'At some point, I might need your friend's details to verify this.'

'Not a problem.'

The sound of crunching gravel alerted both men to a car pulling into the drive. Ryan seemed encouraged by the arrival of whomever he'd been expecting. Harry suspected he wouldn't get much more out of him.

Ryan jumped up from the sofa and said, 'My mother is home.'

'One last thing, Mr Levinson, you haven't once asked how Rebecca is doing.'

Consumed with panic and struggling for words, Ryan faced Harry. 'When you said the accident was fatal, I assumed you meant she was dead.'

'Oh, there was a fatality, but it wasn't Miss Heaton. The person driving the other vehicle is deceased. With regard to your girlfriend's well-being, we don't know. She wasn't found at the scene.'

The element of surprise on Ryan's face as his brows lifted and his eyes dilated was quite revealing. Harry's instincts told him Ryan was withholding information, but at this stage, he was keeping an open mind. Keys rattled in the front door, and it slammed shut.

'So, she could be alive?' It was difficult to tell if Ryan was hopeful or disappointed.

'We're optimistic,' said Harry. 'As I'm sure you are. All I can say is we're doing our best to find her.'

The young man's mother appeared – an attractive woman, possibly in her early forties, wearing a figure-hugging white knitted jumper, tight jeans, and white Converse trainers. The uptight expression on her face didn't suit her, but she looked like a woman who could hold her own. She stared inquisitively at Harry, waiting for an introduction.

Harry showed his ID and said, 'Detective Inspector Baxendale.'

She introduced herself as Penny Levinson, and he informed her why he was at their home. Her shock and concern that something might have happened to Rebecca seemed sincere.

'Mrs Levinson, can you confirm your son's whereabouts between seven and eight yesterday evening?'

'He was home. I remember because I'd just made myself a coffee before going for my run at seven. He came into the kitchen to get something to eat and told me he didn't want any dinner because he'd be getting an early night when Rebecca went home.'

'And Rebecca Heaton was here at that time?'

'Yes, but I'm afraid I couldn't tell you what time she left. I don't keep track of all the comings and goings in this house.'

'Did you see Rebecca?'

She paused before answering and stared at Ryan, considering whether her answer would get her son into trouble. 'Well, no, I didn't see her, but Ryan mentioned she was in his room when he came down to make them each a sandwich. I collected the plates and glasses later that night.'

'Do you know what time she arrived?'

'Detective, why are you asking all these questions? Is my son under investigation?'

'No, Mrs Levinson. I'm just trying to establish Miss Heaton's movements before the crash.'

'I see. Her mother must be worried sick. I know I am. She's a lovely girl.'

'Could we go back to what time Rebecca arrived at the house?'

She turned to her son. 'Did she arrive with you?'

'Yes,' he said, clearly irritated. 'I told you we were going up to my room. You never listen.'

'That would make it around four thirty, then,' she said.

'Thank you. Was your son's car in the driveway during the time Miss Heaton was here?'

'I suppose it must have been.'

'Did you see it?'

'I can't remember.'

'You didn't see it when you left for your run?'

'I'm not sure. I'm sorry.'

'It's okay. Are there other members of the household?'

'Just my husband. He's at work right now and usually gets home around six.'

'Could he have seen the car outside last night?'

'No. There was a problem with the machinery. He didn't get home until late.'

'May I ask what your husband does for a living?'

She paused – decidedly unhappy he was asking about her husband. 'I don't see the relevance of the question, but he runs Skippity Do. It's a waste management and recycling company.'

'Skippity Do,' Harry repeated, a faint smile shining through. 'No relevance, Mrs Levinson,' he said, even though there was. He wanted to know what kind of job paid for such a beautiful home. 'Going back to something you said earlier, what time did you collect the plates and glasses from your son's room?'

'Not long after ten, so I could start the dishwasher before bed.'

'And you saw Ryan at that time?'

'Yes.'

'Okay. I have all I need for now. Thank you, Mrs Levinson.'

Ryan led him along the hallway, and Harry sneaked a peek at the tops of the bags by the front door. Jewellery boxes from Diamond Supreme in Mayfair, the same shop where he'd purchased Jenna's engagement ring. Lovely store and service, but pricey. Someone was being spoilt this Christmas. Leaving the house, Harry observed the brand-new Range Rover in the driveway. He'd recently come across a stolen one while working on a different case and knew you wouldn't get much change out of two hundred thousand pounds for the model he was staring at. It surprised him that Ryan was only driving a Mazda MX-5; he imagined a Porsche would have been more to his liking.

Harry stared up at the sky, thankful the rain had stopped for now. He turned to Ryan. 'I almost forgot. Does the name Vincent Perry mean anything to you?'

'No,' he promptly answered. 'I can't say that it does. Who is he?'

'Mr Perry was the fatality at the scene.' Harry watched for a reaction, but if there was one, Ryan hid it well. 'If Miss Heaton contacts you, can you have her call me as soon as possible?' he asked, handing him a card with his name and number.

'I'll be sure to do that, Detective.' Ryan wasted no time in closing the door.

9

December 19

As soon as Ryan closed the front door on the detective, Penny was waiting for him in the hallway. She pointed towards the living room. 'In here, now.' She paused in the centre of the room and stared at the blank wall. Penny's heart thumped – her mind ran wild with a mixture of worry, confusion, and anger.

'What's up?' said Ryan, standing behind her.

She turned to face him. 'What's up? Are you kidding me? What the hell were you thinking, letting her take your car? She hasn't even passed her test yet! Oh my God, she could be lying out there in a ditch. Her mother must be frantic. If something's happened to that girl, I swear I'm gonna slap you silly.'

Ryan lowered his head and stared at his bare feet. 'I was so ill last night and clearly wasn't thinking. It was raining, and she asked if she could borrow the car. Half asleep, I just pointed to the chest of drawers where the keys were. When I looked up a few seconds later, she was gone.'

Tearful, he gazed at her. The urge to give him a hug was too much to resist, and she advanced towards her boy, pulling him close. 'It's okay, sweetheart. I'm sure she's fine. She's probably hanging out at a friend's house, scared shitless because of the crash. You're certain there's nothing you're not telling me? You didn't argue or anything?'

'No. Like I said, I just wasn't with it.' His arms tightened around her.

'Everything will be all right, I'm sure,' she said, pulling back from him. 'I'd say come and help me take the bags upstairs, but I've got some of your Christmas presents in there. Can't have you seeing them.'

'I'm going to see if I can find her, Mum. Like you said, she's probably holed up at a friend's place. Can I borrow your car?'

'Okay, baby. Good idea. The keys are out on the console. No peeking in the bags,' she said as he walked off.

Penny remained in the centre of the room, sensing all was not well. She loved her son dearly, but he wasn't a saint. Much like his father used to be, he had a short fuse and a habit of being economical with the truth. Hearing the car pull out of the drive, she marched down the hall, collected the shopping bags, and headed upstairs.

After depositing the bags in her bedroom, she walked along the landing to Ryan's room, opened the door, and stepped inside. Looking around his pristine and minimalist room, she wasn't sure what she was expecting to find. Her husband liked everything to be spotless – no clutter or posters on the walls. A few years ago, Ryan had felt the back of his father's hand when he'd pinned a poster of the West Ham football team to the door. He never did it again. There was nothing in this room to indicate her son's personality at all. She knew him, but she didn't *really* know him, not any more. She had no idea what type of music he liked, what games he played on his PlayStation, or if he still liked football. All residing under the same roof, yet living separate lives.

Penny walked over to his desk, reached down to open a drawer, and paused. What was she doing? Invading her son's privacy was wrong. Backing away, she glanced at his overflowing wastepaper bin and carried it downstairs to empty it. Watching as the contents dropped into the kitchen bin, she spotted an uneaten sandwich. Thinking back to the plates she'd cleared the night before, she recalled how both had been empty. It now bothered her that she hadn't seen Rebecca in the house and didn't know if Ryan's car was in the drive or not. Her son had lied before, but doubting his version of events on this occasion was unsettling.

10

December 19

With the television on in the background, Harry and Leah made small talk while stuffing their faces with pizza. The large box sat between them on the sofa, with only three slices left. Leah answered her silent phone, became excited about something, grabbed a slice of pizza, and rushed off to her bedroom. Father-and-daughter time had come to an end. Their relationship had changed a lot from what it once was. Yes, she'd grown older, but it was more than that. The sparkle she used to have whenever he was around had vanished – a consequence of Jenna's affair.

Harry and Jenna did their best to conceal the affair, but it wasn't possible. When he moved out of the house for nearly a month, Leah knew something was drastically wrong. They had always prided themselves on their daughter's intelligence, but for some reason, when their marriage started to fall apart, they imagined her to be oblivious. Leah had overheard their raging arguments and picked up a few words here and there; however, she didn't know the truth. When Harry left home, she assumed it was all his fault and that he'd been the one having the affair. He wasn't going to correct her and make her think badly of her mother. A few months passed before she forgave him, but the close bond they'd once shared was broken.

Harry placed the pizza box on the floor, sprawled out on the sofa, and put his feet up. A few minutes to himself wouldn't hurt. He lay in silence but couldn't switch off. What a strange twenty-four hours! His phone rang. He reluctantly reached across the table, saw Lucy was calling, and answered.

'Hi, guv. Just calling to give you an update before it gets too late.'

'Go on then,' he said, yawning.

'I called the Toronto Police Service and was put through to Detective Christopher Tremblay. Annalise *is* from there, and she's definitely *not* on holiday in the UK. Her parents became concerned when she didn't return home after her shift at Landucci Pizzeria. At first, they surmised she must have gone to a friend's house. They tried calling her phone, but it kept going straight to voicemail. Her workplace confirmed she'd left after her shift at three, and her friends had neither seen nor heard from her. Around ten in the evening, Toronto time, Anna's parents reported her missing.'

'She was telling us the truth,' said Harry.

'Yes. There's more. A witness reported a girl being chased by a man not far from Annalise's place of work. The police didn't link the two events until much later and put out an APB on a red SUV. As you can imagine, they assumed the worst. The detective has since contacted her parents to let them know she's safe. Everyone is as confused as we are about how she managed to vanish in Canada and turn up in the UK. The detective ran a check on flights—'

'Hold on – flights?' said Harry, sitting up.

'Well, I'm pretty sure she didn't come over on a broomstick, guv.'

'Hilarious. No, I'm questioning whether it's possible to make that journey in the allocated time. And what about a passport?'

'A flight from Toronto to London is about eight hours. It was around fourteen hours from the minute she went missing to the time she was found the next morning. So yes, even with an allowance for airport check-in, it's possible. *But*, as I was about to say, the Canadian detective checked all commercial airlines bound for the UK around that time, of which there were two, and according to the manifests, Annalise was not on either of them. A little later, her parents found her passport in a drawer at home.'

Utterly baffled, Harry contemplated the car accident involving the missing teenager and the mysterious appearance of Annalise, seemingly from the other side of the Atlantic. Could a man have abducted Annalise in Canada and flown her to England, where she somehow managed to escape? It was a plausible, if not far-fetched, option, but perhaps there *could* be another explanation.

'Okay, when you get a chance, I need you to check this end for any private flights from Toronto. Let's see what turns up. Also, check the government database and find out if Rebecca Heaton was an only child.'

'Are you thinking Rebecca Heaton and Annalise Fournier could be twins?'

'Their likeness is uncanny, so it's worth a shot,' said Harry. 'At this point, I'll take what I can get.'

'So you think these girls might have been up to something, like a prank?'

'I have no idea, Lucy. I'm probably way off. A connection between these girls would at least give us somewhere to start.'

'Does this mean I'm working the case with you, guv?' He detected excitement in her voice.

'Yes, but only if you stop calling me guv.'

'Done.'

'I'll talk to DCS Falconer first thing. What's happening with Annalise?'

'Arrangements are underway for her to fly back to Canada.'

'Good. It's best she gets back home to her family.'

Harry ended the call and reached for a cold slice of pizza. It pleased him that Annalise's parents knew she was safe; nevertheless, it wasn't the news he'd expected to hear. He considered calling Owen but opted to update Lenny instead.

11

December 19

At the kitchen table, Lenny perused the information Harry had sent. The printed documents lay scattered on the glass around his laptop. Usually, he'd be tired and in bed by now, but reading through the case notes fuelled his enthusiasm. The latest news about Annalise Fournier piqued his interest. As for Rebecca Heaton, with Harry pointing towards the notion of something more sinister going on, he trusted the detective's instincts. Harry's confidence in his own abilities may have taken a beating, but Lenny's belief in how good a detective he was had not changed.

Lenny examined the pictures of both girls and looked through recent online news articles in Canada and the UK, searching for blonde teenage girls who had been murdered or reported missing. Some of the Canadian links weren't accessible, but then he came across Reagan Scott: blonde, nineteen, presumed to have disappeared on the eighteenth of December – the same night as the other incidents. Checking an online map, he found that the last sighting of Reagan wasn't far from where Annalise was attacked.

His painstaking search continued into the early hours. Struggling to keep his eyes open, he discovered another girl who fit the same profile, this time in the UK. Manchester, to be exact. Eighteen-year-old Louise Norris was reported missing by her parents at the end of November; her body was found a week later. She had been badly beaten, raped, and strangled to death. Could these girls be victims of the same person? If so, Annalise was lucky to escape with her life.

The cat jumped onto the table. 'Come on, Phoebe, you know you're not allowed up here,' he said, running his fingers through her thick fur. 'All right, just don't do it if we have guests.' Phoebe stared at him, appearing to mock his last statement. He laughed. 'I know – fat chance of that happening, right, girl?'

He looked again at the faces of Rebecca Heaton and Annalise Fournier. They could easily be mistaken for sisters, and Harry's reasoning was understandable. As far as Lenny was concerned, a connection between the two was unlikely. Staring at Annalise, he said, 'How on earth did you wind up in this country?'

He got to his feet, walked over to the cupboard, and poured himself a glass of Talisker ten-year-old single malt whisky, gifted to him by a neighbour for helping her get a chest of drawers up to her apartment. He glanced at all the papers splayed out across the table. 'Oh, Olivia. Why the hell am I getting involved in all this again?'

'Because you love it,' she answered. Seated in his favourite armchair, she said, 'You need it like you need a fry-up in the café down the road most mornings.'

'I don't know about that,' he said. 'To say "most mornings" is a bit excessive.'

'It's stupid o'clock, and look at that table. You've been going over it for hours. You love it, Lenny, and there's nothing wrong with that.'

'I'm just – I dunno, bored, I guess.'

'You're not bored. You are lost. You've had no purpose for a while, and now you have something to focus on. This is just what you need,' she said, walking towards him.

'Do you think?'

Olivia placed her hand on his cheek. 'Oh, my love. I'm certain. There is a man out there who is murdering young girls. Catching monsters is what you do best, and you need to stop him.'

'I miss you so much,' he said.

'I know.' She put her arms around him and laid her head on his shoulder.

12

December 20

Shrouded in a hangover from the previous night's miserable weather, dark clouds lurked menacingly in the early morning sky. Sweeping winds pinched the skin on Lenny's face as he trudged across the open field, away from the site of the crash on the M2. Vast areas of long, green grass remained compressed, highlighting the various routes taken by members of the search party. He forced his way through a thick hedge and onto a narrow road where he'd left his car. As he settled behind the wheel, a van belonging to the collision investigation unit passed by and parked in front of him. Soon after, a police minibus pulled up. Several constables piled out, talking loudly while smoking cigarettes. Stupidly, it hadn't occurred to him the search was ongoing, and if they had caught him out in the field, he might have had some explaining to do. Harry would have been far from pleased, as he wanted to keep Lenny's involvement in the investigation under wraps.

Suspicious eyes glanced Lenny's way as he drove past the police vehicles. In less than a minute, he parked outside St Michael and All Angels Church and wandered towards the main entrance. He took a chance and tried the door. Locked. He sauntered along the path until he came to the graveyard at the rear of the impressive building. It would have been nice to see exactly where Annalise had been found, but unless the reverend showed up early, there wasn't much chance of that happening. He only had himself to blame. Before the crack of dawn, impatience got the better of him, and with hardly any sleep, he was out the door.

Wandering between long-abandoned graves, a loud croaking noise urged him to pinpoint the source. Perched on top of a headstone was a bird, at least a metre tall, with grey, black, and white feathers. It had a strikingly long, pinkish-yellow beak. The bird croaked again. He recognised it as a grey heron from a recent Kent wildlife programme he'd seen. Harry was right: too much time on his hands and far too much TV. Another flew overhead, its wingspan around two metres. The one he'd been observing launched from the headstone. Mesmerised, Lenny watched the spectacular birds disappear over the trees.

He regarded the stone where the bird had stood and wandered closer. About to turn away, something grabbed hold of his hand. Though he saw nobody beside him, he sensed someone was there. The slow drum of his heart thundered in his ears. An extraordinary electrical sensation flowed under his skin like a gentle caress as he was pulled forward towards the grave. He read the name aloud: 'Mary Elizabeth Martin.'

Turning his head to the side, a young girl dressed in a flowing, tattered white gown stared back at him. There appeared to be fresh injuries on her face, as though she had been beaten. Her neck was bruised and indented, indicating some sort of ligature had been applied. The left side of her face was severely scarred but had healed, suggesting it was older. Despite her physical condition, she had the most bewitching smile he'd ever seen – warm and full of life. Her manifestation gradually faded. The croak of the grey herons drew his eyes skyward as they flew over him, and the strange force that had restricted his movement ceased.

*

In light of his supernatural experience, Lenny waited for Reverend Strathearn. Though certain, he wanted confirmation that Mary Martin's grave was where Annalise was found. Any information regarding the young girl buried there would be a bonus. Lenny posed his question to the reverend as soon as he arrived. He recalled a member of his parish telling him a story about the grave a few years earlier. He had assumed it was a tall tale passed down through the ages. In the storeroom, they opened dusty boxes and scoured through old folders. The reverend checked his watch and left Lenny to search alone while he attended to some church business. He returned an hour later, carrying two cups of tea.

Taking a break, Reverend Strathearn asked, 'I know you said you're helping Detective Inspector Baxendale, but how does a girl who has been dead for over 245 years relate?'

'It's complicated,' said Lenny.

'Now I am intrigued, Mr Grey.'

'You'll probably think it sounds crazy.' Lenny explained everything except the part about his ghostly encounter.

The reverend stood there, mouth agape, his eyes wide and full of surprise. 'I must say, it's incredible that the girl I found in the cemetery was attacked in Canada and ended up here, but there must be a logical explanation.'

'If there is, we haven't found it.'

Buzzing with exuberance, the reverend said, 'And now you're looking into the past, perhaps searching for some kind of – dare I say it – a miracle?'

'I'll be honest, Rev – I'm not sure what I'm looking for. I kind of let events guide me.' He hoped he didn't sound like a madman.

'Guidance is often the best way to get to the bottom of most problems. I'd be grateful if you'd let me know the outcome.'

'Will do,' said Lenny, taking a sip of his tea.

Changing the subject, Reverend Strathearn said, 'You'll have to forgive me, but I can't help noticing a heavy weight about you.'

'I suppose I am carrying a few extra, Reverend.' Lenny patted his belly. 'But I have, in fact, *lost* weight over the past year.'

'Huh! No, you misunderstand. I wasn't talking about your weight. I meant that you seem greatly burdened by something.'

'Oh, I see. It's nothing. Well, it's obviously something. I'm dealing with it, though.'

'Are you? As I often tell my parishioners, bottling things up is unhealthy. That's why talking helps.'

'It's not so easy when the one person you would have turned to for help is taken from you by a bloody psychopath.' Lenny was aware of the rising anger and pain in his voice. 'I'm sorry for swearing, Reverend. I know I shouldn't, not with this being' – he glanced to the heavens – '*His* house and all that.'

'Not to worry. I do it all the time,' he said. 'May I ask how she was taken from you?'

'A killer I was pursuing came looking for me. Instead, he found my Olivia. We weren't together long, but I loved her. I know I did.' Once again, Lenny's emotions came to the fore.

'Love is not measured by time, Mr Grey. Love is both heart and soul. You're angry, and rightly so. To lose a loved one is truly devastating for us, but to have them taken from us in such a brutal fashion is just plain cruel.'

'I imagined you'd be telling me she's in a better place and all that guff.'

'Not at all. I find the phrase condescending. Who's to say where a better place is? The best place to be is with the ones we love and who love us. The soul in Heaven may not be suffering as much as the soul in Hell, but I'm pretty sure that in most cases, neither is happy for the sorrow they have left behind.'

'Yeah, you could be right.'

'Just remember, God created the world to carry us, not for us to carry the weight of the world. If you have nobody else and ever need to talk, I'm a good listener.'

'That's much appreciated, Reverend.'

'Right, let's see if we can find something that may be of help to you.'

Within the hour, the reverend had found a timeworn folder and a dusty old brown book, bound with string to keep them together. Blowing off the dust, he uncovered the faded name of William Martin. The men shared a palpable sense of enthusiasm as Reverend Strathearn pulled the string to unbind the items so they could take a look.

13

December 20

Alone at the kitchen table and ready for work, Harry consumed his scrambled eggs, toast, and coffee. Off school for Christmas, Leah was having a lie-in. No doubt she'd been up most of the night messaging friends online as usual. Perhaps he'd have done the same if all this social media malarkey had been around when he was young. Jenna hadn't arrived home until the early hours, and he assumed she'd be going to work later than usual. He'd taken a cup of coffee up to her, but the muffled groan of appreciation from under the covers made him doubt she'd stayed awake long enough to drink it.

He hadn't got much sleep himself, not with the mystifying events of the case swirling around in his mind and a couple of visits to the bathroom – an all-too-regular occurrence since reaching his mid-forties. When he finally nodded off, the familiar chuckle of a taxi's diesel engine caused him to stir. He tapped the screen of his phone to life, strained his eyes, and saw it was half past two. She hadn't come home in her car, which meant she'd been for a drink. She'd tiptoed into the bedroom, but stealth had never been her strong suit.

Thinking about the day ahead, he hoped for a positive breakthrough and that Rebecca Heaton would be found alive.

His first job this morning was to update DCS Falconer and ask for Lucy Fenton to be assigned to assist him. She'd spent most of yesterday with him and was now familiar with the case, so he hoped it wouldn't be an issue. Before making breakfast, he'd spoken with Owen, who'd discovered Vincent Perry was no stranger to crime. Owen had also warned him about Luton Road in Chatham, where Perry had lived with his older brother. It had become notorious over the years for all the wrong reasons, such as knife crime, assaults, arson, and murder. He scraped the remnants of his breakfast into the bin. It was going to be a long but interesting day.

In the car, Jenna's late-night drinking session played on Harry's mind. Presumably, her firm had won a big case and gone out to celebrate. She'd previously used such events as cover to hide her affair. Not wanting to dwell on the past, he turned up the volume on the radio – Katy Perry's 'Firework' had always been an uplifting distraction. No doubt he'd receive a message from Jenna later, telling him off for not waking her. Driving past the police station, he spotted Lucy walking up the steps and through the dark brick and glass-fronted entrance.

Harry found his usual space in the police car park and entered through a rear door. At his desk, he fired up the computer. The station looked as outdated and timeworn on the inside as it did on the outside. In front of him was an A4 sheet of paper containing the flight data he'd requested. There were two cargo planes and two privately owned jets on the list. One belonged to Marvin Collingwood and had been hired by an English folk singer and his band, while the other had been piloted by Peter Mullings, the managing director of a popular bank. As expected, Annalise's name wasn't among any of the passengers. To add further woe, there were no women included on either of the flight manifests.

All the people on those planes were suspects, and unless he and PC Fenton got lucky, they'd have to interview every single one of them. If he didn't get around to interviewing Mr Mullings today, he'd go and get a statement from him tomorrow. Flying his own jet gave him the means to bring Annalise into the country, and that alone made him a person of interest. Lucy must have done some unpaid overtime to have all this waiting for him. He appreciated her help and effort.

Since questioning Ryan Levinson the previous day, Harry had been eager to run Ryan's father's name through the Police National Computer. 'I had a feeling you'd be on the system,' he said, reading through the content on the screen.

Carl Levinson had two convictions for assault in his early twenties. As well as the waste management company, he also ran a scrap metal business. After those convictions, plenty of rumours surfaced, specifically involving narcotics, dealing in small arms, and the corruption of police officers. Numerous investigations had failed to tie him to any wrongdoing until finally, his actions caught up with him, and he was imprisoned for twelve years. Since his release fifteen years ago, not a peep, which didn't necessarily mean he'd gone straight.

Harry checked his inbox. There were two emails from Owen Carrick, the latest of which revealed that Ryan Levinson had no criminal record. The earlier email referred to Vincent Perry, who was about as clean as a Wuhan lab technician's coat: shoplifting, burglary, street robbery, and assault. 'Not so sure the world's going to miss you, Vincent,' he said.

Another email appeared, this time with information about Vincent Perry's brother. Both were registered at the same address, and surprise, surprise, they shared a similar criminal background. Harry double-checked the name – Frederick – *Fred Perry*. He couldn't imagine his parents being fans of the legendary tennis player from the 1930s.

Owen had gone out of his way to provide him with more details than he'd asked for, even giving him a heads-up about the kind of person he would be visiting. Given Mr Perry's violent past, two constables had accompanied a Family Liaison Officer to break the news to him the day before. That same afternoon, Fred had identified his brother's body through carefully taken photographs in a sitting room at the morgue.

On his way to see DCS Malcolm Falconer, Harry collected a piece of paper from the printer, folded it, and put it in his pocket. He knocked and was beckoned into the office. Harry lingered in front of the desk.

Busy scribbling away, Malcolm said, 'I'll be with you shortly.'

In his late fifties, the DCS was fast approaching retirement. A traditionalist, Malcolm followed the rules but had grown tired of the continued modernisation of the force and the ever-increasing paperwork. He'd done his bit and was counting down the days until he could spend more time sitting in his garden, overlooking the sea, with his wife beside him. Malcolm Falconer had a presence that *demanded* respect. The deep stress lines on his face hid the stories of many embattled years of service. Though Harry hadn't been there long, he'd found him to be one of the best senior officers he'd worked with.

Malcolm laid down his pen and said, 'Right. All done. How's the case going, Harry?' Having already shown plenty of interest, the DCS was even more intrigued after receiving his update; nevertheless, he was convinced the reason behind such strange events would soon come to light. 'Anything else?'

'Yes, sir. After yesterday's mix-up at the hospital, we had a forensic officer attend the Heaton residence to collect samples from personal items belonging to Rebecca. We've prioritised a DNA test to find out if it was her blood on the steering wheel and dashboard of the Mazda.'

'Good. It sounds like you're on top of things.'

'Is there any chance we could get a warrant to search the home of Ryan Levinson?'

'Based on the lack of evidence at this time, it's not a good idea. For starters, we don't have a body, and witnesses clearly state she was in the car at the time. I'm also concerned about this being the residence of Carl Levinson. There is a lot of history there, including corrupt officers and police harassment charges upon his release. So tread carefully. Of course, if you find something of significance, a warrant will not be a problem.'

'Very well, sir,' said Harry, disappointed.

DCS Falconer got to his feet, gathered his paperwork ready to leave the office, and clocked Harry wavering in the doorway. His wide-eyed stare and slight tilt of the head signalled Harry to speak up.

'Would it be possible for Lucy Fenton to continue working with me on the case? She's been fairly insightful so far, and I could use the extra help.'

'I don't see why not. She was eager to assist in the first place.'

'Eager, sir? I assumed you'd assigned her.'

'I did indeed, but only because she waltzed in here before anyone else and pleaded to work with you. It seems you may have gained a fan or two after all that Joseph Webster business. I'll make the arrangements immediately.'

Knowing how hard Lucy had pushed to work with him was marginally unsettling, but after his career setback, it gave his confidence a modest boost. 'Thank you, sir.'

'This will mean more blasted paperwork,' said the DCS as Harry left the office ahead of him.

Despite forming a good working relationship with DCS Falconer since moving to Kent, the boss had a favourite: Detective Inspector Samantha Jennings. Harry was often overlooked when it came to high-profile cases, so he hoped this particular investigation would nudge him ahead in the race for the vacant DCI role in the new year.

14

December 20

Settling into his armchair, Lenny's heart raced with excitement. At this stage, there was no way of knowing whether this had anything to do with the case, but Harry did say to follow his instincts, wherever they might lead. He opened the aged folder to continue from where he'd left off earlier. Though reluctant to let the items leave church property, the reverend considered the circumstances and made an exception on the condition Lenny returned them when he'd finished. Lenny found both the folder and the book enlightening.

The Martins moved from London to Hartlip in 1760, a year after the birth of their twin daughters, Mary Elizabeth and Emma Rose. The sisters were born with their skin and some cartilage fused together from the face to the hip and had undergone difficult and comprehensive surgery to separate them. Other than scarring and slight damage to their hips on one side, the girls were perfectly healthy. Lenny's research revealed that the first successful recorded separation of conjoined twins occurred in 1689.

Mary Martin's burial in the church cemetery came three years after she was falsely accused by four younger girls in the village of witchcraft and of stealing a necklace from one of them. With her father, William Martin, away on business and unable to protect her, she was dragged from her bed in the night and beaten. The following morning, she was subjected to an unfair and illegal trial by the small village community and was hanged from a tree. They tossed her body into an abandoned pit and left her to rot. The injuries suffered by Mary were identical to those of the girl he had seen in the cemetery.

On William's return, the church refused to let him bury her within their grounds, so he buried her remains on the outskirts of the village. He tried in vain to have her murderers brought to justice. Even the statements he had gathered from the few people in the village who were opposed to what had happened were not enough. Two of the four girls who'd accused her eventually came forward and admitted they had lied about everything at the behest of their friend, who, for some reason, deeply disliked Mary, particularly the scars on the left side of her face. It was no coincidence the supposedly stolen necklace belonged to the same girl. William presented his evidence to the church, and three years after her death, he was allowed to have her remains interred in the consecrated ground of the cemetery.

Towards the back of the book were entries for a one-off payment followed by subsequent payments every three months between 1759 and 1769 by Lord Claxton Chambers. What could that be about? Blackmail sprang to mind. But why did the payments stop? Glancing at other financial figures, it appeared times had become difficult for the family after the payments ceased.

William noted that his wife, Elizabeth, died of typhus in 1773, shortly after visiting her sister, Susan Kirby, who lived with her husband and their three sons in London's Whitechapel. She had gone to say goodbye as the family was moving to British America to settle in New York. William held them partially responsible and asked if they would take Emma with them to New York, as he was struggling financially. From a combination of guilt, sympathy for William's plight, and perhaps the prospect of an extra pair of hands to help with domestic duties, they agreed to take her.

Though he didn't believe in witchcraft, Lenny had witnessed strange occurrences he couldn't explain, and after what had happened in the churchyard, this case was certainly heading in an inexplicable direction. It wasn't going to be easy to figure out the connection between the appearance of Annalise Fournier on Mary Martin's grave and the disappearance of Rebecca Heaton, but Lenny was convinced there had to be one.

His head pounding, Lenny placed the book on the arm of the chair and climbed to his feet. He poured himself a glass of water in the kitchen, took two paracetamol, and lumbered to the bathroom to take a shower. Resting his head against the ceramic tiles, he closed his eyes and let the water run over him. It was still morning, and already he was tired. A lack of sleep and having a headache didn't help. He stared at his foot, where his big toe used to be, and couldn't help but smile, remembering how he'd accidentally shot it off when slipping in a bathtub – a disastrous suicide attempt.

In the living room, wearing only his white boxer shorts, he stood in front of the large window. Looking over Stratford and beyond, Lenny contemplated whether he'd made a mistake by assisting Harry in his investigation. He proceeded to rub moisturising cream over the scars on the left side of his body, a forever reminder of why one shouldn't run into a burning building. Walking along the hallway, he stopped outside the bedroom that held such painful memories. Not a day had passed without Olivia entering his mind. If only they'd had more time. He wrapped his hand around the door handle, hesitated, and went inside.

Lenny glared at the bed and chastised himself for being so weak. Averting his eyes, he peeled back the duvet and climbed onto the mattress. Lying on his side, he focused on the pillow next to his.

'You should look,' said Olivia.

'I don't want to.'

'Sometimes, when you don't want to do something, it often means you should. Just look, my love.'

Lenny turned his head to view the vast bloodstain from where Olivia had bled out.

'You needed to do this. You've been avoiding it for too long.'

'It's hard to face up to you being gone.'

'I'm still with you.'

With glassy eyes, he gazed mournfully at Olivia's heavenly face and placed his hand on her side. A tear trickled and tumbled over his nose. Phoebe startled him when she jumped up onto the bed.

'You shouldn't be in here,' he said, reaching out to stroke her.

She pranced around for a short while before snuggling under his arm, purring loudly until they both fell asleep.

15

December 20

Lucy was openly thrilled to be working on the case. She also had permission to wear plain clothes, which was an added bonus. Before going off to change ahead of their trip to Luton Road, she informed Harry of her findings from the government database. Rebecca Heaton *was* an only child. Not long into the working day, there were already more questions than answers. Harry waited for the constable by the car and called Mrs Heaton to confirm their appointment that afternoon.

As he ended the call, Lucy approached wearing a leather jacket, jeans, and black trainers. The pale complexion of her face stood out against her contrasting brown, shoulder-length hair, and for a moment, Harry was captivated. Full of self-reproach, he turned away, opened the car door, and climbed into the driver's seat, hoping she hadn't caught him staring. Silly sod! This wasn't like him, well, at least not since his indiscretion nine years ago. Perhaps his paranoid insecurities surrounding his marriage were to blame. Whatever it was, he wouldn't allow himself to go down that road again.

Lucy got comfortable, buckled up, and said, 'Were you checking me out?'

Harry stuttered, 'N-no, I most certainly was not.'

She smiled. 'Relax, guv. I'm only teasing. A little icebreaker for our first official day as partners.'

'Terrific! Give me a panic attack, why don't you?' He smiled back, although he couldn't tell if her comment was coincidental or if she had noticed him looking her way.

On the drive to Chatham, he learned she had been a police officer for five years and hoped to become a detective inspector in another two to three. Harry complimented Lucy on her good work and suggested she should consider it sooner. Lucy said she'd think about it and steered the conversation towards their destination, Luton Road, a place where she'd previously attended two major incidents: once after a man had been brutally attacked in his own home and the second time when a woman had been badly beaten in the street after an argument. Considering Harry had only worked in Kent for a few months, she wasn't surprised he was unaware of the road's notoriety.

They parked in the first free space they came across, close to a Chinese takeaway opposite an off-licence and a fried chicken shop. The terraced house they were visiting was just along the road. From what he'd been told, he half-expected the place to look like a battleground, but in reality, it appeared no different from any other residential road. Sometimes, an area's reputation is built on a couple of newsworthy incidents that drag its name into the gutter for the foreseeable future. Harry knew this all too well.

Born and raised in Hackney between the 1970s and mid-80s, Harry remembered how parts of the area were like an adventure playground, with empty, crumbling buildings and burnt-out shops. Dangerous but fun. Everybody knew who you were and looked out for you. Harry was happy there until he was introduced to the hellish reality of life. In 1985, Sidney Cooke raped and murdered a young boy in a flat not far from where Harry lived with his mother, sister, and younger brother. It proved to be the final straw for his mother, who set about making arrangements to move out of the area. A year later, they relocated to Colchester, and the name *Hissing Sid* was never mentioned again.

Heading towards the front door, the pair were aware of the frosty stares they were attracting from a small group of youths loitering inside and outside the shops across the road. A couple of lads tore chunks from chicken drumsticks with their teeth, while others dipped their hands into the takeaway boxes for a share of the fries. They had obviously been identified as police officers, though Harry was certain they had a more unpleasant name in mind. The youths continued to stare as Lucy knocked on the door. This was the kind of place where some residents stuck together, but all knew exactly whom to avoid.

After the third knock, a tall, burly man opened the door, wearing jeans and a grey T-shirt with a logo that read, 'Hell is empty, and all the devils are here.' Harry didn't know what to make of a career criminal wearing a shirt with a quote from Shakespeare's *The Tempest*.

Both officers showed their warrant cards, and Harry inquired, 'Mr Frederick Perry?'

Without saying a word, the man headed inside, leaving the door wide open. They entered the house, and Lucy closed the front door, noticing a couple of youths on their bicycles right outside the gate, watching closely.

Along the short, narrow hallway, they stepped into a messy living room, barely large enough to swing a cat – not that you'd choose to. The thick stench of nicotine and alcohol lingered in the air.

'Mr Perry, I'm Detective Inspector Baxendale, and this is Police Constable Fenton. We're sorry for your loss. We'd like to ask some questions regarding the death of your brother, Vincent.'

Frederick flopped into the armchair and pointed across the small coffee table littered with empty beer bottles to the two-seater sofa. 'Take a seat,' he said, his voice rough and dry.

Scattered about the walls were movie posters, *Apocalypse Now* and *Reservoir Dogs*, being the most notable. A life-sized cardboard cut-out of Kurt Cobain filled the alcove behind the television, close to the window. As they perched on the edge of the sofa, Harry examined Frederick's tattoos, noting the word 'DAD' inked on the middle fingers of his left hand, just like his brother's.

Being fairly well-read, Harry couldn't resist mentioning the quote on Frederick's shirt. 'I see you're into Shakespeare.'

'*Westworld*,' he answered. Seeing their confusion, he elaborated, 'The quote was used in the TV show. I liked it, so I bought the T-shirt.'

'Ah, I see,' said Harry, normality restored.

Fred reached for his cigarettes and lighter next to the overflowing ashtray on the coffee table. 'What do you need to ask me?'

Harry said, 'Did you see your brother on the day of the collision?'

'As far as I'm aware, "collision" implies guilt,' said Fred.

'During investigations, the term "accident" can be misleading.'

'That's because of the blame culture in the society we live in today. Someone always has to be responsible. Is that what you're trying to do, pin this on my brother cos somebody's car got damaged? You can go fuck yourself.'

'Frederick, I could breeze through this investigation and let them hang your brother out to dry, but I'd like to find out exactly what happened so the blame isn't placed where it doesn't belong. If this wasn't Vincent's fault, I'll prove it.'

Frederick quietly reflected. The tension around his neck and shoulders eased. Had Harry earned himself a little trust? 'Of course I saw him. He lives – lived here. We were having a smoke and a beer right before he went out. But he wasn't over the limit, if that's your next question. He'd had one bottle and didn't even get to finish it.' He gestured to what must have been the bottle on the table in front of them. 'If you test his blood or whatever it is you do, you'll find out for yourself.'

'Any idea where he was going?'

'Didn't say. He got a phone call and left soon after. He wasn't himself, though.'

'How do you mean?' asked Harry.

'His mood changed. It didn't register at the time, but after I received the news of his death, I couldn't stop thinking about that night – the look in his eyes. We went through some shit as kids, and he suffered with his mental health. Tried to top himself once. I hoped he'd put it all behind him. For a good few years now, he'd been fine, and even better since we'd stopped with all the bullshit to try our hand at odd jobs, gardening, and other stuff. But whoever he spoke to sent him back to a dark place.'

Lucy said, 'Do you have any idea who called him or what it was about?'

'Not a clue. Though I wouldn't mind having a word with them. When can I have his phone back?'

'At the moment, it's evidence,' said Harry. 'All the calls made to your brother's phone will be checked, and hopefully, we'll find out who he last spoke to. Mr Perry, since you brought up your brother's mental health problems, do you think he could have crashed deliberately – to harm himself, I mean?' Harry braced himself for a furious backlash of denial.

'I wish I could say no. I want to say no. But I've seen people do some crazy, unexpected shit in this life. All I can tell you is he was all right until that phone call.'

Frederick's calm, honest, and sincere reply surprised Harry. 'Is there anything else you can tell us?'

'I wasn't going to say, but before he left, he stood in that doorway and said, "Don't be a fuck-up." I should have known right then he wasn't coming back.'

'Why is that significant?'

'Because it's what our father said to us right before he walked out of the front door and disappeared. Less than a week later, he was found hanging in an abandoned warehouse. He'd killed himself. Soon after, our mother met some right fucking bastard who beat the shit out of us and did worse to Vincent. You know . . .'

Harry nodded, reading between the lines. 'Do you think your brother specifically used your father's quote to indicate he wasn't coming back?'

'It's likely.'

'Okay,' said Harry, rising from the sofa, with Lucy less than a second behind. 'Thank you, Mr Perry, you've been extremely helpful.'

'Why wouldn't I be? He was my brother,' he said, his eyes welling up.

Harry reached out a hand, which Perry shook. 'If something isn't right about your brother's death, I promise – I will find out.'

The gang of youths, some on their bikes and some on foot, stalked them all the way back to the car. Once they'd buckled up, Lucy turned to him and said, 'Well, that went better than expected. I was surprised he was so helpful.'

'Why? As he said, it was his brother. People don't always end up where they are by choice. Not everyone gets to willingly lead a life. For some, life leads them.'

Harry and Lucy's next destination involved a trip to the seaside to see Rebecca's parents. Mrs Heaton's estranged husband, Derrick, would also be in attendance. Derrick had visited the police station several times to rant at the staff behind the front desk, demanding that more be done to find his daughter. On every occasion, an officer spoke with him and escorted him from the premises. Nobody could blame a frustrated parent's short fuse.

16

December 20

Dozing with the cat didn't last long, and for a moment, Lenny was uncertain what to do next, though at some point today he wanted to visit the British Library to do some research. He'd considered calling Harry to let him know about Mary Martin, but until he knew exactly how she was linked to their investigation, it would sound like the ramblings of a lunatic. Instead, he sent an email telling him to look into the death of Louise Norris and mentioned Reagan Scott, who was missing in Toronto.

Since Joseph Webster's death, Lenny had kept a promise his friend Elaine hadn't and stayed in contact with the boy he'd helped rescue. He'd visited Daniel Logan a few times to see how he was coping after his horrific ordeal. Elaine had said she wanted to move on with her life and focus on her children, and after everything she'd been through, he couldn't blame her.

From across the road, Lenny watched the Logan family unpack the car and enter the house. It looked as though they'd just returned from Christmas shopping. He gave them time to get settled before ambling towards the front door. Daniel's parents always made time for Lenny. Shortly after Danny returned home, they learned of the huge role he'd played in finding their son. If it had not been for his tireless efforts, they would never have seen their boy again. His continued support meant so much to them.

Barely over the threshold, he sensed the couple were tense and on edge. Vivien showed him into the living room while Brendan put the kettle on.

Lenny made himself comfortable in the armchair, alert to Mrs Logan's fidgety demeanour and the nerves in her voice as she made awkward small talk.

'Daniel's up in his room,' she said. 'I'll get him to come down in a bit, *or* you can go up and see him. Either is fine.'

Brendan popped in, placed a large biscuit tin on the table, and said, 'I'll just fetch the tea.' The couple's behaviour was distinctly unusual compared to previous visits. The warmth and welcome remained but lacked the usual gusto.

'Perhaps I'll go up now,' said Lenny, attempting to escape.

'Would you mind going up after your cup of tea? There's something we'd like to discuss with you.'

'Is everything okay?' he asked. Before she could reply, Brendan entered the room with three cups.

'Here we go,' said Brendan, handing out the cups and taking a seat next to his wife on the sofa.

Lenny said, 'Vivien's left me on tenterhooks here. What did you want to talk to me about?'

Brendan seemed troubled; they both did. 'Ah, yes. I suppose we should get straight to the point. We're becoming increasingly concerned about Daniel.'

'How do you mean?'

'His behaviour is ever-changing. It's difficult to keep up.'

Danny's inevitable struggle with his mental health was always going to materialise. Lenny's fear had been how it would manifest and to what degree. 'I can't say I'm surprised. Your son has been through something no adult, let alone a child, *ever* should. At some point, his mental scars were bound to surface. Have you spoken to his therapist?'

'Of course,' said Brendan. 'The thing is, we've had to cancel his last three appointments because he was extremely abusive to Mrs Hurley. Thankfully, she was sympathetic to the circumstances and willing to continue, but Daniel is refusing to go back.'

'I see.'

'We discussed calling you,' said Vivien. 'But you've already done so much. We didn't want to impose.'

'Don't be silly, it's fine,' said Lenny. 'Look, it could be he's just lashing out, letting off steam over what happened.'

Brendan hesitated to speak, rose from the sofa, and gently closed the living room door. 'Is it possible he would lash out in a violent way?'

Now Lenny was worried. He knew violence could breed violence in someone so young. He'd witnessed it at close quarters, but the last thing he wanted to do was panic the distressed parents further. 'I'm not a psychologist, so it's not my field of expertise. Has he struck either of you?'

'No, nothing like that,' said Brendan. 'But Haylcy claimed she'd entered Daniel's room and caught him holding the dog in the air – by its neck. She said he had his hands around Muttley's throat.'

Vivien added, 'We're not naive enough to think our eight-year-old daughter wouldn't lie – it's just – this is not the kind of thing she would make up.'

Lenny said, 'I suggest getting him back to therapy.'

'We've tried to convince him, and it never goes well, but you – you have such a rapport with Daniel—'

'You want me to try, don't you?'

'I know it's cheeky of us to ask,' said Vivien.

'I'm not sure he'll take any notice of me.' Staring at the stressed couple, he couldn't possibly refuse. 'I'll do what I can. I'll even tell him to leave the dog alone.' Lenny smiled, attempting to make light of the situation.

The Logans glanced at each other and then back at Lenny. 'The dog's dead.'

'Dead?' His concern deepened.

Brendan said, 'Muttley somehow managed to run off when Daniel took him for a walk. The next morning, when I was leaving for work, I found the poor thing on the doorstep. The dog was cut into pieces and its head was missing. We don't want to imagine our son capable of such an appalling act, but sometimes it's as though the boy who came home is not our son at all.'

Lenny played it down, suggesting Danny was unlikely to be responsible. He told them about a spate of animal killings that had occurred across the country and how the family pet would be left on the doorstep in much the same way Brendan had described. They appeared reassured. Whether it was blissful ignorance or they truly believed their son didn't have a hand in the dog's demise was anybody's guess. As for Lenny, he wasn't convinced Danny had decapitated the dog. He would have to tread carefully when broaching the subject with Danny. Preventing him from going down the same monstrous path as Joseph Webster had to be his priority.

With his headphones on, engrossed in a world of loud music and gunfire, Danny was at his desk playing a shoot-'em-up game on the computer. Lenny approached and sat on the edge of the bed, choosing not to disturb him. He didn't have to wait long for

Danny to turn and see him. He paused the game, removed his headphones, and apologised.

'It's fine, I haven't been here long. I did knock, but you were never going to hear me with those things on. So, how have you been?'

'I suppose they've been talking about me downstairs?' snarked Danny.

'Of course,' Lenny answered bluntly and truthfully, then broke into a smile. Danny couldn't help but follow suit.

'How is school?'

'Awful. I hate it. There are a couple of boys who constantly tease me about what happened before.' Danny lowered his eyes.

'Unfortunately, bullies want you to react, and they'll twist every word you say and throw it back at you. So don't worry about what they think or say.'

'I worry because the other kids listen to them.'

'Who cares?'

'I care.'

'No! You don't. You're trying to convince yourself you care because you think that's the norm. Your normal vanished the day you were abducted. There is no reset, Danny – we've talked about this. Acceptance is your weapon. Your experience, no matter how traumatic, is now your armour. Those boys can't hurt you. You are beyond their childish nonsense. Rise above it.'

'You're right,' Danny replied. 'After what I survived, I am stronger and should know better.'

'There you go. Now, tell me about the dog?'

'I didn't mean to hurt Muttley. I took my anger out on him because of those stupid boys. Despite what my parents think, I didn't kill him.'

Lenny prided himself on being able to read people. With Danny, it wasn't so easy. 'I'm sure you didn't,' he said. 'Let's say nothing more on the matter.' He rose from the bed and wandered around the room, stopping to look at some DVDs and books on a shelf. Among them was *Oliver Twist*, the book he'd sent Danny for his thirteenth birthday.

'I haven't got around to reading it yet.'

'You should. It's a story of good versus evil and inspires hope in desperate times. We could all do with a bit of hope now and then.' Lenny walked over to the window and looked at the back garden. 'How are the nightmares?'

'They're less frequent, though I'm not sure they'll ever stop.'

'Not sure mine will either, but time's the greatest healer, Danny.' Lenny turned and walked back towards the end of the bed. 'Now, one more thing, and I'll leave you to your game. What's all this avoiding therapy business?'

'It's just non-stop talking. I'm not sure it helps.'

'You might not think so, but trust me, it does. So get your arse back there – please?'

Danny sighed. 'All right.'

'Be nice to the lady and make sure you apologise.'

'Mum and Dad didn't leave anything out, did they?'

Lenny smiled and repeated himself more sternly, 'Apologise to Mrs Hurley.'

'I will.'

'You've got my number. If you're struggling and need someone outside your family or therapist to talk to, don't hesitate to call me.'

'It would be easier if my parents bought me a phone.'

'Maybe you'll find one under the Christmas tree this year.'

'I doubt it.'

'Wait and see. Now, I'll stop by to see you again soon.'

'Mr Grey, why doesn't Elaine want to see me?'

'She has her reasons.'

'After she saved me on the boat, she made a promise.'

'Without belittling what happened to you, Elaine has been through a hell of a lot worse. She also has children of her own and a business to run.'

'I only wanted to thank her. She should have kept her promise.' Danny's head dropped, and he stared at the floor.

'Look, next time I speak to her, I'll try to arrange something. Maybe I can get her to change her mind.'

Danny stood, walked over, and threw his arms around him. Other than talking and joking, Lenny's experience with children was minimal. In fact, the only child who had hugged him before now was Elaine's daughter, Emily.

17

December 20

They arrived in Whitstable, with Harry questioning long-distance relationships. 'I don't get it,' he said. 'For instance, Ryan Levinson is dating a girl who lives miles away. What is it with dating people so far from where you live? When I was a teenager in the eighties and early nineties, you went out with someone who lived on the same road or around the corner.'

Lucy laughed. 'A teenager in the eighties? Christ, you're older than I thought. Anyway, Ryan has a car.'

'True, but most young men don't have rich daddies.'

Lucy agreed and explained how internet chat rooms, followed by online dating and social media, had changed the dating world forever.

'I suppose so,' he said. 'But taking public transport to visit a girlfriend or boyfriend sounds like too much hard work to me. Not to mention expensive. Plus, places were further away in my day.'

Lucy laughed again. 'Don't be silly, places were not further away.'

'I'm telling you – they were.'

'You're showing your age now,' she said. 'Besides, when you're crazy about someone, it doesn't matter how far you have to travel – you find a way.'

'Are you speaking from experience?'

'No. Maybe.' She blushed.

Breaking the ensuing silence, he said, 'When I was a kid, taking a ride in a black London taxi was a special treat.'

'Shut up, Harry.'

They parked outside a detached house on Joy Lane, overlooking the sea and battered by the elements. Mrs Heaton opened the front door before they'd climbed out of the car. She appeared overtired, pale, and expressionless, the worry within clawing its way to the surface. Though she was expecting them, the pain of not knowing if she was about to receive hopeful or devastating news endured. Poor woman. On this occasion, it was neither, which often caused more distress.

The inside of the house looked in much better shape than the outside: modern, beautifully refurbished, and clean. As she led them into a bright reception room, Mr Heaton and their twenty-year-old son, Ian, were sitting on one side of a large dining table. Floor-to-ceiling windows and a glass door showcased the beautiful sea view and the immaculate terrace area.

The officers took a seat, and Derrick Heaton wasted no time in speaking. 'I hope you have some bloody news.'

Harry said, 'I'm afraid not, Mr Heaton. But rest assured, we are doing our best to discover exactly what happened.'

'It's not good enough,' Derrick blasted. 'You should be out there trying to find her and asking that tosspot boyfriend of hers some questions.'

'I've spoken to Mr Levinson and expect to do so again,' said Harry.

'Good! Because he hasn't answered any of our calls. Bloody prick is ignoring us. If that's not a sign of guilt, I don't know what is. June has even been to his house. I was thinking of going round there myself this evening.'

'That would be unwise, Mr Heaton. I understand why you'd want to, but I advise you to leave the investigating to us.'

'That's what I told him, Detective,' Mrs Heaton chipped in. 'He'd only end up getting himself arrested or something.'

'Look, I know this is an extremely difficult time for you all, but the sooner I ask you some questions, the sooner I can get back out there and attempt to locate your daughter.'

Mrs Heaton said, 'Of course, you're right. Please, continue.'

Derrick frowned while their son sat quietly and reached for his mother's hand on the table. Mrs Heaton was an anxious wreck, though less riled than at the hospital.

Harry said, 'Mr Heaton, you're obviously not an admirer of Ryan Levinson. Is there a specific reason for this?'

'He's a flash little cunt, that's why.'

'Derrick!' shouted June, angry at his use of foul language. 'He's not a bad boy. Yes, dare I say a little cocksure, but confidence is not always a bad thing.'

Derrick added, 'He's an arrogant prick, is what he is, and at twenty-two, I still say he's far too old for her.'

Being the father of a teenage daughter, Harry would probably feel the same way. He asked, 'How long has Rebecca been in a relationship with Ryan?'

'Relationship! Don't make me laugh,' said Mr Heaton. 'They haven't got a clue at their age.'

'Shh, Derrick. I'm so sorry, Detective. It must be about fourteen months now,' she said.

'Fourteen months, are you certain?' asked Harry.

'Yes, definitely.'

Harry made a note of her answer before the next question. 'Have you ever witnessed Rebecca driving Ryan's car?'

'No, never! I wouldn't allow it,' she said. 'Rebecca doesn't have her licence, and I'm confident my daughter wouldn't be so silly. She certainly wouldn't want to get into trouble with the police.'

'Did any of you see Rebecca on the day of the collision?'

'Yes,' said Mrs Heaton. 'Ryan picked her up between half twelve and one in the afternoon.'

'Did everything appear to be okay between her and Ryan? Was there anything out of the ordinary?'

'Not as far as I'm aware. They're generally happy together. I mean, they have their arguments, but nothing serious. Just petty stuff, mostly about Sarah, a friend of Ryan's. Rebecca isn't keen. I got the impression they were a little too close for her liking. They were going to see her that afternoon. I overheard Rebecca talking on the phone with him in the morning, complaining that she didn't want to go.'

Harry said, 'When did you learn Rebecca disliked Sarah?'

'She told me. Apparently, Ryan knew Sarah long before he met my daughter. Rebecca was under the impression Ryan liked her more than he let on – enough to suspect there might have been some previous history between them.'

Pen at the ready, Harry said, 'I don't suppose you know Sarah's surname and address?'

'Kerr. Sarah Kerr. She's some kind of model or actress. Pretty girl. Rebecca showed me some pictures online. As for her address, I'm not sure, but I'm certain it's easy for *you* to find. It's a penthouse at Chatham Maritime Marina. There can't be many of those down there. I picked them up once in the early hours, outside the place that used to be Dickens World. They went to her flatwarming party a few months back. I dropped Ryan off on the way home.'

Harry stared at Lucy; she read his mind. 'On it, guv.' She left the room to call the station and find out Miss Kerr's address.

Harry continued, 'I assume you've contacted Rebecca's friends?'

'Of course. Nobody has seen or heard from her. Not that she hung out with many friends since meeting Ryan. He liked to keep her to himself.'

Harry took out the paper he'd printed earlier and showed them a picture of Vincent Perry. 'Do you recognise this man?'

Mrs Heaton scrutinised the picture closely and shook her head. 'No. He doesn't look familiar to me.'

She slid it along the table to Mr Heaton, who also said no. As he pushed it back across towards Harry, Ian put his fingers on the paper and pulled it back to take a closer look. 'I've seen him before,' he said.

'Ian, can you tell me where and when you saw this man?'

'A few weeks back. I bumped into Rebecca and Ryan at a nightclub in Maidstone. I remember this guy because he and Ryan were talking while I was asking my sister how she managed to get into the club, what with her being underage.'

Harry's eyes lit up. 'You're sure Ryan Levinson knows this man?'

'Yes, I'm certain. Ryan called him Vinny.'

'What's the name of the nightclub?'

'Phantasm.'

'Can you remember the date and the time you entered and left the club?'

'It was my mate's birthday. Let me check my messages.' Ian scrolled through his phone.

A rush of excitement energised Harry. Ryan knowing Vincent confirmed that something underhand was going on. This could be the breakthrough they needed.

'Here we are, November twenty-sixth. We arrived at the place at about ten thirty and left at quarter past two, but I'd say I saw them around eleven, as my sister arrived not long after us.'

Having already noted the name of the club, Harry wrote the date and time underneath. He'd try to get hold of the CCTV from the club. If he could get footage showing them together, Ryan couldn't possibly deny it.

Derrick asked, 'Who is this man? Has he got something to do with all this?'

'I'm afraid I can't say at this time, Mr Heaton. It's a line of inquiry we are looking into.'

Harry couldn't reveal Vincent Perry was the man who'd crashed into the car their daughter was allegedly driving – not now there was a connection between Perry and Levinson. Before leaving the house, Harry asked permission to take Rebecca's laptop in for examination. Her parents were happy to oblige.

As they set off to visit Miss Kerr in Chatham, Harry asked Lucy to look into Sarah on her phone while he kept his increasing anger towards Ryan under control. Showing the picture of Vincent Perry was a long shot, but his instincts told him Ryan Levinson was hiding something. Harry was thankful Ian Heaton had been present. After constant dead ends, he finally had something to get his teeth into.

Lucy said, 'I can see why Rebecca was worried about Sarah Kerr. She's gorgeous. She's been in a couple of films and a few TV shows, mostly bit parts as far as I can see. She comes from a wealthy family. How come we're paying her a visit?'

'She was one of the last people to see Rebecca. Mrs Heaton confirmed Rebecca and Ryan had visited Sarah's place that afternoon. Ryan played down how long he'd been seeing Rebecca. He said it was only seven months, whereas Mrs Heaton stated with certainty it was fourteen.'

'Quite a discrepancy, I'll give you that, but men are useless at remembering dates.'

'Usually I'd agree, but to be seven months out, I'm not so sure. He's trying to minimise the importance of the relationship to us, pretending it was nothing serious. More importantly, he denied knowing Vincent. While you were out of the room, I showed them a picture of Vincent Perry – Ian recognised him. He saw Ryan and Vincent together in Phantasm nightclub. Ryan called him Vinny.'

18

December 20

During their quest for a parking space close to the shops, Lucy pointed out where Dickens World used to be. Eventually, they managed to park outside a row of busy eateries. The pair strolled alongside the dock to the front entrance of the apartment building and received no response from the buzzer. Harry suggested they get something to eat and try again later. They entered a place attempting to replicate an American diner from the 1950s. Making themselves comfortable in the tacky red leather seats of a booth by the window, they ordered chicken wings, fries, and Diet Cokes.

The window seat proved advantageous when Harry spotted Sarah Kerr walking away from her residence with a male companion. She was a striking young woman, instantly recognisable from the Instagram posts Lucy had shown him. Harry was irritated she had chosen to ignore her entry buzzer earlier, as it was more time they could ill afford to waste. When the person beside her came into view, Harry identified Ryan Levinson, no doubt giving Sarah a heads-up that the police might be paying her a visit. There was nothing to suggest they were romantically involved, but it was enough to convince him there was more to Rebecca's disappearance. They parted ways outside the entrance to the shopping centre. Ryan headed towards the car park, and Sarah disappeared through the automatic doors to the shops.

Lucy asked, 'What do you want to do?'

'Finish our meal and wait,' he calmly replied.

'Good, because I'm loving these chicken wings.' She pointed a bone in his direction. 'Is it true your middle name is Caius?'

'Yes, though it's not a name I particularly like.'

'Shakespeare used it a few times, so he must have liked it.'

'Caius was my father's name. Anyway, how did you find out?'

'People talk. You have star status down here in the sticks. You helped take down Harper Darmody and Joseph Webster, two of the most infamous killers of the modern era. Everyone was thrilled when they heard you were coming to work here.'

'I was the lead detective, but I didn't help take down anyone.'

'Take the credit. Most would in this job.' Lucy picked at her fries. 'Darmody's body was never recovered, and rumours persist that he's still alive. Between us, what do you reckon?'

Harry didn't answer her question; however, his suggestive smile and the glint in his eyes betrayed him.

'Oh my God. Do you know for certain?'

'Not for certain, but Darmody's as tough as they come. I know for a fact he fought and killed Webster to save a young boy. Make of that what you will.' Harry put down his Coke and jumped to his feet. 'There she is. I'll get her to come inside for a chat over a cup of tea.'

'Want me to come with you?'

'No. Stay here and finish your wings.'

Harry left the restaurant and stopped Miss Kerr in her tracks. He showed his warrant card and explained why he'd come to see her.

'To be honest, Detective, I didn't know Rebecca Heaton at all well.'

'You're speaking about her in the past tense. Do you know something we don't?'

'No, I didn't mean it like that.'

'Why don't we pop into the diner over there where my colleague is waiting? We won't keep you long.' Reluctant to follow, Harry said, 'Come on, I'll buy you a cup of tea.'

They entered the diner, and as he pointed to the table they were sitting at, Sarah was on her way towards Lucy. At the counter, Harry ordered three teas. On his way to the table, he perceived that the girls were engaged in an amiable conversation.

Shuffling awkwardly along the padded banquette, Harry remarked, 'You two seem to be getting along.'

'It's not often you get to meet a celebrity,' said Lucy.

Sarah smiled, bared her pristine, milk-white veneers, and said, 'Oh, I'd hardly call myself a celebrity. Not yet, anyway.' Her laugh was coy and somewhat annoying. 'Well, this is all strange and exciting. Like being in a movie.' She settled quickly, her voice smooth and refined. 'As I mentioned outside, Rebecca and I aren't close, so I don't know what I can tell you.'

Harry said, 'How well do you know Ryan Levinson?'

'Ryan?' She paused, as though the question was unexpected. 'We met a few years ago at a charity function. Ryan's father was the host. We have seen each other a handful of times since, but that's all there is to it,' she said, with all the confidence of the actor she was.

Harry asked, 'When did you last see him?'

The waitress arrived with the tea. She pretended to think. 'That would be a few days—'

'Let's not waste each other's time, Miss Kerr,' said Harry.

'You saw me with him just now, didn't you?' she conceded with a cheeky grin.

Lucy confirmed it with a nod, and Sarah reached for her cup and sipped her tea.

No sugar for the health-conscious, Harry observed. He said, 'Tell me about when they came to see you on the eighteenth of this month.'

'Ryan and Becca showed up around two in the afternoon. We had a drink and a chat. A couple of hours later, Ryan felt unwell, and they left not long after four.'

There was a strong possibility Ryan had coached her on what to say. Harry asked, 'This drink, did it involve alcohol?'

'No, just coffee. I tell a lie – Ryan had a few sips from a bottle of beer as soon as they arrived, but he poured the rest down the sink and had a coffee instead. Perhaps that's when he started to feel a bit queasy.'

'Any drugs involved?'

'None. I don't know if Ryan and Rebecca use them, but I will not tolerate drugs in my house or around me. My older brother died of an overdose, so you see, my feelings are emphatically against drug use of any kind.'

Lucy asked, 'Did they argue at any point?'

'Not at all. They seemed perfectly happy. They always do. Young love, I guess.' She smiled.

Harry said, 'This might seem personal, but have you ever been in a relationship with Ryan?'

'God, no. I mean, he's tried it on with me a few times, but I've always turned him down.'

'So you knew he had a thing for you, yet it didn't stop you from seeing him?'

Sarah toyed with the handle of her cup and smiled. 'Detective Inspector, most men, and even some women, want to sleep with me. Some just want to be seen with me. Do you suggest I lock myself away from everyone?'

'You never led him on at all?'

'No. He isn't my type. If I do go for a man, I prefer him to be older.' She grinned, winked at Harry, and took another sip of tea.

Harry didn't react or show any emotion to her mock flirtation. 'When was the last time he tried it on with you?'

'If you're asking whether he's made a move on me since he and Becca have been an item, then yes, he has. But I'll stress once again – I politely declined.'

Lucy asked, 'Were you aware Rebecca knew Ryan had a thing for you?'

Sarah paused to glance out of the window before turning back. 'No, I wasn't. If Rebecca *was* aware, she kept it well hidden.'

Lucy followed up with, 'What was he doing here just now?'

'He came to pick up his laptop. He left it here the other day.'

Harry knew she was lying. Ryan wasn't carrying anything when he walked past a short while ago. He chose not to confront her about the laptop. If he needed to question her again, it was prudent not to let her know she'd aroused more suspicion.

Sarah asked, 'Are we done? I have to be on set in three hours.'

'One last question,' said Harry. 'What do you think of Ryan Levinson?'

'Honestly? He's a bit full of himself.'

'Thank you for your time, Miss Kerr,' he said.

Having barely touched her tea, Sarah pushed her cup into the middle of the table and exited the booth with considerably more grace than Harry had entered it. She reached into her Gucci purse, pulled out a card, and placed it on the table next to his hand, letting her fingers lightly brush against his. 'If you need to reach me again, don't hesitate to call.' With her head held high, shoulders back, and a slight swivel of her hips, she sauntered out of the door.

Locking eyes, Harry and Lucy couldn't help but laugh. She said, 'I think someone has an admirer. I'm guessing there was a reason you didn't call her out on Ryan not carrying a laptop?'

Harry replied, 'It's better if she remains confident and assumes we're done questioning her.'

'You won't have to worry about that girl losing her confidence,' said Lucy, brimming with sarcasm.

Watching Sarah through the window, he said, 'I'd love to have forensics examine her penthouse, but unless I can find evidence to suggest something happened to Rebecca inside, there's no way I'll get a search warrant. You know what's funny? First, Ian said Ryan knew Vincent as Vinny, and just now Sarah referred to Rebecca as Becca. Name shortening suggests familiarity.'

They stopped by Phantasm Nightclub on their way to the station to view the CCTV. The head of security was dismissive and unhelpful. Fortunately, the manager showed up and permitted them to take a look. Examining the footage in a back room, he saw Rebecca talking to her brother, and then there they were: Ryan and Vincent, standing by the bar at 11.04 p.m. Ian had been spot on. Let's see the little shit wriggle out of this. Harry recorded the scene on his phone. As it continued to play, he spotted Fred Perry talking with Sarah Kerr. Unbelievable! Harry asked if he could have all the door footage from when the club opened at 10.00 p.m. The manager was happy to copy the CCTV onto a memory stick and hand it over so he could look through it later that night at home.

Harry had barely set foot in the station when he received news from the laboratory: the blood on the steering wheel and dashboard of the Mazda *was* Rebecca Heaton's. The witness statements could no longer be disregarded, and any lingering doubts he had about the teenager being in the car were gone. He slumped into the seat at his desk. Ryan Levinson's connection to Vincent Perry was his biggest lead and the best place to start. It might be a good idea to question Fred again; if his brother knew Ryan, there was a strong possibility *he* knew him as well. Video evidence also suggested Fred and Sarah Kerr were on friendly terms.

He'd instructed Lucy to take Rebecca's laptop to digital forensics and carry out a background check on Peter Mullings. There didn't appear to be a link between the two cases, but it still had to be dealt with. He called Owen Carrick, hoping he'd had more luck as he continued to comb the area where Rebecca had disappeared. Along with regular officers, he had help from special constables and volunteers from the community. Some of Rebecca's friends had also shown up to help.

Checking his inbox brought more bad news: the e-fit from the composite artist had flagged nothing on the criminal database. Examining the image himself, the suspect wouldn't be difficult to recognise in person. He looked like a creepy villain from a zombie apocalypse series. Annalise had done remarkably well to remember so much detail. Next up, an email from forensics revealed the findings of Vincent Perry's phone data. The last two calls were to different numbers within an hour of the incident. One would definitely have been the call he received at home. The second was later, an outgoing call several minutes before the crash. It was the only time these particular numbers featured on the list. The technician's report stated that both mobiles were either switched off or destroyed and were most likely burners, which meant there was no way of knowing whom Vincent had spoken to before or after he'd set off on his fatal journey.

Along with all the latest information, Harry emailed the e-fit to Lenny and clicked on an earlier email from him. He glossed over the missing Canadian girl and immediately looked into the unsolved murder of Louise Norris. Their similarity in appearance was undeniable, but Harry considered whether Lenny was reaching. If he were to research homicides involving young women over the last few decades, many of them would fit the same profile; however, he spoke to a detective in Manchester and asked to be sent more details about the case. Lenny had an eerie knack for being right, so ignoring his advice could prove to be a mistake.

For the next hour or so, Harry worked his way through Vincent's contacts, hoping to find the last two callers, possibly on different numbers. Most turned out to be customers of the Perry brothers, many of whom were full of praise for the work they'd carried out. It seemed Frederick was truthful about the pair trying to turn a corner. Two other numbers on the list showed up frequently. One turned out to be a self-employed carpet fitter who'd worked with the brothers, and the other, with the last four digits being *4129*, connected to an automated voicemail belonging to Kent Property Care. He left a message and searched for both businesses online. The carpet fitter was genuine and easy to find. The other proved more difficult and wasn't registered with HM Revenue and Customs.

He leaned back in his chair and checked his watch: 5.20 p.m. Time to call it a day, at least in the office. He'd get Lucy to finish going through the list tomorrow. On the way home, he wanted to stop by and question James Harding, the boyfriend of Melanie Hillingdon, who had been with her on the night of the crash. Harry doubted Mr Harding had seen much in the rear-view mirror but couldn't afford to leave any stone unturned.

19

December 20

Penenden Heath in Maidstone wasn't too far out of Harry's way. Due to high rents and inflated house prices, James Harding, like many youngsters in their early twenties, still lived with his parents. Mrs Harding answered the door, and after stating his business, she escorted the detective to the living room and excused the mess, which baffled Harry as the room appeared to be spotless. He made himself comfortable in the armchair while she fetched James from the shower. Harry detected the distinctive odour of a cat, recognisable from his monthly visits to his mother's house for Sunday roast.

James entered the room, his mop of damp brown hair soaking the thin cotton of his white T-shirt. Nervous from the outset, he apologised for keeping him waiting. He took a seat, and Harry asked questions. Restless and unable to sit still, James anxiously picked at the skin on the ends of his fingers. Other than not seeing the girl in the car, his answers about the immediate aftermath were much the same as Melanie's. He came across as a pleasant, respectful young man, but something bothered Harry. It all seemed too familiar. Similarities from witnesses about the same incident were common; only this was different – manufactured. The forced confidence and subtle pauses before speaking, as though remembering what he was supposed to say, reminded him of Ryan Levinson and Melanie Hillingdon.

He recalled his interview with Melanie and how her words had raced across her lips before they'd entered her mind. She might not have had the deceptive self-assurance of Ryan, but the same fidgety behaviour and nerves were on show. He'd originally put it down to her being shaken up by the crash. Now he wasn't so sure. Harry's headmaster from many years ago had called them mechanical lies – fabricated words rehearsed over and over until they rolled off the tongue. Had they all revised from the same script? The idea they were all involved seemed absurd.

James showed Harry to the front door. The commotion of a bus attempting to navigate past a car along the narrow road drew his attention. A man jumped from the front of a parked blue van and rushed across the front of the bus towards them. The bus driver brought his bus to a stop and beeped his horn. The young man turned to the driver and held up his middle finger.

Coming up the path, he said, 'Did you see that? There's plenty of room to get by. Fucking dickhead!'

James said, 'I'm just getting ready to go out, mate. I've been answering the detective's questions about the accident.'

The shaven-headed man acknowledged Harry with a nod and breezed into the house. Harry thanked James, and as he returned to his car, a loud horn and raised voices made him glance along the road. He cast his eyes towards the van belonging to James's friend, but the bus crawled along and blocked his view.

Jenna had messaged to say she was going Christmas shopping after work and asked him to prepare dinner. Leah was up in her bedroom watching Netflix with a friend, which gave Harry a chance to unwind with a cup of tea. On his way to the bathroom for a shower, he stopped by the airing cupboard to fetch a towel.

As he pulled a large one from the middle of the pile, several fell on the floor. With a sigh, he picked up the towels and spotted a plastic carrier bag hidden under a spare pillow at the back of the cupboard. Replacing the towels on the shelf, he cautiously removed the bag.

In the bedroom, he unfurled the carrier bag, noting the pretty red bows and holly printed on the outside. This must be his Christmas present. To look or not to look? He'd never been good at surprises. Inside was a black leather box. He popped the lid open and stared in confusion. A new watch, not too dissimilar from the expensive one Jenna had gifted him last Christmas. Why would she have bought him another, or had she?

Harry's heart raced, and his blood boiled. Consumed with anger, he restrained his urge to lash out. Maybe he was jumping to conclusions again. Should he ask her tonight or wait until Christmas morning? If it turned out Jenna *had* bought it for someone else, what then? Another Christmas ruined for Leah, that's what. He pictured his hands around Benjamin's neck when he'd caught them together, almost wishing he hadn't come to his senses and let go. For now, Harry placed it back in the bag and left it on the bed.

With his shower out of the way and a chicken stir-fry prepared, Harry lay on the sofa, contemplating the two cases and how he would confront Jenna about the watch. When they'd moved to Kent, he'd trusted the promise of a new start, but mostly, he'd put his faith in her. What a mistake that was turning out to be! As for work, there were tough days ahead. Progress on either case had to be made soon.

Harry had set the table for dinner with a bottle of wine at the ready. He'd even lit a candle, not to romanticise their meal but to put pressure on her to eat at the table, where it would be easier to broach such a sensitive subject. Most nights, depending on what they were eating, it was usually plates on knees in front of the television. He'd cooked Leah something beforehand and allowed her to take it up to her room.

When Jenna finally arrived home, she was tired and wanted to go straight upstairs to take a bath. Recognising the trouble he'd gone to, she let out a disgruntled sigh, relented, and turned on her loving smile. Once she'd taken a seat, sipped some wine, and tucked into the stir-fry, she appeared to loosen up. Sitting across from each other, she talked about her day and complained about how busy the shops had been.

'To be fair, it is Christmas,' said Harry.

The seconds of silence increased to minutes. Harry had always been slow at eating, and when Jenna finished her meal before him, she poured herself a second glass of wine. She was itching to leave the table and take her refilled wine glass up to the bathroom, so he placed his fork on the plate and pushed it aside. It was time.

Harry said, 'Did you pick up my present today?'

'No, not yet.'

'What are you getting me this year?'

Jenna smiled. 'I told you, socks. To replace all the moth-eaten ones in your drawer.'

'No, seriously,' he said, forcing a smile.

'Jeez, you're like a child. Don't moan come Christmas morning when you haven't got a surprise under the tree. I haven't picked it up yet, but through a friend of a client, I managed to get hold of that particular turntable you're always banging on about.'

'The Garrard 401?'

'Yes, and I'll tell you this much – it wasn't cheap.'

It baffled him that she'd gone out of her way to find such a vintage gift. 'I'm speechless,' he said, happy but, at the same time, lost in the mire of sorrow. She'd confirmed the watch he'd discovered was not for him.

Seeing his lack of enthusiasm, Jenna said, 'What's the matter? I thought you'd be over the moon. Ah, I bet you're disappointed you know about it now.'

'I am disappointed,' he said, reaching under the table to the chair beside him. 'Because I found this.' He placed the box on the table and lifted the lid to reveal the watch.

Eyes wide, her smile vanished. She blinked slowly and relaxed, embracing acceptance. Relief replaced shock. Jenna didn't say a word – didn't need to. They both stared at the small box of despair that contained the end of their marriage. A bitter stillness of time and silence lingered like a ghost of past mistakes come back to haunt them.

Harry rose from the table and, as he passed by, placed a gentle hand on Jenna's shoulder. Pressing her cheek against his hand, her falling tears touched his skin. Their love remained intact, but their togetherness lay in tatters. He collected the bag he'd prepared earlier from the cupboard under the stairs and glanced up at Leah, who was sitting on the top step. The landing light revealed the tears streaming down her face. He'd spoken with her already and, without mentioning her mother's affair, told her he was leaving.

'Sometimes, even love isn't strong enough to keep a marriage together,' he'd said.

Angry and upset, it came as no surprise when Leah stormed into her bedroom. The only person truly hurt by their actions was her, and without knowing all of the facts, she blamed him. Perhaps she was right; after all, he'd laid the first foundation of heartache.

20

December 20

Lenny arrived at the library in the late afternoon. As a regular visitor and knowing it closed at 8.00 p.m. on weekdays, his preference would have been to get there sooner to give himself more time. His painstaking search through the archives of the eighteenth century produced little, though he managed to find out why the trial of Mary Martin had been illegal. The Witchcraft Act of 1735, which commenced the following year, made it a crime for any person to accuse another of having magical powers or practising witchcraft. The law brought an end to the hunting and execution of witches in Great Britain. However, as he'd recently discovered, a number of sham trials took place in rural villages and towns after the Act was passed.

Moving on to the vast collection of microfilm, which contained tens of millions of articles from newspapers dating back centuries, he knew it would involve plenty of scrolling. With limited information, Lenny's search for William and Elizabeth Martin yielded no results, but fortunately, he had the name of Lord Claxton Chambers. Chambers was a soldier and politician whose peerage was created in 1755 after his heroism in both the First and Second Carnatic Wars between 1744 and 1754. His death in 1769 was the result of tuberculosis at the age of fifty-one. There was little else to go on, but there had to be information about his personal life somewhere in history.

After searching through several newspapers of the time, including *The Daily Post* and *The London Gazette*, where his death was announced, Lenny discovered something interesting in *The London Chronicle*. A small article reported the death of Lord Chambers' wife, Isadora, and their two children during childbirth in 1759. His search for death certificates proved futile, as not all births and deaths were recorded at this time and wouldn't become compulsory until 1878.

Mary and Emma were born in 1759, and the payments to William stopped upon the death of Chambers in 1769, which led Lenny to surmise the conjoined twins were the legitimate children of Lord Chambers and his wife, Isadora. And let's not forget the one-off payment. It wasn't blackmail after all; he'd paid a married couple to raise them. There was no mention of the Martins having any other children, so perhaps they couldn't conceive. No doubt Chambers paid for the surgery to separate his daughters. The reason *why* he didn't want them could be perfectly innocent, but with his children being conjoined, it could have garnered attention that someone of his stature did not want.

Back home in the comfort of his armchair with a glass of whisky, Lenny ruminated over the information he'd uncovered. He'd love to know what had happened to Emma Martin. Maybe when he had more time, he'd delve deeper. It could prove difficult due to her moving to a country where the American Revolution was about to erupt, but it was worth a go. Who knows, perhaps she'd settled comfortably in New York, got married, and had children of her own. Lenny yawned. His scrupulous research had left him exhausted. He closed his eyes. Five minutes of sleep couldn't hurt. He'd call Elaine about Danny afterwards.

21

December 20
Toronto

Wrapped up tight in his thick green parka and wearing black gloves, Detective Christopher Tremblay trampled through the snow and stood over the body of Reagan Scott, a teenage girl who'd been missing since the eighteenth of December. Her half-naked body had been found in Lambton Park by a middle-aged couple walking their two dogs. Early signs indicated she'd been beaten, raped, and strangled. She was one of two girls reported missing that night, the other being Annalise Fournier. He had yet to find out how her situation had come to be, but right now, he was more concerned about the pretty blonde at his feet. The young lady had disappeared less than two miles from where the attempted abduction of the Fournier girl had occurred. No coincidence.

The previous evening, Annalise's bag, containing personal items including her phone, had been found in the bushes of a nearby churchyard. She had informed UK police that she'd lost it while hiding from her assailant. Detective Tremblay had yet to call PC Lucy Fenton to provide an update, and now he had even worse news to report. Not only did he need to inform her about the body of a young girl, but also about the discovery of a burned-out red SUV on an industrial estate, with little hope of retrieving fingerprints or DNA. They couldn't link the vehicle to a suspect, as it had been reported stolen the day before the girl's murder.

Sixteen years as a detective, and staring down at a young victim never got any easier. As a father of two teenagers himself, it always hit him hard. Tremblay left the coroner to finish up and returned to the diminishing warmth of his car, immediately starting the engine to generate more heat. He removed his gloves and placed his hands directly in front of the vent. With much more snow predicted in the coming days, if they hadn't found Miss Scott now, it could have been weeks before they recovered her body. He'd identified Reagan from a photograph her parents had provided, and now he had to pay them a visit and deliver the harrowing news.

Finalising his report at headquarters, a constable approached Tremblay with information about an unidentified young girl who may have been attacked by the same man on the night of the eighteenth. She had been spotted traipsing aimlessly along St Clair West when she wandered out into the road and collapsed. She was admitted to the hospital in the early hours of the nineteenth, having suffered severe head trauma. The officer explained he'd just been to visit the young lady, but with her fractured jaw, it was difficult to tell if she could speak or not. Since waking up a few hours earlier, she hadn't communicated with anyone. Being of a similar description to the other girls, the constable determined the news might be of interest to the detective. Tremblay grabbed his coat and hastened to Mount Sinai Hospital.

The doctor informed him the girl had suffered a severe concussion from multiple blows, sustaining fractures to her skull and jaw, which would make it difficult but not impossible for her to speak. She'd also lost a lot of blood from numerous lacerations and needed stitches to her right temple, forehead, left eyebrow, and the bridge of her nose.

Though warned in advance about her injuries, Tremblay entered the room and paused in disbelief. Traumatised and fortunate to be alive, the poor girl lay asleep on the bed. He approached slowly, observing her heavily bandaged head. Sensing someone in the room, her eyes snapped open with fear. Despite her horrendous wounds, he recognised similarities to Annalise Fournier and Reagan Scott: height, age, complexion, and blonde hair. The killer had a specific profile, and despite his failed attempt to abduct Annalise, he had held his nerve and stuck to type.

'I'm Detective Christopher Tremblay. I can see you're afraid, and I'm sorry for whatever has happened to you, but if you'll let me, I'd like to help in any way I can.' He doubted she was ready or, as the doctor said, able to communicate, but he had to try. 'Is there anyone I can reach out to on your behalf?'

She failed to respond, her desolate stare bereft of substance. He pulled a pen and notepad from his inside pocket. 'Can you write your name for me?'

About to give up, the girl held out her hand. Christopher passed her the items. She wrote something and handed him the pad.

I don't remember my name. I can't remember anything.

'That's a start,' he said. 'I'll let the doctor know.'
Again, she reached out for the pad. She wrote:

I'm scared

'I know you are. Memory loss is fairly common after a head injury, so try not to worry. I'm sure everything will come back to you soon.' He looked into her sad eyes and placed his hand on hers. 'You'll be okay.' He smiled reassuringly. 'I'll get the doctor to come and see you.'

She lifted the pad and wrote:

Will you come back and see me later?

Faced with those tearful eyes and her bruised, battered, and frightened face, he said, 'Yes. I'll come and see you later. I promise.'

Despite all the horror she'd been through, she did her best to curl her lip in an attempt to smile.

Back at the station, Tremblay sat in his chair with a thud and sighed. The doctor had said the girl's memory loss could be post-traumatic amnesia, which meant her memory might not come back for months. He'd asked to be informed immediately if there were any changes in her condition. He sent an update to PC Fenton and DI Baxendale about finding Annalise Fournier's bag and the discovery of Reagan Scott, who had been murdered not long after the failed abduction of Annalise. He also mentioned the young girl in the hospital and how it was conceivable that all three girls had been attacked by the same man on the same night.

22

December 20

The frozen ground weakened Lenny's knees as he dashed through the forest. Lost and alone, he stopped to catch his breath and look around. The huge trees loomed menacingly, refusing to show him a way out. *Bang*! A bullet whistled past his ear. A second shot struck a nearby tree. He dropped to the ground. A third shot flew over his body. Lenny tucked his head under his arms and waited. When all was quiet, he peeked over his forearm. Less than twenty feet away stood a distressed young man, bound with rope to a tree.

'Help me. Please,' he begged. A fourth shot rang out. The man's head jolted backwards and hit the bark with a thwack. A black dot appeared on his forehead, and a dark red line descended, as though painted by an invisible brush.

Tied to another tree was an elderly woman with the same wound. To her left was a young boy, his head dangling to one side. Lenny climbed to his feet. Beleaguered, he walked over and saw he'd met the same fate as the other poor souls. Blaring machine-gun fire forced him to cower at the boy's dirty, bare feet. Continuous shots rang out for around thirty seconds. The hellfire gave way to the haunting sound of sporadic single shots. Back on his feet, Lenny followed the eerie gunfire.

He advanced towards a clearing beyond the trees until he was swallowed whole by a thick, rolling mist. He staggered blindly into the unknown, unsure if his next step would be his last. The shooting ceased, echoing into a long silence. Relief followed the uncertainty of every nervous step. He plunged forward, falling into a vacuum, and landed face down with a thump. Gathering his senses as the mist slowly dispersed, he grasped something beneath him and gazed down into dead, petrified eyes, staring through him into an endless void. He made out the muddied face of an elderly man next to the body of an old woman. Beside her was a young girl, and beyond, he witnessed the gradual unveiling of a grievous pit of death.

Lenny fumbled over bodies in a frenzied panic, slipping and sliding on mud and blood. He clambered to his feet and stared in horror at the many men, women, and children, some holding hands, clinging to loved ones in their final moments. Young ones were encompassed in the arms of desperate parents attempting to protect them from the terrifying spray of bullets. Lenny backed away and scrambled up the slippery edge of the mass grave. Thrusting his arms over the top, he observed a woman holding her side, unable to prevent the steady flow of blood.

'Where were you, Lenny?' Olivia cried. 'It should have been you.'

Lenny tumbled into the pit and opened his eyes, gasping for air. Enveloped in darkness, it took a moment to collect himself and discern that he was in his armchair in front of the large window.

A nightmare he hadn't had for a long time. Well, more of a distorted memory. Disturbing images imprinted in his mind from photographs he'd taken in Bosnia. Olivia wasn't part of his life back then, so for her to feature was a sign that his horrors were merging. Lenny turned on the lamp next to his chair and glanced at his watch. Perhaps it was a little late to call Elaine. He fetched his phone from the coffee table and called her anyway.

'Elaine.'

'Hey, how's it going, Lenny?'

'Okay, I guess. Just checking in to see how you're all doing.'

'You know it's half past ten, right? I'm about to go to bed.'

'I know. I'm sorry.'

A faint sigh followed a small pause before she said, 'We're all good here. As you can imagine, the kids are looking forward to Christmas.'

'Christmas!' His blissful ignorance of the time of year had caught up with him. 'Yes. I bet they are.'

'Are you sniffing for an invite?'

'You know me. I'm not one for celebrations. I'll be fine here.'

'Well, you're welcome to come if you want. I hate to think of you spending Christmas alone. Plus, Emily misses you.'

'Very sweet, but honestly, I'm good. There is something I'd like to discuss, though,' he said, shifting to the edge of his seat, knowing her response. 'Danny.'

'The answer is no, Lenny. I've told you before – I want to put it all behind me and move on.'

'He just wants to see you, to thank you for saving his life.'

'Just tell him there's no need. I did what anyone would have done.'

'But it wasn't anyone else – it was you. You promised him, and it's ingrained in his mind.'

'I promised I'd get him off the boat so he could go home. Nothing more.'

'He's hurting, Elaine. He feels dismissed.'

He hoped her pause was a positive sign. 'I'll think about it,' she said.

'That's good enough,' he said. 'I'll let you get to bed and talk to you soon.'

Possibly sooner than she had imagined. Her response was enough for him to contemplate taking Danny to see her in the next few days. He switched off the lamp, relaxed into his chair, and viewed the city through the window. Harry hadn't got back to him. No updates, nothing. Maybe he didn't need his help after all. A return to monotonous days of passing time in front of the television looked to be on the cards. It seemed all he did these days was pass the time. All those years alone had never bothered him, but things were different now. Olivia had touched his heart in a way no one had ever come close to. Though initially reluctant, he'd hoped assisting Harry might pull him out of the deep hole he'd found himself in – a temporary fix to slow his descent into abysmal emptiness. He'd always been brilliant at helping others, but who was helping him?

'Life will get better, Lenny.'

He looked around at Olivia, leaning against the wall beside the window. 'Fat chance.'

'You have witnessed so much suffering and seen for yourself that no matter how damaged people are, they find an inner strength they weren't aware of and carry on. And so will you.'

His eyes glazed over. 'Most people have others who need them. Loved ones who fuel that inner strength. Who needs me, Olivia? Where will my strength come from?' A tear fell, with a second close behind.

Olivia wandered towards him. 'Oh, Lenny. You still don't get it, do you?' She sat on the arm of the chair and placed her hand against his face. 'You have an incredible gift. You see things others can't. Stop fighting and embrace it. Charlie Davis was the first to gain your attention. He led you to Joseph Webster. Let Mary Martin do the same. You think nobody needs you? You couldn't be more wrong. If you hadn't found Webster, who knows how many more lives he would have destroyed? Find the killer, Lenny – because he's not going to stop.'

23

December 21

The room at Gerty's Guest House in Rochester was compact and bleak. Harry hadn't envisioned another spell in a hotel room. Too much faith and a lack of foresight on his part. For a while, everything about his life had involved adjusting to circumstances: Jenna's affair, the transfer to a new station, the move from London to Kent, and a full circle back to Jenna's affair. He didn't care to ask who she was seeing; it didn't matter. One thing *was* certain – he wanted that bloody turntable she'd bought him.

Harry climbed from the bed, opened the faded curtains, and glanced over the tiny car park at the rear of the building. Worried about Leah, he'd call her later to see how she was doing, though he suspected she'd be reluctant to talk. The difficulties of her parents' marriage had affected her deeply, but she was a determined girl who would soon be moving away to university. He took the momentary win and perked up as he imagined all the wonderful life experiences that lay ahead of her. In no rush to get to work, Harry had a quick shower and opted to have breakfast at the guest house; after all, it was included in the price.

He arrived at the station and observed Lucy at her desk with her head in her hands. She looked up when he called out and said she'd gone through the remainder of Vincent Perry's contacts and turned up nothing of note. She'd also run a thorough check on Peter Mullings. Not a blemish. During her research, she'd discovered he was at a conference in Canterbury. She suggested it would be better to visit him there instead of travelling to London.

Lucy drove, leaving Harry to dwell on the collapse of his marriage. The two cases he was working on seemed irrelevant right now, and come tomorrow morning, unless he had a miraculous breakthrough with at least one of them, he'd be standing in front of DCS Falconer and Owen Carrick, explaining why there were no results. Despite his problems, he'd discerned Lucy wasn't her usual happy-go-lucky self. She asked if he'd seen Detective Tremblay's email.

'Yeah, I did. Sounds like the psycho went on a spree. It shows he can't control his urge to kill when plans go awry. Desperation gets you caught.'

Lucy said, 'What puzzles me is, if the other girls were attacked *after* Annalise, as Detective Tremblay suggests, how did the killer track her down later and bring her to England?'

If he wasn't so preoccupied, he would have picked up on that himself. Why hadn't his Canadian counterpart questioned this? Perhaps he had, but like them, couldn't fathom an explanation. 'He must have returned to the scene and somehow found her.'

'I suppose,' said Lucy. 'Well, he must have. It just seems an unlikely thing to do, given that the police were trawling the area. And also, why not kill her there? Why bring *her* to England and not one of the others? Why bring her to England at all?'

Harry was drowning in a pool of unanswerable questions. His phone rang. A detective informed him there had been a murder. 'Turn the car around,' he said.

*

Before entering the property, they had to jostle through a horde of local residents gathered behind the taped-off area. Forensics hadn't finished in the living room, so Harry and Lucy had to suit up. Lucy paused to take a deep breath before walking through the front door. Seated in the armchair, a thin, deep red line was visible around Fred Perry's neck. The table in front of him, on its side, had no doubt been kicked over as he struggled and fought for his life. Scattered about the floor were empty beer bottles and cans, a bottle of vodka, and the remnants of cigarette ends from a broken ashtray, all of which would need to be bagged and tested for DNA. Physically fit and strong, even if Fred had been drunk, it would have taken brute strength to strangle him in his chair.

Harry moved in and circled the victim, mindful of the debris at his feet. Examining the back of the chair, he crouched to take a closer look. There were two indentations on the material. Starting at the top of the chair, Harry ran his fingers from the top downwards until he came across a gap in the middle where the wooden supports had been broken.

'Ah, I see you've discovered the method used to strangle this poor chap,' said a familiar voice.

Harry popped up from behind the chair. 'Arthur! This is unexpected. I'm surprised to see you out in the sticks.' Arthur Potts had worked as the lead forensic investigator on a few of Harry's previous cases.

'I go where the bodies are, DCI Baxendale.'

'Just detective inspector now,' muttered Harry, still bitter about the ramifications.

'Oh dear. I take it you were part of the reshaping after the Webster fiasco?'

'That's one way to put it, I suppose.'

'Well, at least you weren't part of the cull. Those murders had been going on for years. Heads were bound to roll.'

'Unlike you, I failed to find a positive. Anyway, Arthur, this is Police Constable Lucy Fenton. She's been assigned to work with me on the case.'

Arthur shook hands with Lucy and got down to body talk. 'Catching him unaware, the perpetrator attacked the victim from behind and strangled him with what I suspect to be an elastic bungee cord. If you look here' – Arthur crouched and pointed to the red mark around the left side of Fred Perry's neck – 'you can see green and black fibres.'

Harry squinted to see, and Lucy peered over his shoulder. 'How can you be sure it's a bungee cord?' he asked.

'I've come across this method of strangulation before. I've already taken samples, and I'll get them under a microscope at the lab to confirm. Now' – Arthur moved behind the chair – 'at first sight, you look at the size of the victim and think whoever did this would have to be of a similar stature. Hardly ever true, and not the case here. As soon as the killer placed the cord around the victim's neck, they dropped to the floor and positioned their feet against the back of the chair for leverage, exerting enough force to snap the wooden supports. The scratch marks around his neck are where he clawed at the ligature. He put up a fight but didn't stand a chance. Going by age and build, he would have lost consciousness in between twelve and twenty seconds, and death would have occurred three to six minutes later.'

Harry said, 'So the murderer would have held the ligature in place for around six minutes? They must have been pretty determined.'

'This method of killing is one of the most brutal,' said Arthur. 'When someone chooses to end another's life in this way, they have plenty of time to think and come to their senses. Murder was most definitely on the agenda here.'

Ill at ease, Lucy walked behind and studied the back of the chair. She said, 'Could fibres from the material of the chair be transferred to the killer's shoes?'

'Very much so,' Arthur replied.

'Time of death?' Harry inquired.

'I'd say he was murdered between midnight and two a.m.'

'Which would suggest he knew his killer and let them in earlier.'

'Not necessarily,' said Lucy. 'The murderer could have assumed he was asleep and shown up later.'

Arthur said, 'There were no signs of a break-in, so I have to agree with the detective on this one. It's likely whoever killed him was invited into the house.'

Harry knelt in front of Perry and viewed the deep marks on his neck. 'A loose end,' he said. 'Fred had information that could help the investigation, and someone silenced him.'

Lucy said, 'He was cooperative when we interviewed him, so why didn't he tell us then?'

'Because he wasn't aware of its relevance at the time. We wanted to ask him if he knew of his brother's association with Ryan Levinson or knew Ryan himself. We have our answer.'

Returning to the car, Harry and Lucy faced nasty remarks and taunts about not doing enough to protect honest people. Though he didn't deserve to be killed, Fred Perry was anything but honest. Across the road from the car, Harry recognised the youths who'd previously watched them visit Perry's house. A couple of them appeared to be hiding something behind their backs.

Harry said, 'Quick, get in the car.'

Lucy glanced behind to see a lad on his bike with a brick in his hand. She pulled the door open.

'Murdering pigs!' shouted the teenager, preparing to launch.

'Slag!' yelled another.

Lucy jumped in and pulled the door closed. Harry was soon beside her, shoving the key into the ignition. The brick landed close to the car, with small bits of debris pinging against the paintwork. A constable gave chase, but the boys were already racing away, with a smaller boy discarding a missile in his wake.

Harry said, 'What the hell was that about?'

Lucy contemplated as they scarpered up the road. 'You know how hated we are, especially in these neighbourhoods.'

'Still, it was a little bit strange.'

'They've lost one of their own,' she said. 'They're just angry.'

24

December 21

Despite his lack of sleep, Lenny had woken in a spirited mood, eager to dig deeper into the case. Research into the past was all well and good, but he had to focus on the here and now. Somewhere out there was a missing teenager and a killer to find, and after looking through the most recent information Harry had sent, despite the detective's reservations, Lenny was certain the cases were linked. There was no time to waste, so he arranged to meet with Marvin Collingwood, the pilot who flew the folk band from Toronto to London. He didn't know if Harry had interviewed the pilot or not. It didn't matter. Lenny figured Harry had asked him to get involved because of what he brought to the table: determination to find out the truth by any means necessary.

On the way to Mr Collingwood's address in Hampstead, Lenny stopped at a café for a cup of tea and a bacon sandwich. His phone rang, and after viewing the name, he took his time to answer. 'What's up, Harry?'

'Did you get my email?'

'I read it first thing this morning.'

'Good. Anyway, I'm calling to let you know this case has just got considerably worse. The brother of the van driver has been murdered.'

Lenny set down his cup. 'I see. That is an unexpected turn of events. Is there something you need me to do?'

'We'll shortly be on our way to interview Peter Mullings. Would you be able to go and find out what you can from the other pilot, Marvin Collingwood?'

'Yeah, I can do that.' Lenny smiled and sipped his tea.

'You'll find his address in the—'

'As it turns out, I'm in Swiss Cottage, so I'm fairly close.'

'You're already on your way to see him.'

'You know me, Harry. I don't muck about. By the way, what did you make of the email I sent you?'

'I'm waiting for the details to be sent over. It won't be easy to link Louise Norris's murder to our case, but if anything stands out, I'll let you know.'

'Okay, great. Talk to you soon.' Lenny ended the call and took a large bite of his sandwich.

One glance at Marvin Collingwood ruled him out as the main suspect. He looked nothing at all like the man in the e-fit, and after explaining why he was there, it took less than a minute for Lenny to disregard him as a suspect altogether. His willingness to talk to him, even though he wasn't a police officer, helped. A person with something to hide would have shut him down in an instant. He lived with his wife, and the couple had an adopted son. Lenny asked about the band.

Marvin said, 'Ah, Asa Finch and The Redpolls. For a band, they were fairly quiet and respectable. I've taken a few bands to various destinations, and there have been issues – drinking, arguments, even brawls. Other than a couple of beers, these guys mostly drank coffee, played cards, and slept.'

'Is it mostly musicians who hire your plane?'

'No, all sorts. CEOs, athletes, actors. Tomorrow morning at six, I'm flying the wife and daughter of the Canadian ambassador to Toronto.'

'Have you flown—' Lenny paused as Marvin's wife passed him a cup of tea and placed a small plate of biscuits on the thick wooden coffee table in front of him.

'Thank you,' he said, glancing at the biscuits and recalling a past experience when he'd got a little carried away. He reached out and took one digestive biscuit, determined to leave the rest alone. 'Where was I? Oh yeah, have you flown this band before?'

'No. First time. Mr Finch mentioned they usually fly with Able-Air. That would be Hal Turner, a Canadian pilot with British citizenship based in the UK. I hear he is particularly unwell, though I'm unaware of the circumstances.'

Lenny dunked his biscuit and looked slightly embarrassed when only half of it resurfaced.

'I assume you're a private investigator, Mr Grey?'

The penny dropped, and Lenny contemplated how he'd inadvertently become an unlicensed PI. 'I prefer to think of myself as a police consultant.'

'How exciting!'

'Sometimes,' he said, his mind drifting back to Olivia. Sod it! He reached for another digestive. 'Exactly how many people were on the plane?' Lenny made sure to put his cup on the coaster and searched through his phone.

'Including myself and the co-pilot, six.'

Lenny showed the e-fit of the suspect. 'Was this one of the men?'

'He doesn't look familiar to me. Though I briefly saw them all, I only interacted with two of them. After that, I didn't pay much attention. I focused on safety and flying the plane.'

'Makes sense.'

'Just a minute,' said Marvin. He briefly left the immaculate living room and returned, scrolling through his laptop. 'I happened to look for the band online and watched a clip on YouTube. Here,' he said, resting the computer on the table in front of Lenny. 'You can see for yourself.'

Why the hell hadn't *he* searched for the band online? He supposed he would have got around to it – eventually. Lenny tapped his foot as he watched the video. 'They're pretty good,' he said. 'Though I can see none of these resemble the man I'm looking for.' He finished his tea, took another biscuit, and shook the couple's hands. 'Thank you for your time. I doubt you'll be bothered about this again, and I'm sorry to have troubled you.'

In the car, Lenny messaged Harry, telling him he could rule out Marvin Collingwood as a suspect. By the time he arrived home, he'd become strangely subdued, partly because he didn't know what to do next. Perhaps his heart wasn't in this investigation after all. No, it wasn't that. His growing frustrations were due to there being so little to go on, and he was finding it difficult to focus.

He made a cup of tea and fished a couple of digestive biscuits from his jacket pocket. He'd taken a couple for the road, snatching them from the plate while Marvin and his wife weren't looking. He tossed his jacket on the worktop and got comfortable in the armchair. Phoebe jumped onto his lap and nudged his hand, attempting to make him put his cup on the side, which he did. While running his hand through Phoebe's fur, he reflected with sadness on Olivia and how much he missed her. He recalled what Reverend Strathearn had said about carrying the weight of the world. Taking on cases like this was a great example, reasoning that it was his responsibility to track down murderers and bring justice to suffering families.

'The reverend also suggested this could be some kind of miracle,' said Olivia, who appeared at his side.

Lenny smiled, glad to see her. 'Yes, he did, as well as adding that there must be a logical explanation, so don't go there.'

'I wouldn't rule out the miracle. I mean, where is the logical explanation for you talking to me?'

He huffed and placed Phoebe on the floor so he could dunk his biscuits and drink his tea. Soon after, he dozed off in the chair. A severe lack of sleep had finally caught up with him.

25

December 21

Canterbury Cathedral Lodge was situated within the cathedral grounds. Despite the well-attended event, they were fortunate to find a space in the guests' car park. The lodge looked modern and stylish but was not out of place under the gaze of the ancient and awe-inspiring cathedral. The conical roof of the auditorium added to its unique appearance. Harry and Lucy were shown to the Kentish Barn, where the conference was being held. A member of staff asked them to wait while she attempted to locate Peter Mullings. The pair watched as guests mingled over drinks and canapés.

Harry stared up at the central tower of the cathedral and said, 'Now there's a sight I wouldn't mind waking up to every morning.'

'Are you coming on to me again?'

He acknowledged her sense of humour and continued to admire the view.

She said, 'I never had you down as a religious man.'

'Appreciating a work of art doesn't make me religious, but what makes you think I'm not?'

'I don't know, you just don't seem the type.'

'I've witnessed evil up close, and I've had my doubts, but I cling to the belief that there is something more powerful beyond all of this.'

'Very profound.'

A man in his early fifties wandered towards them. 'Detective Inspector Baxendale?'

'Yes. You must be Peter Mullings.' Harry showed his warrant card and reached out to shake his hand.

Peter said, 'It's a good job you caught me now, as I'm not much of a drinker. A couple more of these and they'd have already carried me back to my room. What can I do for you?'

Harry inquired about his recent flight to Toronto and showed him the e-fit of the suspect.

'He doesn't look like someone you'd forget in a hurry,' said Peter. 'If I'd seen this man in the last few days, I'd remember.'

Harry said, 'I didn't see a co-pilot listed – is that usual?'

'My jet is single-pilot certified.'

'Thank you for your time, Mr Mullings. We'll let you get back to your function.'

Walking to the car, Harry's frustration about Annalise's case grew. He remained hopeful that Lenny would find a breakthrough. Regarding the other case, Fred Perry's death bothered him. So brutal, and just as they'd discovered a link between Vincent and Ryan Levinson.

Lucy asked, 'What now?'

'Let's track down Craig Bishop. He's the only witness I haven't spoken to in person. Maybe he'll reveal something new.'

'Before we set off, I need to use the bathroom,' said Lucy.

'While you do that, I'll give Mr Bishop a call.'

Harry climbed into the car and keyed in the number. No reply. He found Bishop's address in his notes, typed it into the satnav, and waited for Lucy. When she returned, they drove to a hostel close to the high street in Strood. They struggled to find a parking space on the narrow road lined with terraced houses on either side, so they parked around the corner and walked back under the swift advance of dark clouds and sporadic drops of rain. With many vehicles parked on the pavement, it made for a tight squeeze. A few of the houses looked in dire need of repair, while others had been spruced up, painted bright blue or yellow.

The outside of the house they arrived at looked grim. The door was tatty and battered; the lower half had occasionally been kicked in anger. Lucy pressed the buzzer for flat C. The lack of sound and the long delay left them questioning whether it was working. Impatient, Harry beat his knuckles against the door several times. While waiting for someone to answer, he glanced up and down the road. There was no sign of a maintenance van. The door was opened by an unkempt man with a vacant stare. He shuffled past them without a word and headed off down the road, leaving the door ajar.

Lucy said, 'Do you think that's Bishop?'

'I hope not.' Harry pushed the door wide open and stared into the confined, uninviting hallway. Dirty magnolia walls and a stained, threadbare grey cord carpet loomed. The pair glanced at each other, unable to quell their reservations, before walking into the unknown.

The stench of nicotine and weed thickened the air. The scuffed gloss on the doors had yellowed over time, possibly aided by heat and the absence of natural light. Harry knocked on C, and the door nudged open a little. He gave the door a push and called out to Mr Bishop. Hesitant, they entered. Craig Bishop kept an untidy abode. Clothes were strewn across the floor, and empty cans of lager scattered the small worktop in the tiny kitchen area, along with unwashed plates, glasses, and cutlery. Improvement was not to be found in the bedroom. More empty cans and a crowded ashtray lay on the filthy carpet next to the unmade, inhospitable double bed. Huddled in the corner were worn clothes, dirty towels, and soiled underwear.

Harry remained in the living area while Lucy headed off to check the shared bathroom. The television screen displayed a video game on pause. Harry examined the flimsy wooden table in front of the mangy sofa, which contained two joypads, a half-eaten plate of beans on toast, and a cup of tea. He hovered his hand over the unfinished meal and touched the back of his fingers against the chipped cup.

Lucy returned. 'Bathroom's empty.'

Harry said, 'The food and cup are still warm. We must have just missed him. It looks like he left in a hurry.'

'He couldn't possibly have known we were coming. I suppose he could be in someone else's room.'

A voice spoke out before entering the flat. 'Right, I hope you're ready, cos I'm gonna kick your arse.' The man looked surprised. 'What the fuck? Who are you?'

Harry showed his ID and said, 'Detective Inspector Baxendale. We're looking for Craig Bishop. Do you know where he is?'

'No. I came down to see if he was back and saw the door wide open. Why are you here?'

'Police business. We need to ask him a few questions about the accident he witnessed the other day.'

'Accident? He never mentioned anything to me.'

'Do you know him well?'

'Yeah. I sometimes work with him. We also have a few beers together and play video games.' The man appeared more with it than the zombie who'd opened the front door when they'd arrived.

'And you are?'

'Greg. I live upstairs.'

'How long has Mr Bishop been gone?'

'Ten minutes, maybe more.'

'Where did he go?'

'I dunno. He got a text, said he had to meet someone and wouldn't be long.'

'Did he walk or take his van?'

'I assume he took the van, cos he snatched his keys off the table and was out of here in a flash.'

Harry asked Greg to phone Bishop, knowing he was more likely to answer a friend than an unknown number. Nevertheless, the call was directed straight to voicemail.

Harry handed Greg a card. 'When Mr Bishop returns, tell him to give me a call. Oh, out of curiosity, do you happen to have a picture of Craig on your phone?'

At first reluctant, Greg pulled out his phone and showed him a photo of himself and Bishop in the stands at a West Ham United football match. 'We'd just beaten Chelsea.'

Harry recognised Craig Bishop as the cocky guy who had shown up when he'd finished questioning James Harding. 'This isn't a selfie. May I ask who took the picture?'

'A mate of Craig's – Ryan.'

Harry pulled out his phone and showed a picture of Ryan Levinson. 'Is this him?' Backing away and clearly nervous, Greg didn't want to say. 'Look,' said Harry. 'This won't come back on you. I just need to know if this is the man you were with.'

Greg nodded and shifted towards the door. 'I'm not sure what's going on, but whatever it is, it has nothing to do with me.'

'I know,' said Harry, easing Greg out of the flat. 'Thanks for your help.' He turned to Lucy, savouring the new information.

She said, 'A witness to the crash knows Ryan Levinson.'

'Bishop also knows James Harding. That's no coincidence,' said Harry. 'The only problem is we still don't have a body.'

*

With the day pressing on, Harry opted to question Ryan Levinson the following morning and returned to the station to write up the report on Frederick Perry's murder. Being unable to talk to Craig Bishop was a blow, though he remained hopeful of interviewing him before going on to see Ryan. Meanwhile, he'd asked Lucy to run the names of the witnesses through the PNC to see if anything interesting showed up. She found nothing notable, and by the time he'd finished his report, Lucy had gone home.

In his inbox was an email containing the file for Louise Norris. The case remained unsolved. He clicked on the attached folder, which brought up the report and harrowing images of eighteen-year-old Louise, who, like Reagan Scott, had been strangled. Reading the report, Harry discovered Louise had been attacked at around 8.30 p.m. on her way home from work. The back of her head had been struck with a blunt object, causing her to fall to the ground. She had also been injected with suxamethonium chloride, a neuromuscular blocking agent.

Harry recalled Annalise telling him that the man who'd tried to abduct her had injected something into *her* arm.

Louise was then bundled into a car and driven to a nearby park. A second dose had been administered into her thigh before she was dragged across the gravel car park and laid out on the grass. The coroner concluded that Louise had remained conscious throughout her attack but was unable to move due to the effects of the drug. The perpetrator raped and strangled her. Death occurred approximately twenty minutes after her abduction, and no DNA match was found in the database. The report was horrific and uncomfortable to read, but it revealed they were dealing with a sadistic bastard who liked to look into his victims' eyes as they died. Control. Power.

Harry had more than enough to link the two cases and emailed the hospital to inquire about the results of Annalise Fournier's blood test. He also emailed Detective Tremblay to find out about Reagan Scott's autopsy results. If they'd all been injected with the same drug, he would send him this file and all the other information he'd gathered. Tremblay would need to know they were dealing with an international serial killer.

At the guest house, Harry placed a carrier bag containing Chinese food on the bed and called Leah to see how she was doing. The call lasted less than two minutes, and the conversation was decidedly frosty, with plenty of awkward silences. With no cutlery in the room, he picked at his food while watching an old James Bond film. Soon full, Harry put the leftovers in the plastic bag, turned off the television, and collapsed backwards onto the bed. After a rest, he would spend the evening going through the CCTV from Phantasm nightclub. It wasn't as if he had anything better to do.

Within seconds of lying down, the vibration of his phone on the bedside table had him reaching across to answer. 'Hey, Owen. What's up?'

'We've called off the search for Rebecca Heaton's body. There's nothing out here. It's as though the girl has vanished into thin air.'

For Harry, the news wasn't unexpected. 'I don't get it either.'

Owen said, 'We had the dog units out this afternoon, and the most bizarre thing happened. After giving them her scent, they led us not to where the car she was in came to rest on the grass verge, but straight to where the car had been impacted.'

Harry's eyes shot open. He sat up on the edge of the bed, unable to grasp how the dogs had picked up her scent from inside the car before it was hit. 'Where did the dogs go next?'

'Nowhere. They lay on the ground. The guys said they'd never seen anything like it.'

'But that's ludicrous. Doesn't that indicate she never left the car?'

'That's exactly what it means. Not on foot anyway.'

'Are you suggesting someone removed the body from the car?'

'If you've got another theory, Harry, I'd be happy to hear it. Also, forensics have finished searching through Rebecca's laptop and found nothing helpful at all. According to their findings, the girl is an absolute angel.'

After updating Owen on his own findings throughout the day, Harry opened the laptop and plugged in the memory stick. He watched from when the doors opened at 8.00 p.m. Ryan Levinson showed up at the club with Rebecca Heaton just after 9.00. Close behind them was Craig Bishop, and Ian Heaton arrived at 9.30. Next through the door at 9.40 were the Perry brothers. All he needed to conclude tonight's viewing was Sarah Kerr, and she arrived alone at 9.52. James Harding and Melanie Hillingdon made an appearance not long after. Though not all were pictured together in these images, things finally started to make sense. He'd already considered that three of the witness statements seemed manufactured; now he was certain. Something awful happened to Rebecca Heaton on December 18, and everyone other than Frederick Perry attempted to cover it up. With so much on his plate today, he'd failed to provide Lenny with the latest information from the detective in Canada. Harry peered at his watch: a quarter past nine.

26

December 21

Asleep in the armchair, Lenny stirred to the violent rumble of his phone in his trouser pocket. Phoebe jumped from his lap onto the floor as he moved to retrieve it.

After apologising for not calling earlier, Harry said, 'Anyway, Peter Mullings is not a suspect, and it's likely Louise Norris was killed by the same person who attacked Annalise Fournier. There are striking similarities, plus Louise had been injected with a fast-acting neuromuscular blocking agent, causing temporary paralysis. I'm waiting for the toxicology report on Miss Fournier's blood test results, but I'm confident they'll find a match for the same drug.'

Lenny scratched his stubbly cheek. 'Thanks for letting me know. We need to catch this bloke, Harry, because he will kill again.'

'He already has.'

'Let me guess, Reagan Scott?'

'Yeah. She was murdered after Annalise escaped. I've asked Detective Tremblay for her autopsy report. I fear the MO will be exactly the same. They found Annalise Fournier's bag close to where she worked, and there is another unidentified young girl in the hospital over there suffering from amnesia due to head trauma. The detective suspects she could be a victim of an attack on the same night.'

'Angry about the Fournier girl getting away, I'd imagine,' said Lenny.

'I agree. If I get the results I'm expecting, I'll need to let my DCS know what we're dealing with. The Serious Crime Analysis Section from the NCA will no doubt be called, and the case may well be given to a higher-ranking detective.'

'Given you helped take down two high-profile killers last year, do you reckon that's likely?'

'We'll find out soon enough.'

When the call ended, Lenny rested his head on the back of the chair and stared at the ceiling. 'Shit!'

Come tomorrow, Harry might not be in need of his help any more. He pulled himself out of the chair and marched to the bathroom to use the toilet. He washed his hands, splashed cold water on his face, and observed his pale complexion in the mirror. The strain of an irregular sleeping pattern and not eating properly was beginning to take its toll. At least he hoped this was the reason for his muddled thinking. Despite being assured by a doctor that a strong genetic link exists for rarer types of dementia, his paranoia about inheriting the disease from his father remained.

On his way to the kitchen, he stopped in front of the main bedroom, hesitated, and opened the door, ready to torture himself once again. He stared at the bed, always hoping to see Olivia lying there, reading or working on her laptop, but he knew the reality, and this was a nightmare that had no end. His chest tightened with an overwhelming sense of loss, guilt, and anger. With a hand on either side of the door frame, he fought to keep himself from entering and pulled the door closed.

'Why didn't you go inside?' said Olivia.

'Because there's something I need to do. I just don't know what that something is, and it's driving me mad.' Lenny walked into the kitchen, fetched a glass, and reached for the bottle of whisky.

'Alcohol isn't going to make things clearer.'

'Maybe not, but at least it'll get me pissed.'

Olivia placed her hand over his. 'Don't pour that, Lenny. I know you're struggling right now, but as you said, there's something you need to do.'

'What, Liv? What can I possibly do? As of tomorrow, nobody is going to need me.'

'Well, you certainly don't have to stop looking for the killer.'

'Stop looking? I don't even know where to start.'

'That's because you're not thinking. Come on, Lenny. Who held your hand and directed you to uncover the past? Who first brought this murderer to everyone's attention, and where did the incident take place?'

Lenny's eyes lit up, accompanied by the faintest hint of a smile. 'Where's my phone?'

27

December 22

At first light, wearing white coveralls and gloves, Harry stood on a vast area of concrete wasteland overlooking the River Medway. He'd dragged himself out of bed at six thirty after a call from the station regarding the discovery of a body. Now he was staring at a man in the front seat of a van with multiple stab wounds to the neck. Despite the considerable amount of dried blood on the victim's face, Harry recognised Craig Bishop.

While Arthur Potts examined the inside of the cab and bagged whatever samples he could find, Harry inspected the outside of the dark blue van. A glance through the open back doors as he passed revealed a disarray of tools and materials. Mr Bishop appeared to have treated his van as an extension of his grubby apartment. As with the other side, large, filthy white signage read C.B. Maintenance & Care, followed by a mobile number that did not match the one on Vincent Perry's phone records. If Harry had glimpsed the initials on the van outside James Harding's house before the bus shielded his view, he would have worked out a connection between them all sooner. Above the lettering, he identified a large faded *K*. Beneath it was a faded *P*. On closer inspection, he made out the previous signage, three words in vertical format:

KENT

PROPERTY

CARE.

Harry grabbed an old cloth from the back and wiped the side, revealing the outline of a previous number containing the last four digits: 4129. He finally had a match for the number that showed up frequently on Vincent's phone. The Perry brothers and Bishop had worked together often.

For the moment, what had happened to Rebecca Heaton remained a mystery, but Harry was convinced Ryan Levinson, Sarah Kerr, James Harding, Melanie Hillingdon, Vincent Perry, and Craig Bishop had conspired to hide the truth. Now, including Fred, three of this ragtag bunch were dead, and someone was attempting to cover it up. If only he'd had the chance to test Bishop's resolve. Showing the picture of Ryan and Vincent together might have been enough to encourage him to come clean.

Keeping a short distance away, Harry watched Arthur at work, his white suit smudged with blood. A moderate but piercing breeze bounced off the river as he observed members of Arthur's team scouring the vicinity. Harry's phone rang, and he was happy to see Lucy's name. He informed her of the victim's identity.

'Want me to come down there?' she asked.

'No, it's okay. I've got it covered. It's bloody freezing down here anyway.' He wandered aimlessly, phone to ear, kicking the odd stone.

'I hear it's an extremely unpleasant crime scene?'

'News travels fast. Yeah, it's grim. Arthur has identified at least seven stab wounds to the neck and top of the shoulder,' he said, edging closer to the river.

'Seems like they wanted to make sure he didn't survive.'

'I agree. It bears all the hallmarks of the determination used to kill Fred Perry. Someone isn't taking any chances.'

'What are you doing now?' she asked.

'I'm staring at a submarine moored in the middle of the river while waiting for Arthur to finish collecting evidence.'

'Ah, the old rust bucket. It's a former Russian sub from the Cold War, now privately owned. I read somewhere that the owner is trying to restore it.'

'Not quite what I expected to see this morning. Anyway, Arthur has just called out. I'll collect you from the station in a bit, and we'll go and see what Ryan has to say. Meanwhile, check if the hospital has provided us with Annalise's blood test results. If not, give them a call. It's important. Also, check if Detective Tremblay has got back in touch.'

'No problem. See you soon.'

Arthur informed Harry he'd removed blood, fingerprints, and hair samples, but emphasised they wouldn't necessarily belong to the murderer. 'Any Tom, Dick, or Jane could have been a passenger in this van, and I guarantee not all, if any, will be identifiable.'

'Okay,' said Harry, his tone highlighting his flagging optimism.

Arthur climbed into the cab and inched across the double passenger seat. Bishop's head rested against the side window, revealing the gaping wounds. 'You said he'd come here to meet someone at around three in the afternoon. That would tally with the time of death. This was a close, ferocious, and frenzied attack, leaving the victim helpless and unable to defend himself.'

Harry said, 'I'm almost certain it's the same person who killed Frederick Perry. Both victims worked together and ran with the same crowd. I'm confident these murders are linked to a crash on the motorway a few days ago and the disappearance of a teenage girl.'

'If that's the case, you could be right. The killer was intent on ensuring neither victim survived. Mr Bishop here bled out from a severed artery. I'll run checks between the evidence gathered from both crime scenes and see if anything matches. I can't tell you any more until I do a post-mortem. I'll finish up here and have my team give the area a thorough going over. You never know – we could get lucky.'

'Thanks, Arthur. Will you be doing the autopsy today?'

'This afternoon.'

'Excellent. I'll drop by later.'

When Harry arrived at the station, Lucy had news: Annalise's blood test showed traces of the same drug found in Louise Norris. The autopsy report provided by Detective Tremblay on Reagan Scott was even more informative. Not only did it identify the drug used on Louise and Reagan, but a tiny sample of Annalise Fournier's blood was found at the injection site on Miss Scott's arm, meaning he had used the same needle containing the drug he'd failed to fully inject into Annalise's arm. This was conclusive proof that the two Canadian girls were attacked by the same man.

Harry emailed his findings and everything on the Fournier case to Detective Tremblay. The National Crime Agency might well take the case off his hands, and he could be reprimanded for sharing such information, but he determined it was the right thing to do, especially if it meant another detective was trying to find the culprit. Before going into DCS Falconer's office, where Owen Carrick would also be in attendance, Harry called Lenny to give him the latest. Directed to voicemail, he left a message explaining the details.

The meeting with DCS Falconer and Owen Carrick didn't go as well as he would have liked. Regarding Rebecca Heaton, the DCS said that while there were grounds to bring them all in for questioning, at the moment there was no victim, and the evidence alone was circumstantial and not enough to make an arrest. He suggested interviewing each individual again in the hope that one of them would let something slip. As for Frederick Perry and Craig Bishop, knowing each other was not enough. Evidence was needed to show their murders were connected to the Rebecca Heaton case, or Harry had to at least find a link between the crime scenes. Arthur Potts would hopefully discover something later today.

Moving on to Annalise Fournier, DCS Falconer couldn't deny she and Reagan Scott were attacked by the same man, but at this time, he refused to link the death of Louise Norris in Manchester to the same killer. Nevertheless, because Annalise Fournier had somehow turned up in England, he agreed that all information should be passed on to the National Crime Agency to see what they could find. The decision on whether to open an investigation into a serial killer in the United Kingdom would lie with them.

28

December 22

The gravel crunched beneath their feet as they approached the Levinsons' front door. Lucy knocked, and Penny Levinson was quick to answer. Harry said they had more questions for her son, and Penny unexpectedly responded by asking if there was any news on Rebecca. After his initial uncertainty, Harry no longer doubted her genuine concern.

She showed them into the living room and, before calling Ryan, said, 'You should probably know that Derrick Heaton turned up spouting all kinds of accusations late last night. Carl confronted him, and they almost came to blows. A neighbour intervened and managed to get Derrick to calm down and leave.'

Harry asked, 'Did you report the incident?'

'No. To be honest, I felt for the man. He must be going through hell. If he does it again, though, we'll have no choice but to call the police and have him arrested.'

Harry said, 'I'll have another word with Mr Heaton and warn him to stay away.'

As Penny left the room to fetch Ryan, Lucy turned to Harry on the sofa and mouthed, 'Great house.' Harry nodded in agreement.

Ryan entered the living room with an unabashed swagger. Was his unbridled confidence inspired by the silencing of Fred

Perry and Craig Bishop? Nothing would surprise Harry with this arrogant prick.

'Mum said there is no news, so how come you need to speak to me again?'

'We need to clear up some discrepancies from your previous statement,' said Harry.

Penny sat in the chair opposite, and Ryan perched on the arm beside her. 'Sure,' he said. 'Not sure I can add much to what I've already told you.'

'Let's see, shall we?' said Harry, hoping to unsettle Ryan. 'You said last time that you'd only been seeing Rebecca for about seven months.'

Mrs Levinson said, 'Well, he's got that wrong for a start. What is it with men and dates? It's been over a year.'

Ryan said, 'Wow. Has it been that long?'

At this point, Harry couldn't tell if Mrs Levinson would be a help or a hindrance. Although acknowledging her son had been incorrect, she'd also reinforced Lucy's observation regarding men's inability to remember important dates.

'So you had no idea how long you'd been in a relationship with Miss Heaton?' said Harry.

'Obviously not.'

'Okay. Let's move on. When I asked before, you said you'd never heard of Vincent Perry. Why did you lie?'

'I didn't. The name means nothing to me.'

Harry fished his phone from his inside pocket and selected the video. 'I'd like to show you something, Mr Levinson,' he said, rising from his seat and moving closer to Ryan. 'This is you, right?'

'Yes,' he answered, appearing unconcerned, which bothered Harry.

'The person you are talking to in Phantasm Nightclub is Vincent Perry, the man you claim not to know.'

Ryan smiled. 'No,' he said. 'That's Vinny.' His expression turned serious. 'Wait, are you telling me this is the dead guy from the crash?'

'Witnesses state that Vincent Perry intentionally drove his van into the car Miss Heaton was supposedly sitting in – your car. A strange coincidence, don't you think, Mr Levinson?'

'This is madness,' said Ryan, getting to his feet and pacing the room.

Penny said, 'Does my son need a solicitor? If so, this stops now!'

'I knew him as Vinny,' said Ryan. 'I didn't know his last name. I have many friends whose last names I don't know. We weren't close.'

'You expect me to believe that?' said Harry.

Enraged, Ryan stepped up to him, their faces inches apart. 'I don't care what you believe.'

Mrs Levinson pulled her son away from the detective. 'Right, it's time you both left,' she said.

Harry had clearly provoked Ryan, but none of this proved his guilt. 'What about Vincent's brother, Frederick? Have you heard of him?'

Temper subsiding, Ryan said, 'I knew Vinny had a brother. I met him once, maybe twice. But I wasn't good friends with either of them. I'd occasionally bump into Vinny around town.'

'My son can't help who he knows. It doesn't make him guilty of anything.'

'Mrs Levinson, I'm just trying to establish whether your son is telling me the truth so I can locate Rebecca.'

'Look, I don't know anything,' said Ryan. 'But if you're telling me the Perry brothers had something to do with her disappearance, shouldn't you be questioning Vinny's brother?'

'Frederick Perry is dead, Mr Levinson. Someone strangled him in his living room two nights ago. And this morning, Craig Bishop was found dead in his van.' He turned to the detective. The colour visibly drained from his face in what appeared to be an authentic look of shock.

'Dead?' Ryan questioned.

'Yes. I take it you knew Craig Bishop?'

'Err, no. I didn't know *him*. I was referring to Frederick.'

'You can't help yourself, can you, Mr Levinson? Stop lying. We have a witness who places you at a West Ham football match with Craig Bishop.' Harry was bluffing. He doubted he'd ever see Greg from the hostel again, let alone get him to testify in court.

'What the hell is going on, Detective? Are you accusing my son of murder? Because if that's the case, you need to either arrest him or leave right this second.'

'At this time, I'm only accusing your son of lying.'

'Look, I meet a lot of people,' said Ryan. 'Friends of friends. I can't remember every name or face. But if what you say is true, I have no idea what's going on or *why* these men are involved with Rebecca. Please, just find her.'

Harry wasn't buying Ryan's air of innocence and was convinced he had something to do with the collision. As for his involvement in the deaths of Fred Perry and Craig Bishop, he wasn't so sure. 'Ryan, if you know anything that can help us, now is the time to speak.'

With an angry glance in the detective's direction and without saying another word, Ryan stomped out of the room.

Mrs Levinson marched the officers from the house. 'Next time you want to question my son, I suggest you give us advance warning so we can have a solicitor present.' She slammed the door behind them.

Once they were settled in the car, Lucy said, 'Well, that was quite an experience. You certainly rattled his cage.'

Harry said, 'Do you think his surprise about the murders of Perry and Bishop was sincere?'

'Yes. I'd also say he looked concerned.'

'I agree. I was hoping he would cave and tell us what he knew at the end there, but I'd already surmised he would shut down and walk away.'

'So, what now?' she said.

'Now we wait on the main road and see if he goes anywhere.'

29

December 22
Toronto

At 6.00 a.m., Lenny was buckled into a seat on Marvin Collingwood's plane as it zoomed along the runway, headed for Toronto. He'd called him the night before and asked if he could hitch a flight. Marvin agreed, but as the Canadian ambassador had hired the plane for his wife and teenage daughter, he had to first seek their permission. Once the couple knew the circumstances, they were more than happy to oblige and politely declined Lenny's offer to pay for his seat. Considering he'd researched how much it would cost, he was quite relieved.

The flight took a little over eight hours, and they landed around 9.00 a.m. local time. Lenny thanked Marvin and his co-pilot, and Marvin warned him the plane would be returning to London at 1.00 a.m. the following morning. He had around fourteen hours to do what was necessary before making the flight back. Stepping off the plane with his small holdall, the cold bit at the skin of his face. Marvin had warned him to wrap up, as the temperature was around minus three.

Lenny hailed a taxi outside the airport and instructed the driver to take him to the Toronto Police Service – 11 Division, on Davenport Road. In the back seat, he listened to the message from Harry and immediately knew he'd made the right decision to come here.

At the front desk, he asked for Detective Christopher Tremblay. Several minutes later, he arrived, curiously bemused.

'I'm Detective Tremblay. Is there something I can help you with, sir?' He had a kind, easy-going manner about him.

Lenny reached out and shook the detective's hand. 'Lenny Grey. I'm here on behalf of Detective Inspector Harry Baxendale.'

'Oh, I see. This is quite unexpected. I had no idea they were sending someone over. So, you're a cop?'

'Er, no. I'm more of a consultant,' said Lenny.

The detective's puzzled expression returned, and he scratched the side of his head. 'Do you have some form of identification?'

Lenny unzipped his jacket and reached inside. 'Yes, I have my passport right here.' He handed it to the detective, who scrutinised it for a few seconds.

'May I ask why you're here, Mr Grey?'

'I'd like to see where Annalise Fournier and Reagan Scott were attacked on the eighteenth of this month. I'm also aware of a third girl who may have been attacked on the same night.'

'I don't mean to sound disrespectful, but until I check this out with Detective Baxendale, I'm afraid I can't discuss the details of these cases with you.'

'Fine by me,' said Lenny. 'I'm assuming you've read the email he sent you about the suxamethonium chloride used on the girls?' By mentioning the email and the drug, he revealed information to the detective that only someone close to the investigation would know.

'Take a seat, and I'll be back in a few minutes,' said Tremblay, disappearing through a side door. He returned wearing his parka. 'Come on. I'll buy you a coffee.'

In a small, quaint coffee shop close to the station, the detective remained reluctant to talk about the case, instead making polite conversation about Lenny's flight and the cold weather.

Tremblay said, 'You know, your name rings a bell.' He sipped his coffee.

'I've written a couple of books, and I appeared on the news last year, but I'm sure you wouldn't have heard about that over here.'

Tremblay snapped his fingers in excitement. 'You helped catch those killers with Detective Baxendale, Webster, and what's his name? Darmody! That made headlines here.'

'Really?' said Lenny, a big smile on his face.

'Yeah. It was a big deal. Arthur Darmody made the news a few years ago. A massacre or something.'

'Harper,' he corrected, 'but yes, you're right.'

'Of course. I should've remembered. Wow! You must be quite something back in the UK.'

'No. I'm relatively unknown.'

'I'm sure you're being modest.' Tremblay's phone pinged. 'Excuse me,' he said, and read a message. 'Well, Harry has vouched for you, so how about I take you to those crime scenes?'

Lenny downed his coffee and grabbed his bag.

They parked on St Clair West, close to Kenwood Avenue. Lenny was thankful it wasn't snowing, but there was plenty of snow around, though it had mostly turned to black slush on the roads and pavements.

Tremblay said, 'Watch your footing. It's quite slippery.'

Lenny slipped and grabbed the detective's arm. 'Yeah, I see what you mean.'

Tremblay pointed. 'Miss Fournier worked just up the road there, where you can see the pizza sign. But this is where she was attacked, and the attempted abduction took place. She fought him off and ran down this way.'

They walked along the road a little. 'She crossed somewhere about here and hid in the churchyard across the street.'

They crossed over, and Lenny noted the name of the church: St. Michael & All Angels. The same name as the church where Annalise was found in the UK. What were the chances? Eager to discover the history of the church, he headed inside, the detective trailing close behind. The archdeacon was away until the next day, but his wife, Lay Pastor Ellie Roy, *was* available. She informed him the church was founded in 1907 with a tent and flourished from there, with no noteworthy reason that could explain Annalise Fournier's situation. No sordid history of burning witches or anything of the sort. They thanked her and left the building.

A slim man exited the door behind them and approached. 'Excuse me. I'm Tim Cote, the property warden. I overheard your conversation inside, and I'm curious. What kind of information are you looking for?'

Lenny replied, 'I was hoping the church dated back further and that there might be a dark history of some sort in the area.'

'You'd be hard-pressed to find a human-occupied area of this planet untouched by dark history. Do you have a specific date in mind?'

'1773 to 1785.' The bewildered expression on Detective Tremblay's face brought a smile to Lenny's.

Mr Cote said, 'I've researched much of the past here, and those dates are quite early for recorded history in these parts, but there might be something of interest.'

'I'm all ears,' said Lenny.

'After the Treaty of Paris was signed in 1783, colonists who had remained loyal to the Crown flocked to the Province of Quebec, a colony of British North America, looking to settle. Many of them were compensated with land grants, and some chose to make what we now call Ontario their new home. I recall a diary entry from around that time by . . . oh, I forget now, but I know it was an unpleasant story about the death of a young woman in 1783.'

Lenny knew this could mean nothing, but a tingling inside stirred his interest. 'Do go on.'

'I'd need to look through my books, but if you've got time for a coffee, we can go back to my office and check.'

'I'd prefer a strong cup of tea,' said Lenny.

They followed him into the church, and after he'd made them a cup of tea, he searched the well-stocked bookcase that ran the length of one wall. It didn't take him long to find what he was looking for.

'Right, here we are. Some of the settlers were loyalists, while others had fought for the British Army. One such person was Samuel Davis, a former New York businessman and soldier. His account is coming back to me now. A small group, mostly men, camped somewhere around here. Davis claimed that during their travels north, they had picked up a few stragglers, including a young woman travelling alone. He noted how some of the men had taken an unsavoury interest in her.

'They snatched her while the rest of the camp slept, carried her off into the woods, and, well, I'm sure you can imagine. Davis followed and remained out of sight. When they'd finished with her, he watched them beat the poor woman with rifle butts before stabbing her with their bayonet knives. He'd wanted to put a stop to it but feared for his life.

'Later that night, he gathered his belongings, put the young woman's body into his wagon, and found a peaceful spot to bury her. Needless to say, he didn't return to the group. The incident had always haunted him. Towards the end of his life, his guilt led him to write about it in his diary in an attempt to ease his burden in the eyes of God. He died a few days later.'

Beyond intrigued, Lenny asked, 'The woman, I don't suppose he named her in his diary?'

'As a matter of fact, he did. He even wrote it on a little wooden cross he'd placed on her grave – Emma Martin.'

Though it was the surname he'd expected to hear, Lenny's jaw almost hit the cold, hard ground beneath his feet. He'd found the connection to the past he was searching for but didn't know what it all meant. It wasn't the ending he'd hoped for Emma Martin.

He said, 'Out of curiosity, did he mention the day and month her death occurred?'

'December eighteenth.'

'Thank you for all your help, Mr Cote.'

They strolled back towards the car. Tremblay said, 'Are you gonna tell me what this is all about?'

'I'm not sure I understand myself yet, but I'll fill you in later,' said Lenny. 'Where was Reagan Scott attacked?'

'A couple of miles or so back in that direction, past the church. I'll show you on the way to where her body was discovered. But in case you wanted to know, the unknown girl in the hospital was seen wandering along the middle of this road moments before collapsing. She's lucky she wasn't hit by a streetcar. I think you Brits like to call them trams.'

30

December 22

Waiting for Ryan to make a move took its toll on Lucy, so she passed the time messing around on her phone. Still taken aback after responding to Detective Tremblay's text, Harry contemplated Lenny going all the way to Toronto. Lenny had a habit of going above and beyond to get to the bottom of things, but this was another level. Harry couldn't fathom why he'd gone to Canada before he'd received the message about the lab results. Did Lenny know something *he* didn't? Knowing him, probably.

Ryan pulled out of the driveway in his mother's Range Rover, and they tailed him to a busy supermarket car park, where he appeared to be impatiently waiting to meet someone. Eventually, he exited the vehicle and paced around, his phone pressed tightly against his ear. Judging by the number of attempts, whoever he wanted to speak to wasn't answering. Half an hour later, an agitated Ryan climbed back into the Range Rover, and they followed him all the way back to his house. It would have been nice to know who he'd arranged to meet, but one thing was clear: something had made him nervous.

Lucy said, 'You don't suppose the person he was meeting spotted us in the car park?'

'No. At least, I hope not.'

'You're probably right. If they did, surely they would have answered and told him.'

'Not if the person meeting him had already killed two people.'

Owen called Harry and urged him to return to the station. As soon as they arrived, Lucy walked off to get herself a cup of tea, while Owen followed Harry to his desk to insert a memory stick into his computer.

Owen seemed oddly distressed. Harry asked, 'Is everything okay?'

'Uh, yes. Not too bad. Though I might be coming down with something, so don't get too close,' he said. 'Now, with the images enlarged, I went over the CCTV from the cameras on the motorway again. Only this time, a couple of things caught my eye.' Owen settled into the chair, and Harry watched over his shoulder. 'This is from when the Mazda pulled onto the hard shoulder. The camera is quite far away. It's dark, and the rain doesn't help. Just to be clear, we can't see whether Rebecca Heaton is inside the vehicle. For a while, nothing happens. But then – look.'

'What? I can't see anything,' said Harry.

Owen rewound the video and touched his index finger to the screen. 'It's not easy to see, but watch the top of the car on the passenger side.'

Harry moved forward and looked closer. 'What the?' he said, seeing the passenger door briefly open and close. 'Show me again.'

They watched it a few times, and again when Lucy returned.

She said, 'Rebecca could have been throwing litter out of the door. I don't see how this helps us.'

Harry said, 'That could be Rebecca leaving the car.'

'Then where is she?' said Lucy.

Owen said, 'This is a little while before the crash. Don't forget, her blood is all over the driver's side. It would also mean the witnesses were mistaken. Not to mention, the dogs would have picked up her scent if she'd left the vehicle.'

Harry thumped the desk and shouted, 'Look, she wasn't in the wrecked vehicle, so she must have bloody well left it!' Owen and Lucy's startled reactions made him aware of his outburst. 'I'm sorry,' he said. He paused for a breath and continued, 'Other than Philip and Vanessa Ainsworth, who did not see whether anyone was in the car, the credibility of the witnesses is dubious. You're right about the dogs, though.' Harry stared at the screen. 'This could be someone else in the car with her. They could have driven the car there, swapped sides, and sneaked out of the passenger side.'

Lucy said, 'We shouldn't rule that out as an option, but without seeing the person, there's no revelation here. We're no further ahead in the investigation, and Rebecca Heaton is still missing.'

Harry hated to admit it, but she was right. This gave them nothing regarding evidence. Although that could be Ryan Levinson climbing out of the vehicle and skulking away before the van hit, it wasn't worth pursuing. 'Let's move on. Owen, you said you had something else to show us.'

'Yes. This second clip is from the impact. In all my years, I have never seen anything like it.'

They watched the van speed towards the car in real time, and there didn't appear to be anything out of the ordinary.

Owen said, 'Focus on the inside of the car, not the collision. I'll slow it down.' They viewed the incident again and observed a bright flash.

Harry said, 'What the hell was that?'

'I'm completely flummoxed,' said Owen. 'The inside of the car seems to light up.'

Lucy said, 'Could it be the interior lighting – a short circuit caused by the impact?'

'Something I considered but ruled out when I slowed it down further. Watch again.'

The flash occurred milliseconds before contact. Harry said, 'Perhaps it's a fault with the traffic camera.'

'What about a camera flash?' said Lucy, echoing Harry's attempt to explain what they'd seen. 'Rebecca could have been taking a selfie. People do it all the time these days.'

Owen said, 'The traffic cameras are in good working order. I've examined the incident from all available angles and can't imagine anything that could have caused such a luminous effect. The flash of a camera is a possibility, but not recovering Miss Heaton or her phone at the scene doesn't help.'

Harry sighed and backed away from the desk. 'I was hoping you were going to show us something that could assist us, but it's just more confusion thrown into the mix.'

'I'm sorry it's not more helpful,' said Owen.

'Don't worry about it. This case has got us all going out of our minds looking for answers.'

'Look,' said Lucy. 'Let's drive out to the crash site and search the bushes along the hard shoulder. It's a long shot, but maybe we'll find evidence to prove someone other than Rebecca got out of the car.'

Owen said, 'Officers scoured the area thoroughly. I know their main focus was to find a body, but anything of significance would have been discovered.'

'True,' said Harry. 'And with all the wind and rain since then, any further evidence would probably have been destroyed.' His phone rang – No Caller ID.

Greeted by silence, he was about to hang up when a seemingly nervous woman said, 'I have information. Meet me within the hour at the coffee shop by the escalator on the upper level of The Mall in Maidstone.'

She ended the call before Harry could respond. Hard to be certain, but it sounded like Melanie Hillingdon. Perhaps it was *her* that Ryan had arranged to meet? He could have told her about Fred and Craig, and now she was afraid.

On their way to the car park, Lucy saw it was raining and turned back to fetch her coat.

Owen asked, 'Do you have a main suspect?'

Harry said, 'I'm quietly confident. If the woman we're meeting is who I think she is, I'm hopeful we'll have him in custody by the end of the day.'

'Well, whatever happens, I'll be happy to see the back of this one.'

Owen left as Lucy returned, walking alongside Detective Constable Jerome Henderson. Harry had worked with the DC a couple of times, though he didn't know him on a personal level. A little raw to the job but efficient, he looked to be around Lucy's age and, by all accounts, was a bit of a ladies' man.

31

December 22

Harry picked a table where he could observe the escalator while Lucy kept a lookout for anything of interest from one of the shop doorways opposite. On their way to the mall, Lucy seemed distant. He'd asked if anything was wrong, but she'd downplayed it and thanked him for being kind to her during the investigation. With time to spare when they arrived, Harry managed to buy a couple of special gifts for Leah. He opened the box to examine the silver necklace and earrings, certain she'd be thrilled with them. The seconds ticked into minutes, and the hour was almost up. This close to Christmas, the mall was naturally crowded. Was she already here, watching and making sure it was safe to approach? Across the way, Lucy shrugged, expressing doubt that anyone would show up.

She glanced to her right and froze, aware of someone approaching the coffee shop. Lucy nodded towards the corner near the escalator and turned around, pretending to browse in the shop window. Unsighted, Harry kept his eyes on the corner. A woman wearing a yellow hoodie appeared, her head bowed low to hide her face. Moving apprehensively closer, she looked up and paused. Had she recognised someone? Visibly anxious, she glanced in his direction. Melanie.

Seeing Melanie's distress, Lucy approached quickly. Melanie surged forward onto the escalator and leapt up the steps, pushing past weary shoppers. Harry jumped to his feet, his chair scraping along the floor behind him. He advanced quickly to catch up with Lucy, who had stepped onto the escalator in pursuit. She nudged her way through the chaos and came to an abrupt stop ahead of Harry. Lucy turned to face him, her eyes wide and mouth agape, holding the side of her stomach. He caught sight of the blood seeping between her fingers. She slumped onto her backside. A child screamed, and space opened up around her as people scurried away in fear. Harry raced up the moving steps, already calling for an ambulance. He crouched down beside her, moved her hand, and lifted her shirt to see how bad it was. So much blood.

'I-I don't know what happened,' she said, her voice faint and drained of energy.

'It's okay. An ambulance is on the way. You're going to be fine,' he said.

The escalator came to a standstill as they neared the top. Someone must have pressed the emergency button. Harry held her, keeping his hand pressed tight against the wound. People looked on as he tried to make sense of what had just happened. He frantically scanned the crowd for Lucy's attacker but found only concerned and anxious faces.

Harry sat in the waiting room, which looked remarkably similar to the one where he'd met Lucy for the first time four days ago. With so much happening since, it seemed longer. Elbows on his knees and using his hands as a mask, Harry hid from the world, devastated. He'd grown fond of Lucy. She could have been killed, and he blamed himself, though he could never have foreseen today's outcome. Fortunately, she wasn't in surgery for too long. The blade hadn't gone too deep, and there was no major damage.

He replayed the event in his mind over and over, attempting to tap into his subconscious to see what he'd missed – a weapon, a face, anything. He recalled the fear in Melanie's eyes. Whoever she'd seen approaching on the other escalator had caused her to run. Melanie was almost halfway up when Lucy was stabbed. There must be something. And there it was: a figure wearing a long navy-blue parka, hood raised, with the thick fur lining concealing their face. The person turned sharply from one escalator onto the next, ahead of Lucy. As she barged through and neared the suspect, Harry recalled a drop of the shoulder as the culprit plunged the knife into her stomach. As Lucy turned in shock and fell, her attacker cast a sideways glance and took long strides up the moving staircase. He hoped Melanie had escaped and was hiding somewhere safe. She knew the killer of Fred, Craig, and possibly the fate of Rebecca Heaton. Harry's thoughts were interrupted by a text from Arthur, asking him to swing by the lab as soon as he was able.

'You can go in and see her now,' said the doctor. Harry glanced up and put his phone away. 'Don't be too long, though. She needs rest, and plenty of it.'

Harry entered the ward and reluctantly approached her bed, heavy with the burden of guilt. He knew the killer was relentless, so he should have been better prepared, for Lucy's sake as well as Melanie's. Now, one of them was in hospital, and the other was scared and probably in hiding.

Lucy's head rolled to one side. She raised a smile and said, 'Hey.'

'Hey there. How are you doing?'

'The doctor said I was lucky, and in a few weeks, I should be as good as new.'

'That's great news.'

'It is, but even with the drugs, it's bloody painful. The blade hit my rib, apparently. Anyway, what happened to Melanie?'

'I don't know. We're doing our best to find her. Lucy, I just want to say how—'

'Shh. Don't apologise. It's not your fault. I guessed she'd been spooked by someone and should have had my wits about me. I just wish I'd seen who it was.' The sound of voices made Harry turn. A couple who looked to be in their late fifties approached the bed. 'My parents.'

Harry said, 'Okay. I'll try to come back later.'

'Don't you dare. I'm going to need a long sleep after they leave.'

Harry reached out and gently touched her hand before slowly retreating, leaving her to face the onslaught of worrisome questions from her mum and dad.

Passing the smokers outside the hospital doors, he called the station for an update on Melanie. She was still missing. He asked if they'd acquired the CCTV footage from the mall. Detective Constable Jerome Henderson was viewing it right now.

Harry said, 'Put me through to him.'

'Hi, guv,' said Henderson.

'Please tell me they caught the incident on camera?'

'I'm afraid the only camera that captured what happened was above a doorway next to the coffee shop. All we can see is a side-on view from a fair distance away. A second camera close to the escalators doesn't seem to have been working.'

'How convenient!'

'I know it looks that way, but it happens frequently, guv. How's Lucy doing?'

'She's doing fine,' said Harry. 'Listen, are you in front of the computer now?'

'I am.'

'Check the escalator for someone wearing a navy-blue parka.'

Henderson responded promptly. 'Found them. The person's face is obscured by a hood – not that we'd get a clear view from this angle.'

'Right, I need you to search every available camera before and after the incident. Find the moment this person enters and leaves the mall. Better still, search for Melanie. She shouldn't be difficult to spot in her bright yellow hoodie. If you find footage of her leaving the mall, I'm sure the suspect won't be far behind.'

Exasperated with both cases, Harry fastened his seat belt. This all started with a routine car crash. Now he had a police officer in the hospital, a missing driver, three dead bodies, a young girl in hiding, and a potential serial killer on the loose. Against his better judgement, he drove to the Levinson house to confront Ryan and find out if he'd left the house since returning home earlier.

He parked next to the Range Rover and placed his palm on the bonnet. Cold. Harry trampled across the gravel. Two thumps on the door, followed by a hefty third.

Mrs Levinson hauled the door open and said, 'Not again. What do you want now?'

'I need to speak to Ryan.'

Her eyes lowered to the blood on his shirt and trousers. 'Oh my, you're bleeding.'

With all that had transpired, Harry's bloodstained clothes were the last thing on his mind. It dawned on him that he should never have come here, at least not until he'd changed. His temper abated. 'It's not my blood. My colleague was stabbed at the mall.'

At first, Penny Levinson looked sorry. It didn't take long for realisation to set in. 'And you think my Ryan is responsible?'

'Yes. No. I don't know.' The trauma of Lucy getting hurt had scattered his senses to the wind. His anguish was clear for her to see.

'Come inside. I'll make you a cup of tea.' She covered the chair at the kitchen table with a tea towel and didn't need to tell him where to sit. 'I'll put the kettle on.'

The events of the day had got the better of Harry. With the job and the goings-on in his personal life, everything was bloody awful. Yet, here he was, charging into this woman's house, accusing her son of murder. And here she was, being kind and making him a cup of tea.

Penny stood by the table. 'Your colleague, is she . . .?'

'No. She's going to be okay.'

'Thank heavens. I assume it was the woman who came here with you last time?'

'Yes.'

'How do you like your tea?' she said, fetching two mugs from the cupboard.

'Milk, please. No sugar.'

She brought the cups to the table and pulled out a chair opposite.

'Thank you, Mrs Levinson.'

'Penny will do.'

Harry smiled softly and sipped his much-needed cup of tea.

Penny said, 'He didn't do it, you know. Other than nipping out earlier for about half an hour, he's been upstairs all day. The truth is, I'm worried about him. He seems different since Rebecca disappeared – more so in the last couple of days. After you left this morning, I'd go as far as to say he's nervous. I've asked him if anything is wrong, but you know how it goes. All you get is "everything is fine" and "leave me alone."' The impression of her son was pretty accurate.

'I have a teenage daughter, so I know exactly what you mean.'

'Then I'm sure you understand why I'm so protective. I'll tell you this much, though – if I find out he has anything to do with Rebecca going missing, I'll drag him down to the nick myself.' She sipped her tea.

Harry smiled. Penny wasn't covering for her son at all. 'I don't suppose Ryan owns a navy-blue parka, does he?' Judging by the clothes he'd seen him wearing so far, he already knew the answer.

'Not since he was about six years old,' Penny said with an amused smile.

32

December 22

Penny was glad the detective inspector chose not to talk to her son. He thanked her for the tea, and she showed him to the door. For whatever reason, she found it difficult to dislike him, but no matter how shaken up he was, he had no right to come knocking on her door, thinking her son was capable of attempted murder. She emptied the remnants of the tea into the sink and placed the cups in the dishwasher. She turned and jumped at the sight of Ryan standing nearby.

'I wish you'd stop sneaking around. You'll give me grey hairs,' she said.

'What did he want?'

'He had a couple of questions.'

'About me?'

'Yes, about you. But I told him you've barely left the house.' Penny unloaded the washing machine, separating the T-shirts and jumpers from the rest and tossing them into a basket.

'Why did he want to know where I'd been?'

'Because somebody stabbed his colleague in a shopping centre, and she's in hospital.'

'And he thought it was me? Wanker! If I'd done it, the bitch would be dead.'

Penny stopped what she was doing and glared at Ryan. 'What did you say?'

'I said if I'd done it, the bitch—'

Penny lunged at her son and pinned him against the wall. 'Think it's clever, do you, all the big talk? I don't care how you speak with your moronic little mates, but while you're under this roof, you'll show everyone respect. Do you understand me?' The alarm in his eyes was telling as his body trembled in her grasp. She had shown him a side of her he'd never seen before.

'Yes. I understand.'

She released her grip on his shirt and backed away. 'Things have to change. You need to either get yourself a job or go and work for your father. You can't keep loafing around, playing video games, drinking, and smoking weed with your friends. Yes, don't think I don't know what you get up to. You need to learn some bloody responsibility.'

He huffed and walked away.

She said, 'Where are you going?'

'Out.'

'Don't you dare take my car!'

'Fine!' With a rattle and thump, her keys hit the console in the hall, and the front door slammed soon after.

Penny sat at the table, surprised at her reaction. It had been years since she'd told him off for anything. What the hell, he had it coming. She deliberated on why the detective kept coming back. Did he know something about her son that she didn't, or was it simply because of his dad's criminal past? She went back to sorting the washing. The uneaten sandwich in his bin sprang to mind, and doubts stirred within her.

Outside her son's bedroom, Penny questioned her loyalty as a mother and backed away. She pressed forward, opened the door, and hesitated. Despite another attempt to convince herself she was being foolish, she failed to realise she'd strayed inside. In a room with not much personality, there was nothing obvious.

She caressed the handle of one of the drawers and said, 'Sod it. Get this over with, and you can forget about all this nonsense.'

Penny rummaged through every drawer, looked under the bed, searched the wardrobe from top to bottom and, other than half a bottle of Jack Daniel's and a small amount of weed, found nothing. She had no idea what she was searching for in the first place. Enraged that she'd been taken in by the detective's unhealthy obsession with her son, she turned to leave. About to pull the door closed, she regarded the ottoman at the end of the bed – the only place she hadn't checked.

Even after berating herself, she was drawn towards the chest. Her hand faltered over the lid before lifting it to reveal layers of boxed video games and a couple of spare controllers. Penny was about to close it when something caught her eye – a bright white shoelace with a red stain. She reached down to pick it up but found herself pulling something heavier through the pile of games. It was one of his new white training shoes, spattered with large, dark red spots. Dried blood. She dropped the shoe, stepped back, and covered her mouth with her hand.

Her mind raced back to December 18. She had just finished her coffee before her evening run when Ryan entered the kitchen to make a sandwich for himself and Rebecca. She went to fetch her running shoes in the hallway and had to move Ryan's *spotless* trainers because they were sitting on top of hers. She couldn't recall if they had been there when she returned. The same could be said for Ryan. The next time she saw him was when she collected the plates and glasses around ten. He could have easily sneaked out of the house and come back between the time of her run and later that evening.

'Oh, Ryan, what have you done?' She reached into the chest and pulled out the other training shoe. It looked as new as the day he'd opened the box. Penny tossed it on the floor next to the other one and made sure there were no more shocking surprises in the chest. She looked through his drawers and wardrobe again. It was difficult to tell if any of his clothes were missing. She sat on the edge of the bed and tried to remember what he was wearing. Oh, what did it matter? He had probably disposed of them by now. But, being a typical young man, he couldn't bear to part with his expensive new trainers. He'd even made a half-hearted attempt to clean off the blood.

What to do? Was it worth confronting him? He'd only come up with some plausible excuse. He always did when he was in trouble. Even when she knew he was lying, she'd let it slide. Perhaps this was her fault for being too soft. His father wasn't as strict as he used to be. In recent years, he seemed to have lost interest, especially since Ryan point-blank refused to have anything to do with the family business. Those two had been drifting apart for a while.

Penny stared at the trainers. She'd told the detective *she* would personally drag him to the station if he had anything to do with what had happened to Rebecca. What if it wasn't her blood? There could be another explanation, and the last thing she wanted was to get him into trouble for an entirely different matter. Why should that change her mind? She was kidding herself, looking for excuses. There was no way she could turn in her own son. Penny tidied the room as though she hadn't been there, picked up the trainers, and headed down to the kitchen. She turned on the cold tap to fill the sink. She'd learned many years ago that soaking her husband's bloodied clothes (as well as her own) in cool water for an hour broke up the stain, making it easier to remove when she put them in the washing machine. Sometimes it took a few attempts; failing that, an enzyme cleaner usually did the trick.

With the sink full, she dangled the bloody trainer over the water, delaying the drop. Was she doing the right thing? Wasn't it a mother's job to protect her child? If it was the right thing to do, her conscience disagreed. She reached into the sink, pulled the plug, and watched the water drain away. She'd wait. If Rebecca turned up safe and accused her son of something terrible, she'd let it play out in court, and they'd accept Ryan's punishment as a family. If they discovered her body, she'd have a big decision to make. Penny took the trainers into the utility room, removed the plinth under one of the units, and tucked them away.

33

December 22
Toronto

Other than a few ramblers and children playing in the snow, Lambton Park was fairly quiet. A large section where Reagan Scott had been murdered remained off-limits to the public while officers combed the area with dogs, searching for evidence. Approaching a small clearing in the woods, Lenny hoped his instincts would pick up on something supernatural, but all he sensed was the cold nipping at his ears. He dropped to his knees and placed his hand on the spot where her body had been discovered. Nothing. He'd witnessed his fair share of strange occurrences, so to him, his actions were rational; but glancing up at the detective and seeing his bewildered expression, he knew Tremblay must be wondering if he was a complete nutcase.

Recalling what Tim Cote had said, he brushed the fresh snow aside until he set eyes on the dirt beneath. He removed his gloves, clawed ineffectually at the surface, and knocked his knuckles against the frozen ground.

'What *are* you doing?' asked Tremblay.

'I don't suppose you have a shovel in your car?'

'Yeah, I carry one around with me everywhere I go.'

Lenny detected sarcasm. 'You don't have one, do you?'

'Nope. Why don't you tell me what you hope to find?'

'Emma Martin.'

'You're not serious?'

Lenny smiled.

'Oh, you've got to be kidding me!' Tremblay reluctantly asked a couple of constables to collect shovels and a pickaxe and told them where to dig. While indulging Lenny's folly, the detective suggested getting something to eat, which pleased Lenny because not only was he hungry – he was freezing his arse off.

Burger, fries, and a cup of tea. Lenny kept it simple. Tremblay ordered the same, perhaps to make him feel at ease. An unnecessary act of kindness, as feeling out of place was a rarity for Lenny. Once held up in traffic by a funeral procession, he followed the horde of cars all the way back to the house and helped himself to the buffet and whisky. He'd even had the cheek to get comfortable on the sofa and pay his condolences to the widow while stuffing his face with mini sausage rolls and vol-au-vents.

The burger and fries arrived, and Lenny's overzealous use of tomato sauce mortified the detective.

Lenny bit into his burger and said, 'Oh, beautiful. I can't even remember when I last ate.'

'You shouldn't talk with your mouth full, but judging by the way you're going at it, I'd guess it's been a while,' said Tremblay, picking at his food. 'So tell me, what makes you think Emma Martin from, what was it, seventeen something or other, is buried in that exact spot?'

Lenny shoved fries into his mouth and washed them down with tea. 'Instinct. I know it all seems like a load of nonsense, but if it turns out I'm right, I'll explain everything to you. Though, even after I tell you, it still won't be believable. Not to your good self or to me.'

With a modest shake of his head, the bemused detective continued to eat. They'd nearly finished their meal when Tremblay received a phone call telling him to return to Lambton Park. He paid the bill, and they left the diner.

As Lenny and Tremblay approached the constables, one of the men stepped forward to meet them. He appeared to have something in his hand.

Tremblay asked, 'What have you got for me, Constable Evans?'

'We assumed we were wasting our time, and just when we were about to give up, Leonard found this.' Evans held up a rotting piece of wood to reveal the letters: *RIP*. 'There's another small piece with a single letter. It could be a *W*, or maybe an *M*.'

Tremblay stared at Lenny as they continued onwards.

Evans said, 'We dug a little more and discovered – well, see for yourself.'

They glared into a shallow grave containing human bones. Open-mouthed, Tremblay glanced at Lenny, uncertain what to make of it all, and turned to his officers.

'Okay, cordon off the area around the grave and get forensics down here immediately. I wanna know who this body belongs to. You' – he pointed at Lenny – 'with me.' The detective was clearly flummoxed.

Lenny followed and said, 'Forensics won't be able to tell you who she is unless Mary Martin's body in the UK is exhumed, but I'd imagine they'll be able to tell you roughly how old the bones are.'

'Do not say another word,' said Tremblay. 'I don't want the constables to hear.' As soon as they were in the car, he said, 'Right, enough with this crap, Mr Grey. Tell me what the hell is going on?'

'The skeleton in the grave belongs to Emma Martin, and deep down, I think you know I'm right.'

'Don't presume to know what's going on in my mind when I'm not even sure. Just tell me how you knew someone from over two hundred years ago was killed and buried in the same spot as a young girl several days ago.'

'Oh, Emma Martin wasn't killed here,' said Lenny. 'This is just where Samuel Davis buried her.'

'Samuel Davis, the guy Mr Cote was talking about?'

'Yeah.'

'And I bet you have a theory as to where she was killed. Would you like to share?'

'The churchyard. Presumably the spot where Annalise Fournier disappeared. Do you want to know where Annalise was found in England?'

'Sure. Why stop now?'

'A reverend discovered her on the grave of a seventeen-year-old girl at a church of the same name as the one we were at earlier. I bet you can guess the name on the headstone?'

'I don't know about the first name, but I'm guessing it ended with Martin.'

'You're getting the hang of this now, Detective Tremblay. I'll fill you in on the rest later, but right now, I'd like you to take me to see the girl at the hospital.'

The mystified expression on Tremblay's face said it all. He turned the key in the ignition, and off they went.

Few words were exchanged on the way to the hospital. Lenny knew the detective was struggling to comprehend what was going on, and in truth, *he* didn't know either. Of course, it helped to have attained relevant historical knowledge along the way, but other than his natural instincts, he was more or less letting events unfold, be they supernatural or not. He simply followed the breadcrumbs.

While waiting for the lift, Tremblay asked if he knew about the girl's amnesia. Lenny said Harry had explained everything. The doors opened, and they stepped inside to join a pregnant woman in her dressing gown, presumably with her partner standing beside her. To the rear was a nurse, and in the corner, a bespectacled doctor, his head hung low, stared at a clipboard. The young couple exchanged angry whispers. It sounded like he'd been out to wet the baby's head before it had been born, and she wasn't at all happy. Lenny couldn't help but smile.

They all stepped off on the same floor. The nurse trailed behind the bickering couple, and Lenny followed the detective in the opposite direction. The doctor from the lift overtook them as Tremblay stopped to use the restroom. Lenny waited in the corridor, taking in how busy it was: organised chaos. Glancing along the corridor, he contemplated the doctor, who was staring through windows and opening and closing doors to different rooms, obviously looking for someone. Surely a doctor would know which room their patient was in? Finding it a little odd, Lenny wandered towards him. The doctor glanced sideways at him and entered a room, closing the door behind him.

Lenny assumed it was nothing, turned away, and stopped short, confronted by the pale, begrimed face of a young girl. He couldn't move a muscle. The air was sucked from his lungs. Her long, dark hair was dishevelled and caked in mud. The naked flesh of her body had been butchered and torn from the bone. The grievous older scarring on the right side of her face and body was evident. She slowly raised her arm, pointed in the opposite direction, and walked through him. He gasped for air and turned. The ghostly figure glared at the room the doctor had entered. Lenny raced along the corridor and barged through the door.

Beside the bed, the supposed doctor pressed a pillow tightly against a patient's face as their legs kicked frantically against the bed sheets. The man scowled at him, and for the first time, Lenny saw his face clearly. The thick-framed spectacles concealed the slight disfigurement of his eye, and his long black hair was tied in a ponytail. He also lacked dark stubble, but it was him – the man Annalise had described.

The man released the pillow and charged towards him. Lenny threw a punch but missed, and before he knew it, they were grappling at close quarters. They wrestled each other to the ground, both attempting to gain the upper hand. A knee plunged into Lenny's groin. The sharp pain weakened his grip, and the hard thump of a fist against his cheek sent bells ringing in his ears. The man climbed off him, jumped to his feet, and ran for the door. Detective Tremblay stepped into view, only to be knocked violently to the floor, his head smacking against the wall. By the time Lenny got up and gingerly walked into the corridor, the killer was gone.

Tremblay looked up from his position on the floor, holding the back of his head. 'What was that all about?'

Between heavy breaths, Lenny said, 'Reagan Scott's killer. You need to stop him from leaving the building.' Lenny hurried back into the room to check on the patient, who was now sitting upright in bed. Distressed and terrified, Rebecca Heaton stared back at him.

34

December 22

After a quick change of clothes at Gerty's guest house, Harry stood with anticipation at DC Henderson's desk. He was shown a clip of Melanie Hillingdon rushing from the mall less than three minutes after Lucy's attack. As Harry had predicted, the hooded suspect was close behind. Thankfully, Melanie had more than enough time to get away. Jerome had examined every entrance to the mall from the recorded CCTV inside, but due to the vast number of people wearing dark blue coats, finding a clear view of the suspect had proved difficult. He suggested the person could have put the coat on after entering the mall, which seemed plausible. Harry told Jerome to keep looking.

Though he'd stopped smoking a long time ago, during times of stress, Harry couldn't help himself. He bummed a cigarette off a colleague outside and leaned against the wall. Scrolling through the latest football news on his phone, Lucy's name popped up as it rang.

'I'm bored shitless in here,' she said. 'How's everything going?'

'We're still trying to find Melanie. Listen, I'm glad you called. I've been unable to stop thinking about what happened and can't work out why she ran.'

'What do you mean?'

'Having seen me, she could have come over, knowing I'd protect her. Instead, she chose to run. Why? Who could have posed such a threat that she deemed it safer to run than to turn to the police?'

'Too scared, maybe. Running away is a natural instinct. Unless she doesn't trust us.' A lengthy silence prompted her to ask, 'Are you still there, Harry?'

'Give me a second, I'm thinking,' he said. She had specifically called *him* when she could have simply gone to the police station. And why did she want to meet in a public place? Harry said, 'It's not us Melanie doesn't trust. Somebody informed the killer she would be there. The question is, who? As far as I'm aware, other than Melanie, only three of us knew about the phone call. I'll contact Owen and see if he told anyone else. Unless you happened to mention the meeting to somebody.'

'No. Wait! Yes, I did. Jerome Henderson asked how the case was going when I was on my way back from fetching my coat. I told him someone who could provide us with important information had come forward. Shit! I'm sorry, guv.'

'Look, it's possible Jerome knowing had nothing to do with it. The killer may have been stalking Melanie. Just get some rest. I'll call you later.'

Regardless of what he'd said to Lucy, he wasn't so sure. But looking into a fellow officer wouldn't go down well, and it was something he would have to do on the quiet. He had second thoughts about contacting Owen. Although unconvinced he'd be sharing information with the killer, right now, he couldn't trust anyone. He stubbed out his cigarette and put it in the wall-mounted bin. Time to visit Arthur Potts in London.

*

Arthur's practice was situated in a stylish, modern building with rounded walls and plenty of glass. An assistant buzzed Harry in and took him into the lab, where Arthur was working. The body on the slab could be Craig Bishop, but with his chest splayed apart, it was difficult to focus on the face. Standing over the body of a victim in a mortuary always made Harry uncomfortable, as though he were invading someone's privacy.

'Be with you in a sec, Harry.' Arthur finished cleaning his instruments and covered the body with a white sheet. 'Right. How are you?'

'To be honest, not great.'

'I asked more out of courtesy, but if you'd truly like to share, I'm willing to lend an ear.' With his heart in the right place, Arthur had always been honest to a fault.

'No, it's fine.'

'Good. On to business. DNA and fingerprints lifted from Fred Perry's house mostly belong to him and his brother. Craig Bishop's van produced *his* prints and those of the Perry brothers – yet more evidence to suggest they all knew one another. The remaining fingerprints from both crime scenes match nothing in our database. I'll send the documentation for further analysis. However, I *can* tell you that none of the prints belong to Ryan Levinson.'

Harry said, 'That is disappointing.'

'Moving on.' Arthur gestured towards Bishop's body, not the one Harry had set his eyes on earlier. 'As you can see, these wounds are closely bunched – eleven, to be precise. The attack was swift, and, as with Frederick Perry, the killer showed no mercy, hoping at some point to strike an artery, which they succeeded in doing twice. They sliced through the subclavian artery first and severed the common carotid artery soon after. Our victim didn't have a hope in hell of surviving. He'd have bled to death in a matter of seconds.'

Harry stepped back from the table and ran a hand through his hair. It occurred to him that the person who did this had probably stabbed Lucy. 'You said, "as with Frederick Perry." Does this mean?'

'Not necessarily the same killer, but given the level of brutality involved and the victims' connection, I wouldn't rule it out. I found a short strand of blonde hair on top of the fresh blood, which would imply it came from the attacker.'

'That's excellent news,' said Harry, thinking of Ryan's blonde hair.

'Don't get too excited. While we're suggesting they are victims of the same person, unfortunately, there are no follicle cells attached to the hair.' Harry's puzzled expression forced Arthur to elaborate. 'Which means you could take a sample from your main suspect, and though it may share similar characteristics, that doesn't necessarily mean the hairs are from the same source.'

'So how does any of this help the investigation?'

'Right now, it doesn't. But say you find the killer and can only tie them to one murder. If you can prove a connection to another victim, along with a motive – a near-matching hair sample will help place them at the scene. On that basis, a jury would likely convict the person of both murders.'

Harry said, 'I suppose that's something.' His mind switched back to Lucy.

Arthur must have wrongly sensed a lack of enthusiasm. 'The good news is that there's been a major breakthrough in extracting DNA from rootless hair, but it's an expensive technique, and it could be a while before it's widely available. It'll be a game changer for solving existing and cold cases, meaning this piece of evidence can be tested again if needed.'

Harry turned away and fixed his gaze on a blank wall.

Arthur said, 'Something is wrong. I can tell you're not yourself.'

'It's nothing. I just want this day to end.'

'Anything you want to share? On this occasion, I mean it.'

Harry faced Arthur. 'The constable I was with at Fred Perry's house is in hospital. She was hurt in a knife attack earlier today.'

'Oh dear, that's awful. Is she going to be okay?'

'She will be, physically at least.'

'Yes, the mind can take longer to heal, and sadly, for some, it never does. Did you catch who did it?'

'Not yet. But it's conceivable she was knifed by the same person who killed Perry and Bishop, and seeing him lying there made me appreciate how fortunate she is to be alive.'

'Indeed. I now understand your melancholy. I've known you for a few years now, Harry. I've seen some of the cases you've worked on and the murderers you've tracked, and despite the odds being against you, you've always come up trumps. I have every confidence you'll find the monster responsible for these terrible crimes.'

Harry smiled softly. 'Thank you, Arthur.'

Instead of calling it a day, Harry waited in his car outside the police station car park, and when Jerome Henderson exited through the electric gates, Harry followed. Unfortunately, he drove straight home. To kill time while waiting to see if Jerome went anywhere, Harry made some calls. First up was his mother, who was on her way to bingo and looking forward to seeing him at some point over Christmas, if he could make it. He called his brother, who rarely answered. No change there. Next was his sister, whom he hadn't spoken to for a while, and she made sure to let him know. Why did people always complain about you not calling them when they'd spent the same length of time not calling you, and yet somehow it was always *your* fault? He then spoke to Leah, who was finalising her plans for New Year's Eve: a big party at a friend's house. Her excitement convinced him not to discuss the negative impact of his breakup with her mother. Instead, he said he would pay for her new outfit and ended the call with her on a high.

His final call was to Lucy, who'd slept little and only out of boredom. She detested being in the hospital and wanted to be back at work, suggesting that staking out Jerome Henderson on a cold December night was better than lying in a warm hospital bed. A close call, but she was probably right. A taxi pulled up, and Jerome came out of the apartment block and got in the back. He said goodbye to Lucy and followed the car. Jerome was dropped off at The Sad Dog's Smelly Breath, a pub on Chatham High Street. Harry was in two minds about whether to follow him in. On the one hand, he needed to know if he was meeting someone of interest, but on the other, what reason would he have for being there if Jerome saw him? He puffed out his cheeks and opened the car door.

Keeping his head low, Harry walked up to the bar. The busy pub was larger than it seemed from the outside and forked off in different directions. There was no sign of Jerome. He ordered a pint of lager and wandered around, attempting to remain inconspicuous.

A tap on his shoulder. 'All right, guv.' He'd been rumbled.

Harry turned. 'Jerome, what are you doing here? Not following me, are you?' He sipped his pint and casually stared towards the nearest exit door, which was closing. Had the person Jerome had met with just left? *Shit!*

'I was about to say the same thing.' (The reason Harry had said it first.) 'What brings you here?'

'Tinder,' said Harry, with the first believable excuse that came to mind. 'I'm supposed to be meeting someone, but it looks like she's a no-show.' It vexed him that he couldn't walk out the door to see who'd just left.

'Yeah, it happens a lot. I'm sure I heard you were married. Not that it's any of my business.'

'Separated, so I wanted to see what it's like out there in the world of dating.'

'Oh, I'm sorry. I didn't mean to pry. Though personally, I don't recommend Tinder for dating.'

'My date not turning up proves your point. Anyway, what are you doing here – is this your local?'

'No. I occasionally drop by for a few beers when I'm bored. Plus, they get some nice-looking birds in here.' He gave a cheeky grin.

Harry bought him a pint, and Jerome got the next. They talked about work and the horror of what had happened to Lucy. It wasn't easy to tell whether his sorrow was sincere. They caught the second half of a football match on the big screen, and when Jerome offered to get another round, Harry declined. When driving, two was his limit, and he didn't want to leave it too late getting back to Gerty's. He bought Jerome another and left him watching the post-match analysis. Outside, it was raining heavily, and Harry hurried across the road to his car.

35

December 22
Toronto

After such an eventful day, both men deserved a couple of drinks. Detective Tremblay picked the place, and as long as they served something resembling whisky, Lenny didn't give a . . .

The young bartender was welcoming, and it seemed like a popular place. There were a number of wooden tables, many occupied by couples and friends drinking and eating. The background music was pleasant and not too loud.

They sat at the end of the bar, far enough away from anyone wishing to eavesdrop. The first bourbon barely wet the glass, and the second followed the same example. The third had a stay of execution as they discussed what had happened at the hospital. Neither of them expected the killer to come for the girl. That he'd got away was a sore point. Unable to speak, Rebecca wrote down something the man had said before he'd placed the pillow over her head: *'You're not the girl.'* He'd likely seen the story online about an unidentified girl in the hospital and assumed she was the one who'd escaped him that night. Annalise Fournier had seen his face, and he'd wanted to make sure she couldn't identify him. Even after he'd discovered it wasn't her, he remained undeterred in his attempt to kill Rebecca.

Fearing the killer might find out Annalise's address, Tremblay had a patrol car stationed outside the family home. He wasn't taking any chances.

The pub became busier as the evening progressed. Lenny finished his drink. 'Whose round?'

'Mine,' said Tremblay, signalling to the bartender.

Lenny asked, 'What's your next move to find this bastard?'

'We're having a meeting first thing tomorrow. Hopefully, I'll be tasked with setting up a team. I've already assigned someone to search for similar unsolved cases where the female victim has been drugged and strangled, and so far, they've found four in Ontario, one in Manitoba, and two in Quebec. Each case will be thoroughly investigated to ensure we can link them to the killer's MO.'

Lenny had presumed there were more victims and remained convinced Louise Norris in Manchester was among them. It was hard to imagine the killer hadn't left a trail of bodies in the UK. Harry's reply from the National Crime Agency could be enlightening. His mind flipped to the naked girl in the hospital corridor: Emma Martin – it had to be. Her body, so mutilated, and the scarring on her face matched that of Mary's. Mary must have had the same scars down the left side of her body. He'd now seen them both – innocent young girls who'd met tragic ends. The world was a cruel place then, and nothing had changed.

Lenny ordered more drinks and explained everything to Tremblay: the car crash, the previously missing Rebecca Heaton, finding Annalise on the grave of a falsely accused witch, Louise Norris, three dead bodies, two sisters from the eighteenth century – *and a partridge in a pear tree.*

'Your Detective Baxendale must be tearing his hair out. But how is all this linked together?' He emptied his glass and said to the bartender, 'Two more here, please.' Not only were their voices getting louder; Tremblay was slurring his words.

Lenny said, 'I suppose it could be some kind of spiritual injustice.'

'Spiritual injustice?' shrieked Tremblay. 'Someone's had too much bourbon.'

'You're right. It sounds like complete and utter bollocks.'

'Must be something to it all though,' said Tremblay, waving his finger at Lenny. 'I mean, you don't just disappear from one place and reappear somewhere else in an instant. That would be, oh, what do you call it—'

'Time travel?'

'Yeah! Time travel. The thing is, nobody can travel through time.'

'Yet Annalise and Rebecca did.' Both men looked puzzled at the suggestion. 'You know what?' said Lenny. 'I haven't the foggiest and probably never will. But one thing I do know is that I need to take Rebecca Heaton home on the plane tomorrow.'

'It's all being arranged and taken care of. And considering the circum—' Tremblay frowned and attempted to say the word again, 'circumsestances and danger to the poor girl's life, there shouldn't be a problem at all.'

Seeing his drinking buddy's speech deserting him, Lenny said, 'You should probably call a taxi.'

'I reckon you're right. Taxi!'

They burst into laughter, and when Lenny calmed down, he said, 'It's been a bloody long day, and I need to find a hotel for a few hours.'

'You'll do no such thing. You'll stay at mine. We have a spare bedroom.'

'Will your wife not mind?' Lenny sipped his drink.

'No. I'm sure she'll be very comfortable in there.'

Lenny couldn't contain himself, spraying bourbon from his mouth.

Lenny received a warm welcome, and Mrs Tremblay had set a place for him at the table. Despite being a little tipsy, Lenny couldn't miss the sharp stare she gave her husband for coming home half-cut. Christopher pulled a face to suggest he was in the doghouse. Mrs Tremblay showed Lenny to the spare room, and before leaving him to settle in, she insisted he call her Karen. He put his holdall down and sat on the bed to rest. A moment to himself was much needed. He reached into his bag and pulled out a small framed photo of Olivia, which he stared at for several minutes before placing it on the bedside table.

Downstairs, he faced a barrage of questions from the couple's teenage son and daughter, mostly about London and famous landmarks. They also found his Cockney accent amusing. After dinner, the children escaped to their bedrooms, and Karen made coffee. They talked in front of the large, cosy fireplace, and it wasn't long before Tremblay drifted off to sleep in the armchair.

Lenny said, 'I get the impression your husband doesn't drink often.'

'He shouldn't be drinking at all,' said Karen.

'I want to ask why, but I fear it's none of my business.'

'He's not a recovering alcoholic, if that's what you're thinking. He has prostate cancer.' Aghast at her statement, Lenny fumbled to hold on to his empty coffee mug. She leaned forward, 'Here, let me take that from you.'

'I'm so sorry. I should never have let him take me to the pub.'

'Don't be silly. How could you have known?'

'Is it . . .?'

'Terminal? We hope not. He has an operation scheduled for next month. They are hopeful they've caught it early and can remove it.'

'I hope so too. He seems like a good man.'

'He's the best man I've ever known,' she said, smiling adoringly at her husband. 'What about you, Lenny? Is there anyone waiting at home for you?'

'Phoebe Waller-Bridge.'

'No offence, but I assume you're not talking about the actress?'

He laughed. 'No. Phoebe is my cat.' Mrs Tremblay had more than enough on her plate, so he refrained from bringing up what had happened to Olivia.

'A pet can be a great comfort,' she said. 'So, what happens once you get the poor girl back to England? Will she be going straight home?'

'No. We'll have an ambulance transfer her from the airport to the hospital.' He looked at his watch. 'Which reminds me – I need to call the detective back home.'

'It's nine thirty. Are you aware the UK is five hours ahead? I only know the time difference because my brother lives with his wife in Scotland. Edinburgh, to be exact.'

'Ah, I've been there a few times. Beautiful city.'

'It certainly is.'

Lenny climbed off the sofa. 'Regardless of the time, I have to make that call, if only to leave a message. I should also get a couple of hours of sleep before my flight. Karen, I can't thank you enough for dinner and for making me feel so welcome.'

'Don't be silly. It's my pleasure.'

'Do you need my help with Christopher?'

'No, I'll manage.'

Lenny held out his hand. 'It was lovely to meet you.'

She stood, brushed his hand away, and gave him a big hug. 'There's a sadness about you, Mr Grey. Don't keep it all locked inside.'

Mrs Tremblay was sharp. 'I bet Christopher doesn't get much past you?'

'He gave up trying a long time ago,' she said, her face aglow with a subtle smile.

Sitting on the bed in the spare room, Lenny phoned Harry. As much as he would have enjoyed giving him the details about finding and bringing Rebecca Heaton home, he was relieved he didn't answer. He left a long message and informed him they would be landing around two in the afternoon. When he climbed into bed, he stared at Olivia's photo.

'Why did you bring that with you?'

Surprised, he turned to see Olivia beside him. 'I brought it because I didn't expect to see you here.'

She smiled. 'I can go wherever I'm wanted. It's not like I need a passport.'

'I assumed you had to reside where you died.'

'Someone's watched too many haunted house movies.'

'I bet you know who the killer is, but for some unknown godly reason, you're not allowed to say. It would make things a lot easier if you just told me, and it would save lives.'

'I'm a spirit, Lenny, not a bloody psychic.'

'But you've got free movement. You could've followed him from the hospital and found out where he lives.'

'I'm afraid that's not how it works. I can't just wander around anywhere. We only get a short amount of time to come back, and only when we are *truly* needed. You're one of the lucky ones who can see those who wish to reveal themselves, but as you know, it's always fleeting.'

'God should go back to the drawing board with this ghost malarkey. Anyway, you're here now.' He made himself comfortable under the covers and stared into her eyes until she faded from sight and he drifted off to sleep.

Other than the pilots, Lenny and Rebecca had the plane to themselves. The doctors agreed she should be okay to travel, and being back home with family would aid her recovery. Lenny was surprised Tremblay had arranged everything in such a short space of time, even the special travel documents. He couldn't imagine the British police or government being so prompt. At the airport, Tremblay had given Rebecca a new pen and pad so she could communicate with Lenny on the flight. Her first message, though, was to Christopher, thanking him for his kindness and all he'd done for her. Her second message was to say goodbye. Her eyes glazed over, and tears fell as she hugged the detective, who struggled to contain his own. Having promised to keep in touch, Lenny shook the hand of his new friend, knowing it would likely be the last time they'd ever see each other. He didn't reveal that he knew about his cancer. Another time, perhaps.

During the flight, Lenny attempted to help jog her memory but soon realised he was up against it. At least she knew her name now. When she asked if she'd ever remember, he reassured her that everything would be all right and let her read an article on his phone about post-traumatic amnesia. He slept for a short spell and woke to find Rebecca asleep. The poor girl had been through such an ordeal, not only in the hospital but back home in Kent as well. The return of her memory couldn't come fast enough, unless Harry managed to unravel the mystery beforehand.

36

December 23

Harry ignored his phone in the early hours on the basis that Lenny hadn't accounted for the time difference. When his alarm went off, he checked the message and almost dropped his phone. He'd been unable to explain how Annalise had woken up in England, and now it turned out Rebecca was the unidentified girl in Toronto. Surely not Lenny's reason for going there. Though relieved, hearing about her amnesia was disappointing. Melanie Hillingdon not being found only made matters worse. She and Rebecca were the only two people who could clarify what had transpired on December 18 and point him towards who had killed Fred Perry and Craig Bishop.

Forsaking breakfast at Gerty's so he could get to the station early was a no-brainer. He'd already made arrangements with Medway Hospital and requested an ambulance to be on standby at London City Airport that afternoon. The phone call to Rebecca Heaton's parents was a real pleasure. Sharing in their elation was very rewarding. Mr and Mrs Heaton had so many questions, but the one they kept coming back to was how she had ended up in Toronto, to which Harry could not provide an answer.

An hour before the briefing, he'd been preparing the incident room. Now that the case had turned into a double homicide, more officers were assigned to assist with the investigation, one of whom was Jerome Henderson. As far as Harry was concerned, the jury was still out on him. Detective Constables Alex Pence and Stephen Rocastle were to lead the search for Melanie Hillingdon. PC Halilovic was to take a second look through the CCTV from the mall in search of a close-up of the person wearing the blue parka. Wanting to keep DC Henderson close, he was to accompany Harry to question Melanie's boyfriend, James Harding, to find out if he'd been in contact with her.

They visited The Braderman Hotel in Maidstone, where James Harding worked as a trainee chef. James had failed to show up for work for two days running and hadn't bothered to call, which was out of character, as he was generally dependable. The hotel manager had been unsuccessful in his repeated attempts to contact him. Their next stop was Harding's home address.

Mrs Harding answered the front door. Her face immediately paled. She invited the detectives inside, and they followed her to the living room. After taking a seat, she gestured for them to sit.

She pulled a tissue from under her sleeve and dabbed her eyes. 'Where did you find him?'

Harry and Jerome looked at each other. Harry said, 'Find him? Mrs Harding, you misunderstand. We're here to speak to James about the accident he witnessed.'

She raised a hand to her mouth and sighed. 'Oh, thank God. I thought you'd come to tell me you'd found his body.'

Confused, Harry said, 'Why would you think that?'

'He hasn't been himself of late. After the death of his father the other year, he became severely depressed and attempted suicide. I'm worried his mental health is slipping.'

'I'm sorry to hear that. Has he given any signs he may harm himself?'

'It's difficult to know for sure. He doesn't talk to anyone and hasn't been to work for a couple of days. If he's not moping in the armchair by the window' – she pointed – 'he'll be lying on his bed, staring at the ceiling. I assumed he'd broken up with Melanie, his girlfriend, but she came over yesterday afternoon. They had lunch in the kitchen and left soon after. I've not heard from him since. He never stays at her place, and if they spend the night together, it's usually here. Neither of them is answering their phones. In fact, James's could well be switched off.'

'What time did they leave the house?'

'Around four o'clock.'

'I'm sure they are fine, Mrs Harding,' said Harry. 'They've probably gone away for a couple of days or something.' He didn't want to cause the poor lady more stress by telling her the truth.

'I hope so. It's just that, before leaving, he came into the kitchen on his own and said if anything were to happen to him, he knows I did my best and that he loves me. I didn't know what to make of it at first, but I recalled his behaviour when he was depressed. He'd said something similar. I sat at the kitchen table and called the mental health crisis team. He wouldn't answer his phone to them either.'

Harry sympathised with Mrs Harding, though he was glad to learn James knew he was in danger. He and Melanie were scared, but at least they were together. Why wasn't James with her at the mall? Unless he was waiting outside in the car. Find the car – find them.

'I doubt he meant anything by it,' said Harry. 'Kids say the strangest things at times. Well, we all do.'

'Perhaps I am reading too much into it.'

'Something just occurred to me. If we can locate James's car, there's a good chance we'll find them close by.'

'You won't have to look far. It's parked just outside on the road.'

'Ah!' So much for that idea. He said, 'Does Miss Hillingdon drive?'

'No. She gets James to drive her wherever she wants to go. He'd do anything for her.'

'Did they get a taxi when they left here yesterday?'

'I'm sorry, I don't know. I only discovered they hadn't taken the car when I went to the shop a little later. It was quite a surprise because he doesn't usually go anywhere without it.'

The only other option was to apply for warrants to check their financial activity. A carelessly used bank card could be incredibly informative. 'Right, Mrs Harding, I'll leave my card, and if he gets in touch, tell him to call me immediately.'

Back at the car, Jerome said, 'What do you reckon?'

'I'm not sure. Though it's clear she's worried about her son.'

Unwilling to share his true thoughts, Harry harboured serious misgivings about the situation. He could only hope the couple were shacked up where the killer couldn't find them. Staring across the road at the house, he imagined how distressing it would be if he had to come back and tell Mrs Harding her son was dead. They fastened their seat belts.

'Where are we off to now, guv?'

'It's about time I questioned Sarah Kerr again. Who knows, we might even find Melanie and James hiding at her place.'

'If she lets us inside.'

'What makes you think she won't?'

'You know what these celebrity types are like.'

'Have you met her?'

'No. I've seen her on the telly. She was in some rubbish drama, and she's been on the local news a few times.'

'If she doesn't let us in, I'll get a warrant.'

37

December 23

From the car park, Harry glimpsed a figure leaning against the railings of the penthouse balcony. It was impossible to distinguish who it could be from that distance. The figure turned and withdrew from sight. At the entrance door, Harry held back to see if Jerome knew which number to press. He didn't. Recognising Sarah's voice over the intercom, Harry gave his name and said he had more questions. A short pause ensued, followed by a loud buzz and a click to let them in.

Wearing a white vest and grey shorts, Sarah greeted him at the door. 'Detective Inspector Baxendale! What an unexpected pleasure. I see you've brought a friend along.'

'This is Detective Constable Henderson.'

'Nice suit,' she said to Henderson, who smiled at her, seemingly lost for words. 'Any news on Rebecca?'

Harry replied, 'Not yet.' Other than Rebecca's parents, he didn't want anyone else to know she was alive and on her way home. Certainly not a friend of Ryan's.

'Seeing as this is not our first time together, perhaps you'll allow me to call you Harry?' She winked brazenly.

'I'd prefer to keep it formal, Miss Kerr.'

'Spoilsport,' she said. 'I suppose you want to come inside?'

Harry considered that she was assessing whether he was after more information regarding Ryan or if he suspected her of something. To reassure her, he said, 'We can talk right here if you'd like. As I mentioned over the intercom, I just have one or two questions.'

She took a moment. 'No, it's fine. Come on in.'

Entering the apartment, he noted the fresh smell in the air and looked around discreetly. Clearly, she'd had professional cleaners in within the last few days. A coincidence or a regular occurrence? She told the officers to take a seat on the sofa and offered them a drink. Jerome was quick to ask for coffee. Harry observed an unfinished cup of tea on the table in front of the long sofa. Usually, he'd decline, but on this occasion, he asked for a glass of water. Sarah entered the kitchen area, and Jerome made himself comfortable.

Harry walked over to the glass door. 'Do you mind if I step out onto the balcony? The view must be impressive from up here?'

'Please do. It's not as impressive as you'd think, though.'

Harry stepped out and glanced towards the car park. This was where he'd seen the figure standing on their arrival. He surveyed the marina and the historic Upnor Castle across the way. How could anyone not be happy with such a fantastic view? Perhaps appreciating simple pleasures was beyond her. He wandered along the balcony, hoping to get a glimpse through the glass into other rooms. The curtains were drawn.

Sarah called out, 'Here's your water, Detective Inspector.'

Coming inside, he took the glass from her. She sat in an armchair wide enough for two people, and Harry remained standing.

Jerome said, 'You make a nice cup of coffee, Miss Kerr.' His compliment barely raised an eyebrow.

'So, what can I do for you, Harry? Sorry, Detective.' Sarah reached for the cup Harry had previously spotted on the table, took a sip, and grimaced. 'Ugh, cold,' she said, setting it down.

'Walking towards the building, I saw someone out on the balcony,' said Harry, sipping his water.

'Oh, that was me. I may not think the view is great, but I still like to observe the people below, rushing around like little worker ants. Did you know worker ants are all female?'

'I had no idea,' said Jerome. Again, she failed to acknowledge he was in the room. Harry didn't know either, but he wasn't going to admit it.

She said, 'Male ants barely survive more than a week. They are merely sperm donors. Many women would argue that human males are the equivalent. Sadly, they live a lot longer.'

Harry said, 'Sounds like you're not keen on men.'

'Not all of them.' She directed a lascivious smile his way. 'I occasionally make an exception, though my preference is for ladies. Two queens can form one hell of a partnership.'

'We're not here to discuss your sexual preferences, Miss Kerr. But you could tell us how you know Fred Perry?' Her eyelids flickered, and she crossed her arms. A defensive reaction. The question caught her off guard.

'The name *is* familiar,' she said. 'I may have seen him around or met him briefly. I wouldn't say I know him.'

'Then it won't hurt you to learn he has been murdered.' He expected a further display of nerves or stress. She remained perfectly still.

She said, 'That's terribly sad. But as I said, I didn't know him.'

'What about Craig Bishop?' said Harry.

'I don't recognise the name.'

'James Harding, Melanie Hillingdon?'

Calmly, she said, 'Detective, it's no use firing random names at me. I meet so many different people, and I can't be expected to remember every single one of them. Who are these people?'

'You honestly don't know James or Melanie?'

'No. I'm certain.'

She seemed adamant. 'Okay. When we last spoke, you said Ryan came to collect his laptop. You know I saw him leave, so where did he put it – up his rear end?'

'All right. You've got me. I lied because I was frightened.'

'What did you have to be frightened about, Miss Kerr?' said Harry. Her shoulders dropped. She closed her eyes and sighed, as though she were about to divulge important information.

'Ryan came to tell me Rebecca was missing, and that the police suspected he had something to do with it. He said it was ludicrous and wanted me to provide an alibi by saying I'd shown up at his house as soon as Becca left and that we'd spent the night together.' She shifted in her seat and locked eyes with Harry. 'But I said no. I told him I had too much to lose and wouldn't jeopardise my career by associating myself with a scandal.' Close to tears, Sarah got to her feet. 'He lost his temper and forced me hard against the balcony door. He . . .' Her cheeks reddened, and she sobbed. 'He reached down and groped me. He said I'd teased him long enough, and if I didn't go along with it, he'd come back and fuck me whether I wanted to or not. I'm now afraid to leave my apartment.'

Jerome said, 'You should have reported it to the police. You still can.'

Though convincing, Harry didn't know whether to believe her story. When she'd said goodbye to Ryan outside the diner, it didn't look as though an incident like the one she'd described had taken place. At the same time, he wouldn't put that kind of behaviour beyond Ryan. He supposed she could have been, as she'd pointed out – frightened.

'No, I don't want to report it. They're not the kind of headlines anyone trying to make it in the entertainment industry needs. Many would view me as trouble.' She sat and composed herself. 'People would say I'm making it up to gain attention. I don't want to add fuel to some of the disgusting comments I already get on social media. You can't imagine the abuse I have to put up with.'

Jerome said, 'Get rid of it. Lots of celebs have chosen to do so.'

'That's all well and good when you've made it, but these days, it's difficult to build a career in the industry without a platform.'

Jerome sympathised with her situation. 'It can't be easy for you. We could have a word with Ryan Levinson and tell him to stay away from you.'

Harry said, 'You'd be better off taking out a restraining order. You should know that I'll probably have to bring this up the next time I speak to him.' He wanted to see her reaction.

'You need to do what you have to,' she said, wiping away her tears – not the response he'd hoped for.

'Okay. We'll leave it there for now,' said Harry, reaching down to grab her cup from the table. 'Let me take this for you.'

He walked over to the kitchen sink and placed the cups on the side. Away from view, he dipped his finger in her tea and tasted it. Sugar. Her show of disgust wasn't because it was cold. At their first meeting in the diner, Sarah did not take sugar. A second unfinished cup in the sink led him to presume someone else was there, unless they'd left in a hurry when he'd rung the intercom. In a panic, she'd put the wrong cup in the sink. There was something amiss about Sarah Kerr, and he was positive he would find out soon enough.

She showed them to the front door. 'Thank you for your time, Miss Kerr,' said Harry.

'Yes, and thank you for the coffee,' said Jerome, passing between them to answer his phone.

'No problem,' she said, raising a smile. 'Oh, I meant to ask, how is your cute lady detective doing? What happened to her was just ghastly.'

Miss Kerr had obviously seen a report of the incident on the local news or online. Although he refrained from showing it, her question caught him by surprise and stirred sentiments of anger.

'Recovering well,' he said. 'She'll be spending time with family at Christmas.'

'Lucky for her.'

Pacing towards him with his eyes bulging, Jerome said, 'Guv, we need to go.' In the lift, he said, 'That was DC Pence on the phone. A body has washed up on the beach in Sheerness. He tried to call you, but your phone must be on silent or something.'

Harry looked at his phone; the battery had died. Fortunately, he could charge it in the car on the way.

38

December 23

Harry and Jerome trudged across the beach towards the body, the clatter and grind of pebbles ringing in their ears. Along with the intermittent rain, a bracing late morning wind slapped against their faces. The police kept onlookers at bay as they watched intently from the promenade and the long, thick concrete steps below that extended far into the distance. Many held their phones aloft, filming and taking pictures. Harry never understood why anyone would want to take pictures of dead people. Head to toe in white, Arthur Potts's assistant pathologist photographed the body. Of course, there were exceptions.

Harry's stomach turned as he speculated on the identity of the corpse, and within seconds, he was looking down at James Harding, wishing he'd been wrong. Harry cast his eyes to the unsympathetic clouds, contemplating his return to Mrs Harding to deliver the devastating news. Failing to spot Arthur, Harry asked the pathologist where he was. He pointed to a wall where the promenade above curled around, extending across the beach towards the sea. Harry left Jerome and slogged through the stones and shingle. Rounding the corner, he discovered Arthur in his white coveralls, halfway up the sloping sea wall.

'Arthur!'

'Ah, Harry. Good timing,' he said as he carefully descended. 'You've seen the body?'

'Yes. And as I suspected, it's James Harding. Suicide, I presume?'

'Someone wanted it to look that way, but I'll bet my third nipple it isn't.'

'How can you be sure?'

'There is blood on the back of the young man's head. Now, if you were going to drown yourself in the sea at this location, where or how would you proceed to do so?'

Harry scanned the vicinity. 'I'd probably do it from the beach. Swim far out to sea and let myself go under.'

'Me too. Countless others have chosen the same way. But if this *was* suicide, we'd have to presume Mr Harding scaled the railing and jumped from the promenade above.' Arthur pointed to a stain close to the top of the sloping wall. 'I'm confident that's his blood, which further analysis will confirm.'

'Why would he jump into the sea above a sloping wall?'

Arthur shrugged. 'Exactly. It's more likely he was sitting on the top rail and somebody gave him a firm shove. Fortunately for us, the tide was on the turn, and his head struck the concrete above the waterline. It will be interesting to find out if he died on impact because if he did—'

'There'll be no water in his lungs,' said Harry.

Arthur smiled. 'Someone's watched a lot of forensic dramas.'

'A few. *Silent Witness*, mostly.'

'I should have guessed. Anyway, he had no identification, no bank cards or cash, not even a phone. In this day and age, most people carry something on their person. Before I suspected foul play, I supposed he could have left his belongings in his car.'

Harry said, 'His car is parked outside his mother's house in Maidstone. I'll have the CCTV at Sheppey Crossing and the local train station checked. It might reveal how he got onto the island and who he was with. Do you have an idea of the time of death?'

'Hard to say until I do a thorough autopsy, but definitely between eight and twelve hours ago. However, last night's high tide was just before midnight. If my theory *is* correct, I'd say he died within the following hour.'

'Because the tide turned and the blood wasn't washed away.'

'Exactly.'

Harry walked a few paces and stared out to sea. Suicide or not, another life had ended because of what occurred on December 18. Four men, all killed during his investigation into a missing person who had now been found alive. Were their deaths on him for not solving the case sooner? He questioned his ability and whether his personal circumstances had clouded his judgement and made him miss something critical. Perhaps he should withdraw from the investigation and let someone else step in and clean up his mess.

Arthur arrived by his side. 'There are three masts sticking out of the sea somewhere over there, unless they've removed them.'

'The wreck of the SS Richard Montgomery,' said Harry. 'There's always talk of removing them. My vision isn't what it used to be, so I couldn't tell you if they're still there. Is this your way of distracting me?'

'If you like. My father loved war stories. Everywhere we went, he'd always be pointing out Second World War relics – pillboxes, forts, shipwrecks and such. He brought me here when I was a child and told me all about the Montgomery.'

Harry said, 'My dad didn't take us to many places, but one particular day, he took my little brother and me to Southend, just across the estuary there. He handed us both a money bag of two-penny coins, directed us towards the arcade, and vanished into the bookies. I'm sure he had a big win because, two hours later, when he found us waiting outside, he had a smile on his face, something of a rarity. Instead of going straight home, we walked along the seafront. He told us about the ship, the explosives on board, and how they were too dangerous to remove. We even took a boat tour around the wreck. I remember asking why he was taking us so close to a dangerous ship. He gave me a clip round the ear and told me to shut up and enjoy myself.'

'Ah,' said Arthur. 'The same kind of parenting method favoured by my father. Listen. Don't speak. And don't ask silly questions.'

'When we arrived home, I hurried to my room to change and add the leftover coins to the thirty pounds in my plastic bottle bank. It was empty. My brother said he'd seen our dad empty it before we left and was warned to keep quiet. He'd had the coins changed into notes at the bank on the way to Southend. The money he'd used in the bookmakers and given us to spend in the arcade was mine. When I confronted him, he beat the shit out of me.'

'Perhaps not quite the same parenting method,' said Arthur.

Harry stared at the body of James Harding. 'I visited Harding's address this morning. His mother answered, and because of his mental health history, she'd assumed I'd come to deliver bad news. Now I have to go back and tell her he *is* dead. This one hurts, Arthur.'

'I can tell. But you can't blame yourself, Harry.'

'I question whether I could have prevented all this.'

'If you could have, you would have. You can't predict the actions of psychopaths, and that's exactly what we're dealing with here.'

'The thing is, I got this so wrong, Arthur. I imagined Rebecca Heaton was going to be found dead, and I'd prove her boyfriend, Ryan Levinson, guilty of murder. Now it turns out she's alive, and I'm no longer sure about Ryan. I'm almost certain he didn't kill Fred Perry, Craig Bishop, or James Harding.'

'So trust your instincts and look for another suspect.'

Harry agreed with a nod and contemplated. If Ryan hurt Rebecca and his attempt to cover it up backfired, who would go above and beyond to protect him? With close ties to a criminal past, there was an obvious suspect: his father, Carl Levinson.

Delivering the harrowing news to Mrs Harding was something he wanted to do alone, so he dropped Jerome at the station and told him to talk to Melanie Hillingdon's lecturers at the University of Kent. It wasn't inconceivable she'd trusted one of them enough to share information relating to her current whereabouts. In his car outside Mrs Harding's house, Harry ruminated on how he would tell her. In truth, he was stalling. There was no easy way to tell a mother she'd never see her child again. He rubbed his hands over his face and sighed.

Mrs Harding opened the front door with a different demeanour from earlier – a hopeful smile and bright eyes, as though expecting Harry to say he'd found her son shacked up with his girlfriend in a Brighton hotel. The silent pause and mournful look on Harry's face soon turned her sanguine expression to utter anguish. Seeing her legs buckle, Harry stepped over the threshold to stop her from falling to the floor. She cried on his shoulder as he escorted her into the living room and sat her down.

'No words can express how deeply sorry I am for your loss, Mrs Harding.'

'I can and, at the same time, can't believe this has happened. Does that make sense?'

'Under the circumstances, it makes perfect sense. A family liaison officer is on the way to offer help and advice about support options, but I wanted to come here first. Do you have a family member or close friend you could call?'

'Yes, I'll call my mum. She only lives a couple of miles away.'

'Okay. Why don't you call her now?'

She said, 'I sensed an emptiness when I woke up this morning. Your words gave me hope, but deep down, I knew. How did he do it?'

'Mrs Harding, this is going to be difficult to hear. I suspect your son was murdered.'

Eyebrows raised, she stared at him. 'Murdered? That can't be right. You must be mistaken. Everybody liked James.'

Harry said, 'The first time I came to see him, a friend of his showed up.'

'Yes, that was Craig. They hung out sometimes and played on the computer.'

'Did James tell you what happened to Craig?'

'No. What are you talking about?'

'Craig Bishop was murdered two nights ago.' In her confused state, she screwed up her face and looked at him as if he were crazy. 'I suspect James was a victim of the same killer.'

She stood and walked over to the window. She gazed at a framed photo on the wall unit next to her and picked it up. 'This was taken the day he passed his NVQ level two in cookery. We went out to celebrate. He wasn't going to stop there. He wanted to work his way up to a level three diploma and own a restaurant or two.'

'Sounds like he was an ambitious young man.'

'When his depression left him alone, there were no limits to what he could achieve.' She put the frame down and turned to him. 'So why – why did this happen?'

'As you're aware, on December eighteenth, your son and Melanie Hillingdon witnessed a serious car crash. We're confident the crash was staged. A man was killed, but the target of the crime was a teenage girl. Fortunately, she survived and is slowly recovering. Details of the incident are still being investigated, but a connection between nearly all those involved has since come to light.'

'James never mentioned anyone was hurt.'

Harry said, 'The older our children get, the less they tell us, and the less we seem to know about them.'

Mrs Harding returned to the sofa. 'You said they were known to one another. Who was the man killed in the crash?'

'Vincent Perry.'

'I know Vinny,' she said, unaware her restless fingers tugged at a frayed piece of wool on the sleeve of her jumper. 'He and his brother did some work in the garden. When I read about the accident online, the name of the deceased man wasn't disclosed. I asked my son if that was the crash he'd witnessed. He said it wasn't. I can't remember the name of the missing girl.'

'Rebecca Heaton,' said Harry.

'I don't know her.' Her dolorous eyes looked upwards. The tears finally came. 'Why did he lie to me? When his father died, we agreed to always be open and honest with each other. I suppose I had no right to expect that of him.'

'Our children have their secrets, Mrs Harding. Just like we did at their age.'

Mrs Harding jumped up from the sofa and paced the room in anger. 'Why did he let himself get mixed up in something like this?'

'I've seen people from all walks of life get caught up in things they would never have dreamed of,' said Harry, attempting to appease her.

She said, 'I bet this is *her* doing.'

'Melanie?'

'Yes, Melanie! I liked her, but she had this unhealthy hold over him.'

Harry recalled Mrs Harding saying this morning that James would do anything for her, but surely this would be more to do with James's friendship with Ryan Levinson.

The doorbell rang. Harry knew it would be the FLO and said, 'I'll get the door while you call your mother.'

Harry brought Vivien up to speed in the hallway and led her into the living room.

Mrs Harding tossed her phone onto the sofa. 'My mum will be here shortly.'

'This is Vivien Whitmore. She'll explain the next steps in more detail and assist you in any way she can.'

Mrs Harding said, 'I should probably get the kettle on and make some tea.'

'I'll come and give you a hand,' said Vivien.

Mrs Harding stopped in front of Harry. 'Thank you for coming to tell me. I hope you find whoever is responsible.'

'I won't stop until I do. You have my word.'

39

December 23

The wheels of the plane hit the tarmac, and Lenny opened his eyes, refreshed after several hours of much-needed sleep. Rebecca passed him his phone. She'd been reading news articles about her disappearance. With a disturbed frown, she handed him her pad, which contained a message she'd written while he slept. It read how strange it was to see her face but not remember anything about herself. Lenny could only imagine how frustrated and confused she must be. Once the plane had come to a stop, Lenny showed his appreciation to the pilots, especially Marvin, who'd gone above and beyond to help – something of a rarity these days.

Lenny departed the plane holding a bottle of Bridgeland Moscato Brandy. He smiled at the sight of Harry, waiting at the bottom of the steps. On his way down, two paramedics passed by on their way up to help Rebecca. 'Here, I bought you a present. Award-winning, apparently,' said Lenny, handing him the bottle.

'Very kind of you.' Harry glanced at the label and said, 'How is she?'

'Difficult to say. Just go easy on her. She has no idea what's going on or why some bloke attempted to smother her with a pillow in hospital.'

'Somebody tried to kill her? You didn't mention that in the voicemail.'

'I wasn't sure how much time I had before it cut out.'

Harry looked to the heavens. 'Was it our killer? Did the police catch him?'

The paramedics were about to escort Rebecca down the steps. Not wanting to alarm her, Lenny put his hand on the small of Harry's back and walked him away from the plane. 'No, he got away. It was him, though, Harry, the man Annalise Fournier described. He'd mistaken Rebecca for Anna and tried to finish the job. Now we all know what he looks like.'

'That's not necessarily a good thing. He's probably trying to change his appearance as we speak.'

'He has a slight but recognisable disfigurement, Harry. All he can do is cut or dye his hair. We've now got police on both sides of the Atlantic searching for him. It won't be long until he's captured.'

'I like your optimism.'

'The poor girl has been through a lot. I just hope when she remembers what happened, she doesn't have a setback.'

'Me too,' said Harry. 'Her parents are waiting at the hospital. I want to get her settled before springing them on her.'

'Good idea.'

'We have a lot to discuss, but we can talk later. I imagine you want to get yourself home after all your excitement.'

'Not half,' said Lenny.

'Detective Constable Rocastle is waiting outside the airport. He'll drive you home. I don't know how you did it, Lenny, but well done on finding Rebecca and bringing her home.'

Before leaving, Lenny introduced Rebecca to Harry and said goodbye. She squeezed his hand and attempted to smile.

*

Lenny opened the door to his apartment, greeted by a meowing Phoebe as she purred and brushed against his leg. He made sure she had plenty of food and water before he left, so perhaps she genuinely missed him. Who was he kidding? She most likely wanted some fresh food. He'd get to that, but first, the toilet. Five minutes into the journey home from the airport, he felt the urge to go. Typical. How he longed for the glory days of full bladder control.

He stripped down to his boxers and ran a bath. The idea of a whisky while having a long, hot soak had circulated in his mind since boarding the plane in Toronto. Phoebe wouldn't leave him alone; she was at his heels with every step. Even after making a fuss of her on the bedroom floor, she wouldn't let up.

'Okay. Come on, let's get you fed.'

She overtook him in the hallway, eager to get to the kitchen first. He washed out her personalised bowl and filled it with another pouch.

'She's taking advantage of you, Lenny.'

Lenny turned to see a familiar face stretched out on the sofa under a blanket. 'Well, well, well. Harper Darmody. Back from the dead – again.'

Harper smiled. 'Who saw that coming, right?'

'You're like a turd that won't flush.'

'Come on. You must have suspected I was still alive?'

'I wasn't certain, but yes, I suspected. What name are you going by these days?'

'Simon Smith.'

'Lovely. Now, why don't you tell me what the hell you're doing here and how you got inside my apartment?'

'Whoa, slow down, fella. One question at a time.'

'Forget how you got in. As long as nothing's broken, I don't care.'

'Then I guess we'll begin with why I'm here.' Harper climbed from the sofa. 'First up, I need my morning coffee.'

'It's the middle of the afternoon.'

'Is it? You'll have to forgive me, Lenny. I didn't get here until the early hours. I did knock, of course. I knew you wouldn't mind if I let myself in.'

'I do mind. I'll put the kettle on, but you'll have to make do with tea.' Lenny filled the kettle, switched it on, and remembered he'd left the bath running.

He turned off the tap and perched on the edge of the bath, unable to comprehend what possible reason Harper, a psychopathic mass murderer, could have for showing up at his gaff. He hoped he'd seen the last of him. Hiding in the bathroom wasn't going to provide any answers.

Lenny made the tea, passed a cup to Harper, and sat in his armchair. 'So, come on, why are you here?'

Harper sipped his tea, paused, gave him a deadpan stare, and said, 'We have unfinished business, and I'm here to settle it.'

Not much scared Lenny, but having seen up close what Harper was capable of, his skin grew cold.

Harper broke into a smile. 'You should see your face.'

'Well, when my legs stop shaking, I'll go and look in the mirror.'

'Relax, Lenny. I always had you down as someone with a good sense of humour.'

'It's been a hectic couple of days, and I'm tired. Are you going to tell me why you're here or not?'

Harper pulled out a bottle of pills and took two. Lenny couldn't see what they were but guessed they were antipsychotics, which didn't make him feel any safer.

'Okay,' said Harper. 'I'm here because Alice and I have split up. Only she wouldn't have found out until this morning. I left her a note before sneaking out late last night.'

'How considerate of you. So, all this time, you've been living in perfect harmony with Alice?'

'Yes. Though I wouldn't say it was always harmonious – leaving them was the hardest thing I've ever done.'

'Wait, them?'

'Oh, you don't know. Elaine doesn't tell you much, does she?'

'Not when it comes to you.'

'I have a daughter called Milena. You should see her. She's a little beauty.'

'The surprises just keep coming with you, don't they? So what happened?'

'I got sick of hiding in the closet.' Was this another bombshell to rock Lenny's sanity? Harper continued, 'And to be clear, I mean hiding every time her family or friends dropped by.'

'Ah. I can see how that would be problematic.'

'For a while, I didn't mind. But it became a regular thing. She was living two lives, and I was this shameful secret.'

'You were literally the skeleton in your own cupboard.'

'Precisely. I wanted to be more involved in her life. We argued, and I sulked. You know how it goes. It was no way to carry on, and although she hid it well, I know Alice felt the same. My past would always haunt us. With Milena getting older, it would have become more difficult. She'd have questions, we'd forever be lying to her, and in time, we'd be making her lie for us. How would that be fair?'

'It wouldn't.'

'Alice would have carried on. She loves me too much to say anything, and I love them both too much to be the perfect storm that would one day drag them to the depths of my personal hell. Elaine warned me there would be no happily ever after.'

Following a short pause, Lenny said, 'While I'm tempted to say a sarcastic "*boohoo*", I can tell how difficult a decision this must have been. In my opinion, you made the right call.' He finished his tea and climbed out of his chair. 'Right, I'm going to pour myself a whisky and get in my bath before it goes cold.'

'Is it okay if I stay for a while?'

'Where else are you gonna go?' He emptied the bottle into the glass. 'Besides, Elaine owns this apartment, and I'm pretty sure she'd want you to stay here.'

Lenny marched off and broke his stride as Harper said, 'Thanks. And just to be clear – you have nothing to fear from me.'

'I know.'

Lenny closed the door to the bathroom and let his fingers drift down to the lock. He wasn't taking any chances. Once in the bath, he let the hot water run until the foam bubbles were level with the rim. He took a large sip of whisky, placed the glass on the side, and leaned back.

'Are you asleep?'

Keeping his eyes closed, he smiled contentedly at the sound of Olivia's soft voice. 'No, my love. I'm just thinking.'

'What about?'

He stared at Olivia, sitting on the edge of the bath, gently caressing the water with her fingers. 'Rebecca, Danny, the Martin girls, and how much they've all suffered. How humans have an endless capacity to be cruel to one another. I hope the twins can rest now Rebecca and Annalise are safe. Is it possible this was all about the sisters?'

'You should know by now that all things are possible.'

'It must have been,' said Lenny, closing his eyes. 'The timing, the location of both events. Somehow, what was going to happen to Rebecca and Annalise opened a door.'

Olivia said, 'Stop obsessing, and the answer will come.'

Lenny smiled and relaxed. 'Yeah, I'm sure you're right. Perhaps I'll try it your way.'

With a burst of excitement, he sat up. 'What if—'

Two identical dark-haired girls stood beside the bath: one in a ragged white gown, the other naked, their wounds fresh and raw. He splashed around in panic and slipped under the water. A tsunami flowed over the side of the bath. Once he'd found his footing, he came up gasping for air. The girls were gone. He'd seen manifestations before, but this was so unexpected. Mary and Emma had revealed themselves again. This *was* about the sisters. He just didn't know what they wanted. Lenny climbed out of the tub and snatched the towel to cover himself.

'Right, that's the last bath I'll ever take.'

40

December 23

Reuniting Rebecca with her family wasn't an easy watch; after all, she had no idea who they were. Uncomfortable and eager to get back to the station, Harry backed away in an attempt to sneak out of the room. Rebecca glared his way, urging him not to leave, clearly not ready to be left alone. He waited patiently in the corner of the room, watching as Mrs Heaton showed her daughter numerous photographs and talked about family occasions. When Rebecca seemed a little more at ease, Harry reassured her he would be back to see her soon and left a police constable guarding the door to the room.

Earlier, he'd told Police Constable Dean Halilovic to suspend exploring the CCTV from the mall and check the camera feed at Sheerness train station. If James Harding stepped off any of the trains arriving after 4.00 p.m. the previous day, Harry wanted to know exactly who he was with. Failing that, he had asked him to check the CCTV at Sheppey Crossing and run the number plates of all vehicles leaving the Isle of Sheppey from midnight until 3.00 a.m.

PC Halilovic informed him Harding wasn't on any of the trains and handed him a list of all the names and addresses of the vehicle owners who'd left the island over the crossing during those hours. As Harry had asked, he'd already discarded all lorries and crossed out vehicles registered to addresses on the Isle of Sheppey. Whoever he was looking for, Harry was confident they did not live on the island.

Harry examined the list. 'You've certainly narrowed it down. There are still plenty of names – it's just a shame I don't recognise any of them.'

Halilovic said, 'I've gone through them all, and none appear worthy of further investigation. There's something else you should know. It's probably a glitch, but I discovered there are thirty seconds of camera footage missing. Other cameras along the A249 revealed the same issue.'

'Okay. I'll look into it. It's disappointing not to have found a lead, but good work. I'd like you to resume checking the cameras from the mall.'

Harry wasn't hopeful that Dean would find anything. As for the missing thirty seconds, he wasn't sure what to make of it, but he knew someone who might be able to help. He called Owen and asked if missing footage on live camera feeds was a common occurrence.

Owen said, 'It happens regularly if the cache isn't cleared. It's called frame skipping.' If there was such a thing as luck, it wasn't on Harry's side during this investigation. Owen changed the subject. 'Great news about Rebecca Heaton. How is she?'

'A couple of nasty injuries, but the doctors are hopeful she'll recover her memory soon.'

Owen asked how Rebecca had ended up in Toronto and if he was any closer to making an arrest. Embarrassed, Harry didn't have an answer to either question. When Owen hung up to take another call, Harry reasoned that now Rebecca was safe, he could focus on discovering who had murdered Vincent, Fred, and Craig.

*

Skippity Do was Carl Levinson's business and place of work. Harry showed his warrant card at the gate and drove into the yard. Taking a good look around, it seemed Mr Levinson had branched out into recycling. The site covered a vast area, with lorries and JCBs skirting off in different directions. He parked in what he assumed was the staff car park, and after asking a couple of people, he found his way to the boss's office.

'Carl Levinson?'

A heavyset, middle-aged man rose from behind the desk and leaned across to shake hands. 'Yes. And you are?'

Towering over Harry, it hit home why some people would feel intimidated. He showed his ID. 'Detective Inspector Baxendale.'

Levinson's grip tightened around his hand. 'Ah, so you're the one who's been bothering my family and accusing my son. It's complete and utter nonsense.'

'I wouldn't call the disappearance of a young girl nonsense,' said Harry.

Mr Levinson slumped into his chair. 'Maybe not, but it is to suspect my son had a hand in it. He adores Rebecca.'

'From what I've discovered, she's not the only girl he adores.'

'Sarah Kerr? You're barking up the wrong tree with that one. Ryan's always liked her, but there's nothing going on between them. As far as I'm aware, the stuck-up little wannabe prefers women. Anyway, I'm a busy man.'

'Yes, it looks like quite a big operation out there. All above board, I hope?'

'You can dig around in my affairs all you like. You'll find nothing illegal here.'

'I assume you have a solid alibi, but I still have to ask – where were you last night?'

'I was tucked up in bed with my wife until six thirty this morning. Why are you asking?'

The chair in front of the desk was too tempting, and Harry made himself comfortable. 'Do you know James Harding?'

'Rings a bell. Could be one of my son's mates. Why? You're not telling me he's dead as well?'

'His body was discovered on a beach in Sheerness this morning.'

'Shit! Should I be worried about Ryan's safety?'

Despite Carl Levinson's concern, Harry kept pushing. 'I don't know, should you?'

'I had nothing to do with these murders. I've never killed a man in my life.'

Harry expressed disbelief and quietly observed Mr Levinson.

'Look, Detective Inspector, I know what's going on here. You know about my past, and I admit, it's not pretty.' He spread his arms. 'Everything I have, including this business, wasn't gained in the most honourable way. But those days are long gone. I did my time at Her Majesty's pleasure, and now I give back to society. I do shitloads of charity work, and I don't do it for praise. Call it guilt. Call it whatever you want. I have nothing to hide, and I'm certainly not behind these murders.'

'All right, Mr Levinson, but I have to know if Ryan has said anything about what happened on the night of the eighteenth. If he has, you need to tell me because there is a strong possibility that someone is tying up loose ends, and he could be in danger.'

'I've asked him several times, and so has his mother. He tells us the same thing he's told you. She borrowed his car and went home. I'm sorry about what happened to her, and I feel for her parents. She's a nice girl. I'd even go as far as to say she's far too good for my son. The boy's bloody bone idle.'

Regardless of Mr Levinson's chequered past, Harry sensed he was telling the truth. 'Okay, we'll leave it there for now, but until we make an arrest, I suggest you advise your son to stay at home.'

Mr Levinson climbed from his chair and held out his hand, which Harry shook. 'I'll have another word tonight, Detective. If I manage to get through that thick skull of his and he tells me anything new, I'll call you.'

Harry handed him a card and walked towards the door. 'Oh, I almost forgot to mention, we have found Rebecca Heaton. She's in hospital with grievous injuries but is expected to make a full recovery.'

The look of relief on Carl's face was evident. 'That's great news. Has she not told you what happened on the night of the accident?'

'Not yet. But she will, Mr Levinson,' said Harry, on his way out the door.

41

December 23

On the way to Lenny's apartment, Harry considered whether he had been wrong about Ryan Levinson. Throughout his career, he'd rarely doubted himself, so why now? What was he not seeing? The ringing of his phone burst through the speakers of the hands-free system. PC Halilovic said he'd found something important on the CCTV from the mall. Harry changed direction and headed back to the station.

As soon as he pulled into the car park, Harry noted PC Halilovic hovering by the rear entrance with a laptop. He marched towards Harry's car and gestured for him to stay where he was.

Once Dean was beside him, Harry said, 'Why all the cloak and dagger?'

'You'll see, but first, who did you get to examine the mall security cameras before me?'

'Jerome Henderson.'

'Okay. I'm not saying Jerome is responsible, but one of the video files reveals that the overhead camera monitoring the escalator *was* working. On a separate file, footage from the same camera around the time of the incident seems to have been deleted.'

'Deleted? Are you certain? Because Jerome told me the camera didn't appear to be working.'

'I can see why he might have come to that conclusion if he hadn't seen the other file and failed to check the history and the logs in the event viewer. If he had, he would have found a discrepancy between the times. It was obvious to me that some files were missing. I had a friend from data forensics help me recover deleted files, and that's when I discovered the log for the file containing the camera footage.'

'Are you telling me you've recovered the video?'

'We tried, but no joy. It's been erased with a professional shredding tool that somebody installed and removed soon after. I called security at the mall, and they assured me the camera in question would have been recording at the time PC Fenton was attacked.'

Harry's suspicions about Jerome appeared to be correct. 'Did you ask security to send us another copy of the recording?'

'Yes, but the person I spoke to was surprised to discover it had also been deleted from their system. A data recovery specialist would be able to restore it as long as it hasn't been shredded or overwritten.'

'Okay, look into it. If we can get it back, I'm confident we'll have a clear view of the suspect.'

'There's something else.' Dean opened the laptop and inserted a memory stick. 'I recorded this footage so it doesn't get wiped. The cameras showing people coming and going from inside the mall may have been searched, but there are a few cameras covering the exits from the outside. Although we still can't make out a face, I found this.'

The video showed Melanie entering the mall in her yellow hoodie, walking beside her – the suspect wearing the blue parka.

Harry's heart raced. He stared at Dean. 'They were together.' His eyes locked onto the screen, and he thumped the steering wheel in frustration. 'It's looking increasingly likely that someone from the force is involved. I need you to keep everything we've talked about quiet until I work out what to do next.'

'Goes without saying, guv.'

Harry sat alone in the staff canteen with a cup of tea, a feeble attempt to alleviate his outrage and reflect. Other than Jerome, he'd contacted all the officers in his team and told them to stop what they were doing and get back to the station for a briefing. Harry also requested more officers to help with the investigation. DCS Falconer sucked air through his teeth, mentioned the Christmas holidays, and complained about staffing shortages. All the usual excuses. Harry's phone rang. Seeing Jerome's name, he debated whether to answer.

'What's up, Jerome?'

'Hi, guv. I heard there's a meeting. Did you want me to attend?'

Word gets around fast. 'No, I'd prefer you to finish questioning Miss Hillingdon's lecturers.' A feasible excuse to keep him away from the station.

'I've got one lecturer left to interview, but I have discovered something of interest. One of the lecturers knows Melanie quite well and said she'd often confide in her. A couple of weeks back, Melanie revealed she was going to break up with her boyfriend because she'd fallen for someone else.'

Harry said, 'James may have known. Because of his low mood, his mother presumed they'd broken up. It surprised her when Melanie showed up at the house the day before he died. Anything else?'

'The general impression is that she's an intelligent young lady who can sometimes come across as a little *too* assertive.'

'Good work.'

'Thanks, guv. I'll get this last interview done, and there's one more thing I want to check before I knock off.'

'Okay. I'll see you here in the morning.' Jerome's actions didn't seem to be those of a guilty man, but right now, everything pointed to him being involved. Best to keep him at a distance.

When everyone was back at the station and seated in the incident room, Harry fumed at their unsuccessful attempts to track down Melanie Hillingdon. For now, he wanted to keep her likely involvement as an accessory to the attempted murder of Lucy Fenton quiet. If Melanie remained oblivious, there was a chance of her reaching out again. He couldn't have Jerome, or whoever, tipping her off.

'The importance of finding this girl cannot be emphasised enough. My instincts tell me she knows who murdered Perry, Bishop, and Harding. She'll be frightened and could be in extreme danger.'

DC Rocastle said, 'Has it been confirmed that James Harding was murdered, guv?'

'Not yet, but I'm confident of confirmation from the pathologist soon. Any other questions?' The room was quiet. 'Right, her parents provided us with a list of all her family and friends. I know you've checked some, but I need you to start over. Somebody must know something. She couldn't have simply disappeared. You've all got your lists of names and addresses, so get out there and find her. PC Halilovic, I want to speak to you.'

The officers jeered and mocked Dean, assuming he was in trouble. When the room was empty, Harry said, 'Put on your civvies and go to Chatham Marina. If Sarah Kerr leaves her apartment building, follow her. I want to know where she goes and who she meets.'

'Why me, guv?'

'Because, right now, you're the only officer I can trust.'

42

December 23

On the way to Maidstone Hospital, Harry toyed with the notion that Melanie and James were responsible for the murders. It wasn't beyond the realms of possibility. Mrs Harding repeatedly mentioned how James would do anything for Melanie. How much control *did* she have over him? Was James wearing the blue parka? It wouldn't surprise him if Melanie showed up at the station in tears, pleading that James had forced her to arrange the meeting at the mall. If they were together at the mall, why did she run? And where did Jerome Henderson fit into it when there was no obvious link between them? What if Jerome was the new someone in her life and mentioned it to remove suspicion from himself? Perhaps he'd killed James.

Surprisingly, most of the beds in the ward were empty. As Harry approached Lucy's bed, her smile told him she was pleased he'd come to visit.

Upon seeing a brown paper bag in his hand, she said, 'Please tell me you haven't gone old school and brought me grapes?'

'Nope.' He tossed the bag on the bed.

She opened it and smiled. 'Oh, Harry, you shouldn't have. Pick and mix with gummy worms and fruit salads. My favourites. How did you know?'

'I didn't. I just scooped up what I liked.'

'Well, even so. Thank you.' She put a gummy worm in her mouth.

'How are you feeling?'

'A little sore when I move, but I'm okay. They said I might be able to go home tomorrow. Apparently, they need the bed.'

Harry looked around with a bemused frown. There was only one other bed in use.

Lucy said, 'I know. I don't get it either. Anyway, how is the case going without me?'

'James Harding is dead.' Harry told her about his trip to Sheerness, the harrowing task of informing Mrs Harding, Rebecca being found alive, and Jerome possibly deleting evidence. He showed her the recording on his phone of Melanie walking into the mall with the suspect wearing the blue parka. She needed a moment to collect herself. Harry poured her some water.

'Sounds like you've had one hell of a day,' she said. 'Do you suspect that Melanie, James, and Jerome are all in this together?'

'There's no question that someone on the inside is involved, and Jerome is the most likely suspect. As for Melanie and James, I just don't know. It's like I'm missing something.'

Lucy put her bag of sweets to the side, drank some water, and stared straight ahead.

Harry said, 'What are you thinking?'

'Why did they want us to go to the mall?'

'I assume they'd planned to kill one of us.'

'If they were covering up whatever happened with Rebecca, how would murdering a police officer help?'

Harry shrugged. 'Perhaps it was a distraction to divert the investigation in another direction.'

'Maybe. But what if *you* were the target? I mean, you're a bit of a celebrity cop these days. You took down two high-profile murderers.'

'I got demoted,' said Harry.

'That's not what the killer sees online. All they'll see is a top-notch detective coming after them. So yes, a distraction, as well as getting Harry Baxendale off their tail. Think about it – why would they want to kill me? I'm just a police constable. If those two walked into the mall together, they arranged to meet you together. They didn't know I was going to be there. Therefore—'

'They wouldn't have needed Jerome to tell them,' said Harry.

'Exactly. That's not to say he didn't delete the camera footage, mind. But you were supposed to be on the escalator, not me.'

Harry excused himself to answer his phone, and Lucy grabbed the bag of sweets, putting a cola bottle in her mouth.

'Okay, thanks, Arthur,' he said.

'Well?' said Lucy.

'No water in the lungs. James was dead before he hit the water due to a head injury. Given the extent of the damage, Arthur reckons it was caused by a hefty shove and not from falling. What if Melanie *was* scared of James, and when the chance to kill him presented itself, she took it?'

Lucy said, 'I guarantee whether she murdered him in cold blood or not, that's exactly what she'll say.'

'I need Rebecca to remember.'

'Here, have a gummy worm,' she said, tossing the sweet his way.

The Christmas tree looked pretty from his car across the street. Harry watched the white lights slowly fade at random intervals, longing to be inside with his wife and daughter. How he wished certain events had never happened. His mother would scold him for thinking this way. She'd taught him to live, make mistakes, and move on. Life was too short for regrets. He could do with one of her occasional boots up the backside right now. Harry turned the key in the ignition, and his phone rang.

'Hi, Dean. You're not still at Chatham Marina?'

'Just about to head home, guv. I've seen nothing of Miss Kerr, but you'll never guess who I've seen loitering around the apartment building for the past thirty minutes.'

'Who?'

'Jerome Henderson.'

When Harry last spoke to Jerome, he'd said there was one last thing he wanted to check. Could it have been something to do with Sarah Kerr? Unless his visit to her was personal.

'Do you want me to hang about and see what he's up to?'

Harry paused to consider. 'No, don't bother. Get yourself home. If he doesn't mention it in the morning, I'll ask him myself.'

43

December 23

A quiet evening indoors with Harper had once seemed unimaginable. But now, here was Lenny, sharing a meat feast pizza and drinking beer with him at the kitchen table. Words were few; yet both men were at ease with silence. With Harper a wanted man and the violent history between them, having him under his roof only added to the tension. Lenny had written about Harper, knew the horrors of his childhood, yet still couldn't decide what to make of him. For Harper, not knowing his origins or birth parents must have been a burden all of its own.

The revelation that Elaine was not his biological sister could only have deepened his suffering. For both to learn that Harper had been abducted and Elaine sold at birth – and that each had been auctioned off to the highest bidder – was a truth almost too devastating to comprehend.

They had survived the unimaginable, refusing to surrender even when the world conspired to break them. Their tormentors had not escaped justice; at Harper and Elaine's hands, suffering had been repaid in kind. Murderers, yes, but somehow Lenny could not help but admire them.

He knew Elaine would be fine. She had her family and nothing to come back and bite her on the arse, but what was next for Harper? Leaving Alice and his daughter proved that his harrowing past made it practically impossible to move on. When he'd asked him earlier, Harper suggested he might leave the country and travel the world, but in truth, he had no idea what he was going to do. As much as Lenny sympathised with his bad lot in life, he didn't want him hanging around his apartment for the foreseeable future.

With a mouthful of pizza, Harper said, 'How did you lose your toe?'

'Bit of a sore point, and I don't wish to discuss it further.'

Lenny grew tired of eating, switched on the television, and sat in his armchair with a beer. Not far behind, Harper climbed under the blanket on the sofa. The ringing of the doorbell had them staring blankly at each other. Lenny traipsed into the hallway and answered the intercom. Harry's voice sent him into panic mode. He pressed the button to open the downstairs door and marched into the living room.

He said, 'You need to hide in the bedroom.'

Harper glared at him. 'What? No chance. I've put those days behind me.'

'There's a detective coming up in the lift. The same detective who was chasing you around the English countryside the other year. This is not the time for a meet and greet.'

'Perhaps not.'

'Now make yourself scarce and take that blanket with you.'

Lenny cleared the beer bottles and plates away, removing any sign he'd had company. He left the door ajar for Harry and put the kettle on.

Over a cup of tea at the table, Harry updated him about recent developments while he had been globetrotting. When asked why he'd gone to Toronto and how he'd discovered Rebecca, Lenny refrained from telling him about the supernatural element and said he'd travelled there to learn more about the killer. Finding Rebecca was pure luck.

Harry glanced around the room with doleful eyes. 'This is the first time I've been in your apartment since . . .'

'I know.' Lenny jumped up. 'Did you want another cuppa?' A clear sign he didn't want to talk about it.

'No. It's been a long day, and I'm tired. I only came by to catch up and to ask if you'd help me find Melanie Hillingdon. I've got my team searching for her, but they're not making any progress. You seem to have a knack for finding people.'

'What about the killer in Toronto?'

'Unless he comes back here, he's their problem. There isn't much we can do from this end. Thanks to you and Annalise Fournier, they have a good description of who they're looking for. Like you said earlier, they'll soon have him in custody.'

'In that case, send me the details in the morning.'

'Already sent. It should be in your inbox. Oh, and unless it's absolutely necessary, stay away from Mrs Harding. She's been through enough, and I don't want her to know her son might be involved until I have absolute proof.'

'Understood.'

When Harry left, Lenny checked on Harper in the spare room, but he wasn't there. He marched along the hallway to his bedroom and found him sprawled across the bed, going through pictures and files of the case he'd been working on.

'Is this what you've been doing?' said Harper. 'Interesting.'

'You shouldn't be looking at all that.' Lenny snatched a sheet of paper from Harper's hand and gathered the rest into a pile.

'I assume you're trying to help catch this guy? I hope you're close because it won't be long before he strikes again.'

'So I've been told. Now get out of my room.'

'He's a psychopath.'

'I suppose it takes one to know one,' said Lenny.

Harper climbed off the bed and strolled out of the room, leaving him to regret what he'd said. Lenny entered the living area and placed the paperwork and laptop on the kitchen table. Harper was on the sofa watching television.

Lenny said, 'How come you didn't hide in the other bedroom?'

Without diverting his eyes from the TV, he said, 'Because that's Olivia's room. You left the mattress uncovered. I watch and read the news just like everybody else. I am sorry for what happened.'

Harper's compassion surprised him. 'Well, if you're going to stay for a while, you should probably make use of the room. It's not healthy for me to keep it as some sort of unofficial shrine.'

'If I'm still around when you're done grieving, I'll use it. Until then, I'll be fine here on the sofa.'

Harper was right; he wasn't done grieving. Lenny grabbed a couple of beer bottles from the fridge and passed one to Harper. Falling into his armchair, he said, 'If you're still interested in looking through those case notes, I'll fill you in after I drink this. DI Baxendale reckons the killer is unlikely to return to the UK, but I'd appreciate any insights.'

Harper smiled and said, 'Because it takes one to know one!'

44

December 23

With his back against the headboard and stripped to his boxer shorts, Harry watched a panel show featuring a handful of comedians trying to guess each other's secret crushes. He could have sworn he'd seen the same bunch of people on a different show an hour earlier. The television was on for company more than anything. With the cold leftovers of fish and chips in a cardboard container on the bedside table, the room was tainted by the strong scent of salt and vinegar. A blast of wind lifted the net curtains. Harry climbed from the bed, closed the sash window, and visited the bathroom, hopefully for the last time that night. He turned off the TV and the light before slipping under the covers.

He hadn't been asleep long when the shrill ring of his phone woke him with a start. He grabbed it from the bedside table and, through bleary eyes, saw it was Jerome. What could he possibly want so late?

'This had better be good.'

Jerome spluttered and gasped, his words stifled and barely intelligible as he repeatedly gurgled Harry's name and said, "Help!"

'Don't speak. Sit tight and leave your phone on. I'm on my way.'

Harry called the station and asked them to trace DC Henderson's phone and send an ambulance. He pulled on his jeans, threw on a sweater, and slipped into his trainers. He already had an idea of where he'd be.

By the time Harry arrived, flashing blue lights whirled in the darkness from emergency service vehicles. Curious onlookers wandered aimlessly, trying to get a better view beyond the police tape. PC Kerry Skelton escorted him towards a tall, defunct dock crane at the end of the pier. Approaching the marina where hundreds of boats were moored, Jerome was slumped against the railings, his head tilted to one side. His blood-covered chin and neck explained the coughing and spluttering over the phone.

PC Skelton said, 'Forensics are on the way. A middle-aged couple came across him on their way home from dinner. They didn't see what happened, but they were with him when he died.'

Kneeling down, Harry examined Jerome's bloodied, light blue shirt. There appeared to be at least five knife wounds to the chest and stomach. Resting in the palm of his outstretched hand was his phone. 'Did he say anything to the couple who found him?'

'He tried, but they couldn't make out any words.'

'Are there any other witnesses?'

'Nobody else has come forward yet, boss.'

Harry said, 'Grab a couple of constables and question people in the crowd. See if there are any staff from the restaurants still hanging around. And knock on some doors. Find me a witness to an argument, altercation, whatever.'

'Will do, but I imagine this must be linked to the other body.'

Harry sprang to his feet. 'What are you talking about? What other body?'

'Sorry, boss. I assumed you knew. The body over there.' She pointed towards the building where Sarah Kerr had an apartment. 'A woman fell from the balcony on the top floor.'

'The penthouse?'

'Yes, boss.'

Harry rushed over to the second body. The paramedics observed his approach. They'd covered her up so people couldn't see. A police constable stepped forward to prevent him from getting closer. Harry showed his warrant card.

A paramedic said, 'I hope you have a strong stomach.'

Harry lifted the corner of the plastic covering. A pool of blood, peppered with fragments of skull, surrounded the woman's head. Noting the yellow hoodie and short black hair, he knelt to examine the side of her face. Melanie Hillingdon. Harry glanced up at the penthouse balcony and promptly turned his attention to the entrance door as it opened. A paramedic, along with Detective Constable Pence, accompanied Sarah Kerr towards the back of an ambulance. He caught up with them and observed the blood seeping through her bandaged forehead. Her left eye had swollen shut. She stared straight through him, as though he wasn't there.

Harry pulled DC Pence aside. 'Is she okay?'

'I'm not sure. When the two police constables entered the apartment, they found her bleeding and unconscious. She came round after a few minutes and became agitated. The paramedics turned up and managed to get her settled. I arrived and took a short statement, and before I could get her to elaborate, she developed a confused look of emptiness and shut down.'

'What did she say happened?'

'Someone knocked on her apartment door, which she thought was unusual because nobody had rung the intercom. She checked who it was and recognised DC Henderson from a previous visit with you. He forced his way inside and shouted at Miss Hillingdon.'

'Melanie was already inside?'

'Yes. She'd arrived earlier, informing Miss Kerr that she was frightened for her life. DC Henderson and Miss Hillingdon argued and fought. When Miss Kerr attempted to intervene, DC Henderson threw Miss Hillingdon onto the sofa and punched Miss Kerr in the face. She fell backwards, striking her forehead against the worktop on the way down. As he stood over her, hurling abuse, Miss Hillingdon appeared from nowhere and plunged a knife into him. Miss Kerr wasn't sure how many times. DC Henderson knocked the knife out of her hand and marched her towards the balcony. Miss Kerr passed out and has no idea what happened next. Though we can probably guess.'

'Okay. Good work, Alex. Follow them back to the hospital. If she says anything else, I want to know.'

Harry approached the ambulance. The paramedic said, 'She's in a terrible state. It might be better if you spoke to her in the morning.' Harry nodded at DC Pence to continue as planned.

As Harry backed away, he fixed his gaze on Sarah Kerr, searching for answers on her expressionless face. He walked to the apartment building and detected intermittent spots of blood on the ground outside the main door. Harry continued down the corridor and showed his ID to the police constable guarding the lift, who had placed a fire extinguisher across the threshold to prevent the doors from closing. Harry entered, avoiding the moderately sized patch of blood in the centre, and dragged the extinguisher inside. Upon seeing a large red smear on the console, he covered his finger with a tissue and pressed for the top floor.

When the doors opened, he blocked the lift and walked along the hallway, scanning the sporadic drops of blood to where a constable stood outside the apartment door, protecting the crime scene. As much as Harry wanted to enter, the right thing to do was to wait for the forensic team to arrive. Downstairs, outside the main door, Harry used the torch on his phone and followed the spots of blood all the way to Jerome. The vast amount surrounding the detective constable had him contemplating the number of wounds and their severity. Why had Jerome's final steps from the door to the crane left a trail of irregular drips instead of a steady trickle?

Waiting for Arthur and his forensic team to arrive seemed like the longest twenty minutes of Harry's life. As they changed into their protective clothing, Harry made them aware of his observations. Arthur pointed out that it was *his* job to examine any blood evidence and ascertain the cause of death. Carrying their holdalls, two pathologists walked towards the body of Melanie Hillingdon, while another headed over to DC Henderson. Harry and Arthur proceeded to the penthouse.

Arthur set to work, looking around the disordered apartment, taking photos and leaving numbered markers on any potential evidence. Harry watched closely but kept out of the way. The coffee table lay overturned in the middle of the room. Broken items from shelves and a display unit, along with sofa cushions, were strewn across the floor. When Arthur finished on the balcony, Harry left him to it and stepped outside, staring at the body of Melanie below. To imagine her falling to her death from such a great height turned his stomach. Such indescribable panic and horror. He tried not to think about the crime itself or Jerome's involvement until Arthur had completed his early assessment. One thing he couldn't shake was why Henderson had called *him* with his dying breath. He also wished he could have understood what he'd said.

'Harry! Shall we?' said Arthur, ready to walk him through the scene. 'Right, it's a bit of a mess in here, and until I've examined both victims and carried out a full forensic inspection of the scene, we can only go by what we see.' On the living room side of the black quartz worktop, Arthur pointed to the drops of blood by his feet. 'Assuming there is no knife wound on the girl, DC Henderson was stabbed here. The spatter on the white panel board beneath the worktop shows the angle at which the blade was withdrawn.'

Harry said, 'Miss Kerr witnessed the attack, though she couldn't determine how many times he was stabbed.'

'From the small amount of spatter, it would have been a quick, single thrust.' Arthur turned his attention to the worktop. 'I'm a little puzzled by the blood on the corner of the worktop and the longer drips on the panel below.'

'Miss Kerr alleges that Henderson struck her in the face, and she hit her head as she fell to the floor. She became unconscious shortly after.'

'The injury to her head. Was it to the front, back, or side?'

'The forehead.'

Arthur gestured across the worktop to the other side of the kitchen. 'As you can see, the largest knife from the block is missing. Probably an eight-inch blade and conceivably the murder weapon. It would be nice if we could find it, but from a quick look around, it's not anywhere obvious.'

Harry walked around to the kitchen area and examined the knives, observing the distinctive silver bands around the handles. 'If Miss Hillingdon grabbed the knife, she wouldn't have just reached over the worktop – she would have had to come all the way around to fetch it. Considering she was on the sofa when Henderson attacked Miss Kerr, she must have moved fairly quickly.'

'I tend to find these things happen in the blink of an eye. Miss Kerr's knowledge of events could be a little clouded.'

'Fair point.'

Arthur continued, 'The lack of blood and the random drops between here and the coffee table suggest that there was a scuffle.'

'DC Henderson was fighting with someone after he was stabbed?'

'I'd say so, yes. Though it didn't last long, and from the trail of blood, DC Henderson's journey from the middle of the room was straight out of the front door.'

'But seconds before falling unconscious, Miss Kerr claims he grabbed Miss Hillingdon and forced her towards the balcony, leading us to conclude he threw her over.'

'The thing is, there's no trail of blood to or on the balcony. I'd say she's either mistaken or *misleading* us.' Arthur's phone rang, and he excused himself to answer. 'That was my colleague from downstairs. There are no visible knife wounds on Miss Hillingdon's body. DC Henderson, on the other hand, was stabbed numerous times. Going back to what you said earlier, if he'd received that many wounds in this apartment, there would have been a lot more blood. In fact, he would have barely made it out of the apartment, let alone the building.'

'Are you saying he was stabbed only once in the apartment and the rest of the wounds were inflicted outside?'

'I'm not saying, Harry. It's what the evidence tells us. My colleague is certain that most of the wounds on DC Henderson's body happened exactly where he was discovered.'

'Could Miss Kerr be lying?'

'Not necessarily. Confusion is highly plausible under the circumstances, and let's not forget about her concussion, but . . .'

'I sensed there was a *but* coming?'

'A couple of things bother me. If you take a look at the worktop where her head struck against it, there are fresh handprints on either side. I'd lay money on these being her prints.'

'And?'

'The handprints are evenly spaced. You said Miss Kerr claimed she was hit and fell backwards. If that were the case, I'd have expected the back or side of her head to have struck the worktop, not the front. But I must stress there are many factors involved, so her account is not improbable.'

'I know that face, Arthur. What's on your mind?'

'It's hard to imagine that in the midst of being punched, she would have placed a hand neatly on either side of where she hit her head. It looks as though she rested her hands to position herself.'

'Are you suggesting the injury was self-inflicted?'

'That's your suspicious mind at work, Harry. I'm saying it might not have happened the way Miss Kerr remembers. Confusion, concussion, and trauma can all play a part. It seems more likely she was knocked to the floor, used the worktop to pull herself up, and her assailant smashed her head into it with brute force.'

'I've had plenty of cases where the victim has a disjointed memory of events.' Harry paused. 'You've got that look again.'

Arthur walked over to the window and knelt beside a sofa cushion. 'There's a bloodstain on this cushion, and it's nowhere near the trail of DC Henderson's blood. At some point, the cushion was tossed over here, hit the window, and left a tiny smear on the glass. Also, if you look around, the small ornamental items look as though they've been swiped off the shelf. Yet the shelf is nowhere near where the scuffle took place. The same goes for the mess beneath the display unit over there. There's no doubt something awful occurred in here, but certainly not in the way your witness describes. The scene is all wrong.'

'It's been staged?'

'Not all of it, just parts. The question is why and by whom?'

'After being stabbed, I'd imagine wrecking the place would have been the last thing on Jerome's mind.'

'I agree, but pain and anger go hand in hand.' Arthur scratched his head. 'The final thing that bothers me is when I opened the dishwasher – the heat was fairly intense. There are just three cups inside. Who washes three items?'

'Seems a little odd. Maybe she has OCD or something. We all have our little quirks,' said Harry.

'Dare I ask?'

'Cotton wool. Can't touch the stuff.'

Arthur gave him a strange look and said, 'Intriguing. My point is, it was set for a mini wash. On average, a mini wash takes around thirty to forty minutes, and for the cups to be as warm as they are, the cycle would have been running within the last ninety minutes. If DC Henderson burst into the apartment as Miss Kerr says, I doubt he was popping by for a cup of tea.'

'So he could have been inside long before events unfolded?'

'Either that or there were more than three people here. Someone went to the trouble of starting the dishwasher *after* DC Henderson was stabbed.'

Harry said, 'Okay, so DC Henderson was knifed once inside the apartment and, according to your colleague, multiple times on the pier. Sarah Kerr claims Melanie Hillingdon stabbed him, which may well be the case. But I doubt Miss Hillingdon chased Jerome downstairs to finish him off, came back up, started the dishwasher, and was so overcome with guilt that she jumped off the balcony. And if Miss Kerr was unconscious, there had to be a fourth person involved, which she failed to mention in her statement.'

'A pretty valid assessment. The crime scene was staged to confuse us. What they didn't count on was someone opening the dishwasher.'

'I'll be sure to ask Miss Kerr when I speak to her in the morning. Right, I'll leave you to give this place a thorough going over. Let me know if you find the murder weapon. If not, I'll get the divers to search the marina first thing.'

Close to the body of Jerome Henderson, Harry rested his elbows on the rail and viewed the boats moored in the marina. The water lapped against the hulls. Shaking his head in disbelief, Harry glanced over at Melanie and turned to face Jerome, wishing he'd pressed him earlier about his final task before heading home. He'd started to doubt whether the detective constable was mixed up in all this, but now he didn't know what to believe. Either he was involved from the beginning, or he'd discovered something that had cost him his life.

45

Christmas Eve

Due to walking Harper through the case and telling him about his trip to Toronto, Lenny didn't get to sleep until well after midnight. Harper's interest surprised him; though once again, he'd shied away from talking about anything supernatural. Opening his eyes, he stared at the ceiling and stretched while yawning. He reflected on not catching the killer but was heartened to have steered the Canadian police in the right direction. Sitting up, he let out a frightful yelp and reached for his chest at the sight of Harper staring at him from the edge of the bed.

'Jesus Christ, Harper. You've got to stop sneaking up on me like this.'

'Sorry, I brought you some coffee. It's probably lukewarm now.'

'Er, thanks. Exactly how long have you been sitting there?'

'About ten minutes or so.'

'I *hope* you know how creepy that sounds.'

'You looked peaceful. It seemed a shame to wake you.'

'Okay. That doesn't make me any less uncomfortable.'

'I'm joking. I walked in seconds ago and saw you stirring. Here.'

Lenny took the cup and sipped. The hot coffee alleviated what was fast becoming an awkward situation.

Harper said, 'I needed to wake you because I've found something that's going to blow your mind. Meet me at the kitchen table in five.'

Lenny watched him leave. The cheek of it, giving him orders in his own apartment. He'd take as long as he bloody wanted. Checking his phone, he saw a message from Harry. Melanie Hillingdon was dead. Not quite the start to the day he was expecting. Leaning against the headboard, he sipped his coffee and closed his eyes. What could Harper have discovered? Eager to find out, he couldn't get out of bed quickly enough. He threw on a shirt and grabbed his coffee.

Sitting at the table with a smile on his face as he spread butter over a slice of toast, Harper said, 'I knew you wouldn't be long. Toast?'

Among the files scattered across the table, along with his laptop, Lenny spotted the rack of toast in the centre and a jug of fresh orange juice next to two empty glasses. 'Yeah, go on,' he said. 'Where'd you get the orange juice?'

'The shop.'

This was all getting a bit weird for Lenny. He pulled out a chair. 'Come on then, blow my mind.'

Harper passed him a slice of toast and said, 'This guy has a high victim rate.'

'What makes you say that?'

'It takes time to master such a brazen method. The first two to four kills would have been messy as he honed his technique. Unless there's DNA evidence, it's unlikely you'll discover his early victims or link them to him, and I doubt he'd ever confess to those.'

'How come?'

'He'll want to convince everyone he has always been in control and will distance himself from acts of clumsiness.'

'But isn't he being clumsy now?'

'No. He is being overconfident. Big difference. It's how a lot of serial killers end up getting caught. That being said, if it hadn't been for a bizarre happening, which I'm not even going to try to get my head around, nobody would know anything about this man. For him to get to the level where he is snatching young women off the street is beyond arrogance. You only get to that stage when you consider yourself invincible.'

Wide-eyed and unaware he'd leaned in closer, Lenny sat upright and said, 'How the hell do you know all this?'

Harper reached for another slice of toast. 'You seem to forget I was imprisoned for many years with the worst of the worst. How they loved to talk and boast. It was tough to sit through, and it takes a strong stomach, but with so much time on your hands, what else are you going to do? By talking about their horrific crimes, they relive them. Some seek notoriety and consider what they've done to be their legacy. That's why they hold back essential information. As the years go by, if only for a short time, they'll put themselves in the public eye, ready to reveal the location of a victim or confess to another crime. But you already know this.'

Lenny said, 'What about you? If you were back inside, would you talk and boast about your crimes to other inmates?'

Harper stopped chewing and put his half-eaten slice on the plate. 'You know my past and have written books about me. It saddens me that you've asked such a question.'

Lenny shifted in his seat, a little unnerved, and pointed to the crime photo of Reagan Scott. 'I'm just curious to know the difference between a killer capable of this and a killer like you.'

'Shame, disgrace, remorse. There are so many words to express how I feel about the innocent lives I took, but I don't regret taking the life of Joseph Webster or the lives of those sick bastards who abused me, Elaine, and countless others. I am a killer, though, Lenny, and that's a fact. So don't ever cross me.' He smiled and picked up his toast.

Lenny poured a glass of orange juice and said, 'Let's get back on track here. Telling me you've discovered there might be a lot more victims is hardly blowing my mind, is it? Because I'm not being funny, Harper, but I imagine the police already suspect as much.' Lenny put the glass to his lips.

'No. I'm telling you I've found him.'

Without taking a sip, Lenny eased the glass away. 'I beg your pardon?'

'His name is Carlton Lee, and I know where he will be tonight.'

'I hope you're not messing with me again.'

Harper shook his head. 'I'm not messing with you, Lenny. Take a look at this . . .' He pushed the laptop in front of him and clicked on the white arrow in the centre of the screen.

A video played, and Lenny watched a live recorded performance of Asa Finch and The Redpolls. 'I've looked into these guys and viewed a number of clips. The killer isn't a member of the band.'

'Keep watching.'

As is usually the case, the camera focused mainly on the singer. The camera zoomed in on the bass player. Next up was the drummer. And finally, the camera panned across to the keyboard player. 'Christ on a bike, that's him.' Lenny leaned in for a closer look to be sure. 'It fucking *is* him. Bloody hell.'

'You're right about him not being a member of the band,' said Harper. 'He's a session musician who's performed on five occasions with Asa Finch's Redpolls, twice in Canada and three times in the UK. Originally from Southampton, he gets hired for recording sessions and live performances.'

'How long did it take you to find this?'

'Not too long. I got lucky. You'd already suspected the band, and with the Canadian connection, I continued to look into them and watched so many of their videos. When I was about to give up and go to sleep, I came across a mobile phone clip from somebody who was at the gig in Toronto, posted the night *before* Annalise Fournier turned up in England. By then, I'd become familiar with the band members, so when someone different appeared, I looked closer and recognised the man from the e-fit. I researched who'd played in the band that night and discovered his name.'

Lenny pointed to the laptop. 'Is this the Toronto concert?'

'No. This one is a recording of the performance in Manchester around the time Louise Norris was murdered. I found this on his website, along with all the bands he's played with and on what dates. I checked for any articles about other murdered or missing young women and matched them to the area and date he was performing.'

'And?'

'Well,' said Harper. 'We know about Louise Norris and Reagan Scott, but I found four other possible victims over the past six years from Brighton, Leeds, Amsterdam, and Ontario. There could be more, but not all news sites from other countries are accessible.'

'Harry Baxendale said the National Crime Agency is looking into the case. They'll be running a search for potential victims. I'm envious, but impressed you managed to put a name to his face. So come on, tell me where he's performing tonight – somewhere in Canada, I presume?'

Harper wore a smile like he'd just found the Holy Grail. 'Here in London, Kentish Town, to be exact.'

Lenny laughed. 'That can't be right. I only got back from Canada yesterday afternoon. The police had a copy of the e-fit. They'd have picked him up at the airport if he'd tried to leave the country.'

Harper clicked on Carlton Lee's website and showed him. 'He's booked to tour with an Icelandic solo artist called Thordia, starting tonight with a Christmas special featuring various bands at the Kentish Town Forum.'

'She'll be short a keyboard player then, won't she? Because there's no way that bloke will be there. I'll wager he's already in hiding.'

'Well, in case he isn't, you should probably call your detective friend.'

'One, he's not a friend, and two, perhaps I should check this music special out myself, just to be sure.'

'I imagine the event was sold out months ago,' said Harper.

'There'll be a tout on a street corner somewhere. There always is at these things. It'll probably cost me a small fortune, though. If he is there, which he won't be. But *if* he is, I can give Harry a call to come and make the arrest.'

'It's going to cost you two small fortunes because I'm coming with you.'

'Not on your nelly. One, it's far too risky, and two—'

'For Christ's sake, Lenny. Do you have to count everything? I'm coming – end of.'

46

Christmas Eve

Exhausted when he climbed into bed, no matter how hard he tried, sleep evaded Harry. He churned away the hours, musing over the disturbing scenes of the previous night and how to proceed with his investigation. In the end, he took a walk and found a busy café. If only for a short while, a full English and a cup of tea appeased what ailed him. As expected, Arthur messaged early to let him know he couldn't locate the murder weapon. Harry anticipated this news and had already requested the attendance of police divers. So close to the crime scene, the marina seemed the obvious destination to dispose of a murder weapon. Whether they would find the knife was another matter.

He had been dreading this morning's briefing in the incident room, one of the many reasons he couldn't sleep. Rocked by what had happened, the officers in his team were quiet and dismayed.

Standing before them, Harry said, 'I know this is difficult, but I want to make it clear that at this stage, there is no hard evidence to suggest DC Henderson is guilty of any wrongdoing. It's up to us to find out exactly what occurred in the apartment and on the pier. I want you to knock on every door in the building. Access any CCTV you can, whether from shops, dash cams, or video doorbells. Check the boats in the marina. Someone might have been aboard at the time and seen something relevant. Find me some witnesses.

And while you're down there, locate Jerome's car.' DCS Falconer entered and stood at the back of the room.

'DC Pence, did you find out anything of significance from Melanie Hillingdon's parents?'

'They revealed she was quite a demanding child and a troubled teenager. She self-harmed, ran away, and attempted to overdose three years ago on her nineteenth birthday. With the aid of private therapy, she turned her life around, started a new job, and met James Harding. Her parents said he was brilliant and helped her a lot. They assumed she was happy and were unaware of Mr Harding's death. Data forensics now have her computer and will provide an update soon.'

'Good to know.'

Alex Pence added, 'Oh, and the financial checks on both James and Melanie revealed nothing of importance.'

'Okay, you and DC Rocastle go to Jerome's home and seize any computers or electronic devices. Give the place a thorough search for anything that might help our inquiries, but be respectful about it.'

When the room had emptied, DCS Falconer closed the door and, in a firm but calm tone, said, 'This is an absolute disaster. I'm being bombarded with calls from the press, and I'm getting grief from my superiors. Was DC Henderson involved in all of these murders?'

'I'd like to prove he wasn't, sir.'

'We can but hope. After our recent bad press, we could do without any further disgrace and embarrassment. Wrap this up, Harry. Don't make me regret putting you on this case instead of DI Jennings.' DCS Falconer's comment stung. He'd been expecting it, though. His only surprise was that it hadn't come sooner.

*

Visiting hospitals was becoming a little too regular for his liking. Fortunately, both Rebecca Heaton and Sarah Kerr were in Medway Maritime Hospital. First, he checked on Rebecca. Her recovery was going well, and she could string a few sentences together before the pain set in. The doctor had good and bad news: Rebecca had recalled some of her past and now recognised her close family; however, she remained unable to call to mind more recent events, specifically those leading up to her injuries. He added that this was commonplace, and her memory could return at any time. It could be a matter of hours or a few days. Hours he had; days, probably not. When he left the room, he warned the police constable guarding Rebecca's door to stay alert and not let anybody enter the room without being certain of who they were.

Like Rebecca, Sarah Kerr had a single room and a police constable guarding the door. Until Harry knew for certain there were no other suspects to apprehend, both women warranted round-the-clock protection. The constable informed him she had hardly spoken and, as of yet, had no visitors. It astounded Harry that none of her family had dropped by to see how she was doing. Sarah was sitting upright in bed, her head heavily bandaged. The swelling around her eye had eased slightly overnight.

Sarah turned to face him. 'Detective Inspector Baxendale. My first visitor.' Her voice was low and tired. He presumed that strong painkillers were the reason for her tranquil state.

'How are you, Miss Kerr?'

'Oh, considering I was nearly killed, I'm just grand.'

'Have your parents been informed?'

'I've spoken to them, yes. They'll be catching a flight from Dubai today, tomorrow, next week – who knows?'

'I'm sure they are deeply concerned.'

'Don't project what you assume they should feel. My parents were not blessed with a caring nature.'

'Is there anybody else I could call for you?'

'If there were, do you not think I would have called them myself?'

Harry was done stalling with the softly-softly approach. 'If you're up to it, I'd like to ask you about last night.'

'Finally, we get to the reason you're here. I'm pretty sure I already answered a ton of questions.'

'Yes, you did. But you were disorientated at the ambulance. After a traumatic event, it's always a good idea to get a second statement to make sure the information is correct. Victims often remember things differently or details they failed to provide in their original statement.'

'Wait, you were there last night? I don't remember seeing you,' she said.

'Does that not prove my point?'

'I must have been in a worse state than I imagined. One might also think you're trying to catch me out. Should I have a lawyer here?'

'Your call, Miss Kerr, but this is merely a formality. A young woman and a police officer were killed due to an incident in your apartment. At this time, you are the only witness we have who can shed light on last night's tragic events.'

'Well, when you put it like that, I suppose I'm still trying to process everything. Poor Melanie.'

'Bearing in mind what's happened, your reaction is quite normal. Do I have your permission to record this interview? It's mostly for my benefit.'

Sarah agreed and explained everything to Harry, and for the most part, it mirrored her previous statement. Though she did alter how she hit her head and fell to the floor after DC Henderson's punch. Now it was time to dissect it and get her to elaborate.

'So, you only opened the door to DC Henderson because you recognised him from our previous visit on the twenty-third of December. You'd never seen him before or since?'

'No. Never. But by the way he barged in and argued with Melanie, it was obvious they were on more familiar terms.'

'What did they argue about?'

'From the moment he entered, it was all such a blur. Lots of shouting until it got out of control. I did pick up one or two words. Something about a shopping mall and what happened in Sheernon or Sheersea.'

'Sheerness?' said Harry.

'Yes, that was it.'

'Okay. In the statement you gave to Detective Constable Pence, you said DC Henderson's punch caused you to fall backwards and strike your head against the worktop. You now say you managed to stay on your feet by using the worktop to steady yourself but were on the floor seconds later.'

'Yes. I don't know why I got that part wrong. Confused, I suppose. I've had a few slaps across the face, but I've never been punched. While holding onto the worktop, a hand clutched the back of my head, and an explosion of silence followed. There was a warm, trickling sensation on my forehead. I reached up to touch it and saw blood on my hand. My legs buckled, and the last thing I recall was Melanie plunging a knife into his stomach.'

'To be clear, you never witnessed DC Henderson march Melanie towards the balcony?'

'No. I must have surmised and formed the image in my mind because I'd heard others discussing the incident.'

'Who?'

'The paramedic. A police constable. Maybe the detective I spoke to. I can't be sure.'

She was right. Anyone could have been speculating within earshot. 'At this stage, we're not certain he did throw her off the balcony.'

'Then who did?'

Harry didn't reply and fired another question her way. 'In the dishwasher were three cups. Is it usual for you to run the cycle for so few items?'

'What a strange thing to ask. I don't see the relevance, but no, I'd wait until there was at least half a load.'

'Can you explain why it had been on around the time of the incident?'

'No, I can't. It shouldn't have been.'

'Miss Kerr, was there anybody else in the apartment at the time DC Henderson entered?'

'Of course not. I would have said so. Wait! The knife block is in the corner above the dishwasher. Melanie could have easily leaned against it when she reached for one of the knives. I've accidentally turned it on this way before.'

Harry recalled the layout of the kitchen. He'd need to check for himself if it was possible. 'You stated previously that you didn't know Melanie Hillingdon. In fact, you were "quite certain." Can you tell me why you lied?'

'I was protecting her.' Sarah paused; her eyes widened. 'Something has occurred to me, and I should probably disclose it now.'

'Go ahead.'

'She showed up at my apartment the day you came to see me with DC Henderson. She was in such a state and said she'd ended her relationship with James Harding the previous night. He'd threatened to do something stupid.'

'Like what?'

'Kill himself. But if I had a penny for every person I've ended relationships with who'd said something similar. She'd also claimed someone wanted to kill her, and she needed somewhere to hide for a few days. I didn't think she meant it. I could tell she was frightened, but I assumed she was blowing everything out of proportion.'

'Had you known Melanie Hillingdon long?'

'Just over a year. I met her through Ryan on an evening out. We weren't close at first and only met occasionally. Oddly, I've seen a lot more of her in recent weeks.'

'Miss Hillingdon was in your apartment when we dropped by, wasn't she?'

Sarah lowered her head. 'Yes, she was. I'm sorry I didn't say. But I couldn't have known what was going to happen.'

'And when I mentioned seeing someone on the balcony?'

'It was her. Oh, God, am I in trouble now?'

'If you had no idea what was going on, I doubt you'll be in any trouble. Melanie never mentioned Jerome Henderson?'

'Never. We weren't close enough to be involved in each other's personal lives. I was just helping out.'

'And yet you knew about her relationship with James Harding?'

'Well, yes, but just through general chit-chat.'

'Did she ever disclose to you that Mr Harding was dead?'

'No,' she said, and pointed to a newspaper on the table next to the bed. 'I only found out this morning. Though – no, it's probably nothing.'

'Let me decide if it's nothing, Miss Kerr.'

'Melanie said hurting him was the cruellest thing she had ever done. I assumed she was talking about ending the relationship.'

'During her time in your apartment, can you describe her general mood?'

'I told you. She was on edge. Afraid.'

'Anything else?'

'What do you mean?'

Harry said, 'Did she display any signs of depression?'

'You think she might have jumped?'

'I don't know, Miss Kerr. I know she had a history of mental health problems, and I'm exploring all possibilities.'

'She was a quiet girl. Sometimes I heard her crying in the bathroom. On one occasion, I entered the bedroom, and she – well, her jeans were around her knees, and she was cutting her inner thigh. She panicked, pulled up her trousers, and I left the room in a hurry. We never spoke about it.' Sarah's eyes glazed over. 'Is it true what they're saying in the news about Melanie and your colleague being murderers?'

Her use of the word "colleague" unsettled Harry, as though it attributed a sliver of guilt to him. 'I have no idea where the media got that story, and I can't comment on an ongoing investigation. Okay, thank you for your help, Miss Kerr, and for clearing up a few discrepancies. If I need to ask you any more questions, I'll be in touch. Here's my card in case you remember anything more. No detail is too small.'

Harry didn't know what to make of Sarah Kerr. Since their first meeting, his opinion had wavered. Was she unfortunate to have been caught up in this mess – or a brilliant liar? He contemplated travelling to Maidstone to see Lucy but called to find out she had been discharged earlier and was now staying with her mum and dad for Christmas. Lucy revealed that while going through all the unread messages on her phone, she'd not long read about the incident at the marina. Harry said he would explain everything later and arranged to meet her for dinner, his treat.

47

Christmas Eve

At Chatham Maritime Marina, police tape remained around the area of the dock crane. Harry stared at the spot where Jerome was murdered. The crime scene cleaners had already been there, and if not for the memory, you wouldn't know anything out of the ordinary had taken place. Although it was still early in their search, the police divers had found nothing.

Outside the empty apartment where Arthur and his team had worked through the night, Harry put on a protective suit and overshoes before entering. The markers and residue of chemicals around the place suggested Arthur and his team had been busy, but it was clear they had more work to do. Drawn towards the worktop, he knelt down to examine Jerome's blood spatter on the white panel board beneath. The longer drips, as Arthur had pointed out, were probably from Sarah's injury.

Harry sat on his backside and observed the room from a different angle. How he'd love to know what had transpired here! He focused on the panel board and skirting. Away from the main body of blood, he discerned a pink spot resembling a paint drip in the curved groove of the skirting. Perhaps a speck of blood had evaded a previous cleaning attempt. Had Arthur or one of his team missed it or simply assumed it was part of the crime scene? Questioning Arthur's ability would not go down well, so unless it was necessary, it wasn't worth mentioning.

Climbing to his feet, Harry walked around the counter into the kitchen area and examined the dishwasher. The preselected cycle was a mini wash. He reached for a knife in the block, repeatedly pressing his waist against the buttons, and on the sixth attempt, he succeeded. Sarah had said she'd done it before, and although it took a few attempts, it was possible. As he left the building, his phone rang. Arthur had news.

Harry entered the mortuary and found Arthur washing his instruments in the large aluminium sink. Two bodies lay out on separate slabs, one of which was Jerome Henderson. He presumed the body hidden under a white sheet was Melanie Hillingdon.

'Ah, Harry. That was fast.'

'Yeah, there was a lull in the traffic. Quick question – if blood has been cleaned from a surface but a pink drip remains, can you collect a DNA sample from it?'

'Unlikely. Cleaning agents, particularly bleach, contaminate and degrade DNA.'

'Do you have any luminol spray?'

'Are you planning on taking my job, Harry?'

'No, I just need to check something.'

'Will you be using it today?'

'Yes.'

'I'll prepare a bottle before you leave, but I should mention luminol has a tendency to destroy DNA as well. So if you're expecting me to obtain a sample from the so-called "pink drip," cover it first.' Arthur walked towards the covered body. 'Right, let's start with Miss Hillingdon.' He raised part of the cover to reveal her right hand. 'If you look here, there are a few marks from the fall, but no blood.' He marched around and uncovered the other side. 'What do you see?'

'Clean hands,' said Harry.

'Clean hands, indeed. Now, it's not always the case that the perpetrator would have blood on their hands after stabbing someone, but we're talking about seven wounds to the stomach and chest. You'd expect to see some spatter on her hands, the top of her body, or the threads of her clothes. But other than some blood on the inner thigh of her jeans due to recent self-harm, there is not a speck to be found.'

'Are you saying it's impossible for Melanie Hillingdon to have murdered Jerome Henderson?'

'Nothing is ever impossible, Harry. She could have washed her hands after the attack – but not her clothes. Nevertheless, it seems unlikely she would have gone to the trouble of cleaning up after committing murder, only to leap off the top of a building shortly afterwards.'

'Normally I'd agree, but I've since discovered Miss Hillingdon had severe mental health problems.'

'Yes. I gathered from the self-inflicted scarring on various parts of her body that she was a troubled young girl.'

Harry said, 'The actions of anyone experiencing some form of breakdown can often lead to bizarre decision-making. I've spoken with Sarah Kerr, and she explained how distressed Melanie was in the days leading up to the incident. She'd also caught her self-harming in the bedroom, and this could have literally pushed her over the edge.'

'What about the dishwasher and the mysterious fourth person?'

'Miss Kerr says there was nobody else in the apartment. As for the dishwasher, she suggested Melanie could have pressed against it accidentally when reaching for the knife. After a few attempts, I established it's possible.'

Arthur appeared disheartened. 'Something about this doesn't add up. Anyway, let's talk about the knife.'

'The divers haven't located the murder weapon.'

'Okay, but that's not what I was going to say.' Arthur walked over to the counter, picked up a folder, and stood over the body of Henderson. 'Look here.' He removed a couple of enlarged photographs and passed them to Harry. 'I had a former colleague at the hospital send me these pictures of Lucy Fenton's knife wound. I also read the report. She was fortunate the knife struck her rib and prevented it from being more serious. Note the faint serrations around the edge of the wound, and now look at the wounds on DC Henderson.'

Harry inspected both thoroughly. 'Several look similar.'

'Don't they just?' said Arthur. 'When a serrated blade is drawn over the skin surface, it can, but not always, leave serrations, which you can clearly see on three of the wounds. With these incidents being so closely linked, there is every chance it's the same knife.'

'If the knife is found, would it be possible to tell?'

'It would in this case. During Lucy Fenton's X-ray to check that there was no further damage, a tiny metal fragment was discovered and removed before she was stitched up. It had broken off from the serrated edge and wedged into her lower false rib. Find the murder weapon, and I bet we'll be able to match the fragment to the blade and determine that the same knife was used on Mr Bishop, Lucy, and DC Henderson here.'

As Harry left Arthur's practice, he called the dive supervisor, PC Richard Kenworthy, and stressed the importance of locating the murder weapon. They'd carry out a thorough search regardless of what he'd said, but he agonised over the possibility of them coming up empty-handed. The new information Arthur had provided sent his mind into disarray. If Lucy and Jerome were attacked with the same knife, Melanie must have taken it from Sarah Kerr's kitchen for someone to use at the mall and sneaked it back into Sarah's apartment later. Was Lucy right about Harry being the target? If Melanie and DC Henderson *were* accomplices, they would have known the net was closing in and conceivably hatched a plan to take him out of the equation. What about James Harding? Maybe he'd discovered what was going on and threatened to use the information against Melanie if she left him. Could she have roped him into her plan? And who was wearing the blue parka – James Harding or Jerome Henderson? Both seemed unlikely to Harry, especially as he had misgivings about Jerome's involvement. As for James, the lad didn't seem capable; however, love had a way of making people act out of the ordinary.

The first thing Harry did when he walked into the station was ask if any witnesses had come forward. The reply was an emphatic no. The quest for CCTV footage regarding DC Henderson's murder was also unproductive. His next step was to find out Jerome's location at the time Lucy was stabbed. A police constable pointed him towards the desk of DI Jennings.

'Hi, Samantha.'

'Harry,' she said with a wide, snarky grin, laying her pen flat on the desk. 'What can I do for you? Finish solving your case, perhaps?'

'Very funny,' he said, unamused.

'I'm serious. They should have given the case to me. I would have made an arrest *before* the body count started to rise.'

'Yeah, yeah. Of course you would.'

'You don't believe me? I bet—'

'Sam, please! I just need to know if Jerome Henderson was with you on the afternoon PC Fenton was stabbed.'

'All right, Harry. Blimey. Yes. We were interviewing a suspect for one of my cases.'

'Great. I had to be sure. I'm sorry if I sound a little off.'

'It's fine. Do you want to talk about it over coffee?'

'Not right now. But thanks.'

Harry slumped into the chair at his desk. It must have been James Harding wearing the blue parka, after all. DC Alex Pence approached his desk and informed him that Jerome's phone was password protected and that his laptop had, so far, revealed nothing incriminating. Harry wasn't expecting digital forensics to uncover anything else and knew it might be difficult to prove Jerome's innocence. His career was going to be linked to yet another police failure. At this rate, he'd be back in uniform doing crowd control at football matches by the end of the month. After the stress he'd been under, policing sporting events didn't sound so bad. Enough with the pessimism! He jerked forward and swivelled in his chair.

'Alex!'

'Yes, guv?'

'See if you can push digital forensics to open DC Henderson's phone. We need access to his Tinder account and private messages to find out if he had alibis for the murders of Perry, Bishop, and James Harding.'

'Didn't he visit Harding's crime scene with you?'

'Yes, he did, but that doesn't mean he didn't kill him. We need to prove otherwise.'

Harry jumped up from his seat, grabbed his jacket from the back, and marched out of the station. He drove to The Sad Dog's

Smelly Breath in Chatham. He'd been meaning to revisit the pub to check the CCTV from the night he followed Jerome there but had struggled for time.

When Harry arrived, he explained the circumstances to the landlady, and without a fuss, she allowed him to view the footage in her office. Jerome entered the pub, ordered a pint, and wandered to the rear of the premises to watch football on the big screen. He spoke to no one until he tapped Harry on the shoulder. Harry fast-forwarded the video to when he left Jerome alone and continued watching to see what he got up to. He spent most of the next hour talking to an attractive woman before escorting her outside, where a taxi was waiting. Jerome watched her leave, returned to finish his pint, and left in a taxi fifteen minutes later at eleven thirty. Harry noted the name of the taxi company and called them. They confirmed they had dropped him home. From what he had seen, Jerome's actions were not those of a man about to jump in his car and drive to Sheerness to commit murder.

Harry checked the CCTV for December 20, the night Fred Perry was murdered, and lo and behold, Jerome was in the pub. Judging by his inebriated state when he slumped into the taxi at chucking-out time, there was no way he was responsible for Perry's murder. It was pointless to check the recordings from the day Craig Bishop was murdered, as Henderson would have been at work that afternoon. Harry saved both recordings onto a memory stick and sealed it in an evidence bag.

Upon his return to the station, Harry discovered Jerome was at his desk at the time of Bishop's murder. DC Pence informed him they had accessed Jerome's phone, and when Harry examined the messages, they matched the video evidence. He marched straight to DCS Falconer's office and knocked on the open door.

'Come in, Harry.' He stopped what he was doing, put down his pen, and reached for his cup, which had the image of an old blue police box on the side.

'Nice cup, sir.'

'Ah, yes, a present from my teenage granddaughter. She's a big fan of Doctor Who.' After a couple of sips, he said, 'By the way you swaggered in here, I assume you have good news?'

'Yes, sir. Jerome Henderson has alibis for Perry, Bishop, and Harding.'

'Better news than I was expecting. What about Miss Hillingdon?'

'Not all of the crime scene can be explained, but there is enough evidence, backed up by witness testimony, to suggest that Miss Hillingdon murdered Jerome and took her own life. According to the witness, Melanie stated that hurting James Harding was the cruellest thing she had ever done.'

'Sounds like a confession.'

'It's possible that's what she was implying. She showed up at Miss Kerr's apartment hours after Mr Harding's murder.'

'Does this mean DC Henderson is in the clear?'

'Not quite, sir. We don't know why he was in the apartment. The witness said that he seemed acquainted with Miss Hillingdon, and they argued about what happened in Sheerness. It turned ugly, and he attacked both women. The thing is, we *know* Jerome was not in Sheerness at the time of the murder.'

DCS Falconer said, 'So we have evidence to suggest Melanie Hillingdon was guilty, but what's your gut telling you?'

'I'm not convinced there was a relationship of any kind between the pair. On the day of his murder, Jerome phoned to give me an update. He'd worked hard gathering information about Miss Hillingdon and said there was something he wanted to check before going home. He called me again seconds before he died. My gut says Miss Kerr isn't telling us everything, and an unidentified person in the apartment killed both Melanie Hillingdon and Detective Constable Henderson. Forensic pathologist Arthur Potts concurs. Unfortunately, we can't prove it.'

'You think the witness is protecting someone?'

'I'm not sure what she's doing, but it seems that way.'

'Regrettably, we can only follow legitimate evidence. At least you've proved DC Henderson is unlikely to have been involved in any of this. That's something to be thankful for and will certainly keep the wolves at bay. Hopefully, when Miss Heaton's memory returns, you can fit the missing pieces together and close this case.'

'I hope so, sir, though I imagine there'll be one thing she won't be able to explain.'

'If you're referring to the Canada business, let's wait and see what she says and not let our imaginations run wild. Sometimes the rational explanation eludes us. As for the main suspect being deceased, all you'll be able to do is tie everything together as best you can.'

On the way to his desk, Harry was stopped by DC Pence, who informed him they had found Jerome's car parked in the Dockside Shopping Outlet close to Sarah Kerr's apartment. He also revealed that data forensics had discovered little on Miss Hillingdon's barely used laptop and nothing to connect Jerome to Melanie on his phone or computer. However, there were emails and messages on both to back up his alibis at the time of the murders. It surprised him to learn that Melanie's computer had nothing to incriminate her or anyone else, which was a huge blow.

Harry returned to working on the case report. A ping on his computer alerted him to an email from Detective Tremblay, claiming the serial killer might have boarded a flight to Heathrow on the twenty-third of December. Tremblay insisted he couldn't be certain it was the suspect and had attached an image of the man, showing only the side of his face. His team was working through the flight manifest of three hundred and seventy-two passengers, and if they learned the man's identity, he would get back to him with a name. Harry zoomed in on the picture, but like Tremblay, he had no idea if it was him or not. He took a photo of the image and sent it to Lenny, asking if this was the guy he'd fought in the hospital. He received a call from Vivien Whitmore, the family liaison officer.

'Hi, Vivien. What's up?'

'I'm at the home of Mr and Mrs Hillingdon, and they've revealed something you should come and hear for yourself.'

48

Christmas Eve

Within the hour, Harry was on the sofa facing Mr and Mrs Hillingdon, aghast at the bombshell they had dropped. Beside him, Vivien Whitmore reacted as though she were hearing the news for the first time. He set his cup of tea on the glass table in front of him and said, 'Melanie was in a relationship with Vincent Perry when she was fifteen?'

'Yes,' said Mrs Hillingdon.

Harry worked out the dates in his head. 'Vincent would have been twenty-four.'

'That's right,' said Mr Hillingdon. 'And we weren't happy about the situation.'

Mrs Hillingdon said, 'Melanie could be a difficult child. She'd often disappear for days, even weeks.' Harry recalled DC Pence informing him about this. She nodded towards her husband. 'Terry picked her up a few times from a squat where she used to hang out. Other times, when we couldn't find her, she'd eventually come home on her own.'

'Did you report her missing to the police?'

'At first, yes, but the police, social services, and the mental health team were not ever so helpful. As time went on, we wanted to keep it as private as possible.'

Harry appreciated their dilemma. It wasn't something you'd want everybody to know. And how people love to gossip. 'Where did she meet Vincent Perry?'

'At a party. You probably think we're terrible parents for letting her go out at all hours at such a young age, but after a friend advised us to give her some space, she calmed down and stopped running away.'

'You're not terrible parents. Dealing with children who have mental health issues can leave parents exhausted and with so few options. How long were they together?'

'Barely a year,' said Mrs Hillingdon. 'As soon as we stopped fighting her about it, she ended things with him, but he was always showing up here, drunk, banging on the door in the early hours, begging her to take him back. She soon put a stop to that.' Mr Hillingdon glared at his wife, as though urging her not to elaborate. She said, 'They bumped into each other occasionally and sometimes spoke on the phone. He wanted something more, but she wasn't interested.'

'Only because he had nothing to offer,' said Mr Hillingdon.

Harry asked, 'What do you mean?'

'She had expensive taste and enjoyed being pampered,' he said. 'There were a number of boyfriends after Vincent, and she hit the jackpot with James Harding. The lad had savings and ambition. He wanted to be a chef with his own restaurant. The poor sod spent a fortune on her and would do anything to make her happy. Even that wasn't enough in the end. She couldn't leave him like a normal person. No, she had to go and kill him.'

'We haven't confirmed your daughter murdered anyone yet, Mr Hillingdon.'

'Judging by the papers, it's only a matter of time,' he said.

'We're looking into who may have leaked information to the press, but most of what the media are saying is based on guesswork and hearsay.' The demeanour of both Mr and Mrs Hillingdon suggested they'd already condemned their daughter. 'Did Melanie tell you she was leaving James?'

'She didn't have to,' he said. 'It was obvious to us she was seeing someone else, getting dolled up and disappearing all night without him. We hoped it was just a fling, but James called and told us he suspected she was going to ditch him.'

'Mrs Hillingdon, what did you mean by "she soon put a stop to that" with regard to Vincent Perry coming to the house?'

Mr Hillingdon jumped to his feet in frustration and stomped over to the bay window. 'Go on, you might as well tell them. They'll probably find out anyway.'

'Mrs Hillingdon?' Harry prompted.

'Melanie knew a young drug dealer who used to visit the squat where she hung out. Many of them were users, you see. One time, when Terry went to find her, he got into a scuffle with this dealer, and Terry pinned him against the wall. That same night, we had a visit from the young man's father, who happened to be a local villain. He knocked Terry down and repeatedly kicked him.'

'He caught me off guard,' said Mr Hillingdon, defending his pride.

'I had to drive him to the hospital afterwards. He had four broken ribs.'

'Just get to the point, love. The detective doesn't need to know every single detail.'

'Anyway, Melanie got this young man to have a word with Vincent. It turned out he knew him, and Vincent never bothered her in that way again.'

Having already guessed, Harry asked, 'This young man, did you ever catch his name?'

'Ryan Levinson.'

Mr Hillingdon said, 'Tell him how she persuaded him to have a word.'

'It's embarrassing, Terry.'

'I'll tell him then, because if that scumbag is involved in any of this, I want him arrested and charged,' he ranted, pointing his finger nowhere in particular. 'While Melanie and Vincent were together, she had him take some nude pictures of her. When they split up, she obviously wanted them back, so she offered Ryan a thousand quid and told him what was on Vincent's phone. By whatever means, Ryan acquired it from him. The thing is, he didn't take any money from Melanie and kept the phone.'

'How do you know he didn't take the money?'

'Because it was my money she was going to buy it back with. I didn't report it. The last thing I wanted was another visit from his father or his bloody heavy mob.'

Harry said, 'Are you telling me Ryan Levinson still has Vincent Perry's phone with underage pictures of your daughter?'

'I assume so,' said Mr Hillingdon. 'He told Melanie it might come in useful one day.'

'I hate to ask, but did your daughter and Ryan ever have a relationship?'

'Not a relationship as such,' said Mrs Hillingdon. 'But we used to hear them in her bedroom.'

'Having sexual intercourse?'

Embarrassed, Mrs Hillingdon hung her head low and said, 'Yes. She wanted a proper relationship, but he wasn't so keen.'

'The bastard used her,' said Mr Hillingdon. 'He'd turn up here, have his way, and sod off.' He pointed to the hallway. 'He'd come down those stairs smirking, showing me he could do what he wanted and there was nothing I could do about it.' Terry's face reddened, and anger took hold as he knocked the ornaments off the nearby windowsill. Mrs Hillingdon walked over and silently picked up the items.

Whether Melanie's behaviour and bad decisions were induced by mental health problems didn't matter. In front of Harry were two crushed parents who'd begun grieving for their daughter long before she'd died. He couldn't comprehend what they'd gone through. How Harry would love to destroy Ryan Levinson. He'd never been keen on the prick, and now he had good reason to hate him even more.

Harry said, 'I assume she was over sixteen when she was with Ryan?'

'She was, yes,' said Mrs Hillingdon. 'It used to be a regular thing, but it became less frequent when he met someone else, and even less so after she'd met James.'

'You mean this was going on while she was with James?' She nodded. 'Is there anything more you can tell me?'

'No, I don't think so,' she said, unable to hold back her tears. Through their anger and disappointment, there was something else about the couple – relief. As though a great burden had been lifted. It seemed odd that the death of a child could cause less grief now she was gone.

Harry climbed from the sofa. 'Oh, one last thing – did Melanie have a mobile phone? We've been unable to locate it.'

'Yes. James bought her a new one not long ago,' she said.

Mr Hillingdon said, 'What about the one you found in her room?'

'I doubt it works,' she said. 'It's a cheap old thing. I found it under her chest of drawers. It must have fallen down the back.'

'Would you mind if I took it anyway, Mrs Hillingdon? I should have it checked for evidence.'

'Of course. I'll go up and fetch it.'

While she retrieved the phone, Harry said, 'Mr Hillingdon, at some point, Ryan Levinson will pay for everything he has done.'

'I don't believe that for one minute. Even if he is still up to his old tricks, I doubt he'll ever spend a single day in prison. It doesn't seem fair, considering all the pain he's inflicted on others.'

Mrs Hillingdon returned and handed him the phone. It was a cheap no-frills pay-as-you-go, but it didn't look too old. The type of phone people used when they wanted complete privacy, typically used by criminals before being discarded. Harry attempted to turn on the phone, but the battery was flat.

'Do you want me to see if I can find the charger?'

'No, it's fine, Mrs Hillingdon. I'm sure I'll find one knocking about the station. Once again, my condolences.'

Harry arrived at Chatham Maritime Marina, having stopped by the station on the way to hand over the mobile phone to the tech team. He had also requested a warrant to search the Levinsons' house, which he planned to do first thing in the morning. He'd assumed the police divers would have finished as soon as it got dark, so he was surprised to see them packing away their equipment. PC Kenworthy informed him their search was complete and they hadn't located a murder weapon – a huge disappointment. Harry thanked him and took the lift up to Sarah Kerr's apartment, his final task before meeting Lucy.

Harry made small talk with the constable guarding the crime scene while he put on new coveralls. Upon entering, he turned on the lights, set the luminol spray on the worktop, and searched the cupboards. He opened the fridge – force of habit – but the bottle of Merlot looked tempting. No, he couldn't. Rummaging through the kitchen drawers, he found a plastic bag and covered the pink spot on the skirting board. Harry sprayed luminol over the panel and turned off the lights. Amid Sarah Kerr's blood, the light blue glow revealed what he presumed to be blood from a previous incident. Someone had been seriously hurt in this room before now, and he'd lay money on that person being Rebecca Heaton.

Harry retrieved his phone from his pocket and took some pictures. After a hesitant delay, he called Arthur.

'Hello, Harry. What's up?'

'I'm down at Chatham Marina.'

'Let me guess, the divers have completed their search and found nothing?'

'You guessed right.'

'That is disappointing,' said Arthur. 'Have they looked in other parts of the marina?'

'I'm confident they've been thorough. Anyway, I'm calling about why I wanted the luminol spray.'

'Ah, the pink drip.'

'I found it in Sarah Kerr's apartment beneath the worktop, close to her blood. It was between the curved groove on the skirting board. I covered the area as you suggested, and the luminol revealed something you should see. I'll send you the pictures now.' Harry waited for Arthur's response.

'That's a fair amount of blood. I'm sure you'll acknowledge we were not looking for what may well be an older crime scene, but the spot you've found is likely a mix of blood, water, and bleach. I can't deny I missed this, Harry.'

'It's fine, Arthur. This could be where Rebecca Heaton was first injured and received her skull fracture. I'm certain you would have found it before you finished your work here.'

'Perhaps.' It was clear Arthur's self-confidence had taken a hit. He said, 'Leave the cover in place. I'll get over there first thing on Boxing Day.'

'You don't have to do that. A few extra days aren't going to make much difference. As you said, it'll most probably be contaminated by bleach.'

'No, it's my error, and I know how desperately you need answers. I'll collect the sample and run a test for DNA. Who knows, we might get lucky.'

49

Christmas Eve

Lenny and Harper marched out of Kentish Town Tube station like a couple of over-excited groupies. Their excitement, however, had more to do with catching a serial killer than seeing any of the performers. They had agreed to get there early so as not to miss out on getting tickets. Lenny had expected to find a tout loitering outside the station; unfortunately, they'd arrived a little too early. The event didn't start for another three hours. With the venue less than a five-minute walk up the road, the pair wandered around in search of a tout. No joy. The familiar strains of Wham's 'Last Christmas' and a profusion of twinkling lights drew Harper's attention to a lively-looking pub on the corner. It didn't take much to persuade Lenny to join him for a festive pint before continuing their quest for tickets.

The pub was rammed with people wearing all sorts of things, from Santa suits to reindeer jumpers. Some were even dressed as elves, complete with pointy ears. The Christmas decorations were excessive, and most of the customers appeared to be much younger than Lenny. Before getting ready earlier, he had rummaged through every drawer and cupboard for something suitable to wear. He eventually found an old pair of jeans to go with his favourite threadbare sweater. Unlike Harper, who could blend in anywhere, Lenny was out of his comfort zone, and it didn't matter what he wore; he was never going to fit in with this crowd.

Surrounded by loud chatter at the bar, Lenny took a welcome sip of his pint and said, 'Getting tickets might not be as easy as I imagined. All this online bollocks has taken the fun right out of everything. I remember when you could go to a top football match and buy a ticket on the day, first come, first served. Not any more. Now it's about being a member or sitting at your computer, hoping you beat everyone else to the punch and the website doesn't crash. It's either that or getting ripped off by touts selling them for a ton of profit.'

Harper said, 'We're not going to a football match.'

'Music, football, theatre – same difference,' said Lenny. 'The touts have probably gone online as well.'

Harper smirked and sipped his lager.

A young man behind them leaned closer and said, 'Did you say you're looking for tickets?'

Lenny swivelled around on his stool. 'Yes, we are.'

'There was a geezer offering tickets in the gents just now. Two hundred and fifty quid a pair.'

Lenny said, 'Is he still there?'

'I'd imagine so. He walked in as I left.'

'Cheers, mate.' Lenny turned to Harper. 'Right, keep my seat warm – I'm going in.'

He bundled his way through the throng towards the toilets, and as the door opened, a small, thin man glared at him as he brushed past in the tight passage. Lenny entered, stared at the men standing over the urinals, and said, 'Who's selling tickets?'

There were laughs and a few expletives fired in his direction. A man using the hand dryer said the tout had just left. Probably the bloke he'd passed on the way in. He rushed out of the door, along the hallway, and tapped the man on the shoulder.

Lenny leaned into his ear and said, 'I'm looking for tickets to the forum.'

The stick-thin man looked him up and down and said, 'Yeah, right. I don't think so, mate.'

'Look, I'm not a copper. I just need two tickets for tonight's event.'

'Shouldn't you be going to see a musical in the West End at your age? Or, better still, at home watching reruns of *Midsomer Murders*.'

Lenny refrained from taking a swipe at the mouthy . . . 'Have you got tickets or not?'

The man eyed Lenny once again and backed up against the wall. 'Okay, two tickets, you say? Five hundred quid.'

'I was told two hundred and fifty for the pair.'

'The price went up.'

'Come on, mate. Don't take the piss.'

'Now they're six hundred.'

Lenny considered whether to pay up. 'Nah, you can shove them up your arse. I'll get them elsewhere.'

The man smirked. 'Please yourself.' And slunk away.

When he returned to the bar, Harper asked how he got on. Lenny said, 'No good. The bloke wanted six hundred quid.'

'You pissed him off, didn't you?'

'No. He just kept putting the price up. It's all right. He's not the only one who'll have tickets.'

'Where is he now?'

Lenny scanned the room. 'See that big bald bloke walking out the door? It's the skinny little fella behind him.'

Harper shook his head in disbelief and said, 'Give me the two hundred and fifty. I'll go and get them.'

Lenny contemplated. 'I don't know if that's such a good idea.'

'Come on, Lenny, before he disappears.'

'All right, but don't do anything stupid.' Lenny pulled out his wallet and stealthily counted the money.

'I won't. I'll buy the tickets and come straight back.' Harper took the cash and hurried after the man.

Lenny watched him leave, hoping he wouldn't come to regret his decision. He glanced around the pub. So many people chatting, laughing, and filling their bellies with food and drink. Everyone seemed to be in good spirits. An attractive woman, possibly in her mid-forties, wearing jeans and a thick striped jumper, approached. She eased her way to the bar and stood beside him. She smiled his way before attempting to catch the bartender's attention. Lenny presumed she was going to the music event, smiled back, and turned away. Best not to mingle.

She asked, 'Are you going to the forum?'

When she repeated the question, he looked around. She *was* talking to him. 'Oh, yes. I hope so.'

'You hope?'

'My friend has the tickets. I'm supposed to be meeting him here,' he said, not wanting to let on that they were obtaining their tickets illegally.

'I see. Well, you have plenty of time before it starts. I'm sure a handsome gentleman such as yourself won't be stood up.'

Lenny took her compliment and soon twigged – she had assumed he was gay. Before he had a chance to explain, she was ordering a round of drinks. After she'd paid the bartender, she moved closer to Lenny.

She asked, 'Do you live around here?'

'No. Stratford. Though I used to come up here a long time ago to cash my cheques at a pub up the road.'

'For a fee, I bet?'

He smiled. 'Of course.'

'My ex-husband used to do the same thing in Shepherd's Bush.'

'Who are you here with?'

'My daughter and her friend. They had a spare ticket and invited me along.'

'Nice of them.'

'Yeah, she's a good girl. I'm a proud mum. I must say, you don't look like the kind of guy who'd be champing at the bit to see Thordia or any of the other bands playing tonight, for that matter.'

'Thordia?'

'Tonight's main act. You've never even heard of her, have you?'

He'd forgotten the name of the artist and smiled awkwardly. 'Not until this morning.'

'It's so sweet you're going to this event for your partner.'

Should he bother to correct her? No. Best to leave it.

She said, 'It's true what they say about all the good men being gay or married.'

He couldn't take it any more. 'I'm sorry, but I may have misled you. I'm not gay.'

Her jovial demeanour faded. 'Do you mean you were pretending to be gay to avoid chatting to me? Jesus, that's a new low for me.'

'No, I wasn't trying to . . .'

Her face lit up. 'I'm just teasing.' She had an elegant smile and laugh. 'I had a feeling you weren't, but I had to keep plugging away to get you to admit it.'

He laughed and said, 'You're a bit of a card, aren't you?'

'So come on. What's your story?'

'I'm waiting for an acquaintance who's gone outside to find a ticket tout, so we can get into this event to see if we can find a serial killer.'

She smiled. 'I don't know why, but I sense there's some truth in what you say.'

'I'm too old for anything but the truth.' Lenny sipped his beer and caught sight of Harper over his shoulder. 'This is Simon Smith, the friend I was talking about.'

'Nice to meet you, Mr Smith.' She stared at Lenny. 'You still haven't told me *your* name.'

'Lenny Grey.'

She reached out and shook his hand. 'Well, Lenny Grey, if not gay, am I right to assume there's a Mrs Grey?'

Aware of the quizzical expression on Harper's face, Lenny said, 'I'll tell you later' – and turned back to – 'I'm sorry, I don't know your name either.'

'You haven't asked. I'm Florence.'

Lenny was sceptical as to whether that was her real name. 'No, I've never been married, but there was a special someone. She died last year.' Saying those words was a little unsettling.

'Oh no. I'm so sorry. I can see I've made you uncomfortable now.'

Lenny looked at her and smiled. 'No, you haven't. I was more uncomfortable weighing up what vibe I was giving off that led you to assume I was gay.'

Florence laughed. 'You're funny. Well, I should probably get these drinks over to my daughter and her friend. I can see her giving me the evil eye. It was lovely to meet you, Lenny. Who knows, perhaps we'll bump into each other inside the forum. Oh,' she said, reaching into her clutch bag. 'This is my card. If you ever want to go out for a drink or maybe dinner, call me. No pressure, of course.'

Lenny took the card but didn't know what to say other than, 'It was lovely to meet you too.'

She'd clearly noted his uncertainty and followed up with, 'You should call. It might be good for both of us.' Lenny watched her walk away and looked at the card: Dr Florence Stone, General Practitioner.

Harper said, 'Someone's been busy. You're punching above your weight, but she certainly seemed keen. What was that about you being gay?'

'Oh, it was nothing. Just banter. Anyway, how did you get on?' Harper gleefully handed him the tickets. 'Why is there blood on one of these? What the hell have you done, Harper?'

'Don't worry, he isn't dead.'

'Jesus Christ. I knew something like this would happen.'

'The man was being an absolute arse, and so was his sidekick.'

'You took on the big fella as well? I'm not happy about this, but I doubt they'll report it. Even if they did, I shouldn't think they'd get much sympathy from the police.'

Harper handed back his two hundred and fifty pounds and said, 'Something didn't seem right about beating him up for being a prick and paying him for the tickets.'

'He was a prick,' said Lenny. 'Another pint?'

'Yeah, go on. But perhaps we should go to another pub. They might come looking for us mob-handed.'

Lenny sank his pint and climbed off the stool. 'Good idea.'

After a couple of pints in a different pub, they sauntered along the road to the venue, deciding it was best to get there early and find a good vantage point. Joining the back of a long queue, it seemed everyone had the same idea. When the doors opened, the line shifted quickly. They presented their tickets, and Lenny panicked when the woman took longer to examine their tickets than the people in front. Perhaps the bloodstain concerned her.

'Ketchup,' he said.

Once inside, they jostled and snaked their way forward until they were standing a few rows from the front. Patience was going to be key, as there were three other performers before the headline act. As time progressed, people forced their way to the front, and the pair found themselves further away from the stage. It didn't take long for a persistent ache between the top of Lenny's back and shoulder to set in. He also needed the toilet. For a man of his advancing years, he'd pushed his luck with that third pint of lager.

He leaned in to Harper and shouted, 'I need to use the bog!'

'What!' said Harper.

'Toilet!'

'If you leave, you'll never make it back!'

'If I don't, I'm going to piss my new Step One boxers!'

Lenny fought his way through the horde. There were easily over two thousand people in attendance. After he'd used the facilities, he considered fighting his way back to Harper but opted to blag his way backstage. He told the brawny security guard at the door that his press pass had been stolen in the toilet. When asked for his name, Lenny gave a false one, and the man headed off to check. Lenny opened the door and furtively followed him along a busy corridor. As the man entered an office, he scurried past, searching different rooms, hoping to catch a glimpse of Carlton Lee. A young performer in one of the rooms asked who he was looking for. She had no idea who he was talking about but directed him to the last room on the left at the end of the corridor, where someone would be able to help.

As he turned the corner, he bumped into someone, knocking them off balance. Their eyes met, and Lenny was dumbstruck. In front of him stood the man he'd fought in the hospital in Toronto. Lenny remained calm as Carlton Lee apologised.

Lee's gaze narrowed as he scrutinised Lenny. 'Have we met before?'

'It's possible,' said Lenny. 'I'm a music critic, so I'm always hanging about these venues.'

'I knew you looked familiar. Well, I suppose I'll see you around.'

Lenny's prompt reply seemed to work, and he watched Lee walk away without turning back. Should he attempt to apprehend him? If it ended in disaster and he got away, he'd never forgive himself. He pulled out his phone to call Harry and viewed the text message asking if this was the man he'd fought in Canada. There was no need to zoom in for a closer look. He made the call. It rang until Harry's voicemail activated. He tried again. Still no answer. He left a message indicating where he was and who he had found.

50

Christmas Eve

The Thai restaurant in Maidstone overlooked the River Medway, and the table where Harry and Lucy sat gave them a lovely outside view. Though dark, the lighting around the river's edge and what looked like a Christmas party boat provided a perfect setting. Despite going home to change into clean trousers, an ironed white shirt, and a pair of decent shoes, Harry's appearance wasn't much different from earlier. Lucy, on the other hand, looked strikingly beautiful in her well-cut trousers and silk shirt. Her harrowing experience didn't appear to be holding her back in any way, but Harry knew appearances could be deceptive.

They had finished their starters and sipped their Thai martinis while they waited for the main course. Harry brought Lucy up to speed on the most recent developments.

'James Harding stabbed me?'

'Unless new information comes to light, yes. Though I suspect Melanie played her part in coaxing him.'

'And do you believe Melanie jumped?'

'According to her parents, she had a lot of problems. Everything she'd been responsible for could have been too much to process.'

'You sound as though you're trying to convince yourself there's nothing more to this.'

'It's not quite done and dusted. Melanie *is* complicit. Guilty of murder? Possibly. However, she didn't act alone, and I'm not talking about James Harding. Going by what everyone has said about him, James was not a murderous psychopath. I'm hopeful Rebecca will regain her memory and give us an accurate account of events.'

'You still think Ryan Levinson is involved?'

'I'm convinced he had something to do with what happened to Rebecca. And with the pictures on Vincent Perry's old phone, there's no doubt he had a hold over Melanie. The Levinsons won't appreciate me turning up on Christmas morning with a search warrant.'

Their eyes brightened as the main course was placed in front of them. Harry said, 'I won't cause too much disruption – I'm not a total grinch. But I'll leave no stone unturned when searching his room.'

'Other than her memory loss, how is Rebecca doing?'

'Great. Her injuries are healing fast, and she was allowed to go home today, so at least *they* can all have a lovely family Christmas.'

'I sense a little resentment in your tone.'

'Not for the Heatons. I'm delighted for them.'

'Ah, I assume there's trouble at home?'

'Something like that. After I'm done annoying the Levinsons, I'll be returning to the house for an awkward exchange of presents. And if nothing else comes up, I plan on sinking a bottle of brandy while listening to my favourite records.'

'Your evening sounds delightful. My mum and dad's house will be full of shrieking kids and relatives who detest each other.'

Harry raised his Thai martini. 'To the joys of Christmas.'

Lucy lifted hers and winked. 'Cheers.'

Harry grimaced. 'I don't know why I ordered this. It's bloody awful.' He signalled to the waitress and said to Lucy, 'I'm getting a pint. Do you want another one of those?'

'Nah, I'll have a pint as well.'

With the main course over, they were picturing dessert when Harry's phone rumbled in his pocket. He had a couple of missed calls and a voicemail from Lenny. Reluctant to check while at dinner, he proceeded to put it away.

Lucy said, 'If it's about the case, you should probably ring them back.'

'No, it's okay. I don't want to be rude.'

'Answer it, Harry. It's not like we're on a date. Or are we?'

'Of course not! Sorry, I didn't mean to sound so—'

'I'm only messing with you. Just go outside and call them back. I'll order our drinks and ask for the dessert menus.'

Out on the terrace, with the sharp breeze slamming against his back, Harry observed Lucy studying the menu through the window. He took out his phone, listened to the voicemail, and after several frustrating attempts to get hold of Lenny, he gave up.

'Shit!' Dinner was over. He messaged Lenny to say he was on his way and he'd get a response team there immediately. He called DCS Falconer, who said he'd inform Scotland Yard.

Harry rushed inside. 'I'm so sorry, Lucy, we have to go.' He signalled for the bill.

'What's going on?'

'You know I said the serial killer might be back in the country? Well, he is, and I've been told exactly where to find him. I need to drop you home and get to London.'

'Bollocks to that. I'm coming with you,' she said, jumping up and swiping her coat from the back of the chair.

'No, Lucy. I'm not taking any risks with you.'

'Too bad. You haven't got time to fart about taking me home. I'll wait in the car if I have to.'

There was no point in arguing. Besides, she was right; he couldn't afford to waste any time.

51

Christmas Eve

Progress was sluggish as Lenny edged his way back to Harper, boxed in until someone in front of him moved. A roar from the crowd had him casting his eyes towards the stage as the band walked on. There was Carlton Lee, behind the keyboard, waving to the excited audience. The young singer walked on to huge cheers, and the show commenced. Lenny checked his phone and read Harry's message. Though relieved, he knew Harry would be annoyed he hadn't informed him earlier. He'd argue that he didn't want to waste police time and had to be certain, while Harry would say it wasn't his decision to make. In which case, Harry would be right.

Lenny glanced up as a flurry of artificial snow descended from the ceiling. The person in front moved aside, and he pressed forward a little more. It was slow going, but he eventually found his way back to Harper, who appeared surprised to see him. Oddly, he looked as though he was enjoying himself, and why wouldn't he? This was probably a new experience for him.

Shouting into Lenny's ear, he said, 'I assume you've seen him up there on the stage?'

'Yeah, I also bumped into him backstage!'

'He didn't recognise you?'

'No! I've informed the police, and they're on their way! You should probably make yourself scarce!' Harper agreed and faded into the mesmerised crowd. All Lenny could do was wait for the arrest and talk to Harry when he arrived.

Knowing the despicable crimes he'd committed, watching a jovial Carlton Lee performing to an unsuspecting audience wasn't easy. It baffled and unsettled him how a talented musician could double up as a vile killer. But he wasn't the first monster to hide in plain sight, and he wouldn't be the last. Lenny checked his watch. It had been over an hour since he'd called Harry. With such a large, pumped-up crowd, he imagined the police were waiting backstage, monitoring all the exits and wanting to limit any disorder. Carlton Lee glanced sideways and appeared spooked. He must have seen the police waiting in the wings. Seconds later, Lenny spotted them as well, inching forward, eager to move in for the arrest. What were they waiting for?

In desperation, Lee picked up the large keyboard and hurled it towards them. Cheers rang out, everyone assuming it was part of the act. Police officers rushed forward from both sides of the stage. Lee barged past an alarmed backing singer. The bass guitarist stepped forward to confront him. Lee rolled up the leg of his jeans, pulled a knife from a sheath, and plunged it into the musician's stomach. He ran in Lenny's direction and launched himself into the hysterical crowd. Lenny couldn't see where he'd landed. Moving abruptly, the spectators at the front caused a surge, forcing people into one another. In the panic, Lenny was bundled to the floor. From his viewpoint, he witnessed the ripple effect, a chaotic scene of bodies falling and being trampled underfoot. Screams filled the air as the snow kept falling. The man on top of him shifted, and Carlton Lee came into view, knife in hand, shoving people out of the way in his frantic bid to escape. Police officers stared in vain at the edge of the stage, attempting to locate the suspect.

Lenny couldn't let him get away and climbed to his feet just as the house lights came on. He glanced at the mass of people behind him, running aimlessly in different directions, anxious to find a way out. Bodies lay unconscious and injured. Bloodied faces were all around. Lenny set off after Lee, paying close attention not to step on anyone. At the exit door he'd seen Lee crash through, a police officer writhed on the floor in agony, his forearms repeatedly slashed from a desperate attempt to defend himself. Lenny dragged the officer away from the entrance to prevent him from getting trampled.

He knelt down and placed the shell-shocked officer's hand firmly over the severed vein. 'Keep pressure on the wound. Help will be here shortly. Which way did he go?'

'That way,' he said, nodding towards the door Lenny had sneaked through earlier.

'I need to borrow this.' He grabbed the police officer's Taser.

The corridor was eerily quiet compared to the pandemonium he'd left behind, but if he listened closely, the clamour of panic and pain endured. He opened one of the dressing room doors, Taser at the ready. Three frightened crew members were cowering in the corner. He gestured for them to leave the way he'd come. He checked the next couple of rooms, but they were empty. A terrified young woman crept around the corner and stopped in front of him. Lenny recognised her as one of the backing singers on stage. He put a finger to his lips, summoned her towards him, and sent her in the same direction he'd sent the others.

Lenny peeked around the corner. There was no sign of anyone. Startled by a tap on his shoulder, he turned and fired the Taser. Harry hit the deck with a loud thud, shaking violently. 'Oh shit. I'm so sorry, Harry. What the hell were you thinking, sneaking up on me?'

Stunned and helpless, Harry's body continued to convulse. Lenny pulled out the darts and supported his head, but it provided little comfort. Harry's fearful expression forced Lenny to look up. Carlton Lee hovered over them a few feet away, his hand at his side clutching a sharp, bloodied knife.

Lenny cautiously stood tall and raised his hands in a calming gesture. 'Nobody else needs to get hurt here, Mr Lee. The police have every exit covered. There's no way out.'

Lee said, 'It's you, the guy from the hospital in Canada. I should have recognised you.'

Searching Lee's eyes, Lenny knew this wasn't going to be straightforward. Lee wasn't going to give up easily. His main concern was Harry, incapacitated at his feet. Lee stepped towards them. Lenny didn't move. He couldn't leave Harry.

'Back away,' said Lee.

'I can't do that.'

'Your call.' Lee advanced, holding the knife in a threatening manner but paused as armed police officers entered the corridor behind Lenny, aggressively identifying themselves.

Lenny raised his hands, and Lee crouched down. Using Lenny as cover, he grabbed Harry by the ankles and dragged him around the corner. About to give chase, Lenny froze at the louder screams not to move. He was thrown against the wall by an officer.

'I'm Lenny Grey. My wallet is in my inner jacket pocket. I'm the one who called Detective Inspector Baxendale.'

'Where is DI Baxendale?' said an officer as another reached into Lenny's pocket.

'You just watched him get dragged away.'

Two officers peered around the corner. One of them turned to alert the others, 'No sign of the suspect or the hostage.'

'He's unarmed, and his ID checks out.' They released Lenny and handed back his wallet. 'Sir, you need to make your way to the foyer, where an officer will take your statement.'

Although he didn't want to do as they'd suggested, their forceful nature didn't leave him much choice. When he entered the foyer, he gave a short statement to an officer and sat on the floor with his back against the wall. The place was teeming with police officers as they escorted people from the building. Paramedics waited patiently outside to provide aid to the walking wounded but were unable to help those inside until the police had secured the premises. The focus of Lenny's concern was Harry. If he hadn't stupidly stunned him with the Taser, together they would have disarmed Lee and made the arrest. A gunshot echoed throughout the building.

Lenny overheard the words *'Building secure'* on a passing officer's radio. For a moment, he assumed they'd shot Carlton Lee, but this was followed by the message, *'The suspect has fled the building.'*

Lenny thought the worst. When an armed officer appeared in the foyer, Lenny climbed to his feet and hurried over. 'Any news on Detective Inspector Baxendale?'

The officer wasn't going to respond but must have recognised him from before. 'Carlton Lee left through a fire exit and carjacked a woman at knifepoint. She said he forced another man, who identified himself as a detective, into the driver's seat. We've locked down the area and are searching for the vehicle. He won't get far.'

Lenny said, 'What about the gunfire?'

'Accidental discharge.' The officer walked away.

A woman standing nearby approached. Producing her warrant card, she said, 'PC Lucy Fenton. I heard something about an accidental discharge. What's going on – have they made an arrest?'

'No. He escaped with a hostage.'

'Who's the hostage?'

'A detective.'

'Harry Baxendale?'

'Yes, how did you know?'

'Because I work with Harry,' she said. 'How do you know him?'

'I've been helping out, but I seriously let him down tonight.'

'You're the one who called him earlier about Carlton Lee.'

'That's right,' he said.

'Who exactly are you?'

'Lenny Grey.'

'I'm sure Harry will be fine,' she said. 'Right, I'd better see if I can offer any help.'

Lenny's quest to apprehend Lee had become a complete disaster. Many people were injured, most with superficial wounds. Fortunately, there were no fatalities – at least, not yet. The bass player was on his way to hospital, as was the police officer with knife wounds. Worst of all, Lee had escaped. The odds of finding Harry alive? His muscles tightened. A visible cloak of dampness layered his skin, and the hideous discomfort of nausea grew stronger. He'd just been handed guilt's calling card. Lenny raced to the toilet and hovered over the pan. The torment of wanting to be sick lingered but didn't materialise. At the sink, he ran cold water over his hands and rinsed his face. His legs weak, he sat on the cold tiled floor. After a brief spell of contemplation, he pulled out his phone and called Harper, but he didn't answer.

52

Christmas Eve

Driving with the point of the knife occasionally pricking the back of his neck, Harry darted along the back roads. While recovering from the effects of being tasered, Lee had taken his phone, and for a fleeting moment, there was a chance of them being tracked by GPS. But a little way back, he glanced in the wing mirror and saw Lee toss it out of the window. He considered speeding up and crashing the car, but hanging over him was the fear of endangering bystanders and of Lee making his escape. Despite the circumstances, Harry still had some control. Every turn led them down a dead end or closer to the forum. Lee shouted angrily in Harry's ear from the back seat as though it were his fault. To be fair, Harry knew Kentish Town fairly well from being stationed in the borough of Camden when he was a young police constable. Although brief, it was long enough for him to find his way around. His plan was to take them back to where there would be plenty of police. As he turned onto Leighton Road, he knew exactly where they were and headed in the direction of Kentish Town train station.

At the traffic lights, a stream of people crossed the road in front of them, making their way home from what had proven to be a tragic night out. With the station on his left and the forum just along the road to their right, Harry indicated to turn. Police cars blocked the road to stop vehicles from entering or leaving the vicinity of the venue without being checked.

Lee said, 'You idiot, you've practically brought us back to where we started. You did this on purpose.'

'I'm unfamiliar with the area,' said Harry, knowing he could have found a way out if he'd wanted to.

'Just shut up and go straight ahead.' The lights turned green, but people continued to cross. 'Edge out – force them to let us pass.'

Harry eased the car forward. A man slammed the bonnet, cursed in anger, and continued on his way with a young woman. Behind him, another man who'd stopped to let them pass caught Harry's gaze. A familiar face, and for a second – *no, it can't be?* The man turned his attention to Harry's passenger in the back. Feeling the knife in his ribcage, he inched the car onward and narrowly missed a young couple as they dashed across the road. When clear of pedestrians, he sped forward to Regis Road, aware that it was another dead end full of mostly business premises and warehouses. In the rear-view mirror, he perceived the man he'd locked eyes with at the crossing, staring in his direction. *No! It's not him.*

Carlton Lee's anger hit boiling point when they came to the end of the road with nowhere to go but back towards an ever-increasing police presence. He writhed in the back seat, tense, frustrated, and swearing quietly to himself. The searchlight of a police helicopter scanned the area close to the forum. Lee knew the net was closing around them and they wouldn't get far in a stolen vehicle. Harry remained calm.

'You should give up,' he said. 'There's no way for you to escape.'

'Shut the fuck up. I need to think.'

'Nobody else has to get hurt. This would go a lot easier if you let me take you in.'

'I said shut it!' The butt of the knife cracked hard against the side of Harry's head. He instinctively reached up and glanced at the blood on his fingers. Lee said, 'Right, park over there, down the side of that warehouse behind the skip.'

With blood trickling down the side of his face, Harry didn't wait to be asked twice. Hidden from view, Lee exited the car and opened the driver's door. 'Get out.'

He shoved Harry towards the warehouse, and going by the contents of the skip, it appeared to be undergoing renovation. The door around the corner was padlocked. Lee ordered Harry to break it off with a long, thin metal bar that was protruding from a pile of rubbish against the wall. Harry could run, but what then? Get the police and come back to find he'd disappeared to kill again. No, he didn't want to lose sight of him. Remaining by his side, the opportunity might arise to overpower him. He needed to bide his time. Harry broke off the lock and pushed the door open.

'Right, inside,' said Lee.

Stepping into complete darkness, Harry felt for a switch on the wall. Of the many fluorescent lights, only a few worked, providing barely enough light to survey their surroundings. The main part of the warehouse had been stripped bare, and from the materials gathered to the side of the electric roller shutter, it looked as though this place was about to become a car repair centre. Lee shoved Harry forward towards the glazed office area. Entering the room, he ordered Harry into the small area behind the desk. Harry screamed in agony as the blade penetrated the back of his thigh. He was pushed to the floor.

'That should rid you of any ideas,' said Lee, settling onto a squeaky swivel chair, the shredded fabric exposing the flattened foam beneath, nibbled away by restless fingers.

Nauseous and light-headed, Harry said, 'You might have hit an artery.'

'Hope so.'

He took off his belt and tightened it above the wound. Energy fading fast, Harry flipped over an old metal wastepaper bin and lay flat on his back, resting his foot on the top to gain elevation.

Lee said, 'You're wasting your time attempting to save yourself. This was always going to end badly for you.'

'Maybe I'll live long enough to see you shot by the police.'

'I'll slit your throat before that happens.'

'Bit of a change for you, killing a man instead of helpless, drugged young girls.'

'Speak again and I'll end your life this minute.'

Harry didn't respond – better to save his strength. He checked the back of his leg; the belt had done its job and inhibited the flow of blood. From recent knowledge, he had roughly two hours before the tourniquet needed to be removed by a surgeon and his wound treated urgently. The helicopter hovered above and, at times, right over the warehouse. For the next ten minutes, Harry watched Carlton Lee grow increasingly agitated, in and out of his chair, pacing towards the door and back, worried the car would be spotted by the searchlight. Lee stopped abruptly in the middle of the room, looked up, and listened. The noise of the helicopter faded as it moved away from their location. As Lee approached, Harry recalled what he'd said about it ending badly for him.

He said, 'Time for me to go.'

Harry anxiously distanced himself until his back hit the wall. 'Armed police could be waiting outside. They'll probably open fire as soon as you walk out of the door.' There were no police. It was merely an attempt to sow a seed of doubt in Lee's mind and save himself, or at least gain a little more time.

'You'll never know,' said Lee.

'You don't have to kill me.'

'You're right, I don't. But I want to.'

Lee knelt over him, about to plunge the knife into his chest. *Shit*! This was it. Utterly helpless, he closed his eyes and pictured Leah.

Lee asked, 'What are you thinking about?'

'I'm not sharing my last memory with you. Just fucking get on with it.'

'Suit yourself.' A loud bang inside the warehouse distracted Lee. He left Harry and went to investigate, reappearing moments later. 'The wind is picking up out there. It blew the door open. Oh, and look at me,' he said, opening his arms and staring down at his body. 'No bullet holes.' With menace in his eyes, he advanced towards Harry. 'You know what? I'm going to give you a fighting chance.'

'I'm too weak to fight you.'

Lee laughed. 'I'm not talking about hand-to-hand combat. Release the tourniquet, hand over your belt, and I'll walk out of here.'

'If I do, the rush of blood could cause more damage. I could also go into shock from the bleeding and be dead within minutes.'

'Well, it's your choice. I can kill you this instant, or you can hand over the belt and see if fate saves you. What's it going to be?'

Both options would likely end in Harry's death, but Lee was right; no matter how minuscule the chance, he had to take it. As Harry tentatively reached down to undo the buckle, the cacophonous sound of smashing glass reverberated around the room. A man crashed through the window into Lee and landed awkwardly, catching the edge of the desk and dropping to the floor with a thump. Harry shielded his face from the glass fragments showering upon him. Observing under his forearm, he saw the two men grapple on the floor, with Lee gaining the upper hand over his opponent. Lee's hand forced the man's face to the side. It was the same man he'd seen at the traffic lights – Harper Darmody. He'd always suspected he hadn't drowned when the Zephyr sank, but what the hell was he doing here?

Both men scrabbled for the knife that lay inches beyond their reach. Harper swung a left hook at Lee's jaw, knocking him across the floor. Lee leapt to his feet and scarpered from the office.

Harper climbed to his feet using the desk and stared at Harry. 'Lenny will be here soon with help.' With no time to lose, Harper pursued Lee.

Lenny! He should have guessed he'd have something to do with why Harper was in town. Harper must have called Lenny after they'd locked eyes at the crossing. As for why he'd followed them down Regis Road, that didn't matter. If he hadn't, Harry knew he'd be dead.

Charging footsteps echoed across the warehouse floor. 'Harry!' a voice shouted.

'I'm in the office!' The relief of seeing a dripping wet Lenny in the doorway was something he'd never imagined possible.

'Where are you injured?' Lenny asked, kneeling beside him.

'Back of the leg. I don't know if he's nicked an artery or not. I've tied it off. Is that rain or sweat all over you?'

'Both. An ambulance is on the way, so you'll be in safe hands soon.'

'Safer than your hands – you shot me with a Taser.'

'Well, you should know better than to sneak up on an armed man. Right, I need to go after Carlton Lee.'

'I saw Darmody.'

'I gathered. I'll explain later,' said Lenny.

53

Christmas Eve

Lenny raced from the warehouse into the pouring rain. A police car pulled up, and he directed the officers towards Harry. Distant sirens alerted him to the flashing lights of an ambulance further up the road, with police cars directly behind. Lenny wandered into the middle of the road and looked for Harper. It was difficult to see through the darkness and heavy rain, but he caught sight of him clambering up a drainpipe before easing himself over a wall onto the railway bridge, hot on Lee's trail.

'Bollocks,' he said, and set off after them.

Lenny scaled the large commercial wheelie bin and pulled himself up onto the roof of a Luton van. He grabbed the drainpipe and gave it a hard tug to ensure it was secure. Halfway up, his foot slipped, and he found himself on his backside on top of the van. Though too old to be chasing criminals on foot and scaling walls, he wasn't giving up. Succeeding on his second attempt, he hauled himself over the wall onto the stones beside the railway track.

Catching his breath, rainwater dripped from the fused strands of his hair as he peered through the gloom in search of Harper and Carlton Lee. Perturbed by the clatter of hard rain against the stones and the crackle and hum from the electric lines overhead, he trudged alongside the tracks. He stopped and placed his hands on his knees, gasping for air. It crossed his mind to give up and turn back, but as he stood upright and peered further ahead, the two men clashed violently.

A gentle tremor and the vibrating rail made him look behind to see the headlights of a train heading in their direction. He scrambled onward. The spotlight of the police helicopter loomed closer and would soon be upon the brawling men. Harper knocked Lee to the ground. Lenny glanced over his shoulder as the rattle and rumble of the train grew louder. Sitting astride Lee, Harper threw punch after punch. Lenny's heart raced, and despite his determination, the same could not be said for his legs. He wanted to prevent Harper from going too far. The helicopter hovered above; the spotlight slowly passed over the fighting pair and drifted back again. Officers were now aware of their exact location.

With the train bearing down on them, Lenny was forced to stand clear. 'Harper! Harper!' he shouted to no avail.

Filling his lungs to shout once again, Harper stared in his direction and got to his feet. Always so bloody casual. Lenny assumed Harper would back away and leave Carlton Lee to the police – but he didn't. He reached down, grabbed Lee by his ankles, and dragged him across the stones, positioning the back of his neck across the rail. Lenny's yell for him to stop was drowned out by a blast from the horn. Harper crossed in front of the train as it breezed past. The arcing between the overhead line and the train's pantograph blinded Lenny, spitting sparks that forced him to crouch down and shield his face with his forearm.

Brakes screeched as the train screamed to a stop further down the line. Over the constant whirring of rotor blades above, voices grew louder behind Lenny as police officers in bright yellow hi-vis jackets raced towards the scene. He scanned the area – Harper had vanished into the black night under a cloak of rain. Lenny wandered into the circle of light that pinpointed the horror and grimaced at the headless corpse of Carlton Lee. Although it would have been his preference to see him charged and prosecuted for his crimes, the families of his victims might have had a different perspective. A police officer escorted Lenny away from the body while others searched for the other man involved. The officer asked if he knew the man who had fled the scene.

'Just a passer-by,' Lenny replied.

He managed to find an easier but longer way back to the warehouse, where Harry was being loaded into the ambulance. Lenny jumped in the back to see how he was doing.

'Hurts like hell, but I'm all right,' said Harry. 'The paramedic said it's not as bad as it looks or feels. I was informed Carlton Lee didn't fare too well.'

'No. I expect they're up there trying to locate what's left of his head.'

'Fucker got what he deserved.'

Harry's comment surprised Lenny. Making sure they were alone, he leaned in and quietly asked, 'Are you going to let on about – you know who?'

'I've always had an inkling he was alive, and I'm glad he showed up when he did, but if our paths cross again, I will *not* be so forgiving.'

'Sounds fair. Well, I'd best let them get you to the hospital. We don't want you losing a leg,' he said, a broad smile on his face.

Watching the ambulance drive away, it occurred to him that he'd have to walk back to the train station in the pouring rain. He called out to the police officers milling about, 'Anyone fancy giving me a lift to Stratford? No? Lovely.' He set off along Regis Road.

*

Looking like a drowned rat, Lenny entered his apartment. Even Phoebe didn't want to know, put off by the drops of water splashing on the wooden floor. In the bathroom, he stripped to his briefs, placed his clothes in the laundry basket, and grabbed a towel to dry his hair. He wandered into the living area to check if Harper was back. Sure enough, there he was in the armchair, with the double-crossing Phoebe now snuggled on his lap.

'Bloody traitor,' said Lenny. Moving closer, he noted small cuts on Harper's face and forearms and the nasty swelling around his eye. 'Whoa, looks like someone's gonna have a lovely shiner.'

'Yeah, he caught me good.'

'You certainly made him pay for it. Did you have to kill him?'

'Of all the people to ask.'

Lenny said, 'Yeah, I s'pose it is a stupid question.'

'I imagine the police will be hunting me down again?'

'Unless your mug is caught on CCTV, you'll be alright. Harry isn't going to say a word. All you have to do is stay out of his way.'

'Sounds fair.'

'Exactly what I said.' Lenny tossed the towel on the worktop and picked up Harper's phone, scrutinising the shattered screen. 'What happened here?'

'Busted during the fight.'

Lenny said, 'Whisky? I reckon we've earned it after today.'

'Not for me.'

'Suit yourself.'

Stroking Phoebe, Harper said, 'I bet it didn't look pretty up there on the tracks.'

Lenny swigged from his glass. 'I forgot you didn't hang around long enough to see your handiwork. No, it wasn't pleasant. I'll be having nightmares for the foreseeable, so thanks for that. They're probably still searching for his noggin.'

'I will have that whisky.'

Lenny grabbed a glass from the cupboard and, along with the bottle, took it over to him. 'Right, I'm off for a shower and quite possibly an early night.'

After his shower, he sat on the edge of the bed with a towel wrapped around his waist and looked at Dr Florence Stone's business card. He gave her a call, and she promptly answered.

'Hi, Doctor Stone. It's Lenny. We met at the pub earlier.' Her silence ruffled him. 'You were with your daughter and her friend.'

She said, 'I'm sorry, I don't recall.' A blow to his confidence.

'It doesn't matter,' he said. It bloody well did. 'I just wanted to make sure you were all okay after what happened this evening.'

'I'm only joking. Of course, I remember. And you don't have to be so formal. Florence will suffice.' That cheered him up. 'It's sweet of you to check on us. We were close to the back and managed to get out before the panic, so we're fine. I stayed to assist with the injured outside.'

'I'm glad you got out safely. I bet they were pleased to have an extra pair of hands.'

'It was the least I could do. There are reports of a serial killer. It seems an odd thing to ask, but please tell me this has nothing to do with what you mentioned when we spoke?'

'It would be even more bizarre if it weren't,' he said. 'I've been helping a detective and was following up on a lead.'

'You do know he's dead? They found his body not long after. The details are a bit scarce.'

'Yeah, I know. My detective friend was taken hostage and got hurt, but he's going to be all right.'

'Oh no, not the man you were with, Simon Smith?'

'No, not him. He was there to lend a hand.'

'Well, that's good news,' she said. 'Look, I have to go. I'm about to take my daughter's friend home.'

'No worries. I'm just glad you're all okay.'

'I have your number now, so I'll call you again soon,' she said. 'Perhaps we can arrange to meet, and you can tell me all about your escapade.'

'Sounds great. Take care.'

'You too.'

Smiling to himself, he tossed the phone on the bed and regarded Olivia's photograph on the bedside table. His newfound enthusiasm instantly turned to guilt and shame. Happiness shouldn't be on his horizon. Grief remained a big part of his life, and he wouldn't have it any other way. Until Olivia, his mainstay had been to live and die alone, and if he hadn't strayed blindly into unknown territory, she would still be alive.

'Stop being so pitiful, Lenny.'

He turned to Olivia on the bed beside him. 'I'm not. Anyway, you shouldn't be allowed to read my mind.'

'I don't need to read minds to know what's going on inside *your* head.'

He flopped backwards onto the bed and sighed. 'I'm not even sure I like the lady. I was flattered more than anything. You might find this hard to believe, but women don't often come on to me.'

'Oh, I don't find that hard to believe at all.'

'What's that supposed to mean?'

'You're not an ordinary man.' Frowning, he glanced sideways. She said, 'In a good way.'

'Ah, you mean I'm a bit special?' He smiled, pleased as punch.

She raised her eyebrows. 'Yeah, if you like. Just don't rule out going on a date with her if she asks.'

'No. I'm not ready.'

'It's not about being ready. Life isn't about perfect timing. When opportunities present themselves, you have to reach out and grab them with both hands. You don't know how long it might be before another woman takes a shine to you.'

'I don't need anyone else. I've got you,' he said.

'No, Lenny – I'm afraid you don't have me any more.'

'Who are you talking to?' said Harper.

Lenny shot upright and saw him in the doorway. 'Nobody. I was thinking out loud.'

'Something you've done often since I've been here. It's quite disturbing.'

'What do you want?'

'Can we order some Chinese food?'

The idea of food gave him a lift. Lenny said, 'The menu is in the top drawer next to the kitchen sink. Pick what you fancy while I put on some clothes. I'll be with you in a minute.'

Stealing a moment on the edge of the bed, it occurred to him that his work with Harry was over. A return to the mind-numbing days before he'd accepted Harry's offer was like being slapped across the face with a pilchard. *Thanks, Monty Python.*

They were told there would be a two-hour wait. What did they expect? It was Christmas Eve. Sitting at opposite ends of the empty table, scattered words were batted back and forth, some of which amounted to a full sentence. Twenty minutes after ordering, with the space between each word growing longer, Lenny excused himself to make a phone call.

'Hi, Mrs Logan, it's Lenny. I hope I'm not disturbing you?'

'Not at all.'

'As you know, Danny's been saying for a while that he'd like to see Elaine Burgess. When I came to see him the other day, I said I'd try to arrange something over Christmas. So, would it be all right to take Danny away on Boxing Day?'

There was a slight pause on the line; perhaps she'd covered the receiver with her palm while she spoke with her husband. 'For how long?' she asked.

'Just overnight.'

The delay was shorter this time. 'Okay. He'll be thrilled. What time?'

'Eight in the morning.'

'We'll make sure he's ready,' she said.

He hadn't planned on going until the twenty-eighth, but Harper showing up out of the blue stirred him into going sooner. Lenny preferred his own company, so maybe Elaine could come up with an alternative living arrangement for her brother. After all, she did own a number of properties. With time to spare before dinner, he remained in his bedroom and relaxed.

When the food finally arrived, Lenny paid at the door and carried it through to the kitchen, staggered to find Harper had taken it upon himself to set the table as though it were Christmas Day. He'd laid out the tablecloth, placemats, candles, and a bottle of wine. There were even Christmas crackers on the table. Harper must have foraged through every cupboard and drawer to discover those because, for the life of him, Lenny couldn't remember buying them. Perhaps Olivia had bought them at some point.

Lenny said, 'Well, well. Don't this look pretty?'

'Do I detect a subtle hint of sarcasm there?'

'Nothing subtle about it.'

'I figured you wouldn't be whipping up a festive feast tomorrow and thought, why not make the most of tonight?'

'So you've gone all out Ebenezer Scrooge on me. Don't let me catch you offering money to children from the window in the morning. The response will be a lot different from the one in the 1840s.'

Lenny placed the carrier bag on the table and chomped on prawn crackers as he laid out the food. Before tucking into their feast of sweet and sour chicken balls, crispy chilli beef, noodles, chicken satay, and egg fried rice, Harper made him pull a couple of crackers and demanded they wear the tacky paper crowns. If there was any good cheer flowing through Lenny's veins, it wasn't finding its way to his face. All but for the chomping and slurping, they ate in silence. Small talk wasn't Harper's forte. As for Lenny, he could gas with the best of them; tonight, though, he just wasn't in the mood. This was already his second Christmas without Olivia. Now his work with Harry was complete; there was nothing to keep him from reverting to the misery of his life. Phoebe brushed against his leg. No doubt the smell of food had stirred her from wherever she had been sleeping. He fed her pieces of chicken under the table. Less than an hour later, Lenny and Harper parted company and turned in for the night.

54

Christmas Day

Harry slept well, considering the events of the previous night. The morphine certainly helped. A CT scan revealed some muscle damage, but nothing long-term. It meant time off work and regular check-ups, but he didn't mind. It would give him a chance to sort out a more permanent residence. He woke around 7.00 a.m. with Harper Darmody on his mind. To be saved by a man he despised left him deeply disturbed. Until Darmody, there had been no line between good and evil; you were either one or the other. Now he'd discovered a grey area that made no sense. Darmody might well have saved his life and brought an end to two serial killers and a number of abhorrent abusers, but there would be no absolution for what he had done at Sablefall Farm. Not now, not ever.

Jenna dropped by first thing with Leah to see how he was and to bring him a change of clothes. Harry had asked for his dark blue sweater and loose-fitting leisure pants, and she'd brought a holdall full of his belongings. He didn't say anything, but it crossed his mind that she couldn't wait to see the back of him. They didn't stay long; not a bad thing. A quick, "Hello, how are you doing?" was about all he could take. The collapse of his marriage was raw. The two cases he'd been working on had given him little time to dwell on anything else. Now it was all he could think about. Leah's tears when he glanced up the stairs before leaving the family home had pierced his heart all over again. Even when she sat on the edge of his hospital bed, though relieved he was going to be fine, he sensed the blame she placed at his feet. He'd suck it up. Perhaps one day the truth would come out. Family skeletons had a habit of falling out of cupboards, but right now, as her life kicked into gear, it was not the time.

Jenna had been kind enough to invite him for a late Christmas dinner. Sympathy, guilt, whatever. Even though he'd been informed his chances of being discharged from the hospital later today were slim, he'd accepted. He couldn't possibly refuse the slightest chance to spend a couple of hours with Leah on Christmas Day. Afterwards, he'd spend Christmas night alone for the first time in his life. Returning to Gerty's to listen to some vinyl on his record player might not be so bad. Thankfully, he had the bottle of brandy that Lenny had bought. Yes, it would most certainly be better than spending the evening in a hospital ward.

Doing nothing was not one of Harry's strong points, and being in a place where he'd spent too much time of late didn't improve his melancholic mood. If he had his phone, he could at least have passed the time with a few games of Wordle. Maybe even called Lucy to wish her a merry Christmas. He recalled the terrified look on her face when she'd turned up at the hospital moments before he was taken into surgery. Their chat was brief, and he'd informed her the injury wasn't serious. Even so, she'd squeezed his hand so tight that he could still sense her touch while he was in the operating theatre. She'd said she would call him later that day. Not that she could. Everything had happened so quickly, and it never entered his mind to tell her his phone lay smashed to pieces on the kerbside of a backstreet in Kentish Town.

DI Samantha Jennings entered the ward. An unexpected visitor, but to quell the boredom, Harry would have been happy to see Boris Johnson. Actually, strike that.

'How are you doing?' she said, standing at the end of the bed.

'I'm fine, thanks. I'll feel even better if I get out of here later.'

'Considering they usually keep victims with knife wounds in for up to four days or more, I doubt you'll be going anywhere. Though it would be nice for you to be home with your family.'

He'd so far kept his marital issues private. He hadn't discussed the subject with Lucy, and he wasn't about to disclose anything to Sam Jennings. 'Yes,' he said. 'It would. Anyway, it's lovely that you've dropped by for a visit.' Harry pointed to the blue leather chair beside the bed. 'Why don't you take a seat?'

'I'm not stopping. I'm merely the bearer of bad news. Early this morning, I attended the scene of a suicide. It pains me to tell you that Owen Carrick has taken his own life. It's my understanding you'd been working closely together.'

Harry gasped in disbelief and, for a moment, remained silent, racking his brain as to why he would have done such a thing. Owen didn't seem like a man on the brink of suicide; however, Harry knew that people with mental health problems were specialists in concealing their emotions from those around them.

'How did he . . .?'

'He hung himself in the garage around midnight. His wife discovered his body first thing. You can imagine how devastated she and his two teenage children are.'

Harry shook his head. 'And it's definitely suicide?'

'Yes!' Sam seemed to take offence but kept her cool. 'I explored all possibilities, even after I examined the note.'

'What did the note say?'

'Just one word – "*Sorry*." I checked with his wife, and although it was only a few letters, she confirmed it was *his* handwriting.'

'Thanks for letting me know. I don't suppose you've had time to execute the search warrant for the Levinsons' house?'

'I'm afraid not. There's one last thing. The DCS couldn't get down here himself and wanted me to pass on a message. This morning, the NCA got in touch, and they've so far linked three further victims within the UK to Carlton Lee. Congratulations on that, by the way.'

'I didn't do much,' he said, never one for taking plaudits.

'You put your life in danger and led him down a dead end. If you hadn't done so, he might have escaped.'

'I got lucky. That's all.'

Despite much hesitation, and on the condition that he rested and returned to the hospital in two days for his first check-up, the doctor relented and agreed to let him go home. Harry arrived by taxi in the early evening, and as usual, Jenna had pulled out all the stops for Christmas dinner. It left him thinking about all the things he was going to miss. Momentarily, he blamed himself, but she was the one who'd rekindled her affair with Benjamin Knightley, and yes, she'd confirmed it.

Harry mused on why she had invited him and not Ben. Perhaps it was too soon for the illicit lovers to spend Christmas together. Leah would most definitely have had questions. Besides, Mr Knightley was probably spending Christmas with his wife and kids. From what he could remember, Knightley's children were quite young. Harry doubted the prick would ever leave his wife, and eventually, Jenna would discover what a fool she'd been. Fuck it! No point dwelling on a bad situation. Best to enjoy his precious time with Leah. They exchanged presents next to the beautifully decorated tree. The expression on Leah's face when she unwrapped her necklace and earrings lifted his spirits. Jenna was equally happy with the expensive handbag Harry had bought her before he moved out. When he opened the large box and set eyes on the record player, the pain in his leg ceased for a few seconds.

By nine o'clock, Harry was back in his room at the guest house, going through his collection of vinyl records. Jenna had boxed them up along with some more personal items he'd failed to take the first time. His records were precious to him, many of which once belonged to his mother. The joy in his heart when she passed them on to him was priceless – picture discs and special editions that collectors would pay a small fortune for. But he would never part with them. As well as representing *his* younger days, they told the story of his mother's life. One of the many beautiful things he'd discovered about music was how it connected unique moments and memories with the past – happy or sad. The first record he placed on the turntable was his mother's favourite. He poured brandy into a coffee mug, placed the needle on the record, and eased into the chair as 'Have You Ever Seen The Rain' by Creedence Clearwater Revival played.

Harry sipped from the mug, closed his eyes, and rested his head against the back of the chair. His reverie was interrupted by a loud knock at the door. Surely it wouldn't be someone complaining about the music? The television was usually louder, and nobody had said a word. He removed the needle from the record and hobbled towards the door, ready to apologise.

'Lucy! This is unexpected.'

'I hope I'm not disturbing you?' she said, glancing over his shoulder to see if he had company.

'Not at all. Come in.' Harry stepped aside to let her pass. He noted the bottle of Merlot in her hand. 'I see you've brought wine?'

'I assumed you didn't have any booze.' She spotted the bottle of brandy on the table. 'But I can see I was wrong.'

'A gift from a friend.' Harry fetched the other coffee mug and passed it to her. 'I'm afraid I don't have any glasses.'

'What does it matter? A cup's a cup, right? Since the other bottle is open, we might as well save the wine.' Harry poured her some brandy. 'Cheers,' said Lucy. 'Oh, and Merry Christmas.'

'Merry Christmas.' Both smiled as they clinked their mugs together. She ambled over to the only chair in the room and held her stomach as she sat, no doubt suffering from the effects of her own injury. Harry sat on the double bed a few feet away. 'How did you find me?'

'I tried to call this afternoon to see how you were doing.'

'Carlton Lee tossed my phone out of the car window.'

'Yeah, I gathered it was something along those lines. Anyway, I called the hospital and was surprised to learn you'd been discharged. While Mum nattered the evening away with my aunt and my dad fell asleep in the armchair, I slipped out and drove to your house.'

'Ah,' said Harry, as though he'd been caught in a lie. 'Jenna told you where I was.'

Lucy nodded, sipped her brandy, and said, 'You could have told me, though I understand why you kept it quiet. Our private lives are nobody's business.'

'That's not the reason I didn't say anything. I've just been caught up in these investigations. To be fair, I only moved out the other day. I haven't had much time to come to terms with it myself yet.'

'This is where you discover exactly how nosy I am. I recall you saying there were problems, but how come you moved out?'

Before answering, Harry drank from his mug. 'I found out Jenna was seeing someone else.' Hearing himself say it out loud for the first time made him aware of just how much it hurt.

'Christ, Harry. I'm so sorry. Is it not something you can both discuss and work through?'

'We've already tried. It was one of the reasons we moved to Kent. Don't get me wrong, I haven't been a saint, but her affair has lasted a hell of a lot longer than one stupid night.'

'I see. Is she in love with this other guy?'

'I have no idea. It's no longer my concern.'

'It must be a difficult time for you. Anyway, how's the leg?'

'Nice change of subject. I'm not going to lie, it bloody hurts. Lord knows how painful it would be without the painkillers.'

'I know what you mean. What a pair, eh? So, this friend who gave you the brandy – his name wouldn't happen to be Lenny Grey?'

The mention of Lenny's name came as a surprise. 'Yes. Do you know him?'

'We met, albeit briefly. I came across him in the foyer at the forum. He told me what had happened and said he'd let you down, though I didn't know what he meant. Who is he, anyway?'

Harry had wanted to keep his acquaintance with Lenny quiet, but it couldn't hurt to tell Lucy. 'Lenny is a non-fiction author and former journalist. He also has a remarkable talent for finding people.'

'I gather he's the one who found Carlton Lee?'

'Yes. He also found Rebecca Heaton in Canada.'

'That explains the Canadian brandy. I'm sure I've heard his name before.'

'Probably. His hard work led us to Joseph Webster.'

Lucy jerked forward, grasping exactly who Lenny was. 'He wrote those books about Harper Darmody. I read the first one. Gruesome stuff. Terrible what happened to him and his sister.'

Now it was Harry's turn to change the subject. 'I assume you've heard about Owen Carrick?'

Lucy turned her head, eyes wide. 'What about him?' Harry explained his suicide. 'Wow! I'm so shocked.'

'He left a note saying sorry.'

Lucy topped up her brandy and said, 'What do you think he was sorry for?'

'I'd imagine he was apologising to his family for leaving them so abruptly. I have no idea what his personal struggles were, but they must have been pretty horrific to take him to the point of no return.'

'Maybe. It just feels a little off.'

'I reacted the same way at first, but we never know what's going on beneath the surface.'

'True. Though I think an apology to your family is worth more than a single word. What if he was sorry for something else? We'd wrongly assumed Jerome Henderson was the one responsible for messing around with the video footage.'

Harry edged forward on the bed, considering her accusation. Could Owen have been the mysterious fourth person at Sarah Kerr's apartment the night Melanie and Jerome died? As for the video evidence, he had access *and* technical know-how. But Owen? He'd been on the case from the beginning and couldn't possibly have predicted how it would unfold.

Harry said, 'Personally, I doubt Owen Carrick's involvement in any of this. On the other hand, I can't afford to rule it out. I'll either pass this on to Sam or look into it at the first chance I get.'

For the remainder of the evening, they sat on the floor, played records, and talked about all manner of things. They'd finished the brandy and moved on to the wine. With their backs against the bed, the tipsy pair browsed through records. Harry entertained her with stories about himself, his remarkable mother, and, of course, his father, and how they didn't see eye to eye. Lucy glanced at her watch every five minutes and repeatedly said she should call a taxi. She never did.

When it was well past midnight, Harry said, 'Do you want me to call you a taxi?'

'Are you trying to get rid of me?'

'Not at all. It's just – late. You're welcome to stay the night.'

'Oh, Harry.' She looked disappointed. 'Now you're trying to get me into bed.'

'I promise you, I'm not.' Harry instantly regretted the tone of his harsh rejection.

'Why? What's wrong with me?' she slurred.

'That came out wrong.'

'Oh, get over yourself. I'm only joking.' She sipped her wine.

He reached out to take the mug from her hand. 'Okay, I think that's enough.'

Lucy leaned into him. 'Just shut up and kiss me, Harry,' she said, placing her lips on his. All night he'd wanted to kiss her but had refrained, not wanting to make an arse of himself. Why would a beautiful, intelligent young woman be interested in a boring, middle-aged old fart like him? She pulled back and said, 'See, it wasn't so bad, was it?'

Harry smiled. 'No. It wasn't bad at all.'

Lucy leaned forward again, ready to go in for another kiss. As she did so, a stream of vomit sprayed violently onto Harry's chest. Harry was the first to break the awkward silence. Although initially horrified, he soon saw the funny side. 'Come on. Let's get you to the bathroom in case there's any more.'

*

In the armchair with a blanket over him, Harry opened his eyes. Daylight flooded through a gap in the curtains. He looked at his wrist and remembered he'd removed his watch along with his vomit-soaked sweater and trousers. Instead, he peered across at the clock on the console: 9.15. He yawned and gazed at Lucy, lightly snoring in his bed. He wasn't sure whether to wake her or go back to sleep himself. Her ringing phone made the decision for him. Lucy stirred in the bed and no doubt questioned her surroundings. She sat up and stared across the room, wearing a tellingly awkward smile.

She asked, 'What time is it?'

'Quarter past nine.'

'Shit. It'll be my dad checking up on me. I was supposed to be spending the night at theirs. I bet my mum's having kittens.'

'Then perhaps you should answer.'

'I should, shouldn't I?'

Not quite with it yet, Lucy grabbed her phone from the bedside cabinet. She apologised to her mother and said she'd stayed at a friend's house. Though in her early thirties, given her recent injury, their concern was to be expected. While she spoke with both parents, Harry put the kettle on and rinsed the mugs in the bathroom sink. By the time he'd made the coffee, she'd ended her call, informing her mum she'd be back around lunchtime. He sat on the bed and passed Lucy her coffee.

'My head is splitting,' she said.

'I can't say I'm surprised. You drank more than I did last night.'

'No way. Doesn't sound like me at all.'

'You were rat-arsed, Lucy.'

'You could have taken advantage of me.'

'Who said I didn't?' He kept a straight face for all of two seconds.

'Maybe you should have,' she said.

'And have you puke all over me again? I think not.'

'I never did that.' Lucy searched her aching mind and recoiled in horror, covering her sheepish smile with her hand. 'Shit. I am so sorry.'

'Don't worry about it. I'll send you the cleaning bill.'

'Well, rat-arsed or not, you had your chance, mister. You might not get another.'

'More my misfortune than yours, I'm sure,' said Harry. 'Right, drink up. I'll take you out for breakfast.'

She grimaced. 'No way. I couldn't eat a thing.'

'You'll feel differently when we get there. A post-hangover fry-up is one of life's greatest pleasures.'

55

Boxing Day

Harry finished off his full English, sipped his tea, and began entering numbers from his notebook into a mobile phone he'd purchased from a shop a few doors down. Thankfully, he was able to keep his old number. Every table in the café was occupied, which came as no surprise – many people liked a cooked breakfast before hitting the sales on Boxing Day. Sitting opposite, Lucy stared into oblivion, occasionally sipping her coffee and taking a bite of toast. Perhaps she was still fragile or, worse, regretting their kiss and contemplating what might have happened if she hadn't been sick. Harry didn't have the courage to ask, and he certainly didn't want to create any awkwardness between them.

When he'd entered his most frequent contacts, he stepped outside to call Arthur. With the phone to his ear, he exchanged glances with Lucy through the large window. She smiled softly, and it warmed his heart. It had been a long time since he'd experienced such an intense rush of excitement, but with the flame barely extinguished from his marriage, was it all happening too soon? Maybe she meant what she'd said about not getting another chance. He didn't know her well enough to gauge if she was looking for romance, but after a one-night stand that had predestined his residency at Gerty's Guest House, kicking up the dust of a previously trodden path was not an option.

Finally, Arthur answered from his hospital bed. He'd been attacked from behind and rendered unconscious the previous evening when he'd popped over to Sarah Kerr's apartment to collect a blood sample.

Harry asked, 'What were you doing there on Christmas Day?'

'Until my wife reminded me, I'd forgotten all about our Boxing Day plans – dinner with family and whatnot. Yesterday was the only opportunity I had. I couldn't let you down, Harry.'

'It's bloody Christmas. You wouldn't have been letting me down. I told you it could wait.'

'I know you did. The truth is, I needed to get it done. I rarely miss anything or make a mistake, but when I do, it plagues my mind. By the way, I'm sorry about what happened to you. You got your man, though. That's the important thing.'

'I didn't get him personally, but thanks. Not sure it's sunk in yet.' He'd had no time to reflect on the events of Christmas Eve, and truth be told, he didn't want to. Nevertheless, Arthur was right about it being important; no more young women would be forced to stare into the eyes of Carlton Lee as he watched them take their last breath. Harry's mind skipped back to Arthur's attack. 'Where was the officer who was supposed to be guarding the crime scene?'

'There wasn't one. They'd probably gone home, hoping nobody would find out.'

'You didn't report the incident, did you?'

'I felt like an idiot as it was, Harry. I certainly didn't want to draw more attention to my mistake.'

Harry was fuming that the officer on duty had vacated their post, but he understood why Arthur didn't want to say anything. 'What do you reckon, a burglar?'

'That was my first thought when I came to, but once I saw the vial containing the blood sample was missing, I had my doubts. I looked around the apartment, and as you know, there were quite a few valuables about the place, none of which had been touched.'

'Maybe they got scared and left in a hurry, thinking someone might be joining you. Doesn't explain why they took the sample, though.'

'No, it doesn't, unless . . .'

'Spill it, Arthur.'

'Unless there's still a culprit out there trying to cover their tracks. It's doubtful the sample would have produced any results, but they weren't to know that. Just be careful, Harry.'

Arthur explained how he'd locked up and returned home, but by nightfall, he'd become nauseous and light-headed. Mrs Potts wasted no time calling an ambulance, and an MRI scan fortunately revealed no fractures or bleeds. They'd kept him overnight for observation. He said, 'The doctor will be doing his rounds soon. It's likely I'll be going home.'

'I take it your Boxing Day plans are in ruins?'

'Not at all. It took some convincing, but I have managed to persuade Rose to go along without me. I foresee an afternoon of Mozart and bourbon. Every cloud, as they say. I am sorry about the blood sample, Harry. If I hadn't missed it in the first place, this would never have happened, and you might have had a few more answers.'

'Don't apologise. I'm just glad you're all right. Besides, I'll hopefully have all the answers I need when Rebecca Heaton's memory returns.'

Arthur said, 'Nobody's told you?'

'Told me what?' Harry's heart raced. 'Has something happened to Rebecca?'

'I'm surprised they haven't called you.'

'I haven't had a phone. Just tell me.'

'DI Jennings popped in to see me. She was here to take a statement from Miss Heaton, who this morning recalled how she got her injuries. She claims to have woken in the driver's seat of Ryan's car. He flew into a rage and proceeded to bash her head against the steering wheel. Unfortunately, the poor girl doesn't remember anything before the incident or the events that followed.'

He thanked Arthur for the information and said he'd speak to him soon. Harry was pissed off. He'd waited on tenterhooks for Rebecca to regain her memory, and when she did, he wasn't able to be there. It frustrated him further that Sam Jennings had been the one to take Rebecca's statement. She was probably making the arrest right now. *Fuck it*! He'd desperately wanted to be the one to slap those handcuffs on Ryan Levinson.

Returning to his seat in the café, he told Lucy all about it.

Lucy said, 'She doesn't remember anything before waking up in the car?'

'No.'

'That's a shame,' she said, consuming her last drop of coffee. 'Maybe it isn't too late for you to make the arrest. Give Sam a call.'

Harry did as Lucy suggested and discovered DI Jennings had visited Ryan's address within the last hour. He'd absconded. It surprised him to learn she'd tried to contact him before he'd purchased his new phone to see if he was fit enough to make the arrest himself. Not the actions of the self-serving detective he'd assumed her to be. She offered to call him if news of Ryan's whereabouts came to light. Harry glanced at Lucy, who'd perked up within the last few minutes, and for some reason, he declined Sam's offer. Arresting and seeing the bastard squirm no longer seemed important. It was time to step back and recover from his injury before returning to work. They'd insist on it anyway.

They left the café, and Harry dropped Lucy back at her car. She'd promised to spend Christmas and Boxing Day with her parents but had so far failed miserably. She thanked him for breakfast (even though she'd only had one slice of toast) and moved in close. They wrapped their arms around each other and kissed. Something was different. It lacked the intensity of the previous night. Perhaps there was a slight awkwardness on both sides. She said she'd call him later, and he watched her drive off.

Limping gingerly towards the guest house, his phone rang – an unknown caller. 'This is Detective Inspector Baxendale,' he said.

'I need to see you.'

Puzzled, Harry asked who was calling.

'Penny Levinson.'

'I'm not working at the moment, Mrs Levinson. You need to call the station and ask for DI Samantha Jennings.'

After a brief pause, she said, 'No. I'll only talk to you. Meet me at Capstone Farm Country Park in one hour.' She hung up.

He didn't know if it was a good idea to meet her and wasn't sure he should get involved, not now that her son was wanted for attempted murder. But before he knew it, he was on his way.

Arriving well ahead of time, Harry waited in the car. Bolts of pain surged through his leg as the medication wore off. He reached into his jacket pocket and took two tablets from the pack. The small bottle of water in the holder was empty, so he swallowed them dry without much difficulty. Tuning through the radio stations, the senseless chatter and adverts forced him to switch it off. Silence was underrated.

He recognised her Range Rover as it entered the car park and climbed out of his car, ready to greet her. She parked opposite and remained inside. A few seconds passed, and she summoned him over. Harry ambled across the car park, making a half-hearted attempt to conceal his limp. He opened the passenger door and pulled himself up, closing the door after he'd settled in. Mrs Levinson didn't turn to face him. She had a look about her that he'd seen numerous times over the years: detached, beleaguered, defeated – like many others who had found themselves in a situation beyond their control.

Penny said, 'You were right about my son.'

Harry kept quiet. Rubbing salt into the wound would not be welcome or helpful.

'And before you ask, I don't know where he is or where he could be.'

She'd answered the only question he had. He faced forward and stared through the windscreen. It was best to listen and let her say whatever she needed to. A car parked next to his, and a woman with her young son walked off towards the woods with a beagle in tow.

'That poor girl,' she said. 'Ryan could have killed her. I paid her a visit. Had to see for myself and ask if it was true. She didn't reply. Didn't have to. Her silent tears told me all I needed to know. What's really fucked up is that I knew but refused to accept my son was capable of such a violent act.' She twisted around and reached for a carrier bag on the back seat. She placed the bag on

Harry's lap. 'Even when I found these hidden in his room, I still tried to convince myself it wasn't possible.'

Opening the bag, Harry contemplated a pair of training shoes, one of which was covered in blood.

'Obviously, you'll have to check, but we both know that's Rebecca's blood. I was going to get rid of them but couldn't go through with it. After seeing her state and looking into her eyes, I'm glad I didn't.' Penny took a moment, desperately trying to keep it together. 'Stuffed inside one of the shoes is a mobile phone. I didn't see it at first. The battery was dead, so I charged it. There were pictures – of a young girl. I don't know how many. I stopped looking and turned it off. There are certain things a parent should never discover about their child.' A prolonged cry of pain escaped her, followed by a sharp intake of breath. She regained control. 'I've been her, you know – Rebecca. Many times. In my experience, men don't change. And Ryan is his father's son.'

Tears rolled down her cheeks. Handing over evidence that would help send her son to prison must have been the most difficult decision of her life. Even more so, knowing her only child would probably never speak to her again.

She started the engine and gripped the steering wheel. 'I need to get back home. I have to finish packing.'

Harry carefully climbed out and closed the door. Penny took a few seconds to compose herself before driving away.

56

Boxing Day

The plan was to leave at 8.00 a.m., pick Danny up along the way, and get to Elaine's house in Helmsley around one o'clock in the afternoon. A journey that should have taken around five hours was no longer possible, thanks to roadworks, a couple of breakdowns, and an accident. According to the satnav, there were ninety-four miles remaining, and at this rate, as they inched along the A1, they wouldn't get there until late afternoon. To top it off, the radiator was overheating, Danny needed the toilet, and Harper was hungry for more than French Fancies. Fortunately, a service station wasn't too far ahead.

Lenny and Harper had spent Christmas Day cooped up in the apartment, watching television and eating Chinese leftovers from the night before. At one point, Harper expressed that he'd had more fun locked up in Rampton Hospital; tragically, Lenny couldn't tell if he was being serious. Up bright and early, Lenny had wandered down to the shop and picked up some snacks to take with them on the journey: Pringles, French Fancies, Hobnobs, and a large box of Maltesers – the remainder of which rattled around in the box on the back seat.

When Lenny informed Harper where they were going first thing this morning, the pair were quite upbeat about their little road trip. Well, that bubble had burst a couple of hours ago, back on the M11. Harper was also unimpressed about having to bring

Danny with them – especially since it meant he'd have to hide his face under a hoodie, sit in the back of the car, and answer to the name Simon. Along with everyone else, Danny probably assumed Harper had died on the narrowboat along with Joseph Webster. The lack of conversation appeared to safeguard their secret.

The minute the grumpy trio pulled into the service station, Danny raced to the bathroom, and Harper strolled inside to get himself a burger and chips. Lenny opened the bonnet and waited a moment before taking the cap off the radiator. Going to Elaine's was fast becoming a regrettable decision, not to mention, he hadn't informed her they were coming because he knew she'd have said no. Lenny opened the back door and reached for the Maltesers. There were two left. Who the hell leaves two Maltesers in the box? He put them in his mouth and locked the car. Like Harper, he needed something a little more substantial to eat.

As Lenny approached the main building, Danny exited through the automatic doors and put on his woolly hat. 'Come on,' said Lenny, 'I'll treat you to a Big Mac.'

'I don't like Big Macs.'

'Choose something else, then!' Lenny's patience was wearing thin.

The trio ate in silence, and Harper kept his head down.

Danny said, 'You don't have to hide your face. I know who you are.'

Lenny froze midway through taking a bite out of his double quarter pounder, and Harper's hand had paused over his fries.

'I'm not stupid,' said Danny. 'How could I not recognise the man who helped save my life?' Lenny stared at Harper, who in turn eased his head up, deadpan, and locked eyes with the boy. 'Don't worry, I'm not going to say anything.'

Harper turned to Lenny, who winked and quietly mouthed, 'It's fine.' They continued to eat. Lenny said, 'Danny, when we get to Elaine's, you need to continue calling him Simon. Elaine's children know of their uncle but have never met him. As far as they know, he's dead.'

Danny laughed. 'I bet that was an uncomfortable conversation.'

'Yes, I imagine it was. This stays between us, though, okay?'

'Sure. I won't say a word.'

They finished their food and returned to the car. Lenny trailed behind after popping into the shop to buy a couple of two-litre bottles of water. He topped up the radiator and checked for leaks. Everything seemed okay. As Lenny climbed into the car, Danny was now in the back, and Harper was riding shotgun.

Harper asked, 'What was the problem?'

'I was the problem. I haven't been myself of late and can't remember the last time I checked the water level. It should be all right now.' As the car pulled onto the A1, the traffic seemed to be moving a lot quicker. 'Things are looking up already.'

Harper said, 'Do you think you should have called Elaine back at the services to let her know we'd be arriving a little later than planned?'

'Yeah, about that . . .'

'You haven't told her we're coming, have you?'

'Not in so many words. Not in any words, really.'

'I'd hate to be in your shoes when we get there.'

<h1 style="text-align:center">57</h1>

Boxing Day

There were a few cheers and several pats on the back when Harry returned to the station to drop off the evidence supplied by Mrs Levinson. He feigned a smile of appreciation here and there, but as far as he was concerned, the high praise was unwarranted. Lenny found Carlton Lee. All he'd done was stumble into Lee's path, become his hostage, and if it hadn't been for Harper Darmody, he'd be pushing up daisies. It left a bad taste in his mouth.

Not planning to stop for long, he made straight for Sam Jennings and placed the carrier bag on her desk. 'Ryan Levinson's trainers. He was wearing them when he attempted to kill Rebecca Heaton.'

She glanced inside. 'Is that—?'

'Yeah. It's blood,' he said. 'There's also an old mobile phone that belonged to Vincent Perry in the bag. It all needs to be booked into evidence.'

'Will do. May I ask how you came by this evidence?'

'His mother.'

He thanked her for trying to reach him earlier about making the arrest and let her know where Ryan might be hiding. On the way to the station, he'd remembered Melanie's parents mentioning a squat Ryan used to visit to sell drugs. He'd phoned Mr Hillingdon and asked for the address.

She said, 'It's worth a shot.' She immediately readied her team and turned to Harry. 'Why don't you come with us?' His hesitation didn't go amiss. 'You don't have to get out of the car. If he isn't there, I'll drop you straight back here. If he is, do you not want the satisfaction of seeing him handcuffed and forced into the back of a police car?'

They'd located the flat above a kebab shop close to Chatham High Street. From the comfort of Sam's car, parked less than a hundred feet from the entrance door, Harry watched as six police constables and four detectives, including Sam Jennings, marched towards the squat. One of the constables rammed the front door with an enforcer to gain entry, and the officers raced up the narrow staircase. A few people had stopped to see what was going on, while others didn't seem to care. Staff and customers drifted out of the kebab shop to watch.

A silver Vauxhall Astra pulled up beside him and quickly reversed into a space two cars behind. Harry returned his attention to the flat. Whether Ryan was inside or not, this would all be over in a matter of minutes. He imagined Ryan cowering in a dark corner, praying they hadn't come for him. From the moment their paths crossed, Harry had him sussed. A self-entitled young man piggybacking on his father's criminal past. A wannabe with plenty of temerity but severely lacking the kind of toughness that isn't handed to you on a silver platter.

Across from Harry, a car pulled out and set off down the road. The empty space was quickly taken by the silver Astra he'd noticed previously. A constable stepped out of the doorway and signalled to the police van parked further along the street. They'd made an arrest. Seconds later, two more officers appeared and waited outside the front door. The van reversed along the street and stopped in the middle of the road, outside the property. Sam Jennings appeared, followed closely by Ryan Levinson, his hands cuffed behind his back. Detective Constable Alex Pence held the prisoner's arm. Ryan's shoulders sagged. He looked so small. Perhaps that was the idea: to shrink himself as much as possible and not meet anyone's gaze.

An engine revved loudly and furiously. Harry glanced through the driver's side window towards the silver Astra. The man in the car stared straight ahead. With a sense of unease, Harry strained his eyes but couldn't see well enough. He climbed out of the car, stood by the door, and peered across the roof to get a better view. The car edged out of the space. A perspiring, anxious man sat with his arms straight, gripping the steering wheel in anger. Harry recognised him.

'No, no, no.' Harry slammed the door and moved quickly around the car. 'Mr Hillingdon – stop!'

The engine roared. Terry Hillingdon threw Harry a sorrowful stare, tightened his grip, and charged the car towards his intended victim. DC Pence and Ryan Levinson approached the open cage at the rear of the van.

Harry shouted, 'Get out of the road!' Both men turned, either to the sound of Harry's voice or the car bearing down on them. Too late. A deafening crash followed the echoes of torturous shrieks.

*

An ambulance was on the scene within fifteen minutes. Having avoided the full force of the impact, DC Pence escaped with a broken leg, fractured ribs, and multiple cuts and bruises. Ryan Levinson was killed instantly. He had attempted to dive out of the way but was swept along with the car and crushed against the van. Mr Hillingdon had succeeded in taking the young man's life, but in doing so, had sacrificed his own. Not wearing his seatbelt may have been part of his plan. The force of the car striking the back of the van had jerked his head hard into the deployed airbag. Though he may well have survived the head, chest, and facial injuries, his ensuing heart attack was fatal.

Sitting on the pavement, Harry looked to the heavens as though searching for divine intervention. Two more deaths: the tally in this miserable case was now at eight – nine if Owen Carrick was involved. Sam joined him on the kerb and handed him a small bottle of water. He unscrewed the lid and gulped most of it down.

'I should have seen this coming,' he said.

'How could you?'

'Because if I'd been in Mr Hillingdon's shoes, I would have done the same thing, probably sooner. When I called to ask for this particular address, it must have literally set the wheels in motion.'

'You're being too hard on yourself.'

'You didn't see Melanie's parents. They were broken. With her father, it ran deeper. Humiliation. His pride and dignity were taken away piece by piece, and Ryan and his father were partly responsible. Terry Hillingdon believed he'd failed to protect his daughter, and what we've just witnessed are the devastating consequences. Now I have to tell one grieving mother that her husband is dead, and another that her son has been killed.'

'I'm not letting you do both. This happened on my watch, so it's only fair I take some responsibility,' she said.

'I appreciate that. Can you visit Mrs Hillingdon? I'd struggle to face her again.'

'Sure.' Sam got to her feet. 'I'll meet you at the car in five.'

'Sam!' She stopped to look back. 'Thank you.'

On the way to the station to collect his car, Harry received a text message from Penny Levinson. His immediate reaction was that she'd already discovered the news. It wouldn't be the first time social media had revealed such information before the police. To his relief, she thanked him for not saying a word when they'd met earlier – a situation he'd navigated far better than the one regarding Mr Hillingdon.

As Harry drove around the corner towards the Levinsons' house, he recalled Penny saying she was going home to pack. His doubts as to whether she'd be there eased when he saw her car in the driveway. He knocked on the door and waited, which never helped when delivering news of a bereavement; if anything, it made him more nauseous. She finally answered the door.

'You look as white as a—' She paused. Anguish followed realisation as a tidal wave of grief swept through her body. Before he could get a word out, a piercing yowl filled the air, and she fell to her knees in the doorway.

He helped Penny to her feet, escorted her to the living room sofa, and asked if she wanted him to call someone. Sorrow had numbed her senses. He took it upon himself to fetch some tissues and a glass of water. When he returned, she'd recovered from her sombre state and demanded answers: the where, the when, and the how. Harry sat in the black leather armchair and asked if her husband was around so he could talk to them both. Penny informed him she'd packed her husband's bags and told him to leave. Harry explained everything as best he could. Her son's behaviour towards Melanie and her parents did not come as a shock, and it was hardly a surprise to learn her husband had given the girl's father a good hiding.

'I tried so hard to be a good wife and mother, and I've often wondered where I went wrong. Over the years, I became conditioned to think I deserved to be battered by my husband. That somehow it was his right to slap me down when I answered back or spoke to a particular person too much during an evening out. It took my son almost beating a young girl to death to wake me the fuck up.' She dabbed her eyes with a tissue. 'Ryan's behaviour was appalling and unacceptable. What he did to Rebecca was unforgivable. But in the end, he didn't kill her. I don't accept that his actions warranted a death sentence.'

'I agree. He deserved his day in court, the same as everybody else.' Harry's phone vibrated in his pocket. This wasn't the right time to take a call.

Penny said, 'I suppose Mr Hillingdon will get his day in court and get off with diminished responsibility or something?'

'Mr Hillingdon did not survive the crash.' With her mournful demeanour already on display, Harry wasn't sure how she would react to the news.

She shook her head and sighed. 'How awful for his wife to lose her husband and daughter so close together.' Her empathetic response was unexpected, and not for the first time, she'd surprised him for the better. She said, 'I assume you're going to her house next?'

'My colleague is informing Mrs Hillingdon as we speak. You probably don't want to see your husband right now, but he needs to be told before he finds out some other way. Do you know where he is staying? I should pay him a visit.'

'I'm not sure where he is. I tried calling him when you were out of the room. He didn't answer, so I left him a message to contact me urgently.'

Harry reached into his pocket and handed her a bereavement information leaflet. 'I hate this part, but the loss of a loved one can leave us incapacitated. This explains the next steps. There are numbers on there if you need more information or help. You already have my number, so don't hesitate to call me if you have any further questions.'

Penny stared at the leaflet for all of a second and tossed it on the coffee table. 'What happens with regard to my son and what he did to Rebecca?'

'Since he can't be prosecuted, nothing.'

'What about what was on the phone?'

'The phone wasn't Ryan's. The photos were of Melanie Hillingdon, taken by Vincent Perry. She'd asked Ryan to get it back, which, in part, he did. He just didn't give it back to her.'

Confused, Penny said, 'Why would he want to keep the damn phone?' She frowned and closed her eyes, no doubt imagining he wanted the photos for himself.

Harry said, 'It's not what you think.'

'Then why?'

'Ryan kept them for a specific purpose, hoping they might be useful one day. I'm confident he used them to blackmail Vincent, forcing him to crash the van into his car on the hard shoulder. I'm uncertain whether Vincent knew Rebecca was in the car at the time, but from what we've discovered, it's extremely likely.'

Bringing her hands to her face and gasping, Penny said, 'Jesus Christ! Attempted murder instead of a few stupid nude pictures doesn't exactly make it any better.'

'I'm just being honest with you, Mrs Levinson. You deserve the truth. We know Rebecca was not at your house at the time Ryan said she was, and that his car was not in the driveway. An incident occurred earlier in the day, though I'm not fully aware of the details. I do know Craig Bishop, James Harding, and Melanie Hillingdon were false witnesses at the scene that night, and all three are dead. I know Ryan had nothing to do with their deaths, but I'm certain he could have shed light on how all this started and pointed us in the direction of exactly who was responsible.'

'The news on the television said Melanie and James were the main suspects.'

Harry said, 'Evidence sometimes conceals a bigger picture.'

'You disagree?'

'Oh, they're guilty. I'm just doubtful they acted alone.'

'Your instincts were right about my son. You'd be a fool not to listen to them now.'

For someone going through such a traumatic experience, she held it together well. She had surprised and impressed Harry time and again; something of a rarity.

'My boy wasn't always bad,' she said. 'I tried to shield him from his father's shady activities, but the more he learned about his dad, the more he aspired to be like him, wanting the fat prick's approval.'

Her phone rang, saving Harry from a response. It was her husband. She told him to come to the house immediately.

'You should go,' she said. 'I'll tell him.'

'Are you sure? I can stay if you want.'

'No. It's fine. I can do this.'

'As I said, you have my number. I'm truly sorry, Penny.'

In his car, Harry stared at the Levinson house. He had a lot of sympathy for Penny. She had a good heart, and it puzzled him how she had come to marry a bruiser like Carl Levinson. He considered sticking around in case Mr Levinson lost the plot and took it out on her. It seemed unlikely. If he was going to lay one on her, he'd have done so when she'd thrown him out of the family home. They'd probably console each other and be back together before the night's end. Harry gazed up at the window where he'd first seen Ryan peeping from behind the curtain. He'd taken an instant dislike to him, but he would never have wished for things to end the way they had.

Checking his phone, he saw a missed call from PC Halilovic and called him back.

'Hi, Dean. What's up?'

'I've received the report from the data recovery specialist about the deleted files on the security system at the mall. It's not good news. The file was overwritten. He managed to recover a fragment of the frame from around the time we wanted, but it's not enough and doesn't provide us with a view of the suspect.'

'Shit. How come it was overwritten so quickly?'

'The cameras are recording non-stop, so data is written to the empty sectors of the hard drive, and once a file is deleted, it is marked as available. With high-end security systems, overwritten video footage can be recovered, and the frames can be carefully restored. Unfortunately, the system at the mall does not fall into the high-end category.'

'The part he recovered – do we know when it was deleted?'

'I asked the same question. Apparently, determining the exact time and date a file is deleted is difficult because the metadata, which contains the information, is stripped. It could have been deleted at any time within the twenty-two-hour window from when Lucy was stabbed until the following afternoon when I called the security office.'

'Okay, Dean. Thanks for trying.'

'One last thing – we have the results back from Melanie's pay-as-you-go phone. As expected, she received a call from Vincent Perry shortly before the crash. There were other exchanges between the pair dating back a year or so, but nothing noteworthy.'

To sum it up, whoever deleted the file was either clever or lucky, perhaps a little of both. Even though everything pointed to James Harding as the person who stabbed Lucy, it would have been better to have it on film and know for certain.

58

Boxing Day

They arrived in Helmsley just before dark, and within seconds, Lenny became aware of Harper's heightened sense of awareness. So much history for him here, mostly tragic, painful, and downright horrific. As they passed by the old house in reflective silence, Lenny couldn't help but glance sideways. The gate to the drive was padlocked, but there it stood at the top of the rise, the windows and front door boarded up to keep out trespassers. One could argue it was a feeble attempt to conceal its dreadful past. As Lenny focused on the road ahead, Harper twisted in the passenger seat to look back. A glimpse in the rear-view mirror revealed Danny gazing out of the window, both unable to turn away until the house was out of sight. The dropped jaw and wide eyes full of wonder told him Danny knew exactly what he was looking at.

The voice on the satnav said to take the next left. Less than two miles to their destination, and Lenny's tension about showing up uninvited increased tenfold. If he had turned up on his own, she would have groaned for a few seconds and got over it. Turning up with Harper would likely have got him a peck on the cheek. Danny was the problem. Lenny understood why she wanted to move on with her life and put all that had happened with Danny behind her, but what if there was another reason?

Once again, he caught sight of Danny in the mirror. The smirk on his face while he looked up and to his right was telling, as though he was staring at someone beside him. Lenny adjusted the mirror – Joseph Webster's dead eyes darted his way. He slammed on the brakes; the tyres screeched, and they all jerked forward.

'Jesus, Lenny,' said Harper.

'Sorry. A cat ran across the road. Is everyone all right?' Lenny glanced around to make sure Danny was alone. A car slowed behind them. A short, sharp beep urged him to get the car moving. Often uncertain about his visions, on this occasion, he hoped the long, painstaking drive was playing tricks on his tired mind.

Elaine and Tom's beautiful detached cottage wasn't on the scale of Sablefall Farm, but it was a fairly decent size, clearly extended over time. The front was adorned with twinkling white lights, and a festive wreath hung on the thick, dark oak door. The curtains were pulled halfway, leaving enough of a gap to view the elegant Christmas tree and the welcoming warmth beyond. They piled out of the car and sauntered towards the house. Harper and Danny stood off to the side. One timid knock, and seconds later, the door opened.

Emily beamed with excitement. 'Uncle Lenny.'

'Hello, Emily. I can't always tell if I've shrunk or you've grown taller. Probably both.' She laughed and called out to let her mum know who was at the door.

Drying a glass with a tea towel, Elaine marched along the hall and stopped halfway. 'You're a little late for cold turkey and mash,' she said. 'Though I have got a ham on the boil.'

'I never say no to a bit of boiled ham.'

'Well, don't just stand there letting all the heat out. You don't usually wait to be invited in.'

It was now or never. 'I – er, brought a couple of visitors.'

'Oh, Lenny. You didn't?' She continued along the hallway. 'I told you I'd think about it.'

'I took it as a yes.'

'What I truly meant was no. And now you go and spring it on— Hi, Danny,' she said as he walked into view.

'Hello, Mrs Burgess.' He took off his woolly hat. 'You didn't know I was coming, did you?' Danny frowned at Lenny, who shrugged mischievously.

'I didn't.' Elaine smiled and placed her arms around him, the glass in one hand and the tea towel dangling from the other. 'It would have been nice to have some advance warning, but you're here now.' She directed a stern glare at Lenny and lashed out at him with the tea towel. She pulled back and took a good look at Danny. 'I'm happy to see you.'

'Are you happy to see me?' asked Harper, poking his head around the corner.

Elaine looked up, covered her excited smile with her hands, and hastened towards her brother. Lenny had hoped Harper's appearance would soften the blow of bringing Danny. It seemed to have had the desired effect. While they reacquainted themselves, he led Danny into the living room and introduced him to Elaine's husband, Tom, her sixteen-year-old son, Michael, and her eleven-year-old daughter, Emily, who were playing a video game.

Tom got up from the sofa and handed his controller to Danny. 'Here, you take over for me.' He shook hands with Lenny, offered him a beer, and they left the youngsters to play.

Tom grabbed a couple of cans from the fridge, passed one to Lenny, and said, 'I bet she's far from happy with you.'

'She wasn't too pleased, no,' said Lenny. 'Until Harper showed his face.'

Tom's bright mood faded. He walked over and closed the kitchen door. Keeping his voice down, he said, 'It's bad enough you brought that boy with you, but why on earth did you bring *him* here? Are you mad? If the police find him in this house, we'll all be going to prison.'

'Nobody's going to find him because nobody is looking for him.'

'You'd better be right.' Tom paced the kitchen.

'Tom, calm down. You're stressing yourself out for nothing.' Lenny dragged a chair from under the oak dining table and took a seat.

'Stressing myself out! After everything— He's killed— Oh, what's the point? What is he doing with you anyway? He's supposed to be settled with Alice and the baby.'

'Things didn't quite go to plan.'

Tom said, 'I can't say I'm surprised.'

'Me neither,' said Lenny.

Tom joined him at the table and snapped open the ring pull of his can. The kitchen door opened, and Elaine and Harper entered. Words lingered on their tongues, each waiting for the other to speak, but the longer the silence, the tighter the lips. Harper planted himself next to Lenny. Elaine fetched two more beers, sat beside Tom, and slid a can across to Harper.

Lenny was reminded of the evening before they set off after Joseph Webster. They were gathered around the table at the old house, wanting to tear each other limb from limb. He said, 'Is this familiar to anyone else?'

'Yes,' they replied in unison.

'Glad it's not just me.' Lenny hoisted his can. 'Cheers, all.'

Forced smiles broke out around the table as they half-heartedly raised their cans to join his ice-breaking toast. Lenny observed

Danny watching from the doorway, his expression one of distress, maybe a hint of anger, which rapidly altered to a contented smile when he locked eyes with Lenny. To avoid making a big deal out of it, Lenny turned away, but it was enough to give him pause for thought. Perhaps going against Elaine's reluctance to see Danny wasn't such a good idea. The poor lad had unresolved problems about what had happened, and why wouldn't he? He'd most likely be in therapy for the rest of his life. His own parents had expressed deep concerns about his recent behaviour. Lenny considered whether he was overthinking the situation. Danny was in a strange house with people he didn't know but with whom he'd shared an extremely traumatic experience. To say he was overwhelmed would be an understatement.

Emily walked into the kitchen and sat on her mum's knee. Michael wasn't far behind. He raided the cupboard, brought a box of chocolate fingers to the table, and shared them with Danny. Lenny couldn't resist.

Emily looked at Harper and quietly asked, 'Mummy, who's that man?'

'That's Simon. He's a dear friend I haven't seen for a while.'

Harper smiled at Emily, who tucked her bright red face under her mother's arm.

59

Boxing Day

There were better ways for Harry to spend the rest of Boxing Day than going to the mall in Maidstone. A good example would be watching live football at the pub. However, since recovering the CCTV data had proved as futile as Harry Kane winning a major trophy with Spurs, it was time to follow up on Lucy's suggestion of Owen Carrick's involvement. Though it was conceivable, he didn't suspect Owen at all. If anything, Harry just wanted to rule him out and, in doing so, perhaps find the real culprit who had deleted the files at the mall.

The security guard on duty was Ted Grayson, and fortunately, he'd been the one helping the police with their investigation into the missing data. Ted allowed Harry to look through the recorded CCTV footage from the time it was deleted. The radio was on in the background, with the TalkSport team previewing the afternoon's football matches. At least he had something to listen to while he examined the videos. Going through them was slow and painstaking. The only people entering and leaving the security office were the guards themselves, which could mean either the computer system had been hacked or one of the guards had been bribed to delete the files. Harry suspected bribery, but barring a confession, proving which guard it was would be nearly impossible.

Despite coming to the end of his search, he was still browsing thirty-five minutes later, clearly dawdling because he didn't fancy spending the day alone in his poky room at Gerty's. He wasn't on duty, so perhaps the pub *would* be a better place to kill a couple of hours. Going by the commentary of the match on the radio, if he was quick, he'd get there in time for the start of the second half. His back ached from sitting awkwardly so as not to put weight on his injured leg. He dragged himself from the chair and faced Ted, who was glued to the monitors.

'Right, I'm off, Ted. I appreciate your help.'

'Not a problem. Did you find what you were looking for?'

'Sadly, no. But it was worth a try.' Harry swiped his jacket from the back of the chair and put it on. 'Enjoy the rest of your Christmas.'

'You too. Oh, my condolences for the loss of your colleague. I forgot to mention it earlier. He was a good bloke.'

Harry removed his hand from the door handle and turned. 'Which colleague do you mean?'

'The Welsh fella, Owen Carrick. I just assumed you knew him.'

'I did know him. His body was only discovered yesterday morning, so you'll have to forgive me if I'm surprised that news of his death has spread so quickly. You said he was a good bloke. Were you friends?'

'Not exactly. He was a friend of Gareth's. He brought him into our pub quiz team. It was Gareth who informed me earlier today. Owen had a brilliant sense of humour. Clever too. The man knew his history. We certainly missed his know-how at *Who's on the Bauble* this week.'

'Nice pun. I assume it's a Christmas quiz special?'

'Yeah, the first one he'd missed. He failed to let us know and left us a member short. It didn't go down well, as you can imagine. But I suppose it makes sense now, considering how low he must have been to, you know – do what he did.'

'Who's Gareth?'

'Gareth Jones. He's a security guard here. They went to school together back in Swansea.'

And just like that, Harry had a suspect. Though he hoped it wasn't true, Gareth's link to Owen implied Lucy could be right. 'Do you have a number and an address for Mr Jones? I wouldn't mind having a word and passing on my sympathies.'

Gareth Jones's house was a three-bed semi in the Medway area of Lordswood. Harry had called ahead as soon as he'd reached his car to arrange a visit. During the call, Mr Jones stuttered and sounded fairly nervous, which only added to Harry's suspicions. When he opened the door to let Harry in, Gareth couldn't keep still – shifting his feet, touching his face, and constantly wiping the sweat from his brow, which was rather odd considering it was seven degrees outside and not much warmer in the living room. Gareth's wife was in the kitchen making a cup of tea. She appeared to be a lot more relaxed than her husband. The children were sent to their bedrooms the moment Harry arrived. All three being teenagers, they didn't seem to mind.

Harry took in his surroundings. The Christmas tree in the corner of the room, adorned with an abundance of multicoloured twinkling lights, was a little over the top for his liking, but pretty nonetheless. However, the two-tone foil garlands stretching every which way across the ceiling crossed a line no one should dare to go beyond. Harry and Gareth made small talk about the weather and the lack of Christmas specials on the television these days. With Gareth hailing from the same city in Wales, there were moments Harry could have closed his eyes and imagined he was talking to Owen. Mrs Jones brought in the tea and closed the living room door on her way out.

Harry sipped his tea and said, 'Your wife doesn't know why I'm here, does she?'

After a slight pause, he shook his head. 'No, she doesn't.'

'But you do?'

'I can guess.'

'Why don't you explain it to me?' said Harry, pulling out his phone. 'But with your permission, I'd like to record your statement.' Gareth nodded, and Harry placed the phone on the table between them.

Gareth said, 'Owen came to me, terribly anxious about something, but wouldn't say what. He needed a favour. When he stated what he wanted me to do, I asked again what was wrong. He insisted he couldn't tell me, just that if I didn't do it, he could lose his job, his family, everything.'

'What did he want you to do?'

'You wouldn't be here if you didn't know.'

'It's best if you tell me so we can be clear.'

'I don't suppose it makes any difference now that he's no longer with us. He asked me to delete video footage from a particular camera. I got the impression it wasn't something he wanted to do, but he didn't have much choice in the matter. Taking into account how anxious he was and what has happened since, I reckon he was being threatened in some way.'

'So you did as he asked?'

'Yes.'

'You committed a crime by destroying evidence?'

'Yes. And I'll take what's coming. Owen and I became friends when we were eleven years old. For decades, we've looked out for each other. In all the years I'd known him, I'd never seen him so worried. So scared. I helped my friend.'

'And he said nothing else to you – about who or why?'

Mr Jones reached into his pocket for his phone. 'I don't know why, but I took a picture of the man he specifically asked me to delete from the video.' He handed his phone to Harry. 'The man in the photo has the same stressed look on his face that I saw on Owen's. Whatever was going on, it caused Owen to take his life. If I knew anything else at all, Detective Inspector Baxendale, I'd tell you.'

Harry's eyes were focused on the picture of James Harding wearing the blue parka, just as they'd suspected. He said, 'You could get into serious trouble for this, Mr Jones.'

'I know. But if he asked me to do it again, I would.'

His youngest daughter, thirteen or so, entered the room and asked if she could return to the PlayStation on the floor in front of the television. 'Not yet, sweetheart. I'm still talking to this gentleman.'

Harry picked up his phone and stopped the recording. 'We're all done here, Mr Jones. She's welcome to get back to her game,' he said, getting to his feet. The girl smiled and hurried towards the TV.

Mr Jones showed him to the door. Harry walked down a couple of steps and turned to face Gareth. 'At this stage, all I can say is you *may* be hearing from me again. If you don't, consider yourself a lucky man.'

From the car, Harry called Sam Jennings and asked about Mrs Hillingdon. As expected, the news hit her hard. He also asked Sam to acquire any computers belonging to Owen Carrick. Time to find out what was going on in Owen's world. She had already done so, securing his laptop and phone when she attended the property on Christmas morning. Now he knew why DCS Falconer rated Sam so highly. Finally, with some free time on his hands, he had a chance to visit the hospital to see Rebecca and perhaps check in on Arthur. It turned out to be a wasted journey, as both had been discharged earlier in the day. No more delaying his return to the guest house.

60

Boxing Day

The conversation flowed a little better than it had earlier, mostly due to the alcohol, which had helped ease the underlying tension. Lenny and Harper were in the living room; the children were in the back room playing video games, while Elaine and Tom were preparing the spare room for Lenny and Danny. As seemed to be the way of late, Harper would make do with the sofa. Enjoying the warmth of the open stone fireplace, Harper expressed how strange it was to see Elaine living in a different house. It hadn't occurred to Lenny that, on either side of Harper's unjust imprisonment, Sablefall Farm was the only place he knew her to live.

Harper sipped from his bottle of beer and said, 'On the subject of houses, I know why you brought me here.'

'I brought you here because I want you out from under my feet.'

Harper smiled. 'You can't even be bothered to lie about it.'

'You already know, so what would be the point? I certainly didn't bring you here for a family reunion.'

'And there was me thinking we were getting along.'

'I suppose we were doing okay, but give it a few more days and we'd have turned into Felix and Oscar.'

'I've no idea who those guys are.'

'Of course you don't. My point is, we'd get under each other's skin. It's nothing personal. I just like my own space. If she doesn't have anywhere to put you up, we'll make do, but you'll have to move from the sofa into my room. I'll go back into the main bedroom.'

'Fair enough. I'll have a word with her.'

Lenny said, 'If she doesn't have anything right away, there's always—'

'No! I'm not living in *that* house.'

'I suspected moving back there might be a step too far.' Lenny finished his beer. 'Right, I'll fetch us another couple of bottles from the kitchen.'

'Not for me, thanks.'

Nearing the ajar kitchen door, Lenny overheard Danny talking to Elaine and hovered outside to listen.

Danny asked, 'Why didn't you report what I did on the boat?'

'It wasn't my place to say. You went through a hell of an ordeal, and it should be your decision when and how much you wish to divulge.'

'I'm glad you never told anyone. I haven't wanted to talk about it yet, but one day soon I will. It just would have been nice to thank you for saving me sooner. I'm pleased to be here now, though.'

'I'm pleased too,' said Elaine.

Lenny sensed insincerity behind her last response – something he might not have picked up if they were face to face. He hoped Danny didn't detect her flat, hollow words either. A floorboard squeaked as he adjusted his position. To avoid suspicion, he pushed the door open and breezed into the room, bound for the fridge.

Pointing to the Quality Street between them on the table, he said, 'You two had better not be helping yourselves to all the purple ones.' He grabbed a beer from the fridge and walked over, shuffling through the container until he found one.

'We were just having a little catch-up, weren't we, Danny?' she said.

He smiled. 'Right, I'll take my bag up to the room.'

Lenny said, 'You couldn't take my bag up as well, could you?'

'Sure.'

As soon as Danny was out of sight, Lenny walked over and closed the kitchen door.

Elaine reached for a chocolate. 'I think someone's been doing a spot of eavesdropping.'

Walking towards her, he put his finger to his lips to shush her and said, 'And I think someone's finding it difficult to feign the tiniest hint of sincerity. What is your problem with Daniel? I'm not a fourteen-year-old boy, so don't lie to me. Tell me what happened on the boat, Elaine.'

Elaine sighed. 'Okay. I'll tell you, but you can't repeat this to anyone.'

Lenny joined her at the table and reached for another chocolate. 'I won't say a word.'

She said, 'The other boy on the narrowboat – Connor Doherty. He wasn't killed by Joseph Webster. Danny told me Webster forced *him* to do it.'

'But you don't believe him?'

'Not entirely. When I discovered the body in the hessian mailbag, Danny apologised and cried, but there was no remorse or sincerity. No sense of guilt.'

Lenny couldn't grasp why Danny would have done such a thing. 'Hold on,' he said. 'You can't be sure Webster didn't force him. Considering the circumstances, you could have interpreted it wrong.'

'I didn't misinterpret anything. You didn't look into his eyes or hear the tone of his voice. That's not all,' she said. 'I'm convinced Danny was made to dismember the bodies of Connor, and Colin Hargreaves.'

Lenny shook his head. 'No. This is nonsense. You're assuming the worst as an excuse to keep him away from you. You can't know for certain what happened.'

'You're right – I can't be certain. But I know murder. I know death. I know deceit. And I recognise the eyes of a killer. I see it every time I look in the bloody mirror.'

'Is this why you've never wanted to see him?'

'Danny was being groomed to kill. To take the reins when the time came. Just like Joseph Webster and possibly Ozias Blackwood before him. It's not the kind of thing you simply wash away in the shower. In a few years, his mind may well be in a better place, but right now, he is dancing in the devil's back yard, and until he chooses to walk out of the side gate, he is capable of anything. That's why I didn't want him anywhere near me or my children.'

'And probably why you didn't want him sleeping in their room tonight? Look, I think you're overreacting, but I get it. After tomorrow, I'll never bring him here again.'

The familiar squeak of a floorboard made them look towards the door. Lenny stood and crept across the kitchen. He pulled the door swiftly open. Nobody was there.

As the evening wore on, one by one, they were drawn to the kitchen table, where they talked about old times and their plans for the new year. Instead of demolishing Sablefall Farm, Elaine and Tom had opted to sell the property, hoping another family would fare better and build contrasting memories to their own.

Lenny hinted at becoming a private investigator, though secretly he hoped to pursue a consultancy position alongside Harry. As for Harper, he wasn't sure, though he did express an interest in travelling. He also said he was missing Alice and Milena. When pressed about returning home, he doubted it was an option.

With the young ones tucked up in bed for the last couple of hours, Lenny excused himself, stating his need for sleep. Too tired to care as they teased him about his age and accused him of being a lightweight, he trudged up the stairs. Danny's voice echoed along the landing as he neared the bedroom. He assumed Michael must be inside with him and placed his ear against the door. With no sound but muffled laughter from downstairs, he questioned what he was doing and entered the room. Danny was in bed, asleep. Lenny stripped to his briefs and sat on the bed opposite. He yawned, ran his hands over the light stubble on his face, and regarded Danny. Had this kid been playing him for a fool? He wasn't buying it. The boy was no killer.

61

December 27

The previous night had been quiet for Harry, for which he was thankful. After yet another eventful day, he'd finally had the opportunity to relax and play some of his favourite records. Nevertheless, he was surprised Lucy hadn't been in touch, and although slightly disappointed, it was probably best if a little distance came between them. He might well be comfortably afloat after the sinking of his marriage, but it was far too soon to jump into someone else's lifeboat.

Hanging around at Gerty's all day wasn't going to cut it, so an early morning visit to see how Arthur was doing seemed like a nice idea. His wife answered the door and welcomed Harry inside. She said she'd put the kettle on and led him through to the garden, where Arthur was either tending to his hellebores or reading in the cabin. Unable to locate him in the large, immaculate garden, Harry wandered towards the charming log cabin at the rear of the property. He knocked and entered.

Harry was taken aback by the size, bringing to mind a certain doctor's TARDIS. The immense warmth within also came as a surprise. Arthur was in the corner of the room, bending down, doing Lord knows what.

Arthur said, 'Those pesky ants are back, dear. I'm just putting some powder down, so I'll need the handheld vacuum in a bit.

Is it charged?' Arthur stood upright and turned. '*Harry*! This is unexpected. What on earth are you doing here?'

'I came by to see how you were.'

'How thoughtful. Well, come in and close the door. I prefer to keep the heat inside.'

Harry did as he was told and walked over to the sitting area in front of the wood-burning stove. 'Whoa!' Harry hastily removed his jacket. 'With the amount of heat this is throwing out, it's no wonder there's a colony of ants that think they've been whisked away for some winter sun. I'm picturing ants lying on loungers, sipping margaritas. I bet the walls are insulated as well.'

'Don't you start. The wife says exactly the same thing.' Arthur got comfy in one of the armchairs, and Harry settled into the other. 'And yes, the cabin is insulated.' He smiled.

'How's your head?'

'Battered and bruised.' Arthur tilted his head to reveal a small cut and dark bruising the size of a golf ball. 'A bit like my ego.'

'Don't be too harsh on yourself. There's not much you could have done about it.'

'I disagree. It was my responsibility, Harry. If I or one of my team hadn't messed up in the first place, this wouldn't have happened. I don't mind telling you, it's forced me to consider whether it's time to hang up my Gigli.' Reading Harry's vacant stare, he added, 'Bone saw.'

The cabin door opened, and Mrs Potts brought in their tea and biscuits on an ant-patterned serving tray, which she placed on a small table between the armchairs. Harry scrutinised the tray and looked up at Rose, who smiled with a wry twinkle in her eye.

'See how my wife mocks me, Harry? She purchased this tray last summer and brings it out every time we have guests in the cabin.'

Harry appreciated the familiar and loving sense of humour of the couple. Mrs Potts left them to drink their tea and chat, with Harry doing his best to convince Arthur not to retire. It didn't take long to change his mind. When their cups were empty and they'd polished off the custard creams, Harry got out of the armchair and walked over to examine the ants. Arthur soon followed.

Harry asked, 'Will the powder take care of the problem?'

'Hasn't done so far. I mean, it probably kills most of them. They disappear for a spell, but then a new queen comes along and rebuilds the colony from scratch.'

Harry had a lightbulb moment and said, 'Two queens can form one hell of a partnership.'

Arthur didn't quite catch what he'd mumbled. 'What's that?'

'Was the person who attacked you already in the apartment?'

'I'd closed the door, so unless they had a key, yes.'

Harry threw on his jacket. 'Sorry, Arthur. I have to go.'

Marching to his car, Harry seethed at his failure to bring such a vital clue to mind sooner and sensed he'd been toyed with. He pulled out his phone to make a call.

'Hi, Sam, it's Harry. Do we still have an officer assigned to protect Rebecca Heaton?'

'Not any more. I assumed since she was no longer in danger, it wasn't necessary. You sound worried, Harry. What's going on?'

'I'll get back to you.' Harry ended the call.

Harry parked a few houses down from the Heatons on Joy Lane and scanned all the nearby cars. He froze. Every muscle in his body tightened. He took a breath and closed his eyes in disbelief. Leaving his car, Harry walked towards the house on the opposite side of the road. He took a photo of a car with his phone and called Sam. Glancing at the person in the driver's seat as he passed by, he wanted to be mistaken, but sadly, he wasn't. He pretended to be oblivious to their presence.

'Hey, Sam. It might be a good idea to reinstate a police officer to keep watch outside the Heaton residence.'

'Is there a threat to life?'

'Probably.'

'You'll have to be more specific, Harry.'

'I need to look into a couple of things first. Please trust me on this.'

She said, 'You're not even supposed to be working.'

'I know, but I'm sure you've had new information come to light after you assumed a case was concluded. I need some time, Sam.'

'I'll send a car over as soon as possible and make proper arrangements by this evening.'

'Thanks. I'll wait at the house until it arrives. I owe you one.'

Harry knocked on the door. Mr Heaton answered, invited him inside, and showed him to the living room.

Rebecca was stretched out on the sofa, watching television with a blanket over her, clearly being well looked after by her mum and dad. Considering Mr and Mrs Heaton were separated, he was surprised to see Derrick at the house so early. Perhaps what had happened to their daughter had brought them closer. Harry had seen many times how tragedy could either bring families together or cruelly tear them apart. Derrick turned off the telly and asked Harry if he wanted a cup of tea or coffee.

'I wouldn't mind a coffee, thanks. Milk, no sugar.' Derrick left the room, and Harry turned to Rebecca. 'I had no idea you'd been released when I dropped by the hospital yesterday. I assume you're recovering well?' Harry wandered over to the bay window and stared through the thin net curtains.

'I'm still taking painkillers, but yes, I'm getting there,' she said, speaking a lot more easily.

As he'd expected, the car across the road was gone. They'd no doubt seen him and panicked. 'That's great news,' he said, making himself comfortable in an armchair by the window. 'You had us all worried when we couldn't find you. I was told you'd remembered some of the details about how you received your injuries.'

'Yes, but I'm sure there was something before. I know the memory is there – I just can't access it. It's so frustrating.'

'Give it time. Has anything come to mind regarding how you ended up in Canada?'

'I'm sorry, no. After the car, there's just emptiness. Though I do have this recurring dream of a brilliant white flash. It's silly and probably nothing, but there are two young girls either side of me, my hands in theirs, leading me forward. I feel safe with them.'

The bright flash inside the car before the van struck came to mind. Harry said, 'It's not silly. You were unconscious for a long time. Perhaps when one light goes out, another is switched on so we don't wander alone in the darkness.'

Mrs Heaton entered the room. 'Good morning, Detective Inspector Baxendale.'

'Morning, Mrs Heaton. Please, call me Harry.' She handed him his coffee. 'Thank you. I bet it's wonderful to have your daughter home again?'

'You have no idea.'

Mr Heaton walked through the door, sipped from his cup, and said, 'We know about Ryan. I'm not going to speak ill of the dead, but I, for one, won't be shedding any tears.'

Harry wanted to mention Penny Levinson and what she was undeservedly going through, but he held his tongue. There was no point in aggravating the situation. 'As well as coming here to see how Rebecca is doing, I need to tell you there will be a police car parked outside for a day or two.'

'How come?' asked Mrs Heaton. 'Is Rebecca still in danger?'

'It's a precautionary measure while the investigation is ongoing. We just need to clear up one or two loose ends.'

The Heatons refused to let him wait outside in his car and demanded he make himself comfortable in their home. June made him a ham, cheese, and pickle sandwich, which he appreciated, having only eaten several of Mrs Potts' custard creams that day. Harry concealed his impatience while he waited for the police constable to show up. Inside, he was being eaten alive by anger and itching to get going. There was someone in particular he had a few questions for. Whether they were prepared to answer any was another matter altogether. First, though, there was one other thing he wanted to check. When the PC finally arrived, Harry thanked Mr and Mrs Heaton and said he'd be in touch soon.

Before entering Sarah Kerr's apartment, Harry asked the police constable guarding the door if he was on duty on Christmas night. The officer said he wasn't and had no idea who it could have been. Harry entered and looked around, trying to work out why Arthur's attacker would have been there, but saw nothing of note. He stared at the empty slot in the knife block and shook his head with regret. Harry then opened the fridge and knew exactly who had attacked Arthur.

62

December 27

On the journey to Virginia Water in Surrey, Harry chastised himself for not having considered who had the most to lose. Perhaps a tad harsh in light of how quickly the case spiralled, but frankly, it was typical. His head wasn't in the game early on, and he'd made one or two errors in judgement. If there were any blame to be laid at his door when the case was finally put to rest, he'd accept it without question.

Virginia Water wasn't a place he was familiar with, but seeing the enormous houses brought to mind why the term "stockbroker belt" was associated with Surrey. High walls, tall wrought iron gates, security lights, and cameras; the wealthy wanted to keep what they had and built fortresses to protect it. Harry parked his car and approached, intimidated by the huge gated entrance. Disinclined to show any sign of weakness, he tried his best not to limp. He observed an abundance of large, multi-paned windows looming beyond, and eyes could be on him from any number of them. If there weren't, he could be certain his face was in high definition on CCTV.

Viewing the oversized brass-plated doorbell was as daunting as everything else on the short trek from his car. Nauseous and apprehensive, his muscles trembled, which was stupid because *he* was not the villain in this scenario. He furtively shook his hands by his sides and waggled his fingers to relieve the tension. His focus shifted to why he was here – the victims – living and deceased. Calmer and reassured, Harry raised his finger to the buzzer. Before pressing it, a sharp rattle preceded a mechanical whir – the gates slowly opened. Someone *was* watching.

There were no cars to be seen, possibly underground in some luxurious vaulted cave. Even the crunch of the gravel under his feet was different: soft, fine, and rich. At the large front door, Harry had his warrant card ready. For the first time, it occurred to him that he might not get any further than where his feet were firmly planted. Representatives, lawyers, whoever – there was always some haughty individual close at hand to stop you in your tracks and make things as difficult as possible. The sound of high heels clicking against a solid floor grew louder and closer. The door opened.

A wide smile beamed across Sarah Kerr's face. 'Hello, Harry. I've been expecting you. Seeing as you're not on duty, one can assume you're here in an unofficial capacity, so I'm sure we can skip the formalities.'

He wasn't sure she'd be this welcoming, but perhaps he should have guessed that she would be. Sarah was a narcissistic sociopath with murderous leanings, and Harry questioned whether he was doing the right thing by talking to her alone.

'Come in,' she said. 'Don't be afraid.' Debatable. Sarah walked ahead of him in the grand entrance hall, her flimsy, light beige dress flowing around her knees. As Harry stepped inside, without turning, the words, 'And close the door behind you,' echoed aloud. He did as she'd ordered and noted the automatic locking of the front door. Harry followed, letting her believe she was in total control. In truth, she was. But the only play he had was to feed her ego and find out intricate details that, in the long run, could turn the tables in his favour.

Harry glanced around and said, 'I'm half expecting to get savaged by guard dogs.'

'Are you nervous of dogs, Harry?'

'Only big, vicious ones.'

'I wouldn't exactly call Pomeranians big or vicious, but to ease your concerns, the dogs stay at kennels while my parents are away, so you're quite safe.'

She opened a door, glanced at Harry, and disappeared into a room. He paused in the doorway and took in the enormous room he was about to enter, brightened by a gigantic crystal chandelier to make up for the absence of windows. The maroon walls stretched endlessly upwards to the ornate white mouldings on the ceiling. Flanked by colossal alcoves, a broad, castle-esque stone fireplace took centre stage on the far wall. A sizeable and expensive rug covered most of the dark oak floor. Neatly placed around the room in pairs were eight luxurious wingback chairs, upholstered in dark red Italian leather, with mahogany round tables between each set. It brought to mind one of those traditional gentlemen's clubs, except this was more than a meeting place to unwind with a cigar and an alcoholic beverage – it was a secure space to talk business. He had no idea what her father did for a living, but it was either extremely important or highly illegal. Sometimes, the two went hand in hand.

Sarah sat in a chair in front of the fireplace and said, 'If you want to talk, you'll need to come in and close the door.' Harry entered and observed rubber seals around the thick wooden door. Sarah said, 'My father likes his privacy and has brokered his most significant deals in this room, so no doubt you've concluded it's soundproofed. Also, while recording devices will not work in here, I'd still prefer it if you turned off your phone and placed it in the magnetic bowl on the console by the door.' Once again, Harry did as she asked.

With no interest in pursuing the matter, he said, 'You do know it's illegal to interfere with wireless telegraphy in the UK, which includes jamming audio signals?'

'You'd best discuss that with my father when he gets back from Dubai.'

On the table in front of her sat a tray containing what Harry presumed was an expensive tea set made of bone china. The other tables were empty, confirming that Sarah had indeed been awaiting his arrival. 'I'm guessing you're here in this big house all alone?'

'Just until I can return to my apartment.' She leaned forward and reached for the kettle. 'Tea, Harry?'

He'd had his fill of tea for today. 'Thank you, but I'll give it a miss.'

She looked up with a sly grin. 'Don't worry, I'm not going to poison you if that's what you think.'

Exactly what he thought, though he said, 'I had one before I came.'

'I'll pour you a cup anyway, in case you change your mind.' He wouldn't.

Harry wandered over and made himself comfortable in the chair opposite.

'So, where to begin?' said Sarah, who sat back, crossed her legs, and sipped her tea.

'You could start by telling me how you know I'm not on duty and how you knew I was coming here.'

'Oh, I'm quite resourceful.'

'I'm fully aware of just how resourceful you are and of a certain police officer at your disposal.'

'You don't waste time, do you, Harry? I like that about you.'

'There's no point in messing around – we both know what you've done.'

'You may well know what I've done, but if you had any proof at all, you'd be here with thirty officers, ransacking this house and marching me off in handcuffs.'

'Thirty is a little over the top, but you're right, we have nothing. The only deaths to which you could be linked are those of Jerome Henderson and Melanie Hillingdon, and that's only because they happened in the vicinity of your apartment. Any evidence we put forward to the CPS would be discounted.'

'I must admit, everything has turned out considerably better than I could have imagined. With regard to Owen Carrick, he was a big help, but sadly he is no longer . . . *at my disposal.*' Her arrogant expression riled Harry, but he had to keep his cool.

'You've heard about his death?'

'I'm up to speed on most things I need to know.'

'Did you force him to take his life?'

'No. All his own doing. I think murdering Detective Constable Henderson pushed him over the edge. I may have coerced him on that occasion.'

'Did you use the same coercion to make him kill Melanie?'

'No. I pushed her over the edge.'

Despite what he was hearing – and the temptation to wipe the smug grin off her face – Harry kept his cool. 'What did you have on Owen Carrick?'

'That's for you to find out.' She leaned back, unruffled. Before Harry could press further, she cut in. 'I'm curious – how *did* you work out it was me behind all this?'

'Ants,' he said. Her bewildered frown was his cue to elaborate. 'Two queens can form one hell of a partnership.'

She formed a knowing smile as it sank in. 'Ah, yes.'

'Before coming here, I read up on the subject. It turns out you were right – two queens can rule together – until one turns on the other.'

'You're talking about Melanie?'

'If you say so.'

For a split second, she faltered – just enough for Harry to notice. He'd rattled her ice-cold cage.

'You want me to do all the work here, huh?' she said, her smile now edged with nerves.

'You don't have to say anything. But you've welcomed me into your parents' home and chosen to sit in a room where no one will ever know what is said. It suggests you have a lot more you wish to divulge.'

'Like Mr Carrick, Melanie had her uses. She was under the impression we were lovers and was eager to please me – in more ways than you can imagine.'

'Another person you had a hold over.'

'I may have manipulated her to an extent, but Melanie did nothing she didn't want to.'

With much to learn, Harry worried about how much time he had before she fell silent. At that moment, though, she was loving every minute of disclosing what she'd done. He said, 'Why don't we go back to what kicked off your murderous spree? I know something happened in your apartment when Ryan and Rebecca came over on December eighteenth. Did Rebecca call you out on flirting with Ryan?'

'Has a frightfully jealous streak, that one. Always suspecting that Ryan and I were having sex behind her back.'

'Were you?'

'Occasionally.'

'So Ryan was just another cat's paw?'

'My parents taught me to make the most of those close at hand, be they family, friends, or foes.'

'I bet murder wasn't part of the lesson?' Sarah said nothing and concealed her blithe smile with her teacup. 'What happened in the apartment, Miss Kerr?'

'Why don't you tell me?'

'You and Rebecca fought. She hit her head on the worktop, and you assumed you'd killed her. You tasked Ryan with cleaning up the mess, and I imagine he was happy to oblige. But everything fell apart the moment you all discovered Rebecca's body was not in the car. Not knowing if she was dead or alive must have driven you crazy. So much so that you devised a plan to get rid of everyone involved to protect yourself and your burgeoning quest for stardom. Then she turned up alive and hastened your need to silence your flying monkeys.'

'Ooh, I knew you were good at your job,' she said.

'This all started with a petty squabble, and the irony is – the person whose fallacious death kicked all this off is the only one who is still alive. Do you not have any remorse for all the deaths and misery you've caused?'

'The only remorse I have is for all the inconvenience it has caused me. Convinced she was dead, I wanted her out of my apartment and for Ryan to make it look like it happened elsewhere. When he discovered she was alive, he could have easily driven her to the hospital instead of leaving her in a car at the side of the motorway and arranging an accident. I never asked him to kill her.'

'Ryan did it to protect you, and yet you bear no responsibility for what happened?'

'Why should I? Ryan made the decision to commit murder, or at least to try to. The blame lies with him.'

'Well, just so you know, I have Rebecca under police guard. She *will* remember what happened.'

'Probably. But I'll survive the fallout in the long run. All she can attest to is that we had a fight and I pushed her. I had nothing to do with what Ryan did to her.'

Then why keep an eye on her? Sarah wasn't prepared to take the risk and would kill Rebecca at the first chance she got.

'And thank you, by the way,' she said.

'For what?'

'Ryan. You sowed the seed, and Melanie's father did the rest.'

'And you know this because you have another police officer in your pocket?'

She laughed. 'Oh, Harry, of course not. I use the power of social media. The general public gets the news before the journalists these days.' She placed her teacup on the tray and reached for the kettle to pour herself another. Drips from the kettle landed on the rug. 'Damn!'

Harry reached for a tissue in his pocket. 'Here, it's clean.'

'No bother. The cleaner can do it on Thursday. Are you sure you don't want to drink your tea, Harry? It's getting cold.'

'No. I'm fine.'

'Suit yourself.'

'Right, so I know Ryan was responsible for Vincent Perry's death. I presume Melanie killed James Harding, and Owen Carrick murdered Jerome Henderson before taking his own life. You've admitted to pushing Melanie to her death, and Mr Hillingdon died in the process of killing Ryan Levinson.'

'So far, so good,' she said.

'About Vincent? I just want to clarify something. He made a call moments before he crashed into the car. Do you happen to know who he called?'

'Melanie. He'd always had a thing for her and called an unregistered phone she had to express his love and sorrow for what he was about to do. The man was a pathetic fool. He had no idea she was involved.'

Harry said, 'That leaves Fred Perry and Craig Bishop. Were their deaths your handiwork?'

'Until poor, troubled, and gullible Melanie, I'd never killed anyone in my life.' She placed her teacup on the tray in front of her.

'Nine people are dead because of you, Sarah. Are you seriously telling me that, other than Melanie Hillingdon, you played no part in the actual killing of any of the other victims?'

She smiled, revealing her pearly whites, and held up a single digit.

'Which one?' asked Harry.

She held up two fingers.

'Craig Bishop?' Sarah nodded with ruthless pride. 'His murder was pretty gruesome,' he said.

'Tell me about it. I had blood all over my clothes. And before you go off searching, they've all been disposed of, right down to my new Christian Louboutin shoes. I didn't have time to change.'

'No, I imagine you didn't.' Harry couldn't get his head around how one egocentric young woman could cause so much horror and misery. 'What about Fred Perry?'

'Now *his* murder is the only one about which I have no idea.'

'I know you're lying.'

'Come on, Harry. After everything I've revealed, would I honestly hold something back?'

Harry drilled his fingers into the red leather on both arms of the chair. 'Yes, you would.' Hoping she hadn't noticed, he calmly brought his hands into his lap. 'And I know why.'

'Well, you know more than I do.'

Harry sat forward in his chair. 'I have one last request, and it will be the last time our paths ever cross.'

'That *would* be a shame. Are you sure you don't wish to stay a little longer, keep me company?' The solemn look on his face answered her question. 'What do you want to know?'

'Tell me exactly what happened in your apartment on the twenty-third of December.'

Sarah gulped the rest of her tea, put the cup on the tray, and sighed. 'I was in the apartment all day with Melanie. In the early evening, Owen arrived to let me know he'd deleted some CCTV footage.'

'From the shopping mall?'

Sarah nodded and continued. 'Not long after, there was a knock at the front door. Melanie answered and, stupidly, opened it without checking. DC Henderson barged into the apartment. Apparently, he'd seen Owen and followed him up.'

It occurred to Harry what Jerome was trying to tell him on the phone moments before his death. He wasn't saying Harry over and over; he was attempting to say Carrick, to let him know Owen was the mole.

Sarah said, 'He shouted at Owen, and they got into a fight. Henderson was getting the better of Owen, so I grabbed a knife from the kitchen and stabbed him in the stomach. For a brief moment, everyone froze. Henderson grappled with Owen once more before storming out of the apartment, holding his wound. I convinced Owen to go and finish the job – otherwise, we were all going to prison. He reluctantly took the knife and set off after him. Melanie rushed to the balcony, hoping to see it happen, and as I approached to join her, everything fell into place. DC Henderson showing up had presented the perfect opportunity to pin the blame on him, Melanie, and James. We watched Owen kill your colleague, and all I had to do was give Melanie a shove.'

'Thereafter, you staged the scene and whacked your head on the worktop in the same place Rebecca hit hers.'

'Yes. But as they say – no pain, no gain.'

'Out of curiosity, were you with Melanie when she killed James?'

'You said the previous question was your last.'

'Call me a liar and indulge me.'

Sarah smiled and said, 'The silly girl liked him. She needed a smidgen of coaxing.'

'So that's a yes. You said Melanie was a willing participant?'

'As I said . . .' She wrinkled her nose, bringing her index finger and thumb close together. 'A smidgen of coaxing.'

Harry said, 'I know James was wearing the blue parka at the mall and knifed my colleague. Was he a willing participant?'

'Quite the opposite.'

'And that's why he had to go?'

'We tried to make it look like an accident.'

'I know you did,' said Harry. 'So, was I the real target at the mall?'

'If anyone was going to catch me, it was going to be you. I wanted you gone. But I'm happy to say it didn't work out that way – otherwise, I wouldn't have been able to share all the finer details with you. Now, though, I fancy I've shared more than enough. I must say, it's magnificent to get all this out there. Kind of like free therapy without the danger of being reported.'

'Oh, I could report everything you've said to me, but without evidence, there wouldn't be much point.' Harry rubbed his hands together, rose from his seat, and walked over to retrieve his phone from the bowl.

In the hallway, Harry asked, 'Do you have a bathroom for guests in this place?'

She pointed to a door across the hall. 'There's the guest bathroom. I'll wait for you by the front door.'

Harry appeared several minutes later and walked across the marble-tiled floor, where she waited by the open door, ready to show him out. He said, 'One final thing before I leave.'

'There's always a final question, isn't there?'

'What would have happened if I'd drunk the tea?'

Sarah grinned. 'You wouldn't have walked out of this house. Though, after our little tête-à-tête, I'm glad you didn't. I see fun in our future.'

'Do you? Because all I see is death.'

In his car outside Gerty's, Harry glared through the windscreen at nothing in particular, reflecting on his conversation with Miss Kerr. He'd somehow mustered the strength to sit calmly while Sarah rattled on shamelessly about her actions, as though she were well within her rights to commit murder and manipulate others to do the same on her behalf. His next move would be the hardest decision of his life.

63

December 27

Tom had taken the young ones to the shop, while in the living room, Harper reluctantly searched through Elaine's portfolio of properties in North Yorkshire for somewhere to live. Lenny and Elaine were at the kitchen table finishing off the gammon. Well, mostly him. Refreshed after a good night's sleep, he was ready for the long drive home. As for the others, they were nursing slight hangovers.

Elaine asked, 'What time are you leaving?'

Lenny shoved a slice of gammon in his mouth, licked his fingers, and said, 'About an hour. I'm not taking any chances with the traffic. It would be nice to get home at a decent time.' His phone rumbled on the table, causing his tea to ripple in the cup. He glanced to see who was calling but let it ring.

'Who are you ignoring?'

'Harry.'

'It could be important.'

She could be right. He reached for his phone, hoping there might be more work in the offing. 'Harry, what's up?'

'I need you to look into something for me. I'd do it myself, but I have so much to do and dinner plans later.'

'Aren't you supposed to be recuperating?'

'You know how it is when you just can't let go,' said Harry.

'I certainly do, but I can't help you today. I'm in Helmsley.'

'Helmsley! You're with Elaine?'

'Yeah. As a matter of fact, she's glaring across the table at me with her puffy red eyes. She had a skinful last night.'

'I did not,' she said, tossing a piece of gammon his way.

Harry asked, 'Are you coming back today?'

'Leaving within the hour.' He picked the gammon from his lap and put it on the side of the plate. 'I sense urgency in your tone. Is everything alright?'

'No, it's not.'

'Can't you get one of your officers to look into it for you?'

'It's not a police matter,' said Harry. 'I need someone I can trust.'

'Okay. Tell me what you want me to do, and I'll get to it as soon as I can. If not this evening, then first thing tomorrow.'

'Thanks, Lenny. I'll make arrangements and send you the details later.'

'No worries.' Harry had already ended the call.

'You look puzzled,' said Elaine. 'What's going on?'

'I'm not sure. But Harry sounds troubled.'

'Unusual for him.'

'Yes, it is.' Emily ran into the kitchen. 'Here she is!' said Lenny, a big smile on his face as she sat in the chair next to him. 'Your mum just told me you've got a boyfriend.'

'No, I haven't,' Emily answered, her face turning red with embarrassment as she delved into the depths of her crisp packet.

'I'm only mucking about.' Lenny rubbed the top of her head. The others entered the room, and Danny placed a bag on the table. 'Did you get the supplies?'

'Yes,' Danny replied.

'Even my Hobnobs?' Lenny asked as Danny pulled them out of the paper bag to show him. 'Lovely. They'll keep me going. We'll be leaving soon, so you should probably get your things together and say your goodbyes, or whatever it is you kids do.'

Danny said, 'Should I let Simon know?'

'He won't be returning with us. He's gonna stay here for a bit.'

When Danny left the room, Lenny turned to Michael. 'Why don't you set up the computer and have one last go at your game before he goes?'

'No, I don't think I'll bother. He's weird.'

'What do you mean?'

Tom said, 'Oh, come on, Lenny. Don't tell me *you* can't see it? The kid even gives me the creeps.'

Lenny climbed to his feet and grabbed his cup of tea. 'Granted, he's a bit odd, but is it any wonder? I have to say, I'm disappointed in all of you. After everything you've witnessed over the last three years or so, you should know better.' He walked through the utility room and out of the back door into the garden.

Elaine came out soon after and sat beside him on the bench. 'I get why you're taken with Danny and want to help him.'

'He deserves the same chance to rebuild as you and Harper.'

Taking on board what he'd said, she agreed. 'You're right. Maybe I've been too harsh in fobbing him off. That great big heart of yours is infectious. Look, I'll help where I can. Michael and Emily were quite traumatised after Webster invaded our home. They've been seeing a brilliant child psychiatrist who came highly recommended. I'm more than happy to set up an appointment at her London office. Her services are quite expensive, mind.'

'Extortionate, you mean. Danny's parents aren't exactly rolling in—'

'Which is why I'd be willing to foot the bill.'

'As it turns out, he's not getting along with his current therapist, so it might be a big help. His parents would be grateful, I'm sure.'

'Talk to them, and if they agree, I'll make the arrangements.' Elaine's phone rang. She pulled it from her pocket to see who it was. 'I should probably take this.' She put the phone to her ear and wandered towards the rear of the garden.

Danny appeared and took Elaine's seat. Lenny said, 'You about ready to go?'

Danny nodded. 'Everybody hates me.'

'Don't be silly. I like you.'

'You're the only one. My mum and dad don't even like me.'

'I've spoken to them often, so I know that's nonsense.'

'I just find it hard to make people like me.'

'You can't force people to like you, Danny. It takes time. They have to get to know you first.'

'Zeph liked me straight away. He said he knew I was better than the others.'

'You shouldn't take anything that monster told you to heart.'

Elaine shouted, 'Not a chance!' Her raised voice pricked their ears as she wandered closer. 'And not just because it's the Christmas holidays.'

Her anger was evident, and Lenny couldn't help but listen in.

'I said no . . . You're asking too much. I'm not discussing this. Why don't you just . . .? Look, I'm sorry, but that's not my problem . . . I know you have, but I can't possibly . . . You wouldn't do that . . . Shit! Okay, I'll meet you. But I'm not at all happy about you forcing my hand this way.'

Elaine ended the call abruptly. 'Fuck!' She kicked over a plant pot. 'Fuck! Fuck! Fuck!' Aware that Lenny and Danny had observed her outburst, she walked towards them. 'Looks like I'll be coming to London.'

Lenny asked, 'Is there a problem?'

'Work. Some developer is talking about pulling out of a huge deal. Sorry about the language.'

'Can't say I blame you. What kind of pri—' he glanced at Danny, 'idiot causes a load of aggro over Christmas? They obviously don't have much of a family life.'

'Can I stay at your place tomorrow night?'

'Well, in truth, it's your place. So how can I possibly refuse?'

'Great,' she said.

'You'd better bring the spare key with you. I might not be there when you arrive,' said Lenny.

'Will do.' Elaine sighed. 'Now I'd better go and break the news to Tom.'

'Good luck with that.' Lenny turned to Danny. 'I get rid of one and end up with the other. Thank Christ it's only for one night. Right, come on. Let's go.'

When he arrived at his apartment after dropping Danny off, he checked his phone to find he'd received a photo of Sarah Kerr and a voicemail from Harry with instructions to view CCTV recordings at Maidstone Hospital. Harry had called ahead and informed the head of security what it was about and who to expect. Tired from all the driving, it would have to wait until morning. Thankfully, the return journey had been a lot quicker, and although it was only an overnight stay, he was glad to be home.

In his favourite chair, with a contented Phoebe on his lap, Lenny sipped whisky from a glass and relaxed. Earlier, he'd taken a step towards dealing with his grief and moved back into the main bedroom. As he was about to prepare the room for Elaine's arrival tomorrow, he discovered he wasn't as ready as he'd previously imagined to let someone else sleep in the room he'd shared with Olivia.

64

December 27

Tough days would come and go, but today would stick with Harry for many years. Listening to Sarah Kerr was a gut-wrenching experience. Though he'd recorded their conversation with a hidden device, disappointingly, it picked up nothing but white noise. It pleased Harry to piece together details of the murders, but it pained him not to be able to do anything with her confession. In case he'd missed anything, he scoured his mind for a single clue that could link her to just one of the murders. He drew a blank.

Sarah wasn't kidding when she'd said it had turned out better than expected. Looking through her social media was proof enough – her list of followers growing by the second. He imagined top agents would be queueing up to sign her. Interviews, book deals, movie scripts – offers would be falling like confetti around her. Harry considered letting what she'd done fade into the melt of a vanishing tide. Hadn't he done something similar with Elaine Burgess? Having said that, Elaine was avenging a despicable crime. Sarah Kerr's reason was self-serving and savage. He'd searched his soul and questioned every fibre of his being.

Harry exited his car carrying a bottle of wine and crossed the parking area to a stylish apartment block overlooking a charming lake. He pushed the number *4* on the silver plate beside the entrance door and waited.

'Who is it?'

'Hi, Lucy. It's Harry.' The door buzzed and opened.

She might not be *too* pleased he hadn't called ahead, but seeing as she'd shown up at his place in a similar fashion, he doubted she'd make a fuss. The single flight of stairs was steep and not easy on his leg. Thank heavens for painkillers, though he should have taken the doctor's advice and rested. He'd assumed she'd be waiting with the door open, but she was probably rushing around like crazy, tidying up the place. No point in knocking; it wasn't as if she would forget he was on his way up.

She opened the door and smiled as he presented her with the wine. 'I brought a bottle.'

'So you did. All this bringing wine to each other's houses feels like an episode of *Come Dine with Me*.'

'Does that mean there's food on the go?'

'It means we're ordering a takeaway,' she said.

'Even better. I'm not suggesting you can't cook.' Harry stepped inside and removed his shoes.

'You'd be right if you were. Would you like a cup of tea, or do you want to dive right in and get started on the good stuff?'

'I've gone off tea,' he said. 'So if you've got a couple of glasses, I'll do the honours.'

'It's a nice surprise, but what made you come here?'

'A bad day and the need to refocus my mind.'

'And there was me thinking you'd popped round to resume where we'd left off.'

'Do you mean before or after you emptied your guts on me?'

Looking slightly mortified, she said, 'You're never going to let me forget, are you?'

As one would expect, there had been some obvious last-minute cleaning, but all in all, Lucy's apartment looked orderly. For some reason, Harry had imagined a clash of colours and ancient furniture showing multiple scars of self-repair. He wasn't overly surprised to be wrong. She had many layers, and he was only now peeling them back to discover the real Lucy.

After they had their meal on their laps in the living room, Harry helped Lucy clear away the plates and rubbish. They were soon comfortable on the sofa with their nearly empty glasses.

'You mentioned a tough day,' she said.

'Yeah. Quite gruelling.'

'How come?'

He turned to face her. 'I visited Sarah Kerr at her parents' house in Surrey.'

She downed the last of her wine. 'Why on earth would you do that? You're supposed to be on leave.'

'I am. But I worked out that Miss Kerr was responsible for Rebecca Heaton's original injury and, indirectly, most of the murders since, two of which she admitted committing herself.'

Lucy set her glass on the table and twisted around, lifting her leg onto the cushion. 'Oh my God. She confessed to you?'

'She admitted everything. The sad thing is there's nothing I can do about it.'

'Didn't you record the interview?'

'I tried, but it didn't work.'

'Shit. So what now? We can't just let her get away with everything.'

'There isn't one shred of evidence to tie her to a single murder. It's over. I can write the report and say who killed who, but her name will be left out of it. I could argue against some of the facts, but our superiors and the CPS will look at the existing evidence and want to pin everything on Melanie Hillingdon and James Harding. You know how it works.'

Lucy sat forward and perched on the edge of the sofa. 'She's going to get off scot-free?'

'Yep. I'll probably head into the station and make a start on the paperwork tomorrow. It's going to take forever to write this one up.'

'Doesn't seem fair.'

'No, it doesn't. Some people literally get away with murder. Anyway, I came here to get you to help me take my mind off all this.' He gulped his wine. 'Our glasses are empty. Shall I fetch another bottle?'

'Oh, go on then. If we must.'

Harry returned from the kitchen and caught Lucy staring at her phone. 'I hope my showing up unexpectedly hasn't forced you to cancel any plans – like a date or something?'

'I should be so lucky. No, my dad was ill on Boxing Day, so I was just checking in.'

'It's funny you should say that because I'm not feeling too great.'

'Perhaps there's a bug going round,' she said.

Mindful of his leg as he sat, he placed the bottle on the table in front of her.

She stared at the glass of water in his hand as he took two tablets. 'I assume you're not joining me?'

'No. It could be the booze making me queasy. I'm not supposed to have alcohol with my medication.'

'Me neither.' She filled her glass. 'Is it throbbing?'

'Not yet. Oh, you mean my leg?' They laughed, and for a brief moment, his pain subsided. 'Yeah, it's like a hammering sensation.'

'Another day or so, and it will become more of a dull ache.'

'I forgot to mention – you were right about the knife attack at the mall. You weren't the target.'

'You?' He nodded to confirm. 'Doesn't sound like Sarah held back much.'

'She held back enough,' said Harry.

Lucy moved closer and laid her head on his shoulder. Harry hesitated before putting his arm around her. For a while, they sat quietly, listening to the rain tapping against the window. She leaned forward to put her glass on the table, returned to her previous position, and gazed into his eyes. Her warmth and affection fogged his mind. As she drew closer, her breath caressed his face, a purposeful delay before her lips touched his. Like the beat of his heart, their kiss became faster and stronger. His passion raged, pulling him in a direction he was reluctant to take. Desire was a short road, and reason suggested an alternative route. He tore his lips away from Lucy and eased back.

'I'm sorry,' he said.

'Is something wrong?'

'I'm either tired or coming down with something, and the last thing I want is a repeat performance of the last time we tried this.'

'Not sure I'd like that either,' she said. 'We're not having much luck with this, are we?'

'It's got nothing to do with luck. We've both been through a hell of a rough week or so.'

'You're not wrong there.'

'I'm going to head back to the guest house and get some much-needed sleep.' He prised himself off the sofa.

Lucy said, 'You're welcome to spend the night here.'

'Thanks for the offer, but if I'm going to spend the night throwing up, I'd prefer to do it in the privacy of Gerty's bathroom.'

Lucy seemed disappointed and followed him into the hall, where he took his jacket from the hook. She walked him to the door. 'I hope you feel better tomorrow.'

'Thanks. I'll call you.'

'You'd better.' They shared a smile, and he couldn't stop himself as he leaned in and kissed her on the cheek. He hated to leave her like this. But needs must.

65

December 28

Harry had spent much of the previous evening debating whether to cross the line between right and wrong. In the recent past, he'd straddled that line for various reasons, but now he was about to go beyond the point of no return. Up bright and early, Harry's focus was to prove Sarah Kerr's guilt – no matter the cost. He'd been parked on Luton Road, close to Fred Perry's house, for over two hours. Harry had knocked on some doors and questioned a few people, asking if they'd seen anything on the night of Perry's murder. Most had already been subjected to police inquiries and were not forthcoming, and, as expected, none had been helpful on this occasion. With only a few hours until an important meeting, he had to remain patient.

Harry's eyes were on the corner shop next to Chatham Chick 'n' Chips, where he'd seen the youths hanging out during his visit before Fred Perry's death. If anyone had seen anything suspicious, there was every chance it would be one of those lads. The only problem would be getting them to talk. He'd also forgotten that these weren't the type of youngsters to be up by lunchtime, let alone breakfast. As time ticked on, he needed to stretch his legs and wandered a little way up the road. On his way back, someone came round the corner on a mountain bike and laid it on the ground outside the corner shop. The distance made it impossible to make out a face, so he couldn't be sure if it was one of the teenagers. Harry ignored the pain in his leg and quickened his pace.

A little out of breath, Harry stood by a lamp post outside the chicken shop next door. He didn't have to wait long before the youngster appeared with a plain white carrier bag. Harry recognised him as the lad who'd thrown the brick. The teenager clocked Harry and rushed to pull his bike up from the ground. As soon as he mounted his bike, Harry grabbed the handlebars.

'You're that copper who was here before. You best let go of my bike.'

'Answer a couple of questions, and I'll gladly do so.'

'I ain't tellin' you nothin', so let go of my fuckin' bike.'

'How about I arrest you for throwing a brick at a police officer?'

'Nah, man. That wasn't me.'

'I saw you.'

'Then you'd best get to Specsavers, innit? Anyway, it didn't hit anyone.'

'Doesn't matter,' said Harry.

'You're all the same, you lot. Fitting people up and even—' He stopped short of what he was going to say.

'Even what?'

The boy, probably about fifteen, said, 'Take your hands off my bike.'

'Look, all I want to know is if you or one of your friends saw anything or anyone acting suspiciously on the night Fred Perry was murdered?'

He repeated, 'Take your hands off my bike.'

'Okay, I'm arresting you for multiple public disorder offences.'

'This is bullshit. I didn't see anything.'

'But you know someone who did?'

'I ain't rattin' out a mate.'

'Your friend isn't in trouble, and if he doesn't want to talk, I'll leave it be.'

The youngster looked around to make sure nobody was watching. 'You need to talk to Panda.'

'Panda?'

'You'll get it when you see him.'

'Where can I find Panda?'

'His mum works at Maude's Diner up on Watling Street. During the school holidays, she makes him help out in the mornings, waiting tables and shit.'

Harry let go of the handlebars. 'Now that wasn't so hard, was it?'

'Wanker.' The youth rode off without looking back.

It didn't take long to find Maude's diner on the high street. Without knowing it, he'd driven past the place a few times. Unable to park outside, he found a space just off the main road. Unaware of the boy's proper name, he had to approach this delicately so as not to cause a scene in what was a fairly busy diner. Harry was welcomed in by a woman in her mid-thirties and told to take a seat – she'd be with him shortly. He detected three adults working in the place. No teenagers. Much of the kitchen behind the tall glass counter was obscured by a wall. Harry supposed the youngster could be manning the dishwasher.

The waitress placed the order she'd just taken on the counter and approached his table. 'What can I get you?'

'A cup of tea, please.'

'Anything else?'

'Not right now,' he said.

While he waited, there was still no sign of the youngster. Perhaps the youth on the bike had lied.

The waitress placed his tea on the table. 'Here you go. Any decision on food?'

Harry took a wild guess the woman was Panda's mother and placed his warrant card on the table.

'Oh, what's he done now?' she said quietly and sat opposite. 'He was home all last night, and he's been here all morning.'

Harry said, 'As far as I know, he hasn't done anything, but he might have witnessed something a few nights ago when a local man was murdered in his home.'

'Fred Perry?' she said.

'Did you know him?'

'We went to the same school. He was two or three years behind me, but he was always in trouble, so his name got around. Our paths crossed occasionally, and two years ago he decorated my front room. It's a real shame what happened to him – he was really trying to turn his life around.'

'Did your son know Fred Perry well?'

'They became friendly while he was working at my house. Fred would often take Billy to help him out at work, mostly at the weekends. It was a bit of extra pocket money for Billy, and it kept him off the streets, which I didn't mind at all.'

'What time did he come home that night?'

'He's usually home by eleven. Any later and he's grounded. Sometimes he'll push it, but you know what kids are like.'

Harry smiled. 'Yes, I do. Is he here now?'

'He's out back washing dishes. I'll go and get him, though I doubt he can help you. He would have told me if he'd seen anything.'

Within a minute, the woman returned with her son, who appeared reluctant and not at all happy. They sat opposite Harry. The nickname clicked when Harry observed the dark circles under Billy's eyes. Why had he chosen the kind of friends who would make fun of what was probably a medical condition? Sadly, not all children had the luxury of choice, drifting towards acceptance, whether beneficial or detrimental.

'Hey, Billy.'

'You're a fed. I ain't talking to you.'

His mum said, 'You might not talk to him, but by God, you'll talk to me, or you won't be going out for as long as you live under my roof. Now, this detective thinks you might know something about Fred's death.' Billy looked to the side and remained silent.

Calmly, Harry said, 'Billy, I'm just trying to find Mr Perry's murderer. If he was a friend to you, why wouldn't you want to help catch the person who did it?'

'Billy,' his mother snapped, keeping her voice low to avoid attracting attention.

'I stopped by his house at about nine,' he said.

'Oh my God, you did see something,' she said. 'Go on, spill it.'

'We smoked, watched TV, and he let me have a beer. He talked a lot about his brother. He even cried. I think he'd been drinking for a while because he kept falling asleep.' Billy stared at his mum. 'Like Dad used to.' Harry got the impression there was a backstory, possibly not a pleasant one. 'I left his house just before eleven. As I walked along the road, I saw a woman. I crossed over and watched her knock on his door and go inside.'

Harry pulled out his phone. 'Billy, I'm going to show you a photo. Is this her?'

Billy nodded. 'Yeah.'

'Okay, Billy. Thank you. Don't say a word about this to anyone because *she*' – he pointed at the photo – 'is devious and brutal. I'll need you to make a formal statement in a day or two. Can you do that for me?' Billy looked away.

His mum said, 'Yes. He'll make a statement. Who is she?'

'I can't say any more at this time, but I will need to take some information if that's okay?'

'Of course,' she said.

Billy returned to the kitchen to continue washing dishes while his mum provided Harry with her details. He looked around to make sure no one was listening in. 'Miss Graham, nobody but me knows about your son. Billy is a key witness, and his statement could help solve multiple murders.'

She gasped aloud and said in a hushed voice, 'Jesus Christ.'

'I meant what I said about the woman in the photo. She'll be in custody within forty-eight hours, so please, until then, keep your son at home or with you at all times.'

'Why can't we come to the station now, give you his statement, and you can arrest this crazy bitch today?'

'Because two police officers are already dead, and while I'm pretty sure nobody else is involved, I can't be one hundred per cent certain.'

From one food place to another, his next stop was Cliff's Lunch Box, a food trailer in a B&Q car park in Maidstone. He arrived early, ordered a cup of tea and an egg and bacon roll, and sat at one of the aluminium tables with matching chairs. He'd nearly finished his roll by the time Sam Jennings showed up. When he asked if she wanted anything, she told him not to get up and ordered herself a coffee.

Sam pulled up a chair. 'Finally having a drink together, eh?'

'The first of many, I hope,' he said.

'So, Harry, why did you want to meet here and not at the station?'

'I've found a witness to one of the murders.'

'Which one?'

'I can't say yet.'

'Why not? Melanie and James are already dead.'

'They were not the only ones involved in all this. Someone else was pulling the strings.'

'Why can't you tell me more? Do you not trust me?'

'When this is over, you'll understand why, but for now, I need to keep it quiet. I have a few more things to do, and when the time is right, I'll give you a call. I want *you* to be the arresting officer.'

'Why give it to me and not make the arrest yourself?'

'Do you want this or not? You deserve to be the new DCI, and this arrest will guarantee that it happens.'

'Yes. I'm interested.'

66

December 28

Today was supposed to be a breeze. All Lenny had to do was go to the hospital and carry out a simple task for Harry. However, as he'd frequently come to learn, things were never straightforward. Unable to sit still for any length of time in the waiting area, he anxiously paced around, repeatedly asking for updates.

His alarm had gone off at seven o'clock this morning, and two snooze button presses later, he was up, showered, and dressed. In the kitchen, he cleaned Phoebe's bowl, filled it with mackerel, and placed it on her mat. He put two slices of bread in the toaster and sat at the table to drink his tea while he waited. Just another ordinary day. Except it wasn't. Where was Phoebe? He hadn't seen her this morning. After marching around the apartment, calling her name, panic set in. Had she sneaked out of the front door? A few seconds later, he found her lying on her side behind the main bathroom door. She wasn't moving. Lenny's heart sank. Dropping to his knees, it became evident she was breathing. Phoebe's eyes opened. Speaking to her softly, he tried to encourage her to stand, but she wouldn't. A barely audible meow escaped her. Jumping to his feet, Lenny fetched his keys and slipped on his shoes before racing back to gently scoop her up in his arms. He was out of the apartment in a flash.

People sat with dogs on leads while others had carriers of all sizes by their feet, containing their beloved kitties. There were two treatment rooms, and people were coming and going, with smiles on most faces and concern on others. Beside himself with worry, Lenny buried his head in his hands. Phoebe had been in one of the rooms for an hour. The veterinarian had told him that Phoebe was suffering from a urethral obstruction. They were going to manage the blockage with medication and apply fluids under the skin to keep her hydrated; hopefully, this would relax her urethra, and the urine would flush out the obstruction.

The vet appeared and called him into the room. Lenny froze in the doorway when he saw his baby lying completely still on the examination table. 'Is she . . .?'

'No, she's sleeping. Unfortunately, Phoebe has a complete blockage.'

Lenny tenderly caressed her side and said, 'What happens now?'

'It is life-threatening, but we should be able to physically remove the stone. We'll transfer her to our hospital in Bow. She will be stabilised with intravenous fluids—'

'Doc, I don't need to know the procedure. Please, just do whatever it takes.'

'Okay. So I'll get the transfer underway, and she will probably be kept at the hospital for two to three days.' Lenny's next question was answered before he could ask. 'If you call ahead, they will let you know if it's a good time to visit.'

'Thank you,' said Lenny. He leaned in close to Phoebe's ear. 'I'll see you soon, sweetheart.' He kissed the top of her head, a far cry from the man who'd once told Elaine he hated cats.

*

The worry remained, but Lenny was quietly confident all would be well. In the meantime, it was better to keep himself busy. Per Harry's request, he'd driven to Maidstone Hospital to examine the video footage. In the security office, even though they had been informed of his visit, he endured the rigmarole of explaining to two guards that he was a consultant for Kent Police. Christ, you'd have thought the pair of plonkers were protecting the Crown Jewels.

Lenny's threshold for nonsense slowly diminished until he snapped and said, 'Look, a detective inspector has asked me to do him a favour. I don't need to be here. I don't want to be here. If you're not going to allow me to view the video, just say so.'

At first, the guards stared at each other in sheepish silence. One of them turned to Lenny and said, 'All right, mate, we're only messing with you. It's all set up for the two days requested by the detective and ready to go. Use the mouse to click on play and scan back and forth. We'll leave you to it.'

With the guards gone, Lenny got the photo of Sarah Kerr ready on his phone and set to work. This could take a while, but at least his mind was occupied. It didn't take him long to get to grips with how to fast forward, rewind, and slow it down. Until now, it hadn't occurred to him why Harry wasn't investigating this through official channels. Why didn't he trust his own officers? He must have uncovered something he didn't want to reveal. Not yet, anyhow.

An hour into his search, one of the guards returned with a cold can of lemonade, for which Lenny was grateful. He took the olive branch as a chance to apologise for his earlier outburst and continued. Sarah Kerr was nowhere to be seen on day one. Well into the second day, Lenny finally glimpsed someone who was worth a closer look and rewound the video. He pressed pause and compared the photo on his phone with the woman on the monitor. It was her. Lenny took a photo of the screen and noted the time when she'd entered and left the ward. He called Harry, but it went straight to his voicemail. Due to the privacy of the matter, Lenny left a short message asking him to call back.

On the way home, Lenny was tempted to drive straight to the animal hospital to check on Phoebe, but if she was recovering from surgery, he wouldn't be able to see her anyway. Better to leave it and call them later for an update. As soon as he was indoors, he looked at her full bowl of mackerel, which he emptied into the bin. He stared at the bread in the toaster and the cold cup of tea on the table. In a moment of unbearable solitude, he appreciated how much that little cat had helped him through the darkest period of his life.

'This won't do.' He called the hospital. His eyes glazed over at the news. Phoebe's surgery had gone well, and she could be back home the day after tomorrow. Lifted by an overwhelming sense of relief, Lenny soon had a glass of whisky in his hand. He'd just settled into his armchair when Elaine announced her arrival after letting herself in. She walked into the living area, having dumped her overnight bag by the front door.

'You're here,' she said. 'Why didn't you answer when I called out?'

'I don't know. Just soaking up a second more of silence, I guess.'

'Is everything all right?'

'I'm sure it will be. How did the meeting go?'

'As expected. I have another meeting this evening, so I'm likely to be home late.'

'Sounds important.'

'Oh, it is.'

He placed his glass on the side. 'Come on. I'll show you to your room.' Lenny picked up her bag along the way.

She said, 'You've changed rooms. I could have slept on the sofa.'

'It's barely cold from your brother being on it. Besides, you'll be more comfortable in here.' He dropped her bag on the floor. 'Right, I'll let you get settled. Tea?'

'I'd love one. Where's Phoebe?'

'Let me get the kettle on, and I'll tell you all about it.'

Tucked up in bed, Lenny had turned in early, which had become something of a habit of late. On this occasion, stress had depleted his energy levels, along with nattering away the afternoon hours with Elaine. When his head hit the pillow, he imagined he would lie awake for hours, but he dropped off almost immediately. He was woken by the noisy shower pump in the cupboard outside the main bathroom. He glanced at the clock: 2.25 a.m. Elaine must have only just returned. That was a long, bloody meeting. Lenny rolled over and pulled the covers over his head.

67

December 29

Up early, Lenny had taken another step in the healing process and removed the bloodied mattress from the bed. Olivia wouldn't have wanted him to sleep in a pit of misery and nightmares. A call from Harry interrupted his browsing for mattresses on the internet, and he was out of the door before Elaine had surfaced. She'd probably be on her way back to Helmsley by the time he returned. Harry had said to meet in Greenwich Park by the statue of General James Wolfe. No stranger to the park, Lenny had visited many times over the years, mostly when he was younger.

It took him around forty minutes to get there, and Harry was sitting on a bench in front of the statue with two cardboard cups next to him. Lenny approached from the side and said, 'Many people say this is one of the best views of London. Well, east London, anyway.'

'It's impressive, but you obviously don't agree. Here, I got you a coffee, no sugar.'

'Ta.' Lenny sat beside him. 'I remember this view before Canary Wharf was built. There were buildings and dockside cranes, but nothing on the scale of the monstrosity before us now.' He peeled the lid from his cup. 'This is all a bit clandestine, Harry. You haven't been snapped up by MI5 or anything, have you?'

'They couldn't afford me. Did you find anything on the CCTV?'

'You know I did. We wouldn't be here otherwise.' Lenny showed him the timestamped photos he'd taken.

Harry said, 'This is a big help.'

'Do you want me to send them to you?'

'No. Delete them. I can't have you tied to this in any way, but at least I know she's on video and where to look. If you'd watched a little longer, you would have seen my ugly mug pop up. People would still be alive if I'd got there ten minutes earlier.'

'What's going on, Harry?'

'The less you know, the better. If this goes sideways and comes back on me, you'll be glad you were kept out of it.'

Lenny wanted to press for more information, but he'd never seen Harry like this and sensed whatever was going on could lead to severe repercussions. Being oblivious wasn't always a bad thing.

'How was your trip to Helmsley?'

'It wasn't exactly a mini-break. I just had a couple of things I needed to do.'

'How is Elaine?'

'Stressed about something to do with work. Other than that, she's all right. She had a couple of meetings in London and stayed at my place last night. Judging by the time she got home, I'd say a fair amount of drinking was involved.'

'Sounds like her meeting was a success.'

'Most likely. As you know, solving problems is a specialty of hers.'

'Sorry to cut this short, Lenny, but I have some unpleasant business to take care of.'

'Whatever you're up to, Harry, take care.' Lenny watched him leave and finished his coffee in the cold.

*

Queuing at Blackwall Tunnel due to a broken-down vehicle, Lenny received a call on speakerphone from Danny's father. 'Hi, Brendan. You'll have to be quick because I might lose my signal soon.'

'Then I'll get straight to the point,' said Brendan. 'There was a huge argument earlier this morning, and Danny left the house in a rage.'

'We've all been there. He's probably just letting off steam. I'm sure he'll be home once he's calmed down.'

'Is there any chance you could come to our house now?'

'Is it necessary? I do have a lot on.'

Brendan said, 'We've found something you need to see.'

He could have done without this today, but despite his reluctance, he agreed.

The traffic on the way to Edmonton in North London was horrendous. It had always bothered him how a short journey across the city could take so long. When he stepped into the living room, a cup of tea was already on the table waiting for him. Unusually, there was no biscuit tin. *Bloody hell*, this must be serious.

Brendan said, 'I hope the traffic wasn't too bad.'

Being polite, Lenny replied, 'No worse than usual.' He reached for his cup. 'Now, what's Danny got himself in a tantrum about?'

Brendan glared at Vivien, and she said, 'It's a bit more serious than a tantrum.'

'Okay, I'm listening.'

On the edge of his seat, Brendan said, 'After you dropped him home yesterday, he seemed fine. A little moody, but nothing out of the ordinary. Later, during dinner, for no obvious reason, he snapped at his sister and had a go at Vivien. When I got involved, he threw his plate across the room and stormed upstairs.'

Lenny said, 'We've all seen or had similar outbursts.'

'That's not the worst part,' said Brendan. 'This morning, I was up at six and got ready for work. As I fetched my lunch from the fridge, there was a loud thump on the floor above, in Hayley's room. I rushed upstairs to check, and when I opened the door, Danny was sitting astride Hayley with his hands around her neck. I dragged him off her, and he claimed they were messing around, but Hayley was choking.'

Tearful, Vivien said, 'It wasn't a game. We daren't imagine the outcome if Brendan hadn't gone up to her room.'

Brendan continued, 'We argued, and I swear I could have throttled him. I sent him to his room and tended to Hayley. Vivien came to see what was going on, and the front door slammed. I raced downstairs and out onto the pavement, but I couldn't see him anywhere.'

Lenny said, 'When I took him away, he didn't appear to have the phone I bought him for Christmas.'

'We decided to hold it back until the New Year, after he'd apologised to his therapist,' said Brendan.

'Fair enough. It's just a shame we can't call him.'

'Yes, we're now regretting our decision. Though I doubt he would have answered.'

'I can't have him back in this house,' said Vivien.

Lenny said, 'Okay, I know this looks bad, but I'm sure if we can get him to sit and listen to us, we can all agree on the best way forward. He obviously needs a lot more help than was previously suggested.'

Brendan said, 'You're not kidding.'

'Why did he snap at Hayley at dinner?'

'Because she'd asked him about Zeph. Hayley told us she'd overheard Danny talking to someone called Zeph in his bedroom. We've tried to shield her from what happened to her brother, so she had no reason to use that particular name.'

'Let's not kid ourselves,' said Lenny. 'She could have picked it up anywhere – listening in on conversations, from other children at school, or from the news on TV.'

'Maybe, but I've heard him doing it as well. I could have interfered, but his therapist advised giving him as much privacy as possible. This latest episode forced me to search his room. After a number of failed attempts to gain access to his computer, I tried different variations of Joseph Webster. Nothing worked. It then occurred to me to use the name Zeph. Again, no joy. And then I remembered the name of the boat, Zephyr.' Brendan opened the laptop and passed it to Lenny. 'Take a look at this.'

Lenny browsed through Danny's search history. There were plenty of articles regarding the murders at Sablefall Farm. Lenny recalled the expression on Danny's face when they passed by the house on the way to Elaine's. This explained how he knew about the place. He'd also read everything he could about Harper, Elaine, and Joseph Webster. Dozens of other pages featured grieving parents whose children had been taken and killed by Webster or his predecessor, Ozias Blackwood. Towards the end of the list were links to information about animal and human anatomy.

Lenny said, 'Okay, I agree. This is extremely disturbing.'

'Too bloody right it is,' said Brendan. 'He beheaded and dismembered the family dog.'

'This doesn't prove he did anything of the sort, so let's not jump to conclusions,' said Lenny.

Brendan reached down beside his chair and plonked a large glass jar on the table. 'I found this at the bottom of his wardrobe under a pile of clothes. I'm pretty sure that's a dog's heart, a child's finger, and I can't imagine what the hell the other piece is.'

Lenny leaned forward to get a closer look. He twisted off the lid and then tightened it as the pungent, pickle-like odour of formaldehyde assaulted his senses. 'You're right about the heart.

The finger most likely belongs to the boy who was held captive on the boat with your son. The other is a piece of a nose belonging to a detective friend of mine.'

Brendan shot to his feet. 'For the love of God!'

Vivien said, 'Why would he want to keep such horrid things?'

'Trophies,' Lenny said. 'I'm not going to lie – this is worse than I imagined.'

'No shit!' said Brendan.

'We need to find him. Fast. Any idea where he would have gone?'

'Not a clue,' said Brendan as he comforted his sobbing wife.

Staring at the computer screen, Lenny said, 'Ah.'

'What is it?'

'What time did you say he left the house?'

'Not long after seven. Why?'

'One of the tabs at the top of the screen shows today's train timetable.'

'To where?'

'Thirsk.'

Brendan asked, 'Where the hell is Thirsk?'

'According to this, it's a twenty-three-minute taxi ride from Helmsley.'

'Why would he be going back up there?' cried Vivien.

'I can't be sure, but he did show an interest in the house mentioned on his laptop when we drove past.'

Brendan said, 'Not the house where all those murders happened?'

'I'm afraid so.'

Vivien buried her head in her hands, and Brendan let out a dejected gasp.

Lenny said, 'Just because he looked up these train times doesn't mean that's where he's gone. He could walk through the front door any second.' After everything they'd told him and what he'd seen in the jar on the table, his words were merely a futile attempt to alleviate the couple's anguish.

'I meant what I said, Brendan. I don't want him living under the same roof as our little girl.'

'She's right,' said Brendan. 'We have to think of Hayley's safety.'

Vivien said, 'You must think we're monsters!'

'Not at all. In light of what you've shown me, his actions prove he has serious issues. The police don't have a great record in dealing with incidents regarding mental health, so give me a few hours to find him. If I can't, we'll have no choice but to involve the authorities.'

The first place Lenny thought to check was his apartment. Danny knew where he lived, so he could be waiting outside the front door. If Elaine hadn't left yet, he could even be sitting in his living room. When he finally made it home, he noticed Elaine's bag by the front door and found her eating a sandwich at the table with the TV on in the background. Danny was nowhere to be seen.

She said, 'I helped myself to the last of your peanut butter, so you'll need to pick up some more.'

Lenny mumbled, 'Yes, my lady. I'll be sure to get some in for your next visit.'

'What did you say?'

'I said I'm surprised you're still here and didn't set off earlier.'

'I had a lie-in. I was so tired.'

'You wouldn't have been so tired if you'd come home at a decent hour.'

'Sorry, Dad.'

He said, 'Has the door buzzer rung this morning?'

'Not that I'm aware of. Were you expecting someone?'

'I've just come from Danny's parents. He's missing. I hoped he'd made his way here.'

'If the buzzer had gone off, I'm pretty sure I would have heard it. How come he's missing?'

'An argument with his sister.'

'He'll get over it. Michael and Emily argue all the time.' She took a bite of her sandwich.

'I'm sure. But I bet Michael's never tried to strangle her.'

Elaine put down her sandwich. 'For real?'

'Looks like you were right about him after all.'

'Shit, Lenny. I didn't want to be. It's possible his sister lied to get him into trouble, and it's all a big misunderstanding.'

'I don't think so. His father caught him at it. And when I said you were right, I meant about everything. He'd recently cut the family dog into pieces and kept the heart in a jar – along with Connor Doherty's finger and Colin Hargreaves' nose. The kid's lost the plot.'

'Oh, fuck. Have his parents called the police?'

'I told them not to.'

'Why would you do that? Unless you know where he might be.'

'You should call Tom.'

'What are you talking about? Oh, please tell me he's not going to my place?'

'Maybe. Maybe not, but he had today's train times to Thirsk on his laptop and seemed quite interested in Sablefall Farm. He'd researched everything about you, Harper, and that damn house. I couldn't call the police, not with Harper staying at your place. Tom could drive over to Sablefall and take a look around.'

Elaine pulled her phone from her back pocket and called him. 'Tom's taken Harper to look at a house in Whitby. They left about twenty minutes ago.' Tom didn't answer. 'He never connects his phone to the car speaker.'

'I assume Michael is looking after Emily?'

'Yes.' She tried Tom again. Same result. 'Okay, so if Danny has gone up there, do you even know what time he's due to arrive?'

'Well, if he caught the eight twenty-seven this morning, it's possible he's already there.'

'Oh, I don't fucking believe this, Lenny.'

'He's only just turned fourteen,' he said. 'I doubt he's even made the trip.'

She tried Michael's phone. No answer. She tried the house phone. Again, no answer. 'What is it with these kids never answering their bloody phones? Does Harper have one?'

'Not any more. It's broken.'

Frustrated, Elaine banged her fists on the table. 'Right, come on. We're going to Helmsley, and we're going in my car.'

'I'm not going back up there,' he said.

'Oh yes, you are. This is all your fault.'

'How is it my fault?'

'Because if you hadn't brought him uninvited to my house, he wouldn't know where I live, and none of this would have happened. Now my children are alone in the house, and there is every chance a psychotic teenager could knock on the front door. If he is up there, you can take him on the next train back to London.'

'Okay. You've made your point.' Elaine left the room, and before Lenny switched off the television, the one o'clock news came on. He focused on the headline-grabbing banner at the bottom of the screen: 'YOUNG WOMAN BRUTALLY MURDERED AT HOME.'

'Come on, Lenny! We need to get going.' He turned off the TV.

68

December 29

Behind the police tape, photographers snapped pictures of the house, while bellowing journalists stood with their notepads at the ready, waiting for a comment from officers attending the crime scene. Everyone entering the property wore protective suits, gloves, and plastic overshoes, one of whom was DI Sam Jennings. She came out to meet Harry and escorted him over to the forensic van so he could put on the appropriate attire.

He'd received Sam's call an hour after he had met with Lenny. As soon as Sam informed him about the murder and the victim, Harry finished what he was doing and told her he was on his way. It didn't take him too long to get there. Once he was ready, she walked him into the house and across the hallway. The place was crawling with forensic pathologists and local detectives.

Sam said, 'Forensics have a lot of work to do, so don't touch anything.'

'I know the drill.'

She led him up the wide staircase towards one of the bedrooms. 'For starters, it doesn't look as though this is a robbery gone wrong. There's no mess, no drawers have been rummaged through, and everything appears untouched, even the safe. Her parents have been notified. We won't know for sure if anything has been taken until they return from Dubai.'

They put on their masks, and he followed Sam into the room. He focused on Sarah Kerr, savagely murdered in her sleep. His chest tightened. Of all the gory crime scenes he'd observed, this one unsettled him like never before. Harry recalled the end of their last conversation:

'I see fun in our future,' she'd said.

'Do you? Because all I see is death,' he'd replied.

The wall, headboard, and bedding were soaked in blood. Spatter patterns covered the polished oak floorboards around the bed.

'She was murdered around midnight,' said Sam. 'As you can see, she has been stabbed multiple times. The head pathologist says there are a number of fatal wounds, including two to the heart. And going by the vast amount of blood, both her external and internal jugular veins were severed. He will clarify everything once he has performed a full autopsy.'

'I take it Arthur Potts is not the attending pathologist?'

'No, it's a younger guy – Dermot Mackenzie. Probably the regular pathologist for Surrey Police. He found a single strand of hair on the bed, close to the body. He is fairly confident it doesn't belong to the victim, but this is her parents' house, and apparently, they often have guests staying over, so it could belong to anyone. Hopefully, a DNA test will tell us more.'

Harry moved closer and crouched down next to the bedside cabinet to examine the body. After a few seconds, he got to his feet and leaned over Sarah for a closer look. He said, 'As a matter of urgency, all the pathologists' findings will need to be sent to Arthur Potts.' Harry pointed to the area around Sarah Kerr's neck. 'These wounds look similar to the attack on Craig Bishop. The same goes for the chest area and how Jerome Henderson was murdered.'

'Do you think they were killed by the same person?'

'It's possible.'

'Are you suggesting Owen Carrick didn't kill Henderson?'

'We'll find out soon enough.'

'Okay, I'll let the pathologist know. Anyway, speaking of Owen, we got the results back from his computer.'

'And?'

'No criminal activity, but it did show he was a member and regular visitor to a site called SubRosaDevotee.'

'Sounds like a secret dating site for stalkers.'

'It's a subscription service for those who wish to purchase exclusive content from celebrities, such as photos, videos, and even underwear. We are mostly talking about ex-models, former pop stars, and failed reality stars, all desperately trying to cling to past glories. Many will also pay large sums for live face-to-face streams – one can only guess what goes on in some of those. Mr Carrick regularly paid for live streams with Miss Kerr. We discovered raunchy photos he'd purchased and receipts for underwear she had sent him.'

Harry said, 'Make sure the laptop and any computer devices owned by her are taken into evidence. I'm betting we'll find them quite enlightening.'

'There's no sign of a laptop or phone, but we'll keep looking.'

'Who discovered the body?'

'The cleaner, Mrs Amelia Marques. She comes at the same time every Monday and Thursday. She has cleaned this house and others in the area for over twelve years. She's been thoroughly vetted and has an alibi for last night.'

'In bed with her partner, I imagine.'

'Correct.'

As they left the room, Harry said, 'It's safe to say the killer would have been covered in the victim's blood when they left the scene.'

'I'm sure you're right, but so far, forensics have found no traces of blood and no points of entry or exit.'

'Why didn't the alarm go off? Was it not set?'

As they walked down the stairs, she said, 'This is where it gets interesting. Mrs Marques says it was on when she entered the house. The only logical conclusion at this time is that the perpetrator left via the front door, which has a self-locking mechanism. We just don't know how they gained access or left without setting it off.'

By the front door, Harry pointed to a small white box in the corner of the hallway and said, 'How would they have got past the indoor motion sensors?'

'According to a close friend and neighbour, they have three Pomeranian dogs that roam freely about the house at night, so they're usually deactivated. They must have left them off when they went away, and Miss Kerr obviously failed to activate them.'

'Cameras?'

'The hard drives that stored all the CCTV footage are gone. The killer removed them, and so far, forensics have found no fresh prints. We have officers conducting door-to-door enquiries, looking for witnesses and searching CCTV from nearby houses.'

The detectives left the house and walked towards the forensic van. Sam said, 'Is this a coincidence, or is it connected to the case you've been working on?'

'I suppose it depends on whether anything was taken, but from what you've said and judging by the expensive art still hanging on the walls, I'd say this was a planned murder. So yes, I'm sure it's connected.'

Sam made sure nobody was close and asked, 'What about your witness?'

'This doesn't change a thing.' Harry removed his protective suit and placed it in the back of the van. 'Right, I have one or two things to take care of. I appreciate your calling me, Sam.'

'This is still your case as far as I'm concerned.'

'I'm off duty, just helping out with my inside knowledge. The case is yours now. I'll be in touch soon.' Harry walked away, ignoring the barrage of shouting journalists.

69

December 29

The Boy

Since his traumatic experience on the boat, Danny had found life extremely difficult. He'd struggled at home and at school. He had no friends, and though his family had provided all the support they could, nothing seemed to shake off his agonistic mindset. Aggression seeped into his every thought. He no longer cared about his broken promise to be a good son if he survived his ordeal. Danny had gone down with the Zephyr, and all that remained was *The Boy*.

Zeph taught him to be strong, to fight, and to be decisive; that respect had to be earned, and most importantly of all – murder was easy. His future was supposed to be on the narrowboat. When the time was right, Zeph's life should have been his to take. Elaine, Harper, and, to a lesser degree, Lenny and Tom, had robbed him of his turn to stalk the rivers and canals in search of victims and, eventually, his own replacement. Maybe things could have been different if Elaine hadn't rejected him. Overhearing her conversation with Lenny ignited a surge of anger within him. "Eyes of a killer," she remarked. Elaine had discerned his tainted spirit, an unsettling truth he had not wished to reveal, and she would pay for this insight. They all would, in one way or another.

Michael cheered, 'Oh, yes. Two nil to me.'

'Lucky goal,' said Danny, glaring at Michael beside him on the sofa and then over to Emily in the armchair with her iPad. In the other armchair sat Zeph, who grinned and winked. Yes. They'd all pay.

The landline phone rang for the third time in thirty minutes. Danny asked, 'Aren't you going to answer that?'

'No, it's always nonsense. Mum says it's mostly scams. Three nil!'

Danny said, 'I'm rubbish at this game.' On the sofa close to Michael's leg, the bright screen of his phone drew Danny's attention. *Mum* was calling. No doubt Elaine was trying to get through on the other phone as well. *How silly of him to keep it on silent.* Danny slipped the phone between the cushions, out of sight. 'Let's play a different game.'

Michael paused the football game with his controller. 'Like what?'

Danny said, 'How about scary hide and seek?'

'I'm a bit old to be playing hide and seek,' said Michael.

'You're not too old to play this version.'

Intrigued, Michael smiled. 'What kind of version?'

'It will only work if your sister plays as well. How about it, Emily?' said Danny.

'I don't mind,' she said.

'Okay, great. The rules are simple. One of us plays the kidnapper. One of us plays the captive. And one of us plays the hero. The kidnapper hides the captive and cannot hide in the same place. The hero has to find the kidnapper first to put them out of the game, and only then, even if you've found the captive first, can you save them.'

'Doesn't sound so scary,' said Michael.

'The scary part of this game is that whoever plays the captive has to be gagged so they can't talk or scream, tied up so they can't escape, and have a hood placed over their head so they can't see where they are.'

Michael said, 'Emily wouldn't like that at all.'

Danny looked at her. 'Is that right, Emily?'

'It does sound scary.'

Danny said, 'That's a shame. I'm sure you would have enjoyed the game, but I get that you're too little and scared to play.'

Emily huffed, rolled her shoulders, and declared, 'I want to play.'

'Are you sure?' said Michael.

She looked at her brother. 'Yes. Let's play, unless you're the one who is scared.'

'I'm not frightened of anything,' said Michael.

'Great,' said Danny. 'Why don't I play the captive, Emily can play the kidnapper, and you have to find her before rescuing me?'

Michael regarded Emily, and despite her brave front, it was clear she was nervous. 'No. Emily should play the captive. I'll be the kidnapper, and you can be the hero. Emily will be more at ease if I tie her up and hide her first.'

'You're probably right,' said Danny. 'Now, all we need is a rope, a gag, and a hood.'

Michael said, 'I'll check the garage. I'm sure I'll find a rope in there.' He left the room to gather the items they needed and soon returned with a thin rope, Emily's scarf for the gag, and a pillowcase for the hood. He looked on the sofa and checked his pockets. 'Has anyone seen my phone?'

Emily shook her head, and Danny said, 'I haven't either. We'll search for it after our game.'

Michael fastened Emily's hands behind her back, making sure the rope wasn't too tight. He tied the scarf around her mouth. Emily seemed anxious. He asked, 'Are you sure you're okay with this?' She nodded in agreement, but he sensed her unease. 'I promise, if it takes too long, I'll come and get you.'

'That's against the rules,' said Danny.

Firm and protective, Michael said, 'Well, that's my rule.' He placed the pillowcase over her head.

Outside the front door, a light dusting of snow had covered the pavements. Danny would wait ten minutes and give them time to hide anywhere in the house or out back. He stared at the tiny bus shelter across the road, where he'd escaped the biting wind and snow when he arrived earlier. He had shivered for over two hours, watching the house, waiting for the perfect moment to make his move. Armed with the knowledge that Elaine had business to take care of in London, he was aware she could return at any time. When Tom and Harper came out of the front door and drove off, he shared a boastful sneer with Zeph beside him. Though not unwelcoming, Michael had been surprised to see Danny, believing his excuse that Elaine had invited him back for a couple of days; after all, he had no reason to doubt him.

Danny revelled in the quiet stillness of the afternoon. The roaring voices of the wind in the trees had tempered to eerie whispers full of secrets. He closed his eyes, took two deep breaths, and turned his face to the white sky. He smiled and glanced at his watch. Five minutes had passed.

In the garage, Danny snooped around and found a full petrol can, which he put to one side. He also found an old trunk. Inside were some personal items belonging to Tom, some from his time in the police force, including an old pair of handcuffs with a single key attached. He took those and closed the lid. On the wall above a workbench hung a large number of hand tools. The first thing he reached for was a hammer. After examining a few other tools, he also opted for a sharp, thin chisel with a brown wooden handle, which he slid into his back pocket. On the bench was a plastic container full of long cable ties. He grabbed a handful. Coming, ready or not.

The coats he'd recently seen them wear were hanging on the rack in the utility room, so he doubted they'd gone into the garden and braved the cold. In the living room, he reached between the cushions to retrieve Michael's phone. Elaine had called seven times, and with her most recent attempt, she'd left a voicemail. A rummage through the kitchen drawers produced the keys to Sablefall Farm and a box of matches. He pocketed both. With no sign of Michael or Emily downstairs, he tightened his grip around the hammer and drifted up the stairs. Nobody was hiding in the first bedroom he came across, and nobody was hiding in the bathroom either. He walked past a landing cupboard, stopped, stepped back, and yanked open the door. No hiders to seek in there. A muffled thud from downstairs stopped him in his tracks.

In the kitchen, working his way from left to right, he quietly opened and closed each cupboard door until, 'Boo!'

A startled Emily kicked out, knocking over more cans of food. He viciously dragged Emily from her hiding place across the kitchen floor and sat her in a chair in the centre of the room.

He removed the hood. Setting eyes on the hammer, Emily's screams were stifled by the gag. The terrified young girl looked uncertain if this was part of the game.

Danny pulled the scarf from her mouth. 'Untie me,' she said. 'I don't want to play any more.'

'You remind me of my sister, always moaning and sulking.'

'Where's Michael?'

'I don't know. Why don't you call him?'

While she shouted her brother's name several times, Danny dragged another kitchen chair into the middle of the room and placed it next to her.

'You need to do a little better than that, Emily. The game is over. Perhaps I need to make you aware of how real this is.' He slapped her across the face. She yelled out at the initial contact and appeared shell-shocked that he'd struck her. Her cheek reddened, and her eyes glazed over. Her scream was deafening. There was a rumbling from upstairs – Michael was on his way.

He thundered down the stairs and paused in the doorway, clearly shocked by the sight of Danny behind Emily with a chisel pressed against her neck. On the floor next to the chair was a petrol can.

'What the fuck, Danny? Take that away from her neck,' he said, stepping forward.

'Stop!' Danny drew back the chisel and threatened to plunge it into Emily. 'Do as I say, and she won't get hurt.'

'Okay, okay. I'll do what you say. Just don't hurt my sister.'

Danny tossed the handcuffs to Michael. 'Hands behind your back and put these on.'

Michael snapped them around one wrist and fumbled to get them on the other. 'Done.'

'Now turn around and walk backwards to this chair.'

Michael did as he was told. Danny was soon upon him with the chisel. He tightened the cuffs. 'Keep coming backwards.'

He helped Michael into the chair and used his index finger to access his phone. 'It seems your mum has left you a message. Let me see what she has to say.'

Michael said, 'Please, don't hurt us. We haven't done anything to you.'

'Shhh.' Danny listened to the message. He smiled. 'She's on her way home and wanted to warn you about me. A little late for that.' He grinned at the children.

'You should leave. Tom and Simon will be back soon,' said Michael.

'I hope so.'

70

December 29

The drive from Whitby to Helmsley took them a little over fifty minutes. The memory of the property they'd viewed for Harper had faded into irrelevance amidst Tom's cursing and self-rebuke. Tom had left his phone in the side door and only checked it upon their return to the car. There were more missed calls from Elaine than he'd cared to count. To say she was furious when he'd called her was an understatement. Tom getting an earful had amused Harper until he'd discovered why. They'd agreed it was unlikely Danny would have travelled all that way alone, but their repeated debates conveyed their obvious concerns.

Tom entered the house unruffled, not knowing what to expect and acting as though everything was normal.

'I'm home,' he said. His posturing ceased when he got to the kitchen door and was struck by the strong stench of petrol. Gagged, drenched, and trembling before him on chairs, Michael and Emily's wide, fearful eyes begged to be saved as Danny loomed over them with a match, ready to strike. Tom's shoulders sagged, clearly saddened and disappointed. 'Oh, Danny. Why are you doing this?'

'Where is Harper?'

'He isn't here. I dropped him off in Whitby.'

'Don't lie to me, Tom. I know he's here somewhere.'

'I'm telling you the tru—'

'Harper! Come out now, or I will set fire to your niece and nephew.' He motioned to strike the match.

'Nooo!' Tom shouted. Muffled shrieks of terror came from the children as they squirmed in their chairs. 'Kids, try to remain calm. Everything will be okay. Get out here, Harper.' Tom turned his attention back to Danny. 'You're standing in petrol. If you strike that match, you'll go up in flames too.'

Danny shrugged and said, 'I. Don't. Care.'

Harper appeared in the doorway to the utility room. 'This looks familiar to the situation on the boat when Webster had your life in his hands.'

'The difference is – Zeph cared about me. He had no intention of taking my life. I have no concern at all for these two. They have earned nothing from me.'

Tom said, 'Danny, I have no idea what your intentions are, but whatever's wrong, we can get you the right help, improve your life, and make things better. All you have to do is stop this right now. I have seen people who have been through terrifying experiences adjust and turn their lives around.'

With a slight nod towards Harper, Danny said, 'What, like Mr Changeable over there? Kills a bunch of innocent people, takes vengeance on those just like him, and thinks he's a better man for it? You don't have a clue what this is about. I don't want help, and I don't want to change. Zeph made me just the way I should be.' He reached into his pocket and tossed a set of keys to Tom. 'We need to get going.'

Tom looked at the keys. 'Why do you want to go to this place?'

'A place of evil happenings attracts a certain kind of person. Harper knows what I mean. I'd imagine that's why he was drawn to a particular narrowboat.'

Harper leaned calmly against the architrave. He didn't agree or disagree and said nothing.

Tom said, 'Emily and Michael don't have to come with us, Danny. We can just leave them here.'

'I'm not an idiot, Tom. Now, you and Harper need to walk ahead of us and get in the front of the car.'

Tom was unsure of the situation. 'Harper?'

Danny smiled. 'Oh, you think because he has the darkness he can look into my eyes and see whether I'd be willing to set these children on fire?'

'Something like that,' said Tom.

Danny said, 'So what do you reckon, Harper? Do I have what it takes to be just like you?'

'No, you don't. But you do have what it takes to be like Joseph Webster.'

Danny smiled, lifted his chin, and pushed his shoulders back. 'That is high praise.'

'Not praise at all,' said Harper. 'Webster murdered children.' Danny's eyes filled with rage. Harper had antagonised him, but Danny held his nerve, not fooled by Harper's obvious attempt to provoke him into losing his advantage.

Harper walked towards Tom. 'We should do as he says.'

'Slowly,' said Danny. 'If I lose sight of either of you, I *will* light this match.'

A short distance behind, Michael and Emily followed, with Danny lurking at their heels. He ordered the children to pause in the doorway while Tom opened the back door first and then climbed into the front with Harper. Urging the children forward, one by one, they shuffled into position, with Danny getting in last, next to Emily and directly behind Tom in the driver's seat.

*

Less than three miles from the cottage, Tom exited the vehicle and opened the gate with a key. The light of day was swiftly fading, and glaring up at the house on the snow-dusted hill, it stood out like a beacon, ready to welcome yet more terror. Tom returned to the car and drove up to the parking area.

Danny said to Harper, 'Take the keys from Tom, open the front door, and wait for us on the porch.'

Tom said, 'I can do that.'

'No,' said Danny, leaning into the back of Tom's seat. 'You're not coming into the house.'

Tom turned to face Danny. 'I think it's best if I— Agghh!'

'You all right, Tom?' asked Harper.

In agony, Tom faced the front. 'Yeah. I must have pulled something in my back. Here.' He handed the keys to Harper. 'You go.'

'Come on,' said Danny. 'Get on with it.'

Harper headed towards the house. Danny got out of the car and summoned Emily and Michael. He said, 'Stand there and don't move.' He leaned into the back of the car and said to Tom, 'I almost forgot, open your phone and pass it to me.'

'It's not locked.' Tom passed his phone. 'Please, Danny. I'm begging you not to hurt them.'

'You should be more worried about yourself, Tom. I've given you a chance. It's up to you whether you take it or not. Goodbye.' Danny slammed the car door.

Sweat formed on Tom's forehead and brow. Watching them walk away towards whatever Danny had in store filled him with dread. He had been in a situation beyond his control once before when Harper had shot him in the chest. Despite his injuries, he'd managed to survive that terrible day. All he could do now was hope he'd survive this one. He reached around to his lower back. When he brought his hand into view, it was smothered in blood. Danny had driven something sharp into him through the seat, but he'd downplayed it so as not to panic the children. Fatigue was already taking hold. He needed a hospital – fast. Unconsciousness could occur at any moment. Tom started the car and headed down the drive. As he approached the gate, his eyes closed, and the car veered across the grass before coming to a stop in a hedge.

71

December 29

The car mounted the pavement as Elaine brought it to a stop outside the cottage. Their journey had been frantic, with Elaine pressing Lenny to keep using her phone to call Michael, Tom, and the landline. She'd even made him hold the phone close so she could leave a voicemail for Michael. When Tom finally called back, she snatched the phone from Lenny and let fly with a torrent of fear and anger. Unable to see Tom's car, she concluded he was still on his way back from Whitby.

Elaine raced into the cottage as Lenny tried to reach Tom to find out where they were. After a few rings, he hung up and hurried inside to catch up with Elaine. The thick scent of petrol lingered in the air, and when he stood next to Elaine by the kitchen door, the eerie sight of a jerry can beside two empty chairs in the centre of the room turned his stomach. His shoulder brushed against Elaine; she was physically shaking.

Following Elaine into the kitchen, he said, 'This is bad. It looks like he's poured petrol over the kids. He probably threatened to hurt them in order to keep Tom and Harper under control.'

Elaine blew her top. 'Fuck! I knew it. I bloody knew it.' She picked up a chair and smashed it to pieces against the tiled floor. 'I told you that boy was dangerous, but, oh no, he just needs a little help and a chance, you said.'

Lenny held his tongue. Probably for the best. Her phone pinged in his hand. 'It's a message from Tom. He wants to know where we are.'

She grabbed the phone from his hand and attempted to call Tom. He didn't answer. 'Shit! Shit! Shit! Why won't you answer me?' She tried Michael's number. It rang a few times before *he* answered. 'Michael!' she exclaimed.

'Try again.'

She put the phone on speaker. 'Where are my children? If you've laid one finger on them, what you did to Connor will look like child's play compared to what I'll do to you.'

'I'm sure that's true,' said Danny, a calmness in his tone. 'They're here with me, as is Harper. I'm staring at all three right now.'

'Let me speak to them.'

'That's not going to happen.'

'Where's Tom?' she asked.

'My guess – the hospital. Unless he took a turn for the worse.'

Elaine glared at Lenny beside her, listening in. 'What the fuck did you do to him, Danny?'

'Enough questions. You're wasting time, Elaine.'

'I've called the police,' she said. 'They're on their way.'

'We both know there are no police coming. You wouldn't put your brother in that kind of danger. You know where we are. Come find us.' The call ended.

'Tom's hurt,' she said.

'I'll call the local hospitals on the way.'

'That damned fucking house. I should have burned it to the ground when I had the chance.'

*

On the short journey, Lenny called the nearest hospitals and was informed there were no new emergencies involving knife wounds or anything of the sort. Stressing about her children and knowing Tom could be in a bad way must have been tearing her apart, yet she pressed on, forceful and focused, powered by her darkness to safeguard those she loved. Through the trees, Lenny viewed the silhouette of the house against the brooding sky. The downstairs lights glared like a swarm of fireflies through the holes in the metal shutters on either side of the front door. Though creepy, he'd never bought into the house of horror nonsense that had been bandied about, as most deaths had occurred outside. As far as he was concerned, houses weren't evil; people were. Still, there was no disguising that many bad things had happened there.

As the car turned up the dark drive, Lenny climbed between the seats into the back. Elaine asked, 'What are you doing?'

'Danny doesn't know I'm with you. It could be the only advantage we have.' He spread himself across the seat with no idea how he'd use that advantage. As per Lenny's style, he'd wing it and hope for the best. Elaine reached across to the glove compartment. He heard the rattle of keys.

'Here.' She passed them to him. 'The long silver key opens the deadbolt for the security door at the back. He won't be expecting anyone to come in that way. But open the outer door slowly. These security doors can make a racket.'

The headlights beamed across the house as they approached. Peeking between the seats, a dark figure prowled behind the shutters. Lenny ducked out of sight.

Elaine said, 'He knows I'm here.' She parked and turned off the engine. 'Whatever your plan, I hope it doesn't involve appealing to his better nature because he doesn't have one.' Lenny was about to put forward an argument, but she continued, 'Trust me on this. Some souls are lost forever. And don't think about using me or Harper as an example. We are killers and always will be. Danny should not be underestimated.'

Elaine left the car. Lenny listened to her footsteps fade away until all that remained were her words echoing in his mind. His friend Colin Hargreaves had been taken apart by Danny and shoved limb by limb into a hessian bag. Elaine suspected he'd killed and disposed of Connor Doherty in the same way. And let's not forget what had happened to the family dog, his attack on his sister, and his jar of trophies. His concern for Tom grew. Now, Danny had the lives of Elaine's children in his hands. Whatever the outcome tonight, Danny wouldn't live to see another morning. Lenny raised his head and watched Elaine walk up the steps to the porch and push the door open. With a backward glance towards Lenny, she disappeared inside. He eased open the car door and crawled out.

72

December 29

The Boy

Having read so much about the house and the crimes committed there, it was nothing like he'd imagined. It didn't look old or creepy. There were no cobwebs dangling from the ceiling. He couldn't sense the unholy welcome he'd been hoping for. There was nothing sinister about this place at all. The house appeared to be clean and tidy, and the furniture, mostly covered in sheets, looked practically unused. He'd briefly debated his profound desire to come here, but who was he to question the workings of evil? He'd been chosen and was here to do what needed to be done.

Gagged, restrained, and stinking of petrol, Michael and Emily were cold and terrified on the two-seater sofa not far from the window. The thrill of the fear he'd instilled in Elaine's children sent shivers up his spine. Much more excitement, and he'd be dancing in Emily's endless tears. He glanced at Harper, on his knees in front of the fireplace with his hands cuffed behind his back. While waiting for Elaine, Danny removed the handcuffs from Michael and had him put them on Harper. As with Emily, Michael's wrists were now fastened with cable ties.

The front door had closed behind Elaine, and his anticipation grew. Her shadow stretched out along the floor of the doorway. 'Come and join us, Elaine. We've all been waiting for you.'

Entering the room, she gazed at Harper before turning to face her children. 'Michael, Emily.' She marched forward.

'Ah, ah,' said Danny, threatening to light the match. 'That's close enough.'

Elaine appeared anxious, and so she should be. This wasn't some excessive cry for attention. She said, 'Please remove the gag so Emily can breathe properly. She suffers from panic attacks.'

Danny glanced at Emily and considered her mother's plea. 'Okay. I'll remove it, but if she screams, it goes back on.'

'Don't scream, sweetie. Everything is going to be all right. I promise.'

Danny said, 'I'm not sure you should be making promises you might not be able to keep.' He untied the scarf and pulled it away from her mouth. 'There. Better?' Trembling with fear, Emily nodded in silence as fresh tears tumbled over dry ones.

Elaine said, 'Why are you doing this, Danny? What is it you want?'

'I can't have what I want because you took it away from me. And then you broke your promise and rejected me as if I were nothing.'

'You sound like a petulant little child,' she said. 'Because that's exactly what you are – a child.'

'You should watch what you say to me.'

'For God's sake, Danny, just the other day, Lenny and I were discussing how we could help you.'

'I don't trust anything you say. Where is that stupid old fart, anyway?'

'How should I know? And how can you be so disrespectful? He's been there for you and your parents.'

'I only accepted having him around because of his connection to you. I hoped he'd convince you to see me, but by the time he did, Zeph had come back into my life. I only needed Lenny to show me how to get to you.' Danny glanced over at Zeph, standing tall and beaming with pride, close to Harper. A priceless moment for Danny.

Elaine stared at Harper, who raised his eyebrows and shook his head in disbelief. She said, 'I hate to tell you this, Danny, but Zeph is dead.'

Danny shouted furiously, 'And whose fault is that?'

'I saved your life. In some way, we all did.'

'No! You ruined it. You ruined everything. I was meant to take over something special. Something unique. Find my own successor. But you all took away my legacy. You made me a nobody – a laughing stock to the other kids.'

Elaine said, 'Danny, you're delusional. I've been where you are. Harper has too. Your mind is no longer seeing reality.'

Danny chest pounded as he fumed. 'How is this for reality?' He pulled the chisel from his pocket and rammed it into Michael's shoulder. Michael's muffled, gut-wrenching scream echoed throughout the house. Elaine covered her mouth with her hands. Emily squealed, her wide eyes strained with terror. Harper climbed to his feet as Elaine raced forward.

'Get back!' Danny ordered, threatening to do the unthinkable and burn her children alive.

She stopped. Tears for her son's pain and distress streamed down her cheeks. Danny felt her gaze drilling through him. There may have been tears, but behind her eyes was rage, the likes of which he'd never seen. He feared her, but there was no turning back now.

Danny looked at Harper, who appeared as calm as ever. A dangerous sign. 'You! On your knees,' he ordered.

Michael howled as Danny pulled the chisel from his shoulder. He wiped it against the sheet covering the sofa and stepped into full view. Elaine stared at the smear of blood on the side of his jeans.

'Oh, that's Tom's,' he said. Seeing her angst, he grinned. 'Now you know I'm not messing around – we can get on with this. I'm going to present you with a choice. I suppose it's actually more of a dilemma. But I've just made it a little easier for you,' he said, glancing at Michael, who cried out in anguish. He tossed the chisel towards Elaine. 'Pick it up.'

She knelt down, grabbed hold of the handle, and tightened her grip. 'Tell me what you want me to do,' she said. Given the chance, her expression told him she'd like to plunge it right between his eyes. He kept the match and box at the ready.

'Michael obviously needs urgent medical attention, so I want Harper to do what he chose to do for me and sacrifice *his* life for the lives of your children. If he agrees to let you kill him, you can take them out of here and drive away.'

'Absurd! What kind of choice is that?' she said, staring anxiously at her brother, who remained unperturbed.

'The best you're going to get,' said Danny. 'It's because of me you have this opportunity. Zeph wanted you to kill Harper and have me burn your children right afterwards.'

'How do I know you won't?'

'I know it's a lot to ask, but you'll have to trust me. Besides, if you don't kill him, you're going to lose your children anyway.' Danny enjoyed seeing her in turmoil as she gazed at Michael in agony and Emily, who sobbed quietly.

Harper said, 'Elaine, I know this is tough, but *you* can do this.'

'There we go,' said Danny. 'Our mass murderer turned hero, once again to the rescue.'

She turned with a sorrowful stare. 'I can't.'

Harper said, 'You have to.'

Her eyes teared up again. 'No. I can't do this.'

'Elaine, this is the right choice. The only choice. It's my time.'

Danny watched Zeph circle Harper and couldn't help but admire Harper's sense of self-sacrifice, but that was as far as he allowed his sentiment to go. 'I'm growing tired, Elaine. Make a decision.'

Elaine said, 'Kids, close your eyes. I don't want you to see this.'

'I'd prefer they watched,' said Danny. 'But I'm not completely heartless.'

Elaine glared at Danny. 'You know I'm going to kill you, right?'

He laughed. 'Of course.'

Elaine took a step towards Harper and stopped, her eyes searching the room. She was contemplating, desperate to find a way out of her predicament. Danny had witnessed the same look in her eyes on the boat. Unfortunately for her, he hadn't left much to chance. She edged closer and stared at the floor; her lack of options appeared to sink in.

On his knees, Harper straightened his body and stuck out his chest. He shouted, 'Come on, Elaine. Do it!'

She raised her head and looked her brother in the eyes. 'I'm sorry.' Elaine checked that her children weren't watching, took a breath, closed her eyes, and lunged at Harper, forcing the chisel into his stomach.

Harper yelled and looked up at her. 'Fuck, Elaine. Did you have to do it so hard?'

She yanked out the chisel and backed away. He slouched forward to examine the blood gushing from the wound.

'The stomach,' said Danny. 'So you *do* think I'm stupid. We could be waiting hours. Michael could bleed out before Harper. Stab him again, only this time higher up and to the side.'

Elaine sobbed, shaking her head. She reluctantly stepped forward and dropped to her knees in front of him. Elaine put an arm around Harper, rested her forehead on his, and silently eased the chisel into his side.

73

December 29

Lenny had lingered in the hallway, hearing much of what had been said. He'd waited patiently for a chance to present itself so he could make a move on Danny, but the boy had positioned himself well away from the door and wouldn't give up his advantage. The waiting was killing Lenny. It was definitely killing Harper. He stood in the open doorway with a clear view of Elaine and Harper.

Danny said, 'I bet you're both wishing you'd never saved me now. Stab him again, only this time don't shield my view. I want to see his agony.'

Harper muttered, 'Promise me you'll kill that little fucker.'

Her shoulders bounced with every cry as she agreed. Elaine agonisingly readied herself to thrust the chisel into him once again.

Lenny could delay no longer. 'No! Stop this.' He barged into the room. 'Enough!'

Danny said, 'Well, well. This *is* a surprise, but I suppose I should have known. I'm glad you could join us. Elaine is just in the middle of slaughtering her brother.'

'It's over, Danny. The police are on their way.'

'Not sure that's true, but if it is, they're not here yet, are they? So there's enough time for her to finish him off.'

It pained Lenny to see the look of uncertainty on Elaine's face. She no doubt expected him to have a plan, and he wished it were true. He turned to Danny. 'This is senseless. Look at those children, at Michael. Look at what you've done to him. Do you not remember being at someone else's mercy? How scared and utterly helpless you were? Stop this and let them go.'

'And I will. As soon as she takes Harper's life.'

Lenny drifted closer to Danny as he spoke. 'Take his life for who – you or Zeph?' Danny's eyes opened wide. 'Yes, I know he's here.'

'You can see him, too?'

'No. But I'm guessing you can.' Danny glanced towards Elaine and Harper. 'I take it he's over there?' Lenny managed to get within a few feet. 'I'm going to tell you a secret, Danny. I see people who are no longer with us all the time. I even talk to my dead girlfriend, or at least that's what I convince myself. You see, the reality is I don't know if she's there or not. In all likelihood, she isn't. Just like Zeph isn't here with you. Some people create fantasies to cope with trauma, and it doesn't always bode well.'

'Stay back,' said Danny, striking the match. 'You're wrong. Zeph *is* here, and he wants this over with. Elaine, you have seconds to stab your brother before I'm forced to drop this on your children.'

Taking a few steps back, Lenny pleaded, 'Please, Danny.'

Elaine's eyes lingered on Harper's – bonded by heartbreak and vengeance. She whispered, 'I love you.' With a trembling hand, she pressed the chisel into his stomach.

Danny snuffed out the flame between his fingers.

Elaine dropped the bloodied tool on the floor and put her arms around Harper, pulling him close. Their heads, side by side, cheek to cheek.

Harper smiled softly. 'It's okay.' His head fell onto her shoulder.

She eased his body to the ground and kissed his forehead. 'Don't you dare die,' she said. A determined Elaine climbed to her feet. 'I've done as you asked. Now, let my children go.'

Danny smiled. 'When I said you'd have to trust me, you really shouldn't have.' He lit another match. Elaine screamed and advanced.

Lenny shouted, 'No, don't do it!'

Danny moved the lit match towards Michael. Emily turned her head and blew out the flame. Stunned, Danny fumbled for another. Lenny reached out and snatched the matchbox from his grasp. Elaine lunged at the boy, taking him to the floor.

Lenny pulled the children up from the sofa and ushered them out of the living room. 'Go,' he said. 'Get out of the house and wait by the car.'

He raced back into the living room. Sitting astride Danny, Elaine pounded his face. 'Stop, Elaine! He's had enough.' She placed her hands around Danny's neck and squeezed. 'Elaine! Let the police deal with him now.'

'I promised Harper.'

'Regardless of what he has done, he's a child. You don't want a child's murder on your conscience.'

Elaine gradually loosened her grip around his neck and removed her hands. She glared at Danny as he choked and, after several seconds, reached into his pocket and retrieved the key for the handcuffs. Elaine stood tall and turned to Lenny. Instead of the usual darkness lurking within the depths of her eyes, he discerned the fading malevolence of another entity. An illogical dread prickled his skin, and he stepped aside. Without saying a word, she walked past him and knelt down next to Harper.

His pulse weakening, Elaine removed the cuffs and placed his hand over the wound that appeared to be bleeding the most. 'Keep the pressure on. Help is coming. I'll be back as soon as I've checked on Michael and Emily.'

Elaine had left Danny's face a bloodied mess. Unsure of what to do or say, Lenny held out his hand to help him up.

Danny said, 'Why did you stop her from killing me?'

'Because it was the right thing to do.'

Danny laughed. 'Good old Lenny. Always needing to do the right thing.' He shunned Lenny's hand and pulled himself up using the back of the sofa.

'All I ever wanted was to help you,' said Lenny.

'Well, you didn't help. All you've done is prolong what I have to do.' He faltered around the two-seater and plonked himself where Michael and Emily had been sitting. The aroma of petrol seeped through the fabric of the sofa and rose up from Danny's training shoes.

'You won't be doing anything. I didn't lie. The police are on their way, along with an ambulance.'

'You think this is over? It isn't. I will finish this and take everything she loves away from her.'

Danny attempted to stand, but Lenny pushed him down. 'You're not going anywhere.' Elaine had expressed her fears about the boy, and though he now knew the truth, Lenny wanted it confirmed by Danny. 'Did you kill Connor?'

'He was going to die anyway. Taking an axe to Connor was part of my failed plan to kill Zeph and escape.'

'Was Connor's murder when everything changed for you?'

'No. Zeph holding me in his arms shortly after was the turning point.'

Disappointed, Lenny had no words. Only quiet dismay.

Danny asked, 'What will happen to me now?'

'You'll probably be sent to a young offender institution or a secure hospital, where they'll provide you with professional help.'

'Wherever they send me, you know it won't be for long. I'll convince them I can be normal as easily as I convinced you.' He laid his head back and closed his eyes.

Elaine had said, "Some souls are lost forever." Staring at Danny, he should never have doubted her. How blind he'd been, not seeing the truth behind his lies and lifeless eyes. Two children he loved dearly could have died here tonight, and he'd have been responsible.

Danny said, 'This was supposed to be my night, ending with my death.'

'Oh, it's going to end with your death,' said Harper, spitting blood and staggering towards them. He slumped onto the sofa next to Danny. 'And mine.' Holding his side, blood streamed between his fingers. He glanced at the matchbox in Lenny's hand.

Danny grasped what was happening and tried to escape. Harper grabbed his arm, pulled him close, and held him tightly.

Lenny struck a match and hesitated. Danny struggled and yelled, but Harper was never going to let him go.

Harper said, 'For Michael and Emily.'

Lenny dropped the match at Danny's feet and stepped back. Fire soared up the screaming boy's legs and swept onto Harper, who remained silent and unmoved. The fire spread quickly across the sofa. The flames escalated, and the heat intensified. Lenny eased backwards, unable to avert his eyes from Harper, Danny, and Joseph Webster. The boy thrashed around, but Harper's grip held firm. Fire crept along the floor and crawled up the walls and the curtains. Paint blistered, and glass cracked. The breeze crept through the shutters and fed the flames. Danny's screams abruptly fell silent, his body fused with Harper's, both figures frozen in an eerie stillness, while Joseph Webster's manifestation gradually faded.

Elaine cried, 'What have you done?'

'Allowed you to keep your promise and set Harper free for the first time in his life.'

Holding back her tears, she stood beside Lenny and knotted her fingers through his. 'Come on. Let's get out of here.'

Lenny didn't budge. He'd told Elaine she didn't want a child's murder on her conscience. Now he had one on his. Elaine tugged at his hand. He relented and let her lead him away from the encroaching flames that were now swirling across the ceiling above their heads. They stopped at the doorway and gazed sorrowfully back towards Harper.

From the parking area, they watched the fire engulf the house. A police car sped up the drive, shortly followed by an ambulance. Paramedics were quick to treat Michael's wound. Over the next few minutes, more police cars and a second ambulance arrived. The upstairs windows cracked and shattered behind the metal shutters. Flames breached the slates on the roof. As three fire engines approached, the roof partially collapsed into the house. Bright sparks burst like fireworks into the starry sky.

Side by side, Lenny said, 'Sorry about the house.'

Elaine replied, 'I'm not.'

'Sorry about Harper.'

Her tearful eyes mirrored the orange glow of the burning house. 'Me too.'

A paramedic approached. 'Mrs Burgess, we're ready to take your son to the hospital.'

She turned to Lenny. 'Will you take Emily back to the cottage for me?'

'Of course.' She handed him the keys.

Walking towards the ambulance, she stopped. 'What's going on down there?'

At the bottom of the drive, two police cars were parked beside an ambulance, their headlights highlighting a vehicle partially embedded in the hedge.

Under her breath, she said, 'Tom.' Elaine charged down the sloping lawn. 'Tom!'

Lenny asked the paramedic to take care of Emily and chased after Elaine. His heart pounded. A harrowing emptiness came over him. His jellied legs barely kept him upright. A police officer cordoned off the area around the car. Another constable advanced towards Elaine to prevent her from going beyond the tape, informing her it was a crime scene. The words fuelled her agony, and she pushed the officer.

He glanced at Lenny and said, 'You need to keep her back, sir. We've discovered the body of a man inside the vehicle.'

Lenny grabbed Elaine and held her tight. A deafening scream escaped her as she succumbed to the realisation of Tom's death. She slowly rolled down Lenny's body and collapsed onto the ground. Wails of grief poured from within as she released her devastation. Lenny sat with her on the grass, his arms wrapped around her as she cried into his shoulder. He couldn't fight back his tears. Under the cloaked blush of a deep amber sky, the pair mourned the traumatic loss of Tom and Harper. The horror never ceased to exist in this place.

74

December 29

The last forty-eight hours had been gruelling and unpleasant for Harry – it wasn't about to get any easier. When he'd called Lucy earlier in the day to arrange going to her place for the evening, she had been reluctant. She didn't sound like her usual self, and he'd informed her it hadn't been a great day for him either. He wouldn't take no for an answer and emphasised that they'd be better off miserable in each other's company than miserable on their own. Now, here they were with their fourth bottle of beer, sharing stories from their early days on the force, embarrassing moments, and failed relationships.

Harry pulled out a deck of cards, and Lucy fetched more beer. The radio played in the background while they played a simple drinking game called Higher or Lower. Safe to say, the bottles Harry had brought with him were soon dwindling. When Cyndi Lauper's 'I Drove All Night' came on, Lucy jumped up and mimed along, using her bottle as a microphone. Harry smiled as he watched, mesmerised, unsure whether he was comfortable or not.

Halfway through, she collapsed onto the sofa next to him. Harry said, 'Considering you're always banging on about my age, I'm surprised you're into eighties music. Were you even born in that decade?'

'Cyndi Lauper is a legend. Growing up, my mum and dad played eighties songs all the time, so it was hard to ignore. A decade of fantastic music, and don't get me started on the fashion! Clothes these days are so boring. Hardly anyone expresses themselves any more. And for your information, yes, I was born in the eighties, just.'

She grabbed hold of his hand. The sensational warmth of her touch stirred his emotions. Harry liked her very much – but it wasn't right, and he shouldn't lead her on.

He asked, 'How come you were down in the dumps today?'

'Just one of those days, I guess. What about you? You said you'd had a bad one.'

'Oh, you don't want to hear about my day.'

'Tell me,' she said.

'I assume you've heard about Sarah Kerr?'

'Yes, I have.' Lucy sipped her beer.

'I was at the crime scene this morning. Not a pretty sight.'

She squeezed his hand. 'I can imagine. It's strange to know we spoke to her less than a fortnight ago.' She looked at him. 'I wish I'd met you months ago, before all this happened.'

'Not sure my wife would have liked me sitting on your couch holding your hand a week ago, let alone months ago.'

Lucy said, 'For better or worse, we have the power to change the direction of our lives, but it's scary how we often hand that power to others to change our lives for us.' She held up her bottle. 'To better choices.'

'Better choices,' he said, avoiding eye contact as the bottles clinked together.

Lucy climbed off the sofa. 'Another beer?'

'Yep. Keep 'em coming. I'll shuffle the cards.'

'Honestly, Harry, you don't have to get me drunk to get me into bed.'

'I bet you say that to everyone.'

'You'd be throwing your money away.'

When they'd run out of beer, they opened the wine and listened to soft music while snuggling on the sofa. Lucy said, 'I'm glad you came over.'

'Me too.'

She took the glass from his hand, put it on the table, and sat astride his lap. Staring into each other's eyes, Harry restrained himself from making the first move, fighting to keep his emotions in check, which became more challenging when Lucy placed her lips on his.

She said, 'Shall we go to the bedroom?'

'I'm not quite ready to take things further.'

'Well, whatever's poking me in the groin suggests otherwise.'

'It's not that I don't want to. I just need a little more time.'

'It's fine,' she said. 'I'm happy to stick with heavy petting.'

He smiled. 'Lucy Fenton, are you mocking me?'

'Would I ever?' She leaned in and kissed him again.

An hour later, with another bottle of wine on the table, she was asleep with her head on his shoulder. Harry held her for a while, and though his heart was heavy, his mind remained focused on what he perceived to be the right thing. He made her comfortable on the sofa, grabbed a folded blanket from the back cushion, and covered her. He cleared away the glasses and bottles and tidied up. When he'd finished, he sat on the floor and stared at her. He placed his hand on her soft, warm cheek and let it rest there. After a tender moment, Harry climbed to his feet, grabbed his jacket from the coat rack, and left.

75

December 30
The Arrest

An icy chill clawed through the wind as the bleak early morning burst into life. Multiple police vehicles and a forensic unit streamed into the car park en masse. Officers gathered outside the apartment building, ready to flood through the main door. They entered and stormed up the stairs. DI Sam Jennings rapped her knuckles against apartment four. It took a second, louder knock before the weary occupant opened the door.

Sam showed her warrant card and said, 'Lucy Fenton, I'm arresting you on suspicion of the murder of Sarah Kerr.'

Lucy's rights were read while she argued against her arrest, insisting she'd done nothing of the sort. Lucy was handcuffed and escorted from the building. Trudging towards the open back doors of a police van, she glanced around, her hair dishevelled and trailing in the oppressive wind. Lucy paled at the many faces around her, some of whom were officers she'd worked with. She set eyes on Harry and froze. Her expression changed from unknowing to knowing all. A hand pressed against her shoulder, urging her forward. She dropped eye contact and stared at the ground.

*

Harry never suspected a collaboration between Lucy and Sarah Kerr. That's not to say his subconscious hadn't collected the information. But for certain events – for example, if Lucy's stabbing hadn't happened, there was every chance he would have registered Lucy's involvement sooner. Of course, it didn't help that his feelings for her had clouded his judgement. With all his heart, he'd wanted to be wrong, but when he spotted Lucy's car parked outside Rebecca Heaton's home, he was crushed. Either she was keeping tabs on Rebecca's movements for Miss Kerr or waiting for the perfect time to shut her up before she remembered anything incriminating.

The second it clicked, he pieced it together through flashes of particular conversations and incidents. One of which was the fleeting glimpse of familiarity between Lucy and Sarah in the diner when they'd first questioned Miss Kerr. Billy Graham being able to place Lucy at Fred Perry's on the night he was murdered explained why the youth had thrown a brick and called them murderers after they'd examined the scene. Something else he'd failed to pick up on at the time was Owen Carrick's suicide note. Perhaps it was the alcohol or that Lucy was beyond his suspicion, but when he'd informed her, he'd never mentioned it contained a solitary word: "*Sorry.*" Yet somehow, she knew. Once he'd seen her outside Rebecca's and spoken to Sarah Kerr, his main concern was to form a plan and gather evidence. Billy's statement and Lenny finding Sarah Kerr on CCTV visiting Lucy at Maidstone Hospital after she'd been stabbed would help. He now knew why Lucy had pleaded with DCS Falconer to work with him on the case.

Harry watched the van drive away. His dry mouth and tight chest didn't compare to his emotional state. He'd made some distressing decisions in the past, but this was the most gut-wrenching of his life. He took a deep breath. There was work to do, and he had to focus on the task at hand. Harry entered the building and walked up to the apartment where he'd left Lucy sleeping on the sofa hours before.

Sam approached as soon as he stepped over the threshold and said, 'Forensics are recording and collecting the evidence. We found a blue parka hanging on the rack in the hallway. There appears to be a little blood spatter on the coat's exterior.'

Harry said, 'It'll be Lucy's blood from when she was stabbed. It connects her to her attacker.'

'Too right it does. Why else would she have it? I've had forensics bag all her clothing and footwear as well.'

'Good. There is every chance the fibres from the back of Fred Perry's chair will be on a pair of her shoes. At the crime scene, she asked Arthur Potts whether the fibres could be matched. I'm just surprised she held on to all this evidence. Did you get the picture I sent of her car outside the Heatons' house on Joy Lane?'

'I did. I assume that's how your suspicions arose?'

'Yes. I'm just disappointed I didn't pick up on it earlier.'

'Not easy with so much going on. I have to say, I was taken aback when the forensic report revealed the strand of hair found on Sarah's bed was a one hundred per cent match for Lucy. You should count yourself lucky you didn't become one of her victims.'

'I can't say it hasn't crossed my mind. Have they found the murder weapon?'

A member of the forensic team stepped into the hallway. 'Detective Inspector Jennings, we've discovered a bloodstained knife in the kitchen drawer.'

Sam glanced at Harry. 'They have now. I'll take it from here. Make sure you get the witness down to the station this afternoon to make a statement.'

76

December 30

Lenny stood over the cooker, making scrambled eggs for himself and Emily. Neither of them had much of an appetite, but it was best if they tried to eat something. When two detectives finally left the cottage late last night, Lenny tidied up the kitchen and washed the floor. He'd cleaned elsewhere and sprayed air freshener, but the smell of petrol hovered like a bad memory. Constantly reliving the horrors at Sablefall Farm made sleep impossible, so he'd rattled around the cottage looking for more jobs to do. In between checking on Emily, he'd emptied Elaine's bins and watered the plants in the kitchen. He'd even gone to the trouble of unloading the dishwasher, leaving several pots and a pan he couldn't find a home for on the worktop. Elaine had messaged a while back to say Michael was thankfully going to be fine. A relief, but what a harrowing evening. He'd never seen Elaine so distressed, and rightfully so. Her children had been hurt and left traumatised; her husband had bled to death in the car, and as for her brother . . .

She must be going through a new kind of hell. After Olivia's death, he was inconsolable, and even now, he continued to grieve. Elaine had struggled well into adulthood, but when Harper came into her life, she grew in strength and showed herself to be resilient and indomitable. However, she was not a robot. She would no doubt hide her emotions, but inside, it would take her a while to piece together the fragments of her complex nature. It would take them all a long time to come to terms with such a tragic loss. Tom was a good man, drawn into Elaine's tragic world. As for Harper, well, he was Harper. He would not be missed by many.

It took a while, but once he'd settled Emily down to the extent he could leave her alone in her room, he felt duty-bound to call Danny's parents. Though their grief was obvious, it wasn't easy to assess how they'd taken the news. He sensed they'd been waiting for something dreadful to happen for a while. He'd also called Alice to let her know about Harper. To say she was hysterical on the phone would be an understatement. When she'd briefly calmed herself, she said she'd been going out of her mind, hoping he would come through the door at any moment. It wasn't the first time he'd left her and Milena, but on the previous occasions, he'd returned a few days later. Silly sod. If he'd stayed where he was, he'd still be alive. On the other hand, if he had, the outcome for Michael and Emily might have been a lot worse, and they'd still be trying to catch Carlton Lee.

He turned off the cooker, walked over to the table, and scooped scrambled eggs onto the plates. 'Do you want some orange juice, Emily?'

'Yes, please.'

They sat quietly. Lenny didn't have a clue how Emily was feeling and couldn't find the words to ask. He was out of his depth with young children and had no idea how to talk to one after such a traumatic experience. He ate a couple of mouthfuls and pushed the food around his plate. Emily was doing the same.

She asked, 'Was that man really my uncle?'

'Yes.' No more lies.

'Did my mum kill him?'

He put down his fork and took a moment before answering such a question. 'The other year when that man broke into your house, your mum would have done anything to protect you and Michael, even if it meant getting hurt in the process. Last night, your mother and uncle did the exact same thing to stop Danny. All you need to remember is that Uncle Harper gave his life to save you and your brother.'

'Why did Danny want to hurt us?'

'Danny was a troubled young boy who'd been through a terrible ordeal. People don't always recover from such experiences, and it's distressing for everyone involved.'

'My friend's dad was a soldier. When he returned home, she said he used to cry and hurt himself because he'd seen bad things. Then he died. Is that the same?'

Lenny imagined he'd taken his own life, and the circumstances surrounding his death had been kept private. 'What happened to your friend's dad is heartbreaking. Everyone reacts to trauma in different ways, but yes, it's the same.'

Other than forks tapping on plates, Lenny welcomed the return to silence. After a few minutes, Emily asked if she could leave the table and go to her room. He couldn't refuse. Lenny pushed back his chair as he stood and collected his phone from the worktop where it had been charging. He called the animal hospital to find out how Phoebe was and let them know he wouldn't be able to pick her up until the following day.

Scrolling through the news at the table, he caught a similar headline to the newsflash he'd seen on the television before leaving for Helmsley with Elaine. Sarah Kerr was the young woman who'd been brutally murdered. Even more disturbing was the leaked picture of the police officer suspected of her murder – Lucy Fenton.

He recalled meeting her at the Kentish Town Forum; however, amidst the chaos and panic, it had slipped his mind that he'd come across her name previously. Lenny searched Google for a police officer who had recently been injured in a knife attack at a shopping centre and checked the date. Now he knew who Sarah Kerr had been visiting at the hospital and why Harry had sent him to examine the CCTV.

Harry wasn't answering his phone, no doubt busy. In the living room, Lenny looked in the cupboard where Tom kept a few bottles of spirits. Holding an unopened bottle of whisky in his hands, though tempted, he put it back and closed the door. Sitting in the armchair, he thought about Olivia, Tom, Harper, and even Danny. Out of nowhere, the dam holding back his overflowing heart of pain burst, and he cried aloud.

Two hours had passed before he woke from his unexpected nap. Such misery sapped the spirit. He checked on Emily, who was tucked up in bed, albeit awake and clearly upset. He sat on the edge. 'What happened was truly terrifying, but we're all here for you.'

'Tom isn't,' she cried.

Her words and tears turned him into a wreck. 'No, he isn't. Come here.'

Emily sat up and threw her arms around him, resting her head on his shoulder. She had the tight squeeze of a frightened child and could cling on for as long as she wanted. Her sobs echoed in his ear and tore into his shattered soul. He chose to let his words slumber on heavy-hearted breaths.

With his arms tired and numb, a tap on his shoulder drew his attention. He had no idea how long he'd been sitting there with Emily in his arms.

Elaine whispered, 'She's asleep. Let me take her.' She gently removed Emily from his arms, laid her on the bed, and covered her up. 'I'll be down in a bit,' she said, snuggling under the covers beside her daughter.

Entering the kitchen, Elaine had cleared away their plates, glasses, pots, and the pan he'd left on the worktop. He examined his phone; he'd been holding Emily for the best part of an hour. Harry hadn't returned his call. Probably a wise move. He made himself a cup of tea and ventured outside to the garden. The cold air was bitter, almost spiteful in the aftermath of the previous night, but a little brisk air was a welcome gift – until it wasn't. He returned to the kitchen table to finish his tea and wait for Elaine.

She walked into the room an hour later with a dazed look and tousled hair. After making herself an instant coffee, she said, 'Thank you for taking care of Emily.'

'I didn't mind at all. Emily's unsurprisingly upset about Tom. I'm sure she's got a lot of questions that you'll need to answer truthfully.'

'I know,' she said, leaning against the cupboard and sipping her coffee. 'Thanks for emptying the bins.'

He pointed to the windowsill. 'I watered your plants as well.'

She glanced around. 'They're plastic.'

'Sorry. I was just trying to help. How's Michael?'

'They want to keep him in for a few days. I'll go back over later this evening. I'd appreciate it if you could stay another night and watch over Emily. If not, I can always ask Lila. It's just . . . I wouldn't mind a bit more time before speaking to anyone else.'

'No, it's fine. I can stay. Though I'd like to head home in the morning if that's possible.'

Elaine joined him at the table. 'Shouldn't be a problem.'

They shared the silence until he could hold his tongue no longer. 'Have you heard from Harry?'

'No. Why would I?'

'The night before last, a young woman was killed in a Surrey mansion. She was a suspect in one of his cases. Actually, I'd go as far as to say he was convinced she was responsible for a number of murders.'

'I'm sure he'll find out who did it,' she said.

'Oh, he already knows, because *I'm* looking at the killer. And don't even bother telling me otherwise. I know you far too well. It was Harry who called you in the garden the other day, and that's why you came back to London. Meeting a developer, my arse. Now I know why you came home so late and took a shower at two in the morning. It's also the reason you didn't want me to listen to the news in the car on the way here. What the fuck, Elaine?'

Not only was she too tired to deny it, but she knew any attempt to do so would be a complete waste of time. 'Whatever you think you know, you're more than likely right, but this is not something I'm in the mood to discuss at this minute.'

'We will discuss this now. Jesus Christ, Elaine, what were you thinking? You're not some kind of assassin for hire.'

'I said something similar. Though no money exchanged hands.'

'So you're dishing out vigilante-style murders for free? Terrific!'

'No, it's not like that,' she argued. 'If you'd heard the entire conversation, you would know I didn't want to do it.'

'Then why did you?'

'Because he threatened to let the world know Harper was alive.'

'A shitty thing to do, but surely you knew he was bluffing?'

'Maybe. I don't know.'

'Well, I do. Deep down, you wanted to do it. Just yesterday, you told me you are a killer and always will be.'

She looked him in the eye and said, 'You're forgetting something.'

'What?'

'You're a killer as well now.'

He had no comeback. He could forever try to convince himself he did it to protect Michael, Emily, and who knows how many other lives Danny could have taken, but murder is murder.

His deflated look must have been obvious to Elaine as she moved around the table, sat next to him, and placed her hand over his. 'I'm sorry. I didn't mean what I said. I know why you did it.'

'No, you're right. Along with Olivia's, Danny's death will be forever on my conscience.'

'I've told you before, Olivia's death was not your fault. As for Danny, he was about to burn two children alive – my children. Yes, we stopped him, but who knows what horrors he could have gone on to commit? You did the right thing. A *good* thing. I watched you for a while upstairs holding Emily. Danny could have killed her and Michael last night, and knowing you brought him into their lives is not something you could have lived with. You weren't going to give him a second chance. You're a tough old sod, Lenny. I'm sure you'll find a way to cope.'

'I'm just like you now. I can never hold you accountable for your actions again.'

Elaine moved her hand away and said, 'When our paths first crossed, we detested one another. You saw a darkness in me I wasn't aware of, and yet, here we are. I've lost count of how many times we've been there for each other. There are few people I love in this world, and I have just lost two of them. All I have left are Michael, Emily, and, of course, you. You and the children help prevent me from becoming something much worse. I love you *because* you are nothing like me.'

Lenny said, 'I can't deny you've been good for me.'

'Too bloody right. You were a washed-up journalist, a chain-smoker, a blackmailer, and, quite frankly, a stubborn old bastard who thought nothing of shoving a full English breakfast down his throat at every available opportunity.'

'I still like a full English.' He smiled. 'Why don't we go and sit in the living room? There's a bottle of Glenfiddich in the cupboard, begging to be opened.'

'Sounds like a good idea.'

Burning logs cast shadows across the walls of the dimly lit room. The friends sipped their whisky and quietly reflected on the events that had transpired. Conversations were started and left unfinished to wither on the snap and sputter of kindling. Elaine refused a third refill as Lenny poured another.

He said, 'I'd love to hear how you and Harry concocted a plan to kill Sarah Kerr.'

'Now I know why you wanted to open the whisky, to get me talking.'

'That's what friends are for.'

'Would it make you feel better?'

'It won't make either of us feel any worse.'

She relented. 'As you know, it began with a phone call . . .'

Elaine wandered around the garden. 'Who is this?'

'It's Harry. I need your help with something.'

'Why aren't you calling me on your phone?'

'I'm using a burner, so nobody knows I called you.'

'Okay,' she said. 'What help do you need?'

'I need you to meet me tomorrow and take care of someone.'

'Not a chance!' Elaine shouted. 'And not just because it's the Christmas holidays.'

'Elaine, I've agonised over this decision. The person in question is responsible for so many deaths, and I can't touch her through any legal channels.'

'I said no!'

'You know this is not my style. I wouldn't ask if there were any other way. I can't let this go unpunished.'

'You're asking too much.'

'Elaine—'

'I'm not discussing this. Why don't you just—'

'I told you – I can't get her any other way.'

'Look, I'm sorry, but that's not my problem.'

'I've turned a blind eye to what you and your brother have done. I need you to do this for me, Elaine.'

'I know you have, but I can't possibly.'

'I could easily let the world know Harper is still alive.'

'You wouldn't do that.'

'Are you willing to take that risk?'

'Shit! Okay, I'll meet you. But I'm not at all happy about you forcing my hand this way.'

Harry said, 'Thank you. I'll text you where and at what time.'

'I ended the call, swore, kicked over the plant pot and—'

'Yeah, all right,' said Lenny. 'You can leave out the dramatic effects. Just get to what happened.'

She gave him a look and sipped her brandy. 'I met Harry in an industrial park before coming to yours . . .'

77

December 28
The Murder of Sarah Kerr

'Thanks for coming, Elaine,' said Harry. 'I'm sorry for bringing you into this, but there is nobody else I can trust and no one I know who would do what needs to be done.'

'This is a one off. I don't do this for fun, so let's just get on with this, shall we?' she said.

They left her car behind and drove to Virginia Water. He showed her around the area and the house where Sarah Kerr would be, all the while informing her of the plan, his instructions, and answering any questions she had. When they returned to the industrial park, he passed her a set of keys and gestured towards the car parked next to hers. He told her that was the car she'd be using and that it would be disposed of afterwards. With her hair tied back and wearing a black hoodie and jeans, she left Lenny's at about 9.00 p.m. As planned, she changed vehicles at the industrial park and headed for Virginia Water.

Elaine parked next to London Road, just inside the entrance of a restaurant car park, and waited for most of the cars to leave. When the traffic had died down, she exited the car with a small holdall and followed the fence along the main road. Approaching midnight, the road was busier than she had hoped it would be.

She remembered the waterfall just ahead on the right, and as soon as there was a lull in the traffic, she used the small concrete post opposite to scale the fence. Elaine retrieved a torch from her bag and wandered through the pitch-black woods. Harry had said to go as straight as possible until she came to a small clearing on the left. She'd bet her life he hadn't attempted to do this in the dead of night.

Elaine eventually found the clearing and saw the back of a house, but she couldn't tell if it was the house she was searching for. Aside from one solitary light in an upstairs window, the house appeared dark and still. Turning off the torch, she climbed over the fence, retrieved black overalls from the holdall, and pulled them on over her clothes. Using the trees for cover, she advanced to the side of the house, where Harry had said he'd left a small bathroom window open when he'd asked to use the facilities. Elaine focused on the fading green glow of a small strip of luminous tape he'd stuck to the outside frame.

So far, she'd managed to avoid the motion sensor lights and crept towards the house. She sidled along the wall until she got to the window. The light from the upstairs bedroom cast a faint illumination across the lawn. Past experience had taught her that patience was key. Not wanting to make her move until she was quite certain her would-be victim was fast asleep, she waited for the light to go out, which happened less than ten minutes later. Elaine put on a pair of latex gloves, peeled off the tape, and waited a further ten minutes.

Her biggest fear was the alarm going off as she pulled the window open, but Harry had assured her it wouldn't. His main concern was the indoor motion sensors. He'd warned her it was an old system, and because they had pet dogs, it would probably be disabled. However, if the alarm *were* to go off, he'd told her to get the hell out of there as quickly as possible. Elaine had hoped the unlocked window had been discovered and closed, effectively ending Harry's plan. Pulling it open, she sighed. She put plastic covers over her shoes and hauled herself through the window. Elaine reached into her bag for a screwdriver and the other half of the magnet sensor Harry had removed. She placed them on the windowsill, closed and locked the window, and screwed the magnet sensor into place. Finally, she removed the fridge magnet Harry had used to trick the sensor into thinking it was locked.

About to leave the bathroom, Elaine spied a blinking motion sensor high up in the corner. The alarm wasn't sounding, which suggested Harry's gamble had paid off. Using the torch to light the way, she searched the downstairs rooms for the computer connected to the security cameras. In what must be Mr Kerr's enormous office, she shone the torch over the large, empty desk. Out of the corner of her eye, she glimpsed a flashing red dot in the dark. She walked over and found a home computer. Turning on the monitor, she saw four separate squares on the screen, revealing various camera angles. Elaine turned off the computer, slid the side panel from the case, and ripped out the two hard drives, placing them in her bag.

Highlighting every step, Elaine sneaked up the wide staircase. Seeing the upstairs light from the garden enhanced her ability to locate the correct bedroom. Well, almost. The first room she checked was empty, but the next door was slightly ajar. She eased it open and poked her head around the edge. The glare of the moon through the window outlined a figure under the covers in the large double bed. A quick glance around the room at some posters, large teddy bears, and expensive-looking dolls told her this was Sarah Kerr's childhood room.

Elaine spotted Sarah's laptop and phone on the bedside cabinet and her handbag on the floor below. Standing over the bed, she recognised Sarah Kerr from the photo Harry had shown her. Putting the holdall on the floor, she quietly placed the laptop and phone inside, along with the torch. Going through Sarah's handbag, she retrieved a set of house keys. Stepping away from the bed with the holdall, she put it down and pulled out a large kitchen knife. Elaine prowled towards the bed and eased the duvet downwards, slowly revealing Sarah's body in her pink silk pyjamas. In one quick movement, she straddled her intended victim. Sarah's eyes burst open in fright; her screams thwarted as Elaine plunged the blade into her neck. Following Harry's orders, she continued her ruthless assault with further strikes to the neck and chest area.

With blood spatter on her face and in her hair, Elaine climbed from the bed, listening to the sound of Sarah Kerr's gargling growing weaker. She wrapped the knife in a plastic carrier bag and put it in the holdall. She grabbed the torch and a small evidence bag and walked towards the bed. Setting the torch on the cabinet, she used tweezers to remove a strand of hair from the bag and carefully placed it on the bed next to Sarah's body. Picking up the torch, Elaine stepped back, removed her overalls and gloves, and put everything in a separate bag. She put on a clean pair of gloves and pulled new shoe covers over the ones already on her feet to prevent treading blood throughout the house. Opening the double doors to a wardrobe, Elaine looked through the clothes on the hangers and examined the base of the cupboard. She shut the wardrobe and moved on to the other doors inside the bedroom, the first being an en suite. Total darkness loomed behind the next door. She flicked the light switch, revealing a long, narrow dressing room. Elaine carefully rummaged through every drawer and searched every nook and cranny until she discovered, on the top shelf, the blue parka Harry had specifically asked her to look for. She took the coat, turned off the light, and closed the door.

Elaine put the coat in the holdall and slung it over her shoulder. Standing in the bedroom doorway, she shone the torch once more over Sarah Kerr. The gargling had stopped, and her wide, dead eyes stared at the ceiling. Pulling the door to, she walked down the stairs and used the fob from Sarah's keys to deactivate the alarm. She reset it, marched straight out of the front door, and listened for the automatic lock. Seconds later, the beeping of the alarm stopped. Once over the fence, Elaine removed her gloves and shoe covers and tramped through the woods back to the car. When she returned to the deserted industrial park, she took what she needed from the holdall, left it in the boot for Harry, and sent a text to his burner:

Done. Do not contact me again.

'Wow!' said Lenny. 'Harry had clearly thought it through.'

'Yes, he was quite specific. When he explained what she'd done, why, and how there wasn't a single shred of evidence to convict her, I didn't put up much of an argument. Like you said, maybe deep down I wanted to do it. I warned him that as a police officer, the values he'd held dear would forever be thrown into question. There was no talking him out of it. His mind was made up well before he'd called me. I haven't got a clue what the next part of his plan is.'

Lenny considered PC Lucy Fenton's arrest, grabbed the bottle from the table, and topped up his glass. 'I have a pretty good idea.'

78

December 30

In the police station canteen, with his eyes closed and his fingers entwined around the handle of his coffee mug, Harry reflected on the last couple of days, exploring every detail, hoping he'd got everything right. The last thing he wanted was for all this to fall apart because he'd made a stupid mistake. As far as he could recall, it had all gone perfectly to plan.

He'd visited the industrial park a few hours after receiving a text from Elaine, taken the holdall from the boot, and placed it in his car. When the breakers' yard opened, he drove the car around the corner and paid the guy in cash to dismantle it promptly. That evening, he'd gone to Lucy's with the sole intention of getting her drunk. Despite knowing what she'd done, he was plagued by an overwhelming sense of guilt for what he was about to do. His feelings for her were real, and sadly, he would never know if she'd felt the same way or had simply played him for a fool from the outset.

The glass bottles of beer he'd taken to Lucy's were dark brown in colour, so whenever the chance came, he'd pour his beer down the kitchen sink and replace it with tap water. That's not to say he didn't drink a little more alcohol than he'd wished. When she'd finally drifted off to sleep, he hurried to her bedroom, removed a strand of hair with roots attached from her brush, and placed it in a small evidence bag. He left her apartment, returning a few minutes later wearing gloves and carrying the holdall. He hid the blue parka under another coat on the rack in the hall and put Sarah's laptop in a cupboard. In the kitchen, he removed the bloodstained knife from the plastic bag and placed it in the drawer where he'd discovered it by accident the night he'd visited Lucy after his meeting with Sarah Kerr. He immediately recognised the silver bands around the handle and the tooth missing from the blade. Knowing of Lucy's involvement by then, the plan to frame her had already formed in his mind. When he'd gone to fetch a bottle of wine from her fridge, his true aim was to take one of her knives for Elaine to use on Sarah. He had no idea that when he opened one of the kitchen drawers, he would find the missing knife from Sarah's apartment and the vial taken from the night Arthur Potts was attacked. To keep Arthur out of it, Harry removed the vial and put Sarah's phone in the drawer next to the bloodied knife.

When Sam called him about the death of Sarah Kerr, he was already in the area, waiting. Sarah had previously disclosed which days the cleaner visited the house, so he had a rough idea of when the body would be discovered. Elaine had left him instructions about the house keys, and when he sat on his haunches beside the bed, he dropped the keys back into Sarah Kerr's handbag.

'Harry!' Hearing his name, he jerked forward and opened his eyes. Sam Jennings was sitting across from him. 'Someone didn't get much sleep last night,' she said.

'I wasn't asleep. Just thinking about everything.'

'You've had a couple of rough cases, for sure.'

Harry asked, 'How did it go with Billy Graham?'

'Pretty damn good,' she said. 'We have his statement on record.'

'How's Lucy doing?'

'She's refused the duty solicitor and won't say a word. Perhaps she's in shock.'

'Yeah, maybe,' said Harry.

'An early look at Sarah Kerr's laptop and phone has revealed some interesting things. For starters, her connection to Lucy. Their friendship goes back a few years. During the investigation, while you were following Ryan, Lucy warned Sarah not to meet him. And on the day you both visited Craig Bishop's flat, Lucy sent Sarah a text beforehand telling her to take care of Craig. There were other messages too. On the night of the twenty-seventh, Lucy messaged Sarah, informing her that the investigation was pretty much at an end and they were in the clear. Sarah replied, saying she already knew. Lucy said she was pissed off with her for revealing so much information. Not sure what she was talking about or whom she was referring to, but perhaps Sarah's loose lips gave Lucy a motive for killing her.'

Harry recalled Lucy on her phone when he returned from the kitchen. She'd said she was checking on her dad's health, though he'd guessed that she was lying at the time. He was pleased his name hadn't been mentioned; otherwise, he would have had some explaining to do.

Sam said, 'We have also discovered messages to Owen Carrick and the videos Sarah used to blackmail him.'

'Great news,' he said, struggling with his satisfied pretence.

'Arthur Potts has been busy,' she continued. 'Fibres from Lucy's training shoes matched those on Frederick Perry's chair. And the bungee cord she'd used to murder him was in the boot of her car. Arthur has also confirmed that the blood on the parka is Lucy's, and the blood on the knife is Sarah Kerr's. The knife *is* from

Miss Kerr's kitchen, and though he has more tests to complete, he's confident it was used on Sarah, Craig Bishop, Lucy, and Jerome Henderson. Finding the coat, Sarah's laptop and phone, and the murder weapon in Lucy's apartment is phenomenal.'

'It certainly is.'

'Unless she tells us otherwise, we can only assume Lucy was knifed by accident or to throw us off the scent.'

Harry said, 'I suspect I was the target, and James Harding messed up.'

'That would make more sense. Oh, I almost forgot. As you suggested, we sent a sample of Miss Kerr's hair to Arthur. It's a high percentage match to the sample found at the scene of Craig Bishop's murder. With the evidence piling up, if we can get Lucy to talk, it should be enough to tie his murder to Sarah Kerr.'

'Good to hear,' said Harry.

'We also managed to find video footage from a house close to the Kerrs,' she said. The hairs on the back of Harry's neck stood tall. 'On the twenty-seventh of December, a car pulled up outside the Kerrs' residence, and a man entered through the gate. Less than an hour later, he was seen leaving, but the camera was too far away, and the angle was terrible. We couldn't see the man's face, the type of car, or the registration. The guys searched nearby traffic cameras, but without knowing exactly what they were looking for, it was hopeless.' He could breathe again.

Harry said, 'So now you're just waiting for Lucy to talk?'

'We've had her in the interview room twice now. She just sits there in silence. I'm not even sure she's listening to us.'

'Let me talk to her?' he said.

'Is that such a good idea?'

'What harm could it do?'

'True enough,' said Sam. 'Well, you're welcome to give it a try. I'll see if a room is free.'

'No. Not in an interview room. In her cell.'

Sam looked uncertain.

'If I talk to her without cameras and recorders, I'm confident I can get her to talk to you in an interview room.'

She said, 'Okay, let's give it a shot.'

Harry lumbered down the steps. Confronting Lucy after her arrest was always going to be the hardest part. An officer opened the cell door.

Sitting on the edge of the bed as though waiting for him, she said, 'I knew you'd come and see me.'

'I assume that's why you've said nothing so far,' Harry replied as he entered. Before locking him inside, the officer told him to bang on the door when he was ready.

Harry stood with his back against the door. After several unnerving seconds of silent staring, Lucy said, 'Why are you standing over there? You didn't seem so afraid of me last night.'

'I'm not afraid. I'm just not sure I'm welcome.'

She tapped the mattress beside her. 'Come, sit next to me.'

Laden with guilt, his legs carried him the short distance across to the bed, where he was grateful to take the weight off. Convinced he'd done the right thing, he couldn't fathom why his conscience felt so heavy. Maybe he was wrestling with what Elaine had said regarding his values. Eyes forward, they stared at the opposite wall and the cell door.

Lucy said, 'Sam levelled a lot of charges against me, most of which I'm innocent of.'

'But not all,' said Harry.

'No, not all. But why kill Sarah and set me up?'

'It was the only way I could make her pay for what she did. By leaving a strand of your hair on Sarah's bed, I knew they'd have to check whether it was hers, and when they did, they'd come straight to you and link her hair sample to the one found at Craig Bishop's crime scene. Everything would unravel from there.'

'When did you suspect me?'

'The signs were there from the first moment we met Sarah in the diner, but my eyes were closed. When I saw your car parked outside Rebecca Heaton's, I knew what a fool I'd been.'

'I hoped I'd had a lucky escape that day. I threw up when I returned home.'

'You seem to do that a lot.' A faint smile crossed both their faces. 'Tell me why, Lucy?'

'Who knows why we do such stupid things?'

'If she already had *you* in her pocket, why and how did she get Owen Carrick involved?'

'"Pocket" insinuates she had power over me. I can assure you that was not the case. Our relationship ended a few years back. I was a little older than her, had different interests, and it soon became clear we didn't have a romantic future together. Sarah only ever loved Sarah and did whatever and whoever she wanted. Despite her many flaws and all the shit she brought my way, I loved her. Sarah got Owen involved after I told her there were certain things I couldn't do, like mess with traffic cameras. She told me she did live video streams with a local guy who'd mentioned he was an accident investigator for the police. I looked into him, and as always, fortune favoured her.'

'So she blackmailed him?'

'With the recordings she had of him doing all manner of sexual things, it wasn't difficult.'

'I assume Owen deleted the footage of the attack on you from the police computer?'

'That's what she told me.'

'Did Owen know about your involvement with Sarah?'

'No. I wouldn't allow it.'

'Did you kill Owen Carrick?'

She glared at him. 'No. Why would you even ask?'

'Fred Perry comes to mind.' Lucy looked away. He said, 'I missed it at the time, but at my place, when I mentioned he'd left a suicide note saying sorry, you presumed it was one word.'

She closed her eyes and smiled at her mistake. 'I hoped you hadn't noticed.'

Harry said, 'That was also the moment you knew we'd alibied Jerome and suggested we shift our focus onto Owen. How did you know what the note said?'

'Because I saw it. When Sarah last spoke to him, she said he didn't sound right and was worried he'd turn himself in and tell the police about *her*. She asked me to pay him a visit, not only to collect the knife he'd used to murder Jerome but to threaten him in some way. I parked across the road from his house and waited until the bedroom lights went out. As I was about to text him, the porch light came on, and he stepped out of the front door. He walked over to the garage, pulled up the shutter, and closed it behind him. I waited, and when he didn't emerge, I walked over and raised the shutter. He'd hanged himself from a wooden beam. His legs were still twitching, and maybe I could have saved him, but it seemed more advantageous to let him die. So instead, I watched until he stopped moving.'

Harry's stomach tightened. This was always going to be a harrowing conversation, but he could never have prepared himself for how ill at ease it would make him.

She said, 'He'd left a note on the workbench, apologising to his family and confessing to the murder of Jerome Henderson. He mentioned blackmail and pointed the finger at Sarah. At the bottom, he'd written the word "*Sorry*." I used a Stanley knife to neatly cut the paper and took the rest of the note. And before you ask, I tore it up and threw it in a bin.'

Harry closed his eyes and sighed. 'That could have been helpful. How come you disposed of the note but kept other things?'

Lucy shrugged. 'I don't know. I never imagined I'd become a suspect.'

'What about all the others involved? Did you know them?'

'I'd seen Ryan once, years ago, but only in passing. Fortunately, he didn't remember me. As for the others, no. They came along after Sarah and I broke up. Until all of this kicked off, we'd only had the occasional catch-up over the phone.'

Harry said, 'What about your attack on Arthur Potts?'

'Unfortunate for Arthur. From my perspective, lucky. I knew you'd been sniffing around Sarah's apartment and wanted to find out why. Being a constable, I suspected there wouldn't be an officer guarding the door to an empty property on Christmas Day. Arthur walked in, and when he took a sample from the skirting beneath the worktop, I picked up a heavy wooden ornament and struck him over the head. I took the vial and wiped down the skirting and the ornament. I was sorry to hurt Arthur, but if I'd thought he was seriously injured, I would have called an ambulance.'

'Not all you took, though, was it?'

Lucy furrowed her brow, curious, and caught on. 'The Merlot.'

Harry said, 'I'd seen it in the fridge from a previous visit to Sarah's apartment. After seeing you outside the Heatons, I went back to check.'

'You truly are quite the detective.'

'If I were, I'd have sussed all of these things earlier.'

'Why didn't you?'

'Because I trusted you. And being an idiot, I fell for you.'

She smiled. 'Don't knock yourself.'

'At least I know why you pleaded with DCS Falconer to let you work with me. What I don't fully understand is how *you* got stabbed when Sarah told me I was the target?'

'James panicked and messed up. He was supposed to let me run past and knife you, coming up the escalator behind me.'

'And you were fine with me potentially being killed?' A question he wished he hadn't asked.

'Of course not. I'm glad it didn't go as planned and I took the blade.'

'Oh, my hero,' he said, sarcasm abounding.

'Think what you want, but it's true.'

'You were working against me all along, Lucy. We found messages between you and Sarah. Among them, you warned her not to meet Ryan when we followed him to the car park, and you called her from the cathedral right before we drove to Craig Bishop's address. So why do you expect me to believe you didn't want me dead?'

'At that point, everything was spiralling into chaos. I'd already killed Fred Perry and was in far too deep. I'd argued with Sarah a number of times, but things kept going from bad to worse. Please, Harry, trust me when I say I never wanted you to get hurt.'

'I am hurt.'

She bowed her head. 'I know.'

He asked, 'Was it you who leaked information to the media after Melanie's death?'

'No, it was Sarah. She reasoned it would keep police attention away from her and give her career a boost.'

'She wasn't wrong,' said Harry. 'Look, I hate to talk about this, but—'

'Fred Perry?' Harry gave a reluctant nod. Lucy took a deep breath and said, 'Sarah knew he would throw her name into the mix once we'd, well, you'd investigated further. She begged me to help her. I don't need to tell you what she wanted me to do. Having previously paid him a visit with you, it wasn't difficult to talk my way in. He was quite drunk by the time I got there. I took a bottle of strong vodka for him, and we talked about the case and his brother. I even had a glass myself, which, it turned out, I needed. I sat and watched him get wasted. When he fell asleep, I put on my gloves, moved around to the back of his chair, and wrapped the bungee cord around his neck. Even in his weakened state, he fought hard. And as much as I wanted to, stopping was no longer an option. I wiped down the bottle, washed my glass, and put it in the cupboard.'

Harry said, 'It's impossible for me to picture you doing that to someone.'

'Just like I can't imagine you killing Sarah Kerr and framing me. You might not have done it yourself, Harry, but you arranged it. We're all a whisper away from evil.'

'You're right. There's no dressing up what either of us has done.'

'. . . So, what now?'

'I want the world to see Sarah Kerr for the monster she was, and I want you to help make it happen.'

'I couldn't do that to her.'

'Listen to me carefully, Lucy. I don't know if she was being stupid or overconfident, but Sarah made a remark about two queen ants working together and how eventually one would destroy the other. At first, I assumed she was talking about her and Melanie, but I was wrong. You were the other queen. When I spoke to her, she realised I knew all about your involvement. I bet she didn't tell you?'

'No, she didn't.'

'Take the fall for the murder of Sarah Kerr and accept responsibility for Frederick Perry, but don't go down for more than you should to protect a dead woman who, if it came down to it, would have thrown you off the same balcony.'

From the intense look in Lucy's eyes and her pained expression, she was clearly racking her mind, assessing her situation.

'Wow! I'm going away for a *long* time,' she said, finally coming to terms with what was happening.

'It could be less than you imagine.'

'How?'

'A top barrister could make some kind of deal to get you a lighter sentence, but only if you agree to what I've suggested. You could argue that, as with Owen Carrick, Sarah Kerr blackmailed you into murdering Fred Perry and forced you to tamper with evidence to protect *her* from prosecution. Messages between the two of you could be disputed as misinterpretations. Much of the evidence is circumstantial, but some of it could help your case. If you throw as much as you can at Sarah, the CPS and the judge might just buy it.'

'You'd help me after everything I've done?'

Harry nodded and got to his feet. 'You'll do time, Lucy. That's a given. But maybe not as much as you think.' She had listened and taken on board what he'd said, and that alone was more than he could have hoped for. 'I can't say how long they'll keep you here. They're probably organising somewhere to send you right now. They want you to talk, though, so I'm guessing you have until morning to decide what you want to do.' He raised his fist to bang on the cell door.

'Okay,' she said. 'I'll do it.'

Harry turned and wandered towards her. 'I'm glad. I'll let Sam know you want to make a phone call.' He handed her a card. 'I've spoken to an old friend of mine at a prestigious law firm. All you have to do is call this number. She's expecting your call.'

She examined the card. 'How did you know I'd take you up on this?'

'I didn't. I held on to the belief that you'd do the right thing. There are a lot of families who deserve closure. Sarah Kerr may well be dead, but she needs to be remembered for the crimes she committed and forced others to carry out on her behalf.' He walked to the door and gave it a hard thump. The echo bounced off the four walls.

'Harry?' He turned to face her. Tears had formed in her eyes. 'I'm sorry I disappointed and hurt you. And just so you know, I fell for you as well.'

Words he'd wanted to hear. Did she mean them? As far as he was concerned – yes, she did. Harry smiled. 'Perhaps one day you'll mime 'I Drove All Night' for me again?'

Lucy returned the smile. 'I'll most likely be in my eighties, but if these hips allow, I will certainly give it a try.'

Harry walked out of the cell. The officer slammed the door and left Harry to linger in the corridor, listening to Lucy sob. His heart clanged like a bell on a sinking ship. Holding back his tears, he composed himself and ambled up the steps. The echoes of his footsteps eventually drowned out her burgeoning cries.

79

Happy New Year

A fortnight Harry would not forget. On the eighteenth of December, he'd never heard of Gerty's Guest House, and as quaint as it was, it wasn't somewhere he'd have planned to spend the end of the year. He'd been in the armchair all night. No television. No music. Sporadic fireworks screamed and banged outside the window, but other than that, it had been a fairly quiet evening. After a frantic two weeks, he was happy to switch off, though right now, he'd never felt more alone.

Earlier, DCS Falconer had given him a pat on the back but had fallen short of any congratulations. He'd told him he was an accomplished detective and the Met's loss was their gain; however, Sam Jennings would start the new year as DCI. The right call, as far as he was concerned. There would be another political and internal fallout over the two police officers involved in Sarah's crimes. Whether he'd get dragged into the murky business remained open to question. The only good news, if you could call it that, was DC Henderson's innocence. Unable to explain how Rebecca Heaton had turned up in Canada and Annalise Fournier in the UK, DCS Falconer had told him to mark it as unsolved. Falconer had laughed and said, 'Secretly, we'll call it a Christmas miracle.' *Idiot*! Before leaving the station, Sam had informed him that Mrs Hillingdon was recovering in hospital after taking an overdose. Would the repercussions of Sarah's actions never end?

Harry had disposed of the vial and the hard drives Elaine had stolen for him, along with the holdall and everything else inside. He had also deleted the recorded interview with Mr Jones, the security guard from the mall. There was no point in ruining another life. He'd spoken to Lenny and had been made aware of the tragic events in Helmsley. With all that Harry had seen and been through in recent years, the element of surprise seemed lost on him. Perhaps Danny's actions were inevitable. It was a strange feeling not to be shocked by something so terrible. That's not to say he wasn't sorry about Tom, a good and decent man who didn't deserve to die at the hands of a boy he'd helped rescue. As for Harper – although he'd saved *his* life a little over a week ago, maybe it was for the best. He had wanted to call Elaine to express his condolences, but her last message not to contact her had prevented him from doing so.

Loud cheers boomed from the garden next door, and fireworks screamed into the night sky. The midnight hour. Harry sipped beer from the bottle in his hand and wandered over to watch the celebrations from the window.

People in the garden below acknowledged him and shouted, 'Happy New Year!'

He managed to force a smile, gestured with his bottle towards them, and turned away. With a record on the turntable, he played 'Everybody Hurts' by R.E.M. and returned to his chair.

On the narrow top bunk, with her knees tucked between her arms, Lucy stared poignantly through the bars of the small window. The cell seemed half the size of the one at the police station. The low ceiling didn't help. If one could view the possibility of serving eighteen years as a positive, this morning's discussion with her barrister was promising. It could take weeks, months, or more for both sides to examine every shred of evidence. Rebecca regaining her memory of an argument with Sarah Kerr and being assaulted could be a plus for her case. She was taking nothing for granted, though, and knew there was a good chance she would end up serving closer to thirty. Some would say deservedly so or that it wasn't long enough. Maybe they'd be right.

"My word!" That's what her mother would say when she visited. If she visited. Mortification was easy to read on the faces of family, friends, former colleagues, and Harry.

Recalling the nights Harry had come to her place, she saw it now – his hesitation, his reluctance to take things further, and his immense disappointment in her that he'd done his utmost to conceal. She'd missed it, but it was there in plain sight. *Stupid woman.* Everything ruined, and for what? And that was the worst part: she couldn't bring to mind the what or the why. As others had, she'd just gone along on autopilot, doing whatever Sarah wanted. Did she do it for love, or was she unwittingly drawn into some warped woman's inner circle? Oh, what did it matter now?

Lying awake in darkness, Penny Levinson grieved the loss of her son and the end of her marriage. Startled by a loud bang, she sat up in bed and glanced towards the bright flashes at the window. Looking back at the many mistakes she had made wouldn't make things better, but when forced to question so much about her life, analysing the past was inevitable. No stranger to grief, and with the knowledge that life goes on regardless, she would move forward – eventually. Easing her head onto the pillow, illuminated by an occasional burst of colour, tears rolled from her ever-welling eyes.

In spite of the biting cold, Elaine watched the sky light up from the bench in her garden as locals welcomed the New Year. She emptied the bottle into her glass, sipped her wine, and glanced up at the soft, warm glow from Emily's bedroom window. No surprise, it took a while to get her to sleep. Michael remained in the hospital, though she'd been informed she could bring him home tomorrow. She had declined her friend Lila's offer to come and spend the night with her. Sometimes, solitude was a necessity. Distractions were all well and good, but if experience had taught her anything, it was better to confront bereavement head-on.

A couple of detectives had paid her another visit earlier in the day to follow up on her previous statement. There were bound to be plenty of questions after the death of a former police sergeant and two badly burned bodies. Lenny had given his statement the day after the incident, all true – well, mostly. Elaine had repeated everything he had told them, albeit in her own words. They had confirmed Daniel Logan as one of the bodies but claimed to have no knowledge of the second body, suggesting it could have been a squatter. Elaine and Lenny accepted the possibility of Harper's body being identified, but there were many factors involved and every chance it might not be. Stolen as a baby, he had been given the name Liam Bennett, and to hide him within the system, it was changed to Harper Darmody. There was no way of knowing what records existed or if they were freely accessible. If his remains were identified, they would play the ignorance card again and claim that, as far as they were aware, Harper was already dead.

Losing Harper had become routine, and though it pained her deeply, she would cope, whereas Tom's death had left a tight grip around her heart, with a beastly hand squeezing it every so often. On her return from visiting Michael the previous night, she'd cried herself to sleep. This morning, while Lenny made breakfast, she broke down again. The last of her tears fell at the front door when she said goodbye to Lenny. They say time is a great healer – they're wrong. The severity of the sting may soothe, but anguish is a lifelong process. Elaine looked to the sky. The colourful blaze of fireworks above reflected in the desolate glaze of her eyes. Grief was the bastard that kept on giving.

Under normal circumstances, Lenny would stand at the window and watch the celebratory fireworks light up the city skyline. Not tonight, though. With the lights dimmed, he sat comfortably in his chair and stroked Phoebe Waller-Bridge. After Phoebe's initial snub for being left at the vets, she now seemed content and happy to see him. Getting back home to pick her up had been a constant worry. He didn't want to leave her at the animal hospital any longer than he had to, but if Elaine had asked him to stay another night, he would have considered it, especially with the state she was in. He'd even looked into having Phoebe couriered to Helmsley. Pricey, but she was worth it. When he'd overheard Elaine refuse Lila's company, he'd determined that she wanted to be left alone to grieve in peace.

The journey home from Helmsley wasn't plain sailing, and not because of traffic. Time alone in the car had given him a chance to reflect on what he had done to Danny. He'd wanted so much to help him, but when it came to fighting a losing battle that could cost the lives of more children, the choice became clear. He'd hoped to look across and see Olivia in the passenger seat, ready to say he'd done the right thing, but it was not to be. Perhaps what he'd told Danny was the truth, and everything he'd seen was a fantasy. However, it would leave so many questions about how he had come to know certain things.

Before getting comfortable with Phoebe, Lenny checked the messages on his home phone. He had a worrying message from Karen Tremblay and returned her call. Christopher had become seriously ill a few days ago and had been rushed to the hospital. Further tests were carried out, and doctors discovered that his cancer was worse than first feared. A long battle lay ahead, but with effective therapy, there could be a positive outcome. She'd played it down, but Lenny sensed her anguished undertone. A return to Canada in the new year might be nice; maybe he could even do a little sightseeing. He looked at Phoebe.

'Don't worry, girl. I won't leave you behind.'

80

Three Months Later

The clear blue sky and sunshine were a breath of fresh air after such a daunting and miserable winter. Vibrant green grass and daffodils in bloom – spring had finally arrived. Even the morning birdsong sounded buoyant. Though it could be argued that happiness should not be found in a cemetery, Lenny couldn't help but find contentment as he stood over Mary Elizabeth Martin's grave and watched the coffin of Emma Rose Martin being lowered into the ground. Lenny's findings were enough to convince the authorities that Mary and Emma were indeed sisters and should be interred together. A little help from some friends had aided in her repatriation.

Further discoveries revealed Emma's guardian, Russell Kirby, had joined the British Army to fight against the Continental Army. He and two of his sons were killed in action. As the wife of a soldier loyal to the Crown, Susan Kirby was tainted by association and suffered persecution. With everything she owned confiscated, she set off for Canada to start over with her youngest son, Oliver, and Emma in tow. There were no records after this, so Lenny would never know what happened to Mrs Kirby, her son, or why Emma found herself separated from them. However, knowing the sad and tragic end to Emma Martin's life, he hoped that reuniting Emma with her sister would be a more fitting end to her story.

Harry had joined him to pay his respects, expressing his uncertainty several times over the last few weeks about elements of the case that were unexplainable. Lenny had told him to forget about it and that not everyone's mind was open to the paranormal.

One evening, after a couple of beers in his local, Harry dropped by Lenny's apartment uninvited, unable to let it go. Having previously shown Lenny the CCTV footage of the flash in the car, he had dismissed Lenny's theory that it was the moment Rebecca and Annalise swapped places. Now, putting his scepticism aside, he was open to suggestion.

As soon as Lenny opened the front door, Harry said, 'I need to tell you about Rebecca's dream.'

Lenny grabbed a couple of beers from the fridge, passed one to Harry on the sofa, and sat in the armchair.

Harry recounted Rebecca's recurring dream of a brilliant white flash and two young girls either side of her, holding her hand and leading her forward, making her feel safe. He added, 'She said it was silly and probably nothing, but it wasn't nothing, was it?'

'No, it wasn't,' said Lenny. 'I spoke to Annalise, and she described the exact same dream. You know as well as I do that those girls had never met or had any previous contact. However, I have now put them in touch with each other. While they may never understand exactly what happened to them, perhaps sharing such a unique experience will help them process it.'

Harry said, 'I've exhausted every logical explanation for how Rebecca and Annalise ended up swapping countries. I know you've been researching the topic, so what's your theory?'

Lenny leaned forward. 'I'm no scientist, and it's not my theory, but the best analogy I've found to make sense of how ghosts could interact with our world is quantum entanglement – when two particles are linked so that what happens to one instantly affects the other, even across great distances. Some theorists suggest consciousness could work the same way. Maybe ghosts – especially ones as closely bonded as the Martin sisters – can use that connection to act across space.'

Harry frowned. 'So you're saying the twins' spirits somehow bridged the gap to save the girls?'

'I'm not saying this is exactly how it works, Harry, but thinking of it this way helps me imagine how the impossible could happen. If the sisters' connection survived death, their spirits might allow them to act together from different places. When Rebecca and Annalise were both in danger, the twins could have used that link to intervene – swapping the girls' locations instantly, like particles switching states. Many cultures have stories of spirits intervening during critical moments.'

'Is there any concrete evidence linking quantum theory to ghostly phenomena, or is it just speculation?'

'Science generally starts with speculation before it leads to discovery. We know so little about the mind, what happens after death, or the true nature of energy. Spirits might be a form of energy that can interact with our physical world in ways we don't yet understand.'

'Okay, so what about the Martin sisters? What type of ghosts are they?'

'I'm not sure there is a perfect match, but in myth and folklore, they're just ghosts with unfinished business, said to linger because of a traumatic or unjust death. The sisters' bond and the injustice they suffered might have given them the power to help Rebecca and Annalise and to draw attention to their own story. In some traditions, these are called unquiet spirits.'

'And you think reuniting Mary and Emma in death will give them the peace they seek?'

Lenny smiled softly. 'This isn't just about peace, Harry. It's about injustice, closure, and acknowledging their story.'

'This is a lot for me to take in.'

'I understand your scepticism. Your job is all about physical evidence, but most mysteries will always remain unsolved, and this is just one way to think about this particular case.'

Harry sighed and sat on the edge of the chair. 'Sometimes, stories are all people have to explain the inexplicable. You really believe all this, don't you?'

'Absolutely! Having encountered the ghosts and felt their presence, I have to – otherwise, I'd have to doubt everything I've seen.'

Harry didn't reply, and no doubt remained sceptical, but his eyes revealed that he was willing to accept that some mysteries can't be solved by logic alone.

Lenny and Harry grabbed a handful of soil and let it fall between their fingers onto the coffin lid. They bowed their heads as Reverend Strathearn said a prayer before leaving them alone to reflect. After a moment's silence, the pair ambled away. Lenny responded to an urge to take one last look. Behind the new headstone, Mary and Emma stood hand in hand. They appeared to be younger and without the barbaric injuries they had suffered. Their soft smiles brought tears to his eyes as they faded into history. He glanced at the headstone, which bore both names and the dates of their deaths, along with the added inscription:

No distance too great to keep us apart. Separated twice, together for eternity.

About the Author

Gabriel enjoys writing psychological thrillers with plots that twist and turn. Born in London, he now lives on the Kent coast of England with his wife and two cats.
He left school early to work in the building trade as a painter/labourer and went on to become a carpet fitter, postman, and multi-tradesman, though not all at the same time.
Inspirational books include 'Salem's Lot by Stephen King, Flowers in the Attic by V. C. Andrews, and The Rats by James Herbert.

A Whisper Away From Evil is part of the Godless Creatures series. If you enjoyed this story, be sure to read my other novels.

You can find out more about me, my books, and other exciting info on my website:
www.gabrielblake.com

To receive updates about future releases, exciting news, and special offers, please subscribe to my occasional newsletter:
https://tinyurl.com/Subscribe-to-Gabriel-Blake

It would be fantastic if you joined me on X (FKA Twitter):
https://twitter.com/GabrielBlake_

Follow me on Instagram:
https://www.instagram.com/gabrielblakewriter/

Thank you for reading. If you enjoy my stories, please know that it means the absolute world to me. You can show your support for my writing by recommending my books to others or leaving a rating or review wherever you can. Subscribing to or following me on social media is also a massive help.

www.ingramcontent.com/pod-product-compliance
Lightning Source LLC
Chambersburg PA
CBHW061855310726
48972CB00004B/1029